MIRADEN'S FOLLY

MIRADEN'S FOLLY

HER SOUL OF FIRE ✦ BOOK ONE

Copyright © 2015 J. V. Fahl

WWW.JVFAHL.COM

All rights reserved.

No part of this publication may be reproduced, distributed, or transmitted in any form or by any means, including photocopying, recording, or other electronic or mechanical methods, without the prior written permission of the publisher, except in the case of brief quotations embodied in critical reviews and certain other noncommercial uses permitted by copyright law. This book is a work of fiction. Names, characters, places, and incidents are either products of the author's imagination or are used fictitiously. Any resemblance to actual persons, living, dead or otherwise, events, or locales is entirely coincidental.

Cover and Interior Design by We Got You Covered Book Design

WWW.WEGOTYOUCOVEREDBOOKDESIGN.COM

Ebook ISBN: 978-0-578-25635-1

Softback ISBN: 978-0-578-25636-8

Hardback ISBN: 978-0-578-25637-5

v1.0.1 - Errata can be found at HTTPS://WWW.JVFAHL/MF-ERRATA

HER SOUL OF FIRE ✦ BOOK ONE

MIRADEN'S FOLLY

J.V. FAHL

I would love for you to join my spam-free newsletter.
If you want to join now, please visit **jvfahl.com** and sign up.

LET'S GET YOU TO THE STORY

ONE

THE PRODIGAL DAUGHTER

IN A WOODEN COTTAGE DEEP in Baregorin Forest, Ceychell prepared juniper tea with nutmeg. It was not one of her alchemical specialties, just something for her mother to sip. The kettle whistled above the crackle of the fire in the hearth. As she lifted it from the rung over the fire, she heard a knock at the door. She loosened the top of the kettle and replaced it on its hook over the fire, walked across the fur rug to the door, and opened it a crack.

Standing on the stoop was the old seamstress, Vera, her wrinkled face nearly covered by the cowl of her cloak. Next to her stood the cobbler, Steljen, whose face was a swollen crosshatch of red scratches. Ceychell didn't greet them.

The seamstress sounded like a choking horse as she cleared her throat. "How adorable you look with your hair bundled up like that… Is Curasca feeling better yet?" Vera asked. "This cough, I've had it in the past." Ceychell glowered at her, and her wrinkles folded in on themselves.

"My mother is very ill," Ceychell said. "Yet, you wish for her to care for you?" Ceychell shook her head. "I suppose I'll be helping Steljen first." She opened the door for the fidgeting cobbler. He was half of Vera's age. He didn't argue, didn't even look back at Vera. He just stepped inside and removed his gray, moth-pecked wool cap. There was plenty of room in the house for Vera too, but Ceychell cast her a mean glare and then shut the door behind Steljen.

Twenty minutes later, the door opened again. Out stepped Steljen, groaning, with a pungent balm smeared on his face to suppress the itchweed infection. Vera shivered and hobbled up beneath Ceychell's outstretched arm holding open the door. The old seamstress smiled as she entered Ceychell's warm, juniper-scented cottage and seated herself on the couch.

Thick blankets lay folded next to her. She ran her hand over a soft bear pelt she had sewn for Ceychell's mother nearly twenty years ago. Below it was several colorful, beautifully knitted quilts. Ceychell's younger sister, Kyradel, and their mother still used and appreciated them.

Nevertheless, Ceychell would have preferred not to have her as a visitor this morning. "How long have you had the fever?" she asked.

The old woman's smile drooped, and she coughed again. "Two days… would you be so kind as to share a bit of that tea? It would help ease this old wom—"

"I'm afraid not," Ceychell said, placing her long fingers on Vera's sweating forehead. Ceychell shook her head and felt Vera's throat. She was deliberately brusque in her poking and gripping like testing a hunk of butchered meat for tenderness.

"Ceycha?" her mother's voice rang out from her bedroom. "Ceycha, is that Vera?"

Ceychell's back stiffened as both her mother and Vera fell into coughing fits. She waited for the coughing to subside and then answered, "Yes, mother."

Curasca, nearly engulfed by an earthen-colored patchwork quilt, stepped to the top of the staircase. Her thinning brown hair showed streaks of gray, and her once-beautiful face was jowly and wrinkled. She smiled, though, seeming pleased and eager to have company.

Ceychell stood erect with her back half-turned toward her.

"Have you not offered her a cup of tea?" Curasca asked.

Ceychell's eyes met Vera's. She didn't like the old seamstress, and she resented her rising grin. "I spent an hour picking these herbs for you this morning. I made the tea for you. There just isn't very much."

"Nonsense." Curasca stepped down the stairs. The long quilt trailed behind her like a regal cape of the forest floor. "Why don't you fetch some lunarcaps?" she said. "I'll attend to Vera," Curasca passed Ceychell and grabbed a pad before removing the kettle from the fire.

Ceychell sulked. She didn't want Vera cared for; she wanted her out of her house for meddling with her life. She wrested her coat from a wall hook and shuffled to the door, eager to leave.

"Ceycha?" Curasca called.

She whipped her coat on, turned around at the door, and looked at her mother.

"Have you seen Kyradel this morning?" Curasca asked. "I didn't hear her humming before she left the house."

Ceychell pulled her coat on the rest of the way, sloppily flipped her hair out from under its collar, and grabbed her pumpkin-orange gardening bag from next to the door. It's not as if she spoke to her sister nowadays. If Kyradel wasn't such a dreamer, Ceychell thought, maybe she'd help her with at least some of the chores. Maybe even do them all and give her a day off! "Maybe she is out chopping wood or pulling weeds in the garden." Ceychell laughed, trying to quell her rising anger.

"Your sister is an artist… don't be so—"

Ceychell turned, stepped out the door, and slammed it behind her.

TWO

THE LOST ARTIST

CEYCHELL PULLED UP HER HOOD and breathed in the fresh forest air. Warm wisps drifted from her lips as she walked up the hill toward her vast garden, stepping to avoid every fallen leaf and sprig. She loved to garden, loved bonding with nature, knowing which herbs are ready for clipping and when each mushroom will be in perfect bloom for medicines. It was the one chore that brought her joy and a sense of accomplishment each day.

Ceychell opened the garden gate. She carefully navigated the path between the precious herbs and bountiful vegetables and continued to the mossier side of the hill, where she kept invasive plants under careful watch. She approached a red lump on the earth where red ivy, like a tentacled beast, had strangled and downed a tree. The vine had started to climb up nearby trees in the garden, too, threatening to kill and pull them down as well. Ceychell put on her gloves and drew her copper hunting knife from its holster. She hacked through the vines and untangled them from the trees.

Then she carefully approached the downed tree. As she stepped around it to find the rotted hole where the lunarcaps grew, she wondered how much ivy she'd have to cut away to reach them.

The red monster smelled iron-rich, thick like blood, tickling, and burning in her nostrils.

She heard the faint, crackling laughter of that gossipy harpy, Vera, from down the hill, from her home; it boiled her blood. She enjoyed referring to Vera as a monstrous, winged hag but never to her face. Vera knew her secret, a deep secret. Every time Vera spoke with her mother, Ceychell feared she might reveal it: why she and her sister weren't close anymore. Ceychell seethed, remembering the day; that day Vera saw her—

Ceychell shook her head. She reached into her bag and withdrew a digging spade with an oak handle. The metal was spotted with rust, but it was still her trusty tool. She stepped up to the rotted hole and brushed away a few freshly snipped vines. Inside the dark hole, she could see broken purple stubs jutting from the soggy crumbled wood.

"Looking for these?"

Ceychell jerked and turned around. Miraden stood, leaning against a blue dwarf pine, a line of game hens hung over his shoulder. As usual, the young ranger was dressed in soft brown leather from foot to collar and partially covered in a timber-green cloak. His reddish-brown hair drooped over his face, not quite covering his broad grin—her fondest, most haunting memory. He waggled a bouquet of purple fungus at her. Her sternness wilted his smile.

He looked away. Brushed purple specks from his gloves a moment.

She stepped up and took the mushrooms from his gloved hand. Pushed the caps into her bag without moving her gaze from him. "Shouldn't you be still hunting or chopping lumber? The storehouse is nearly empty."

Ceychell stood tall, and when Miraden tried to smile again, her gaze hardened. She felt his love, his search for hope, for a glimmer of her affection. She wanted to hold him close like she used to but gave him nothing.

"I thought it would be nice—"

"You thought wrong."

His posture weakened. When he looked away again, all the anger inside Ceychell started to surface. But when his eyes became misty, she struggled to maintain her coldness. She clenched her fists. She finally looked away when he turned back to look into her eyes.

"Valdenfest is only a few weeks away, I was—"

"No!" she nearly screamed. "Why keep asking me, Miraden?" Her eyes were beginning to water.

He shifted the hens to his other shoulder. He looked down at his muddy leather boots. Stupidly, he asked, "Are you going with someone else then?"

"I will not be *going* at all!" She stepped up to Miraden and stared down at him. She stood taller than him, nearly half a head. Their faces nearly touched.

She let him stare at her in a brief daydream. She knew he could smell the limebloom perfume she was wearing. It was her favorite, and she could only make it thanks to a single plant that grew in the blue pine flowerbox outside her bedroom window. That limebloom was planted long ago by none other than Miraden. It was always cared for, but not by her.

She cracked a trembling grin at him. She'd not smiled at him in two years. It was enough to make Miraden step back. She grabbed his collar and halted his retreat. When she ran her other hand along his cheek, he shuddered. Years ago, she'd expect a hug from him; she expected it now. She also expected him to run. She pulled the pin holding up her hair. He couldn't take his eyes off of her as her burnished locks fell in a silky veil of autumn colors.

Ceychell whispered, "Each morning, I wake up and wish it was like it used to be." She brushed his hair aside and placed her other hand on his face. "I wish my sister still loved me. Mostly, I wish you and I—"

A scream rang out from the village.

She knew that scream. So did Miraden.

They sprinted down the hill. A crowd of villagers was gathering at the cottage across the road from her own. Miraden and Ceychell reached the edge of the crowd as Ceychell's father, Chieftain Ormus, pushed through them like a mad bull. The dairymaid, Lolia, was wailing into the chest of her husband, Wermen. She shook him violently and howled, "They've taken him! They've taken Kjod!"

Ormus's blond hair looked like the tips of a fierce flame as his face reddened with anger. His enormous figure trembled like a mountain ready to blow. The chieftain sighed through his teeth and put a hand on the stout dairymaid's shoulder to steady her rage before she broke her slender husband in half.

"Ormus, you must do something!" Lolia shouted. "You must! Kjod is the second child this month!"

Ceychell felt Miraden shaking next to her. The ashenkin were getting bolder. They snatched the first local child from an outlying farm. Now the ashenkin had penetrated the center of the village.

Lolia continued screaming, "Please, Ormus, you are our chieftain. Will you do nothing? We must hunt these devils down!" Lolia raised her fists, and some other villagers joined in, shouting for Ormus to do something.

"We have only a few able militiamen," Ormus said, rubbing his square chin. "Should I send them when we can't—"

Another scream cut the air. This time clearly from Ceychell's own home.

"Mother?" Ceychell said, her voice a rasp. She shoved past Miraden and ran toward her cottage. Her father and Miraden were close behind her as they trampled inside, scattering two dogs and a cat toward her mother's wailing.

Ceychell burst into Kyradel's room. She saw Curasca lying on the floor beside the bed, crying. The floor was littered with Kyradel's torn blankets. Blood trailed to the open window where claw marks scarred the sill.

"No. No. It can't be," Ceychell whispered, barely audible. "Please, no."

Ormus pushed past her and stood over his wife. She watched her usually impassive father wail and stumble to the floor next to Curasca. Tears flowing down his cheeks, he embraced her, nearly covering her with his bear-like arms.

Ceychell turned toward Miraden, standing in the doorway. She trembled and struggled to stand. She tried to push him aside.

"Ceycha… what—?"

She punched him in the chest. He allowed it, and she hit him repeatedly until he grabbed her wrists. She wailed and let him wrap his arms around her. It had been a long time since last he held her. Too long. She held him back.

She trembled in his arms, her lips quivering. Drool and tears blotted on his cloak as she screamed against his chest.

"I am so sorry," he muttered. His tears fell onto Ceychell's forehead.

THREE

AN UNLIKELY HERO

THREE HOURS PASSED, BUT THE village still buzzed like a hornet's nest knocked from its branch. Miraden brushed past a group of villagers gathered around a house. They discussed sealing homes with wood boards. He approached Ormus, who buried his face in his enormous hands, and stood before him, unnoticed.

Miraden wanted to cry; he couldn't fathom how his chieftain was coping with the reality of his lost daughter. Ormus was the bravest man Miraden knew, but no man, no matter how brave, could bear such a loss. "Chieftain Ormus?"

Ormus lifted his head as if under great strain and squinted his bloodshot eyes at Miraden. Miraden knew Ormus thought he was a pain in his youngest daughter's side. "What do you want, Miraden?"

"I know you cannot spare anyone," Miraden said, wishing his voice would not quaver so much. "I wish to track the ashenkin and find Kyradel. I will bring her back."

Ormus's eye twitched. "Brave words from a boy who runs from his own shadow, Miraden. Even if you tried, you'd do nothing but sacrifice your life. What could you do against those vicious, burning, soulless beasts?"

Ormus's words doused Miraden's courage. Miraden shifted his weight and took a step back. He wanted to pull his green cloak around his face and hide. Ormus's shadow was crushing him. When he couldn't even face Ormus, he realized the truth: If Ormus, a true warrior, didn't go to face them, what real chance did he have? He heard they were eight feet tall and red as fire.

"Sir, I—"

"Stop wasting my time, Miraden. Go back to your chores."

Chandar, the village carpenter, tall with long graying hair, stepped forward from the gathering, calling Ormus's name. Miraden didn't care for the sawdust-smelling stoic. He never even paid when Miraden cut his wood. Ormus, clearly finished, turned away from him and gave Chandar his attention.

"If we work day and night," Chandar said, "we can construct a wall in a few weeks. We can build watch platforms in several trees surrounding the village. Look here." He pointed to a crude map of the village scratched into the dirt in the middle of the gathering.

Miraden crept up behind Ormus and looked down at the sketch of the village. At its center was a crude representation of the statue of Kaehrn. Surrounding the statue were three pods of shops with the villagers' homes spread around them. Ormus's cottage was at the base of some curved lines showing Kaehrnstone Hill, and Curasca's old herb shop was sketched in a pod at the far end of town. A line weaved around sketched trees and surrounded the village. He saw the line passed close between Ormus's home and the trees.

"It cuts off most of my land," Ormus said. "Smothers our village."

"You lost one daughter," Chandar said. "Would you like—"

"Don't!" Ormus shook his massive head. "Build it."

"We can use lumber we harvested to sell and begin at once."

"What good is the revenue if we lose our children?"

The walls would turn Kaehrn into an encampment, a prison.

Miraden felt it would no longer be the beautiful village he had grown up in. Ormus seemed to feel the same way. He watched Ormus among the villagers, grunting and shaking his head.

"I've heard the ashenkin are as tall as a man with large claws. They are good climbers," Miraden said. "Walls won't slow them for long."

The villagers turned hard stares at Miraden all at once, the hardest from the village blacksmith, Bryndyke. The smith was wider than Ormus but shorter than Miraden, with arms so huge they couldn't rest by his sides but stuck out from his torso. He spat on the dirt and said, "Why don't you go cut some wood and leave this matter to the *men* of the village, eh?"

Miraden was used to this treatment. He shrank back into the gathering of villagers. *Miraden, why don't you go cut firewood? Miraden, why don't you go get a stag? Miraden, why don't you get out of sight and return with something of value, then leave again?*

He was sick of it, but not enough to dare confront Bryndyke or the others, especially today. He wanted to help, not cut firewood. He was tired of being ignored. "Bilore Des has high wooden walls," he said. "Three times taller than the largest man. Children are taken, and the guards never see a thing. Why would this be any different?"

Ormus fixed his gaze upon Miraden. His hard face curled into a scowl that threatened to kill.

As all eyes burned through him, Miraden now realized he had his moment. "I am a poor woodcutter and not a good builder," he said. "But I am a tracker. I'm no help here, and… if there is a chance of bringing Kyradel back, this is it. Please, let me go, right now."

Bryndyke and Chandar leaned away as Ormus fumed like a cauldron ready to boil over. "Bring in the logs," Ormus told Chandar. Then he turned to Miraden. "Let's get you prepared for your journey."

Miraden ran all the way home to his little cottage at the edge of the village, as excited about helping Kyradel and Ceychell as he was fearful of the ashenkin. The house was sadly quiet, as it had been since both his parents had died from the coughing disease two winters past. He missed them terribly. He felt their warmth when he gazed upon the small portrait of them that Kyradel had painted, hanging on the sitting room wall, and remembered his father teaching him how to fletch arrows as a boy. He smiled at them, feeling a new meaning coming to his life in his mission to save Kyradel.

He darted to his bedroom, emptied chests, and shoved trappings into his packs. He took three knives from atop the mantle. He took inventory: the knives, two quivers full of arrows, his best bow made from a blue pine—the same tree from which he'd made Ceychell's flowerbox—along with a tinder box, snares, a blanket, plenty of tightly rolled parchment, quill and ink, dried food, sewing kit, spare sack, raptor glove, sixty aluminum coins or lumins, ten copper kamerans or kams, and an extra wineskin. Then he took a deep breath and looked around his home, hoping he would see it again someday.

Miraden walked out the front door and closed it behind him without bothering to lock it. He looked back and peered through the empty, dusty windows and felt memories of his childhood beginning to fade. Then he turned back and walked down the worn path in the grass and away from the only home he'd ever known. Perhaps its next owners would love it as much as he did.

He walked over to the large maple tree beside his house, put down his pack, and withdrew the thick leather glove from it. Then he held the glove up toward the branches, and a beautiful preddlehawk screeched and descended from the top of the tree. The light shimmered on his deep blue wings. A single bolt of silver feathers ran down his otherwise black chest. Stormrange, Miraden's beloved pet, alighted on the glove and then stepped onto his shoulder.

Miraden removed a dried piece of chicken from his pocket and let Stormrange pluck it from his fingers. Petting Stormrange made him happy, if only for a moment. He stroked the bird's neck and said, "I hope you're ready for an adventure, Stormrange." Stormrange juked his head and fluttered his wings.

When Miraden returned to the village square, Ormus, Bryndyke, and Ceychell were waiting for him. They greeted him with silent nods and stares, and he looked down at the dirt on the road, trying to ignore the twisting in his gut. He fidgeted, then adjusted his pack, checked for his bow, moved to his quiver, checked for his bow again. He sniffed the sap in the air, breathed a big sigh, pulled up his hood, and gazed back at their stern looks.

Miraden found more uncertainty than anger in Ormus's gaze. Bryndyke, sooty arms crossed, held a sheathed sword in one hand. The smith smiled below his brush of blood-red beard. Miraden hoped it was something kinder than the portent of a snide remark he was dying to share. Ceychell no longer stared at him, and he tried not to stare at her. It tore at his heart that she didn't offer even an ounce of kindness. He thought back to her comment a few hours ago. He pondered what she was going to say. He hadn't had time to process it, but now it left a pit in his stomach.

"I am ready," Miraden said. Not even he believed his words. In fact, he'd just as soon flee back to his home, hide under his covers, and disappear.

Bryndyke stepped up to Miraden, held out the sheathed sword as if it were a twig in his bear paw, and offered it to Miraden. Miraden nodded his thanks and took the scabbarded sword. He grasped the hilt, and the sword sang as he unsheathed it. Its curved silver blade bore a greenish hue in the sunlight.

"This is my finest saber," the blacksmith said. "Its grip should fit you, and it is perfectly weighted. I hear the little devils don't like tempered relzyian silver, so be sure you cut 'em plenty." Bryndyke smiled. "Or I'm going to take it back." Miraden looked up from the blade in alarm, just in time to receive a hearty slap across his shoulder that sent him off balance. "Make us proud and go bring Kyra back."

Miraden admired the blade's brilliant shine. It was light and firm in his grip. He attached the scabbard to his belt, then carefully sheathed the blade.

Miraden looked up to find Ceychell solemnly staring through him, her eyes red with tears. He stared at the young woman he'd loved his whole life. The pain and anger poured out from her and threatened to drown him in sorrow. There was no escape. Tears ran down his cheeks, through the stubbled growth on his chin, and onto the dirt at his feet. He remained perfectly still and watched Ceychell's tears fall and meet at the same dirt. Memories from their childhood flashed through his mind. Thoughts of swimming together, chasing her, and finally being kissed by her sat on his mind. This might be the last time he ever saw her. He wanted to tell her so much. Should he die on his journey, everything was for *her*.

"I'll find Kyradel," Miraden said, choking up the words. He already missed her so much. He loved Kyradel like his own sister.

Ceychell pulled a small homespun satchel from inside her tunic and handed it to him. "Drink the green vial if you're sick. The brown is for infection, yellow for poison, blue will slow your hunger. I—" Her lips trembled. She pressed her eyes closed and said no more.

When he took the bag, she retracted her hand and wrapped her arms around her body. He wanted to tell her he did everything for her, all of this, but even that wasn't true. He loved Kyradel as well, just not in the same way. He had to find her and bring her home.

Ceychell cleared her throat and rasped, "You should go. She's getting farther—" Then she covered her face and turned away.

Miraden wanted to run to Ceychell and comfort her, but he knew she wouldn't allow it. "I've brought parchment. I will write to you, Ceycha." He looked for something from her. Anything.

She turned an eye to him and nodded. She bit her lips closed as her chin trembled.

His sight of her was replaced by that of her towering father. Miraden gazed up at Ormus and suddenly felt himself shrink.

"You're brave to go, Miraden. Here," he said, untying a leather purse from his belt. "Thirty kams are all I can spare—I must hire mercenaries to help guard our village. Start north to the Bilore Des. They may have more clues on where the ashenkin… where they…" His voice trailed a bit and for the first time. Miraden saw the golem crumbling. Ormus shook his head, then suddenly embraced him. "Go, boy, please bring Kyra back to me," he whispered, nearly crushing Miraden in his embrace. Ormus's fear terrified him.

"I will, sir. I will see happiness restored to your home."

FOUR

A DEVIL'S COMPASS

CEYCHELL STEPPED OUT OF HER house and delighted at the pattering of raindrops on her head. She pulled her coat tight over her robe and smiled. She smelled the rain, tasted the fresh sap in the air. Her spirit lightened until she pushed the wooden handle of her home closed. Her heart sank as she dropped to her knees. She stared at the names etched beside the door.

CEYCHA KYRA

She remembered the morning they carved it: It was a day just like today. She was no older than ten at the time, her sister nine. The memory was clear as day. She still had the whittling knife she used—the one Miraden gave her. It was sharp and perfect for etching letters into soft wood. She ran her index fingernail over the carvings to pull away bits of moss. Her heavy sigh dragged tears with it.

The forest canopy blocked most of the rain, but some trickled through. She drew back her hood to let it kiss her face and long chestnut hair. It, like all simple things as of late, reminded her of her childhood. Of playing with her sister in the rain for hours on end, something she cherished more than beautiful sunny days. Every day was a rude reminder of the sister that was taken from her just a week ago, a sister that had resented her for the past few years, a sister she loved dearly.

A crack of thunder startled her, and the rain came pouring down. Ceychell breathed in the wet forest scents of earth and moss and pine needles and thought back to a time, perhaps four years ago, when she ran, and the rain fell in torrents like it did this day. It poured so hard she worried it would wash her cabin from the hill, but when the storm stopped, the forest smelled wonderfully fresh, like everything was clean and new. She shared that day with the ranger who had also gone...

As the memories continued to swirl, she didn't feel like gathering reagents. Instead, she strode to the top of the hill behind her home. She'd made the climb a thousand times to lie on the large flat rock near the top, the Kaehrnstone, worn smooth by the weather of uncountable years. For many summers, she had lain on the rock while her sister sang of Kaehrn and their heritage. It was their rock, and it felt like a home away from home.

Ceychell sat down on her favorite smooth spot and looked upon the weathered scrawling from her childhood. She ran her hands over the marks. The little coded messages she wrote with Kyra were now so faded they were invisible to anyone else. She found one from her sister, it used to say *I'll love you forever,* and her tears broke free and mixed with the rain on her cheeks.

A screech pierced the storm overhead. She looked up to see a beautiful hawk circling in the gray sky. The bird dove and landed on the smooth stone next to her. "Hello, Stormrange," she said apprehensively. A ring of twine held a small leather scroll case to the hawk's belly. Stormrange puffed up his silver chest and nudged his long sharp beak against her arm. She ran her long fingers through the bird's feathers and scurried them along his chest until the bird lay on its side against her leg. She untied the leather scroll case and hesitated only for a moment before opening it. Out slid a scroll. After it, three gold coins fell into her hand. She examined the three-headed serpent pressed onto each coin and couldn't believe it. She'd only seen gold coins but never held one before. She smiled, then pocketed the coins and tucked the scroll into her chest pocket under her robe to keep it from getting wet. She wanted to read it but feared what it might say. She feared it might confirm Kyradel's death. She hugged Stormrange and placed the bird upon her shoulder.

Ceychell sat on the Kaehrnstone for a few more minutes, thinking about the message, letting the rain wash down her face. Stormrange squawked and shrugged the rain from his long wings. The preddlehawk danced on her shoulder, careful not to hurt her with his sharp talons until she rose to her feet. He chattered and ran his beak through her hair. She grinned ear to ear, running her nails along his neck.

The coins rustled in her pocket as she walked back to her home, thinking about what she could buy. She wished Kyradel was with her to share the money, as they always used to, but this was so much, she couldn't selfishly keep it all. Especially now that her father needed to hire mercenaries.

Ceychell jogged down the hill—completely drenched—into Kaehrn with Stormrange on her shoulder. The old seamstress was walking in the other direction on the muddy road. Ceychell failed to avoid her.

"Hello, Ceychell," Vera said as Ceychell passed in haste. "Is that Stormrange?"

"It is. Miraden sent a message!" Ceychell shouted and kept running.

"Keep his words close to your heart," Vera hollered after her. "Pray for that boy!" The old seamstress shook her head, grinned, and turned back toward her mossy shoe of a cabin.

Ceychell threw open the door of her own cottage. After slamming it hard behind her, she shuffled past her mother and sat down by the hearth to take off her wet coat and warm herself. She removed the letter from beneath her robe and started to open—

"Did you manage to find any—"

"Be right back, mother!" Ceychell said as she got up and rushed through the family room.

"Ceycha? Ceycha!" Her mother's calling didn't slow her.

Ceychell ran into her room. She nearly tripped over her boxes of flasks and vials. She stepped over a sack of her clothes and sat down between a box filled with cinnamon and a box of various seeds. She shook with anxiety as she looked at her room. She was ready to move into her own place. After a few deep breaths, she pulled the scroll from her pocket.

Stormrange chirped then jumped onto the box beside her. She kissed the bird on the head and then rubbed her face against his cheek. Finally, she unraveled the letter and began reading. Her heart fluttered.

Miraden was nervous since the moment he'd left Kaehrn. He followed the tracks from Kyra's window north through Baregorin Forest, but the cold rain was making it challenging for him to follow.

He wasn't typically frightened in Baregorin, but what he might find beyond its borders did scare him. He knew so little of the ashenkin other than what everyone else did. So far, he hadn't found many footprints, though, so he suspected they were carrying Kyradel and Kjod.

Bilore Des was three days' walk, but he wasn't sure he'd make it there after losing the trail many times. The rain just wasn't on his side, but at least the forest was peaceful and quiet. The blue pines were comforting, and Stormrange chirped to him often.

Finally, it seemed the ashenkin trail used the main road. It was a bit covered in weeds now. The merchant traffic had slowed quite a bit to the south since the ashenkin arrived a few months ago. Their reach had grown steadily. At first, there were only stories of children taken in the dead of night in cities. For them to reach a remote village like Kaehrn meant they were either growing larger in force or having to scavenge further for children. Either thought made Miraden shiver and look over his shoulder more frequently.

The woods were quieter the closer he got to Bilore Des, not as he remembered them. He felt as if he were passing through a place he didn't know. The birds were silent, and a gray gloom seemed to follow him. Luckily, his trek was unabated, and he prayed to the Daughter of Forests that it remained this way. He prayed that he would find the ashenkin quickly and otherwise travel unnoticed. He wrote some of a letter the night before reaching town. It started to rain again, so he put his things away, propped himself up against a tree under a thick canopy, and drifted to sleep.

The next morning, Miraden made it to the long stretch of the wooden wall protecting Bilore Des. Miraden walked through the open gate, got a slight nod from a guard in full chainmail, but wasn't asked any questions. He hoped he would find clues to Kyra's whereabouts in town, but the first thing he found was the horrid stink of wet horse dung, rotting vegetables, and chamber pots that the people had dumped in the street. Miraden tried his best not to cover his nose and appear pompous as he saved his senses.

Bilore Des was much larger than Kaehrn, at least ten times the size. Walking down the muddy, horse-pitted main street, Miraden saw a commotion ahead and approached the angry rabble arguing over a naagling attack. They shouted at a lord who was trying to calm them, but the citizens were yelling threats and appeared eager to feed the nervous man to the naaglings.

"Excuse me," Miraden said to a woman next to him. She had her hair up in a tight bun and a hooked nose. Her wool dress smelled sour. Miraden thought perhaps she was a dairy hand. There was no glimmer of kindness in her eyes. They were dark with anger.

"What you want? You here to join the call to arms?" she said. She turned to shout at the lord.

"No, I was just curious if anyone has spotted ashenkin in the past few days?"

The crowd quieted and looked at him. The lord took the opportunity to start backing away.

The dairy hand clicked her tongue. "What else is new?"

Before they could turn back to the lord, Miraden asked, "So, you have seen some? I'm looking for a friend of mine who was taken."

The rabble exchanged glances. "No one sees them. They're just here," the woman said and snapped her fingers. "Then they're gone with your child, like my Fre—" The woman couldn't hold her sternness any longer and began to weep.

"Those ashenkin were created by the wizards in Kander. Never trust a wizard, boy," an old man missing the end of his right arm whispered. He lifted the nub to his eye, spotted with age and bloodshot. "They sent those things to take our children for their rituals…"

"That's nonsense!"

"They are here because the gods are angry with us. We've failed the Mother of Light!"

Miraden realized he fanned the flames of an angry mob and worried about his own safety as they yelled over each other.

"Can you tell me anything of their whereabouts?" Miraden asked. He asked again, but louder to get their attention.

"Go see the mayor. Someone reported seeing something a day or two ago," a guard said. Miraden didn't notice him, but there were now a few guards. The rabble's enthusiasm quickly died. Miraden used the opportunity to scurry away to look for the mayor.

He walked until he found a city hall. He scrapped his boots for the tenth time, annoyed. He looked over as he wiped the rest of the poop from his boot as the shopkeeper sweeping his porch stared at him warily. He missed the friendliness of home where his neighbors greeted him or invited him in for a refreshment, unlike here.

Miraden ignored the stares and the occasional shoulder bump before stepping up to a large building. It seemed to be impressive at one time, but now most of the wood was split. Weeds overgrew the grounds, and even a few sprouted on the roof. It looked nothing like the office of an important city official. He sort of expected marble pillars and manicured gardens.

Miraden tried to open the door, but it stopped abruptly on something. He heard a strange tapping coming from inside. Miraden pushed with all his strength and squeezed through the opening into cigar smoke and the pong of rotten fruit.

"What do you want?" Heavy bags hung below a man's brown eyes, which reminded Miraden of his father, who always worked long, hard days hunting for his village. But unlike him, Mayor Updinkle was pale and sickly and had a sour lip ready with quips.

He stared at Miraden in his rude way without getting up from his oak desk, which was laden with stacks of papers. His walls were bare, and a few stacks of books were without shelves, just piled up from the floor. He held a letter opener up. Below it, there were thousands of pits in his desk—the tapping had stopped. His crumpled face sagged against his upturned hand. His elbow rested lazily on his desk. He seemed to be a man troubled by much who solved very little. Miraden didn't want to bother him but had no choice.

"A guard told me you knew of ashenkin in the area," Miraden said.

He held his hands behind his back and cleared his throat.

"Bah. No telling where they are. Some of the mercenaries I sent out to hunt them told me they found a few west of the city, but today, it's the naaglings that are my problem. Those people"—he pointed to the window where Miraden had heard the faint cries of the arguing rabble—"were beating my door in to yell at me about it."

"Well, did you—"

"Tell you what, kid. You hunt down the naaglings, you'll probably find the devils with them. There's a bounty for the naags—ten hydras. Whadaysay?" His eyes perked up, and his smile was a bit desperate.

Stormrange screeched when he saw a mouse scurry from under the mayor's desk and into a hole in the wall. Updinkle jumped and knocked the papers off his desk.

Miraden's eyes widened. He'd never seen that much money. Ormus gave him 30 kams, which was the most he'd ever carried. The bounty was three times more! He rationalized getting the money to help him fund the journey and send Ormus's money back to hire protection.

"I'll do it," Miraden said.

"Eh, you will? Good boy, come back to me with proof, and the money is yours. Oh, and boy?" Miraden turned to look at him. "If you see a gate wreathed in yellow flames, you best run."

"A … flaming gate?"

"Rhaellin Ashengates. The ashenkin pour out of them to come for our children, and they'll capture a boy like you. Best to stick to the naaglings."

Miraden considered his advice. "Do you know why they are taking children?"

"The Henslemen say the children are sacrificed to make more ashenkin. They say that dark magic broke the seal to their world…" The mayor was standing now, his hands firm on his desk. "There is a rumor that the wizards of Kander are controlling them and creating something fouler than anything in this world beyond those gates."

Miraden swallowed the knot in his throat. Suddenly, his quests felt even more foolish. He had to get to Kyradel before the ashenkin could reach a gate. He had to hurry. Miraden rushed out of the mayor's office as quickly as he could and left town, heading west.

Miraden regretted not searching for Kyra but hoped the money would fund his journey. He trekked west from Bilore Des nearly a day when small tracks in the mud grew in frequency. Three front and two back claw prints—the tracks of naaglings. There were so many tracks reeling about in every direction he knew there were a lot of them. Littered about the tracks were chewed bits of rind and gnarled bones. They even emptied their bowels directly on the path. He hadn't seen them yet, but from the fresh poop everywhere, he knew he was close. He petted Stormrange and sent him off before getting too close.

Miraden knew naaglings scared easily, or at least that's what his father had told him. His father said they fought like smart dogs but would run when threatened. Even so, the number of tracks worried him.

He finally found a village near a copse of maples. Miraden stopped and hid behind a thick trunk. Several crude huts were built around what looked to be a central fire pit with a pot hanging on a hook over the fire. It was dusk, and naaglings were running about. They were puke-green with thin necks and large misshapen heads. Each had tufts of tar-black hair pulled into a tail tied with bones; some had burns where hair might have been. They wore patchworks of hides held by strips of leather. Some had packs or small bags that weren't as crudely fashioned and most likely stolen. They constantly squabbled, first over a dead bird, then the largest spear, and then berries that were completely squashed by the end of the fight. Luck was with Miraden since they were so distracted that they didn't notice him back up into the heavy undergrowth. He tried counting them, but they scurried around so much that it was hard to distinguish one green menace from another. He got to thirty before he realized he counted the same short naagling three times.

They were so raucous and rude that he found them difficult to watch. Naaglings screamed and shuffled like wild children. Spat constantly. They fought over the most trivial of things. One pulled wax from his ear and ate it, then another swatted him in the face with a large stick and tried to take what was left on the ear-picker's finger.

One climbed out from a tree perch and fell, landing on and killing another naagling. Miraden covered his mouth quickly to keep from laughing. He couldn't believe it: The naagling wasn't fazed by the fall or the murder; he just started to loot the dead naagling's body. Then the entire rabble swarmed to fight over whatever trinkets could be found in the squashed naagling's sack. They eventually finished looting and fighting and then went about their business. It seemed they simply forgot why they were quarreling. Miraden couldn't wait to tell Ceychell about this.

As he watched them, he really wondered how he could go through with this mission. He pitied them and certainly didn't want to kill them. He began considering backing out and just searching for the ashenkin. Then he saw a woman's face, staring blankly from the garbage near the stew pot. Then another, and another. It hit him that what he smelled cooking was the people of Bilore Des. It troubled him; he still didn't like the idea of killing but stayed and pondered options.

Miraden didn't sleep while hiding in the thick brush, but it wasn't hard to stay awake watching them. Some left to hunt with crude spears—or at least that is what he guessed they did. Others chewed on bones or danced around a bonfire. Their village was like a swarm of ants on a heap of garbage. The smell—it smelled as if they were burning their own dung to heat the big crude pot of foul stew. Miraden often breathed through his hood, but it barely helped.

His limbs tingled with sleep by the time his patience paid off. Out stepped an odd naagling from the largest hut in the village. It had red horns jutting from his skull. In his knobby claw, he held a jagged dagger that looked crafted, not crude like the spears the others held. He guessed him to be their chieftain. The creature was gangly and disproportioned like the naaglings, just twice their size. When it barked at the other naaglings, they snapped to face the chieftain and ceased their antics. As it shouted, they scrambled to gather food from the pot.

After getting the rabble to bring it a few charred limbs from the stone pot, the chieftain returned to the confines of its hut. They pulled a few more villagers out of the refuse toward the pot. When Miraden saw a large plume of red hair, he couldn't look away. Flames surged through his chest as the thought that it could be Kyradel was bringing him to tears. She wasn't moving. It took everything he had to not jump from cover, but she wasn't moving. She was likely dead, and they would pay for it.

The night was too long. There were too many of them. Miraden couldn't move into a better position to see if it was Kyradel lying on the pile of corpses. He constantly worried that one of them would spot him, or a fight would spill into the bush where he was hiding. His eyelids became heavy. He couldn't shift or slap himself to stay awake.

Then, Miraden thought of Ceychell on a long summer day. He remembered the day last year. She sat on the bank of Pallow Lake, eating apples with Kyra. They weren't talking or laughing like they used to. It was hard to watch, and Miraden relived the dread that he'd caused it. The sullen thoughts kept him awake.

A few hours past daybreak, the naaglings were snoring, farting, and grunting in their huts. In the rising daylight, he could now see clearly why the village stank so bad. The sticks they built their huts with were held together with dried mud and dung, all of them. Beside the huts were fresh piles of dung covered in flies.

A lone naagling was all that stood guard over the village. It leaned lazily on its spear. Miraden thought most of the night about how he would take them out, but the time to plan was over. He needed to be quiet and effective, or he'd be in their stew by day's end. He considered spreading fire, but it would be difficult to do it quickly before they were alerted. Then the Lady of Rain opened the clouds and extinguished the plan altogether.

After waiting a while to see if the pattering would awaken them, Miraden remembered something his father used to tell him: You'll never get the perfect opportunity twice. Miraden drew an arrow and fired it at the lone guard and pierced his skull. The naagling fell to the muddy ground immediately with little more than a soggy squish.

Miraden crept to the corpse pile to see if the fallen girl was Kyradel. She hadn't moved the entire night. Nothing in the garbage did. He looked over his shoulders and back constantly. The tension that something would see him was bringing his teeth to chatter.

Everything was still, and the village was quiet.

Miraden's hand shook when he reached out to pull her shoulder. He turned over a young woman, roughly Kyra's age, but it wasn't her. But that poor girl was dead. Full of spear stabs. He then realized how many dead people he was standing on and jumped off the pile. He felt terrible but now understood why Bilore Des was so upset about the naaglings.

Miraden moved around the perimeter of the village with ease and snuck into hut after hut. Now that he was closer, he could see the naaglings' pocked skin was covered in boils and scars. His nostrils burned from the reek of their urine-soaked dwellings. The horrid stench of rotting meat and poop was caked on their faces and claws.

The first little pest twitched and swatted its face in its sleep. He took a deep breath and put a dagger to its neck, then pulled it away. It did not feel right to kill it. As Miraden's arm shook, he thought of the dead girl. What if he couldn't do this and hesitated when it was time to confront the ashenkin? It wasn't likely he'd steal Kyradel back or talk them into releasing her.

With deep remorse, he pushed his dagger through its head. Black blood poured from the wound and smelled even worse than the naagling. Miraden vomited in the hut. He tried his best to keep it quiet while he gagged.

Miraden held his breath in each hut to save himself from coughing or sneezing from their filth. Like the first, he ran each of them through and hated every second of it.

Everything was going well until he stepped out of a hut and found a naagling peeing on a log. It stared directly at Miraden, and Miraden froze. He wasn't sure what the naagling was thinking, but they stared at each other for what felt like an hour. The moment it finished peeing, it yelled and drew a dagger. Miraden raised his bow and shot it through its eye.

Miraden ran into the woods. He had already killed quite a few naaglings but was unsure how many were alive. When he looked over his shoulder, the horned naagling stared from the entryway of its large hut. First, its jaw trembled a little, then it bared his fangs, roared, and charged across the village at Miraden. The boy fled, stopping every so often to fire an arrow at the snarling chieftain. He had few clear shots while he dodged trees and jumped over roots. He thought he had hit the chieftain, but his arrows weren't effective. He stopped firing and ran for his life.

But the naagling was faster. It barreled after him, bouncing off trees, stumbling through the brush. Its snorting and grunting grew louder behind him. It roared something at him, or maybe it was just a roar of anger, but it seemed the forest shook and rattled his eardrums.

When Miraden realized it would catch him sooner rather than later, he turned and took a moment to get his footing, then fired an arrow point-blank right into its chest. The chieftain buckled over momentarily, then stood straight and lunged at him with its dagger.

Miraden somehow blocked the blow with his bow but was tackled. The air hissed out of his lungs as his back struck the ground. Miraden dropped his bow and caught its dagger hand and held it off just barely. It chomped at his face. Spit flew into his eyes. Miraden ran his fingers along the sweating, stinking chest and managed to grab the arrow shaft covered in sticky blood. He twisted it and pushed it farther into its chest and twisted it again. It roared. It then grabbed for his hand as Miraden let the arrow go. He drew his saber from its scabbard. He fought with its wrist and stretched his head away from the tip of that black dagger. He suddenly heard a loud squawk from the forest canopy. Stormrange dove through the trees and clawed at the back of the chieftain's head. The distraction was enough for Miraden to awkwardly push his blade through its side. It fought him a few moments, but Miraden forced the blade deeper into it, and finally, it collapsed on him.

Miraden shoved the chieftain off, sat up, and saw a pair of terrified naaglings turn to flee. He buzzed with anxiety and adrenaline, but he was exhausted and couldn't chase them.

Stormrange fluttered above him for a moment and then settled on his shoulder. Miraden was so grateful for him. He petted his companion and pulled a piece of dried meat from his pouch and offered it. Miraden's heart raced like it never had before. He looked down at the naagling chieftain on the ground and knew that it almost got him. If it had, his journey would have been for nothing. Kyra would be lost forever, and he would have just been this thing's breakfast. He was glad and thankful as the Lady of Rain poured onto him. He felt blessed by her.

Miraden decided the chieftain's head was proof of success. It was uglier than the others, and its horns were unique among them. Its face and body were twisted by something unnatural. It almost looked as if another head was growing out of its shoulder.

Miraden wiped his saber clean, sheathed it, and then drew a hunting knife. He sliced through the chieftain's neck, carefully cutting between his vertebrae, and placed the head in a spare sack. He'd dressed and carved up many animals, but this was strange. It felt odd cutting through the neck of something that wasn't an animal. He looked at the knife. It was covered in black blood, just like Miraden. His stomach caught up to his fear, and he grew ill again.

Once Miraden was better, he looted a few small bags tied to its belt and took that wicked black dagger.

Miraden was certainly glad it rained hard that entire day: It *almost* washed the naagling taint off of his clothes, but he knew the tarry bloodstains would never come out.

He returned to Bilore Des late that evening, trudging through the heavy rain. The walls were well lit by guards holding torches or lanterns. He followed its outer wooden wall toward the gate and paused when he saw claw marks reflecting from the lantern light upon the wall. They didn't look like they were made by wolves' claws or even bears' and were definitely too large for a naagling. Rain poured down the wooden logs as he put a finger into a claw mark and traced it up the side of the wall. The deep scratches zigzagged to the top. The stories he heard were, in fact, true—walls don't hold back the ashenkin in the slightest. He'll remember to add that to the letter.

Miraden reached the gate at last, and they let him pass. A guard looked askance at Stormrange on his shoulder but made no comment. Miraden offered them a friendly nod and then walked through the gate and continued straight to the mayor's office.

The few townsfolk in the street, likely returning home from the pubs, took no notice of him. He preferred it that way. After all, if he went into the village claiming victory, one of them might take the reward.

Mayor Updinkle wasn't happy to find Miraden rapping on his door late that evening until he pulled the large naagling head out of the bag. His eyes nearly popped out of his skull when he saw the creature's mutated face and horns. He said he'd never seen anything like it and asked Miraden to stay while he fetched his clerics. He also asked if the bird could wait outside, but Miraden didn't budge on it; after all, he was somewhat of a hero now.

Miraden was cleaning the muck from his gear as best as he could and repairing a few arrows when two clerics returned with the mayor. One was a woman, old and wrinkled, reminding him a bit of Vera, only kinder. The other cleric was a young man, an apprentice, stout and heavy, and closer to his age. He had a tuft of blond hair and a large smile and seemed the friendliest of sorts. He carried a labor of books in his arms.

The mayor led them into a study with walls lined with books and a center table surrounded by padded chairs and a desk, a neater one than in his other office. He laid an old blanket on the desk and asked Miraden to put the head on it, which he did, along with the dagger. The younger cleric and the mayor examined the head quietly, prodding its glassy eyes and rubbing its horns, but the older cleric was most interested in the naagling's dagger. Then they consulted their books while Miraden waited patiently. After a while, his legs could no longer hold him up, and he sank into one of the chairs around the table, exhausted. Stormrange climbed into his lap.

Sometime later, a servant shook Miraden awake and placed a bowl of food on the table in front of him. He didn't realize how hungry he was until he had swallowed two full bowls of the hearty mutton stew and fresh bread. He petted Stormrange and listened to the rain outside. The sound was like music to him as he remembered to thank the Lady of Rain and promised her he'd never wish for the rain to stop again.

Miraden shared his bread with Stormrange and wrote a letter to Ceychell. He told her about clearing the naagling village and returning with a dagger and the head of the chieftain. Along with it, he sent his love and how much he missed her. He'd send it out before leaving Bilore Des, so he wanted to finish it tonight.

The old cleric sat down next to him. "This naagling you killed was an agent of the ashenkin," she began. "Creatures turned in this way are afflicted with the ashenkin magic. They are transformed against their will into servants. This might explain why naaglings are taking children." She held the wicked black dagger up for him to see it closely. There was a red runestone carved in its hilt. She ran the weapon along the edge of a table. Its jagged serrations stripped the wood back as if it were soft flesh. The old woman turned it on end and observed the small etching down the blade. "It is a scrying tool. This one bears the name Hellshy. Watch." She dropped the blade on the floor. It juddered and spun itself a half turn before settling still.

"North," the old woman said. "The direction you must go."

Miraden hesitated a moment, then bent down and picked up the dagger. He was curious, so he dropped it on end himself. The dagger shifted and flopped onto the floor, then turned itself in the same direction as before. "That blade leads its bearer beyond an Ashengate, back to the sacrificial altar from which it was crafted."

"Do… do you know why they are taking children?" Miraden

asked her.

The old woman sighed in unease. "The temple of the Lady of Light believes it is because children are the purest of us, and extinguishing their flames will leave us helpless and futureless."

Miraden looked down. "I heard they sacrificed children to—"

"Make more ashenkin?" she snipped. "Bah, you are listening to those bandit Henslemen. They'd have you believe there is a dark pact between the wizards and those godless creatures. Think they spread that nonsense just for the business of being sellswords." She leaned in. "Pay them no mind."

Miraden looked at the blade and wondered if *it* was used to sacrifice anyone. It sickened him, and shivers ran up his back. As much as he wanted to destroy the tool, he thought it would get him closer to finding Kyradel.

"Thank you for your help," Miraden said. The old cleric smiled and nodded to him before quietly leaving.

Mayor Updinkle stepped into the office where Miraden was writing. He handed Miraden a small sack of gold coins. The mayor smiled enough to show his brown teeth, which were nothing to smile about. He gave Miraden a key to the guest quarters that were currently vacant behind his office.

It was a tiny home that probably had room for little more than a bed. Miraden was exhausted, but he knew he had to leave early the next morning to resume the hunt.

As Miraden walked to the guest house, he let Stormrange loose and heard heavy footsteps and turned to see the cleric's apprentice approaching him.

"Hello, I overheard the mayor say you were hunting ashenkin. That true?"

Miraden nodded.

"I'd like to join you if you'd have me. I want to do more than read books and heal the sick. I want to make a difference and stop these devils."

"Well, I am after them because they have my friend. I will do anything I must to bring her home. So, I'm not on a noble quest to conquer the ashenkin if that is what you're looking for," Miraden said. He wasn't ashamed; he just didn't want to be untruthful.

"I can help you find her, and perhaps we'll kill some ashenkin along the way," he said. Miraden enjoyed his grin and how friendly he'd been since he arrived. The large cleric looked sturdy enough, and he certainly could use the muscle. But he was a bit concerned he wouldn't keep up. He had a large mace at his side and hadn't missed many meals, and Miraden couldn't travel slowly. He doused his judgment and shook the cleric's hand.

"I'm Lovo Lotusboro. See you in the morning."

Ceychell finished the note and was so proud of Miraden. She couldn't believe he'd ever stand up to naaglings, but he shined. She felt guilty accepting the coins but would bring them to her father and let him decide what to do with them. She tried to imagine Hellshy in her mind, falling and unnaturally twisting on its own. She shuddered and leaned in to hug Stormrange.

FIVE

THE BLACKSMITH'S APPRENTICE

CEYCHELL SHRUGGED ON HER BACKPACK and left home early in the morning, Stormrange shuffling on her shoulder, a case of grayfold mushrooms in her hand. Her nose curled from their acrid stink. She'd walked along a path dotted with bits of reagents that didn't make the full trip to her mother's old store. She looked forward to making it her new home.

She rounded the hill from her cottage toward the small shop that sat in the shadow of a large oak. The roof sloped down from a sharp center into gutters that poured into buckets on shelves. They were full of stagnant rainwater. Orange corks were jammed into the base of the large maple buckets, and if removed, water would flow into the fallow herb garden troughs. The once lush herb garden was now filled with weeds and poisonous mushrooms.

She pushed the door open with her foot and stepped inside. A musty smell and the low creak of a floorboard greeted her. The shop was mostly empty. At the front of the shop were a few shelves next to a long counter. Near the center of the front room, two chairs sat next to a small table. A painting from her room hung on the wall over a fireplace with two more chairs, and her sister's musical instruments lay on a shelf behind the counter. And that was it. She hadn't moved her bed into the back room yet; it, too, was small and originally used for storage. The shop felt cold and hollow, unlike in her childhood when her mother maintained it. But it was her means to get out of Kaehrn. She didn't care if it took five years. She planned to save her earnings and move to Crestain. The thought of living in a bustling city lingered in her dreams. She'd been there a few times when she was younger. It was large, full of life, and on the sea—she loved every bit of it. She was meant for more than gardening and making potions.

She set her box down next to piles of carefully separated reagents and a few full boxes yet to be sorted. Most of the spiderwebs were removed. She had relocated the spiders to the weed-covered garden out back, but a few still remained. She kicked her boot against the floor, sent a bit of dust flying as she walked over to the countertop, and brushed her hand along a shelf to shoo away a mouse.

She set her pack down on the counter and carefully removed jars and set them on a shelf. She still had four empty shelves and a few more trips back to the cottage left before she filled them. This was her fourth trip this morning, and her arms ached. She walked over to the two chairs next to the fireplace. Only a single log still flickered from the fire she'd set under the teapot earlier.

The chairs were covered in black bear pelts. She sat down on one and placed Stormrange down on the other. She ran her hands over the soft fur. After a moment's breath, she took Miraden's note from the small table next to her chair and read it for the third time. She took a cloth and grabbed the pot from over the fire, then poured a brewed cup of juno beans into a large iron mug. She closed her eyes, scratched Stormrange's chest, and thought about Miraden's selflessness. She thought of how much she missed him. The warm brew calmed her nerves and refreshed memories of when Miraden would stop by her house when they were young.

When she was younger, she brewed the juno each morning and took a large jug with a cup through town. For a lumin, she'd fill the cup with the fine brew for a villager or a visitor. The money helped her mother buy supplies, and she enjoyed the attention.

Miraden would always meet her to get the first cup as she was leaving her home in the morning. He had no money, and his family was too poor to spare the few coins they had on such luxuries. Miraden did some of Ceychell's chores in exchange for the juno coffee. Then, she would make her rounds in Kaehrn or one of the three neighboring villages of Storjn, Valijn, or her least favorite, Adolehrn. Each day, she'd return and find a box filled with herbs at her back window, or chopped wood stacked neatly beside her cottage, or parcels would be placed inside her room on the blue pine desk near her window.

Ceychell took another sip and wondered if Miraden really loved the coffee or if he was just trying to spend a few moments with her. Her mother would grin at Ceychell whenever Miraden stopped by but rarely spoke to him. Ceychell herself said little as well. It wasn't long before Kyra showed up to steal a few moments of Miraden's time. Her little sister loved him to death.

Ceychell finished her coffee and poured a few fresh beans into a small pouch to send back to Miraden with Stormrange. She was thinking about adding a note when the silver bell at the door jangled. The thought drifted away when she saw Hydracks step into the shop. She reached a hand into her hair and pulled it behind her ear.

He wasn't tall, but he was strong and handsome. His dark hair was the color of the soot on his brown apron. Ceychell loved his light blue eyes and grin. He'd moved to the village less than a year ago, and she didn't know him very well, just that he seemed to work long hours at the smithy.

"Mother of Light this morning, Hydracks," she said with a smile that quickly faded when the sight of blood on his arm caught her eye.

"Mother of Light... I burned my arm at the forge." He stepped up to her and lifted his muscular, sooty forearm to show her a long burn, bubbled and red. She held his arm and closely examined the wound. She heard him inhale her perfume and smiled to herself.

Ceychell dug into one of her wooden boxes and removed a clay jar. "This is cellia spore. It will help with the pain and make it heal much faster. It will be two kam," she said. She didn't really want the coins, though, not on this occasion. She'd kind of wanted Hydracks to spend some time in her shop.

"Can you put some on for me? My hands are filthy," he asked and showed her his calloused hands. They were strong and soot-black. She dabbed the wound with a bit of cool water, then pulled balm out from the glass container and lathered it gently on the burn.

"It's been slow at the forge," he said. "Maybe I could build you a few shelves in here to pay for this?" He looked up quickly when she turned her eyes up to his. She caught him admiring her.

Ceychell didn't answer. She took a cloth roll from another box and wrapped a bit around his wound. She coyly glanced at him before placing the pot of cellia spore on a shelf. She felt him staring. "You can pay me within the week or build me shelves on the wall behind you," she said.

He looked over to Stormrange, who was still sitting on the chair, cleaning his feathers with his beak. He stared for a few moments, then said, "What's Miraden's bird doing here?"

"Stormrange delivered a message." She purposely left out that it was from Miraden.

Hydracks glowered a moment. "Looks like I better start building those shelves. Thanks, Ceycha," he said.

She walked out of the shop with him and stood on her porch. She saw Sulover, the ore merchant from Bondare, riding past her shop on his cart with his hunch-back apprentice, Vargla. Two large horses pulled the cart full of iron and copper stones. Sulover wore a wide-brimmed green hat and a white fur coat that had lost most of its fur. His face was as dirty and wrinkled. He turned and waved to Ceychell and Hydracks.

"Hello! You headed to the shop, Hydracks?"

"I am," he said and walked up to the cart.

"Come, I'll give you a ride," he said, then looked at Ceychell. "Mother of Light, young Ceychell!"

She waved to him before she walked back inside.

Ceychell looked at the bag of roasted juno beans on the counter, then up to the painting Kyradel had given her for her 15th Passing. It showed a vibrant yellow sky that melted into lush green hills surrounding a placid blue lake. It was Pallow Lake, where she had so many fond memories of her sister. She could almost see Kyradel at that moment as if she were giving the gift to her again. Without the painter, the painting lost its life. Just like the flute lying on a shelf behind the counter. She was gone, the sister she had loved more than anything, the sister she had first lost because of Miraden's kiss nearly two years ago.

Ceychell huffed, took Stormrange on her wrist, and stomped out of her shop. She threw him into the air without beans or a letter.

A week passed since she sent Stormrange away. Ceychell spent most of it in silence, avoiding everyone. She kept busy moving her things and lamenting the loss of her two loves.

Ceychell's face was splotched red from the chill. Her coat fluttered in the wind as she ran the last box of supplies into her store. After slamming the door shut with her back, she let loose a heavy sigh and smiled. She was moved out of her parents' house, her first step to freedom. She sat down on the box and ran her hand along the iron frame on her wall. Soon, wooden shelves would be mounted on it.

She had enjoyed Hydracks working in her shop the past week, banging the shelves together, chatting. He flirted, but she didn't return the gesture… at least not much. She was anxious but tried not to let it show. Time was running out, though. Soon, Valdenfest would be here, and Hydracks was the only person she'd consider going with now, even though she really wanted to go with Miraden.

Villagers from Storjn, Valijn, and Adolehrn would visit for Valdenfest since it was Kaehrn's turn to host the holiday. It was a tradition for young suitors in her region to court one another at Valdenfest, and most eventually married as was tradition. It was common for someone of at least 17 Passings to be asked, and she had her 17th Passing last month. She didn't want just anyone asking her, though. After all, she was the chieftain's eldest daughter.

A sniveling bookworm in Storjn, son of the village treasurer, sent her an invitation by way of his sister. Yes, his father held a good position, but she could never respect someone who wouldn't ask her in person. A haberdasher twice her age asked her when she visited Valijn—no, but thanks—and then there were others she didn't care to remember from the three villages, and even a couple from Bilore Des. As she considered her options, the one she lamented most was shooing away the boy from her childhood. He was the one who should be at her side. But that dream was gone, and the sooner she came to grips, the better.

Ceychell pulled on her fur-lined leather coat and left her shop to plant seeds in its back garden for winter tubers. She clipped the hedges out front of the shop and removed some of the invasive ivy entangling the sapling pine trees. She gathered some fallen needles in a pouch to burn in her fire—she loved the smell, even if the smoke was heavy. Her nose was cold, but she enjoyed every breath of sweet-smelling pine.

Gourds and pumpkins grew like crazy in her unruly backyard. She gathered many of them of all shapes and sizes and placed them along her porch. She had so many she might sell some to her neighbors. As she looked at the gourds—greens, yellows, reds, oranges, and blacks—she recalled a pumpkin Kyradel had painted last year. It showed two girls, one on each side of the squash. They were painted as shadows and hung their heads before a landscape of sullen browns and grays. She cried when she first saw it. Now the memory brought tears that burned from the crisp air.

Ceychell brushed the tears from her eyes as she sat down next to a large pumpkin near her front door. She and Kyradel decorated many pumpkins last year, mostly in silence. Ceychell placed the last gourd on her steps. It was covered in green spots and splashed with red. Tears continued to drip from her eyes. She sank to her knees as a hollowness filled her chest. She pondered the long road ahead without her. She wondered why she should still live and Kyradel should not. She would never hear her sister's songs again. She won't grow old and watch their children play together as they so often talked about. Many years ago, they agreed to name each other's firstborns, live in an adjoined house, and spend every day together…

Another dead dream.

SIX

LOVO THE UNFORTUNATE

CEYCHELL SAT ON HER PORCH and prayed to the Mother of Light and the Father of Darkness. She whispered her words for hours in the cold twilight and finally opened her eyes. Her hair fell in tangles in front of her pale face. She squinted at the rays of sunlight piercing through thick clouds, illuminating the porch. Bathed in brief reprieve from her own thoughts, she looked up and shielded her eyes. Cast in shadow, her wooden sign swayed in the morning breeze. Her mother's sign used to hang from the post, but Miraden replaced it in the middle of the night with one he carved for her seventeenth Passing last month. It read *Ceycha's Cauldron*. Its borders were wreathed in carvings of six-petaled flowers: limebloom, her favorite. Her eyes drifted a bit higher from the glare and saw a growing shadow. She was startled as Stormrange landed on the sign. She lifted her hands as he shuffled along the sign and then hopped down to her. Ceychell hugged Stormrange as she ran inside her shop.

She placed the bird on the counter before opening the scroll pouch tied to his belly. She removed the letter, and out fell a ring that skittered on the counter before settling near her hand. She lifted the golden band and peered at it. It was a snake with detailed scales, a pentagonal emerald set at the serpent's coiled neck. The ring was warm and heavier than it should have been. She felt guilty that Miraden sent the token of affection, but she absolutely loved it. She rolled the ring between her fingers and put it on her third finger. Then she eagerly unraveled the letter when her door suddenly opened. Hydracks came in with tools and a few iron fittings.

Ceychell nodded to him and held the note.

"Mother of Light, Ceychell," he said. He was staring at her a bit and didn't properly set his tools on the shelves he was building, so they fell to the floor with a thunderous clatter. Stormrange sprung to flight and flapped out of the shop.

"No! Stormrange, come back!" Ceychell yelled and ran after the bird. She cast a furious glare at Hydracks when she ran past and exited her shop. Stormrange was soaring higher into the sky and was quickly out of sight past the canopy.

"Ugggghhhhhh!" she screamed. She had the beans ready and planned to return a letter to Miraden. Now that was ruined.

"Everything okay? Sorry, I drop—" Hydracks said.

"No, everything is *not* okay," she snapped and left her doorstep. She ran up the hill in the cold and went to the Kaelirnstone to read Miraden's letter.

My dearest Ceychell,

Our journey continued north with Hellshy as our compass…

Miraden was thankful to be out of that stinking town and back in the woods. Today was so beautiful. The sun came through the trees so brightly it reminded him of how it streamed down Ceychell's hill on spring mornings. He was sure the walla mushrooms were growing again near the back of her cottage. He always looked forward to buying a few from her. His mother loved them. He hoped when she picked them this year that she would think of his mother. His mother told him that his path would become hard with choices. Miraden never understood what she meant until that day he saw Ceychell in the forest and kissed her. It was the best and worst day of his life. Strangely, his mother's words felt relevant now as well.

Though they were not far from Bilore Des, Miraden felt like he'd trekked with Lovo for years. Between snacking on apples from his pack, he'd heard far more than he bargained for in this deal. Miraden had never met someone with such diversity in what they were poor at or, at least, someone who so openly admitted their shortcomings. Orphaned when he was seven, he took up living in a stable and liked it so much he worked there as a stable boy for shelter and scraps of food. He went on and on about the horses in detail; he had an amazing memory for them. Miraden's mind wandered until Lovo told him he was bitten by several of them. Lovo showed him his left hand, where a horse took most of one finger with the carrot he offered.

After he left horse care, he was a deckhand on a fishing boat at Arrowheart Lake. Or he was a deckhand until he knocked a full barrel of fish onto the lake one frozen evening. His employer told him if he could walk across the ice and recover the barrel of fish, he could keep his job. The barrel rolled a bit further before Lovo could step down, then it dropped through the ice and disappeared, along with his employment.

He talked about how much he hated wiping the fish scales from his frozen hands each night, anyway, and was glad to be done with it.

Then he found work plowing and planting as a farmer's hand. Miraden stopped listening for a bit when he went on about killing a few crops that season. Then he talked about the farmer's son, Edern.

Edern was close to Lovo's age. He described Edern in such great detail that Miraden could almost see him. Some of his words were *blond hair looked like a bed of vanilla flowers, arms were fit from digging all day, chin like a steel spade.* His details continued, and it was clear he still thought fondly of him. Despite Lovo's incredibly poor luck and constant chattering, Edern took an interest in him. Miraden started listening again and smiled when Lovo came to life. Lovo waved his hands as he depicted how he ran from the old farmer one night when he was caught in the barn with Edern. Lovo said he started laughing when the farmer came into the barn with a shovel, stark naked. He had thought rustlers were stealing his horse. Apparently, the farmer wasn't amused by finding them together. Lovo said he couldn't stop laughing when the farmer approached while shouting threats.

Lovo showed Miraden where the shovel hit him before he turned and ran straight into the forest with only his modesty in his hands.

Lovo said he got hungry lumbering through the forest before arriving at Litton. Miraden thought a man of Lovo's girth could survive for weeks without a meal, but apparently not. He stole clothes off a laundry line and went straight to the first stove he could smell. He was so famished he ate four plates of food at an inn and, of course, had no money to pay. He said the innkeeper, Strod, was missing an eye and smelled as foul as a patch of turned onions. Upon discovering Lovo was broke, Strod lifted his wooden plate and told him it was okay if he had no money. Then Strod smashed him on the head with it and knocked him out. When Lovo awoke, he was in the kitchen with Strod and two town guards. They gave him a choice: work at the inn to clear his debt or spend a few weeks in jail, then come back to work off his debt. As Lovo could do nothing but smell Strod, he decided to go to jail, thinking they were kidding.

They weren't.

Lovo spent two weeks in jail, where he earned the job of emptying the "dump" buckets each day. His first day, he was shuffling, holding steady the waste bucket to take it out back, when a guard tripped him. The gushy details of the fall turned Miraden's stomach.

After two weeks, Lovo was released and brought back to Strod. Lovo said his nose was so burned with the stench from jail, he could no longer smell Strod and looked forward to working in a kitchen where he could eat his fill. But, his first night, he dropped scathing hot soup onto the local prefect's lap, the very one who tripped him in jail.

Lovo said he ran for his life; Miraden wasn't sure how. At this point, Miraden would have questioned if a man of his size could run at all, but it sounded like it was one thing Lovo was actually very good at.

Miraden zoned out for the rest of his tales swimming through his head, but Lovo finally found his place serving under the gods, specifically the Mother of Light. That is, before he decided it was time to help Miraden.

Miraden had half a mind to send him home now, but he could really use help. He prayed to the Lady of Rain and the Daughter of Forests that Lovo's unending foolishness wouldn't become the end of him.

They followed the road north for a few days. The air grew moist. It slowly started to stink. Miraden frequently checked Hellshy, and it kept pointing in the direction they were heading, so they followed.

Later that day, Miraden heard a screech and looked up to catch Stormrange on his arm. He scratched his chest and smiled. He reached into an inner pocket of his cloak where he kept dried bits of meat for Stormrange and offered him a pinch. The bird was happy for his treat. Miraden looked at the opened scroll case and grew sad. He said nothing as they kept pace.

They were approaching a festering bog and decided to camp for the night. They stayed under the thick canopy of large willows. A fire crackled between them. Lovo picked his teeth with a long splinter of wood and hummed to himself. It wasn't nonsensical humming. Miraden recognized the tune—it was one his mother hummed when he was a child. And Lovo had a calming, humming voice to boot.

Miraden started a new letter to Ceychell. He figured she was still upset with him, but he knew deep down she loved him. She just had to; he could see it in her eyes.

"What is that tune?" Miraden asked.

"It's a lullaby from the Manocs. My mother said it's about the Daughter of Forests sleeping too long and all the green undergrowth started to smother the forest floor before a long winter."

"My mother used to sing it to me. I never heard it from anyone else," Miraden said. He shifted and took a sip of water from his wineskin.

"It's common to the west, not out here. My father taught me some music when I was young. Before he left for war and never came home."

Miraden nodded and wrote quietly. He didn't really want to talk about family anymore lest the memories become too painful.

"I've seen you write a few times. Who you writing to?" he asked.

"Ceychell. She's... from my village, a dear friend of mine."

"You are writing to her from all the way out here. She sounds like more than a friend," Lovo said. He flicked the toothpick into the fire.

"She's Kyradel's sister, and you're right." Miraden rolled up the letter. He wasn't going to get much done tonight.

The next morning, Miraden's heart sank once he stepped into the border of Pinderfang Marsh. He held Hellshy on the flat of his palm, and it shifted slightly. He lamented that it pointed directly at the bubbling bog. It smelled like a great compost heap in stagnant water. It was difficult to walk and flail at the swarming bugs, though Stormrange made a meal of them. He swatted them ceaselessly until his arms hung from his sides in defeat. Strangely enough, Lovo didn't seem bothered by the pests. He seemed to be without a care in the world until he looked over and said, "Keep an eye out for me, will ya? I can't swim." Miraden was even more uneasy now.

Miraden had a hard time finding a path through the swamp. Moss beds and thick roots proved easiest to step on though it was almost as easy to take a bad step and drop into the mucky grime. He held onto a branch or vine with each uncertain step after slipping in waist-deep a few times. It was tiring and miserable and cold. He finally rested and leaned against a large old willow with branches that draped like the hair of an old woman. Miraden didn't want to walk anymore as he sat in the middle of that forsaken swamp, such a miserable pit. Stormrange was off somewhere, probably to scout for food.

Miraden rested briefly against the trunk of the willow when he looked up and saw Lovo swing his mace directly for his skull. Miraden ducked, and the mace knocked his hood back and splattered a red-and-black spider the size of a possum against the tree.

Miraden rolled forward onto the muddy earth. Lovo reached a large hand down and hoisted him to his feet as if he were a little kid. He didn't say anything, just smiled and kept moving. Miraden couldn't believe it. He should have thanked him, but he only turned and saw the splattered spider against the tree bark. He didn't recognize it, but it certainly looked deadly. He thanked the Daughter of Forests since he could have died in the swamp had Lovo not killed it.

Stormrange returned early that evening, looking pleased with himself. He probably had his fill on rodents. He chirped and stepped in circles before stopping and looking up at Miraden. He'd seen Stormrange do this when he saw something that frightened him. Stormrange did it a few more times, then jumped to his shoulder. Miraden really wished he could tell them what he saw. And after a long night of taking shifts on a watch, Miraden was exhausted. Despite how tired he was, he couldn't fall asleep. The chirps, squeals, growls, and other strange noises around the marsh kept him on edge. But, at first light, they continued northward. Miraden thought their pace improved when he learned better where to step, though they were still slow as they twisted along the serpentine path. They avoided the deeper water at all costs.

Miraden's knees and feet ached. His fingers were nearly numb and stung from slapping so many insects. Large rodents threatened them a few times, but Stormrange picked one up in his talons and flew off somewhere for a while, and the rest decided to scatter. They trudged forward slowly until Lovo stopped and stared ahead. Then Miraden saw it, too. It looked like a man leaning over another man lying on the swamp floor.

"They are deep in this place. They might need help," Miraden whispered.

"No, I don't like this. Something is not right," Lovo whispered back. The large man crouched and backed away. "C'mon."

"No, we need to see if they need help. His friend could be hurt." Lovo shook his head otherwise.

Miraden nocked an arrow, crept closer, and called out to them, "Hello, are you alright?"

They didn't answer. The one on top was moving, but Miraden couldn't tell what he was doing.

He ventured a bit closer and called out again.

"Miraden, leave them. Let's go!" Lovo's whispers were stressed.

Miraden couldn't abandon someone in trouble. Not in such a place as this.

"Are you alright? Is your friend hurt?" Miraden called. He finally saw the man turn. His eye was sunken into its socket. His decayed face sagged from his skull. Hanging from exposed gums and bloody teeth was a tear of flesh. The victim below him had entire chunks of meat missing from his face and chest.

Miraden had heard of ghouls as a child; they gave him nightmares. He thought they were just stories or at least wished they were. Blood drained from his face and left him with numbing cold. The ghoul's blue-gray eye fixed on Miraden as its next meal, then moaned and rose from its prey.

"Miraden," Lovo said, "I am not afraid to die, but I am afraid to live in death."

They fled. Miraden heard branches snap and heavy grunting behind him as they did their best to run in the swamp. They splashed into mud holes and tripped on roots and vines. Each time Miraden looked back, he saw the ghoul stumbling as well, but it was gaining on them and so focused as if they were its very last meal.

Miraden leaped up a tangle of large roots onto a massive willow trunk and began climbing. Lovo jumped for the lowest branches that were well out of his reach. He clambered at the trunk and screamed for help. Miraden looked down and knew that he could never help him climb without a rope, especially with that ghoul gaining on them. Miraden was so scared he briefly considered leaving Lovo down there as a distraction. It was cruel and not who he was, but he also didn't want to jeopardize his mission. But this was definitely his fault. Miraden wanted to climb higher and knew he could fire on it from out of its reach, but Lovo would surely die.

Miraden slid back down the trunk.

Lovo was porcelain white, his lip trembled, and his hand fumbled around for his mace. Miraden drew his bow, nocked an arrow, aimed at the rambling ghoul, and let it fly. The arrow sank into the dead's chest and merely slowed it a step. He loosed three more in succession, and even the arrow that found its neck did not deter its pursuit. Before Miraden could draw his sword, the ghoul was upon them. Lovo slammed the mace on its shoulder and grabbed its other shoulder, and wrestled with it. Lovo screamed like a child, his large hand pressing the ghoul's face and snapping jaw away from his own face. Miraden dropped his bow and drew Hellshy. He was scared to approach the flailing dead thing as it clawed and spat while Lovo grappled it. Its gory jaw snapped wildly, and blue-gray eye twitched. Miraden closed his eyes, lunged for the ghoul, and drove Hellshy up into its skull. Finally, the creature stilled. It hung limp in Lovo's grasp. Lovo dropped it and frantically stomped it into the swamp water until it was deep in the mud under the water.

Lovo was still trembling and seemed to be almost in shock.

"It's okay. You're okay now," Miraden calmly said, but he was shaking too. Miraden saw no bites or open wounds—he wondered if the Mother of Light protected them. For a while, they just stood there and breathed slowly. Lovo blinked a few times and then shook his head hard, which seemed to bring him back to life. Miraden learned his lesson about approaching strangers. Never to repeat that mistake.

Then Hellshy twitched in his grip.

"What is it doing?" Lovo asked nervously.

"I don't know, it's not twitched like this." It twitched again and pointed northwest. Miraden gave Lovo a final pat on the chest and pulled his pack for him to follow him.

Hellshy's twitching grew in frequency as he followed its directions. He wasn't sure if they were getting close to an Ashengate or what, but his nerves became more frayed as the scrying tool grew more active. Miraden struggled to catch his breath. His skin buzzed; eyes watered. He constantly looked around, trying to find what Hellshy was reacting to.

"Your bird," Lovo whispered and pointed. Stormrange circled above them. He swooped down and alighted on Miraden's shoulder. His return helped Miraden calm down, and they ventured on.

Less than an hour later, Miraden heard the unmistakable screams and grunts of fighting. They slowed their pace and crept shoulder-deep through a patch of high reeds. With each careful step, Miraden was scared that he would drop into a murky pit. He couldn't see anything below his knees, only felt the cold muck as he squished through the swamp. He started to imagine snakes or fish biting him, or worse, a ghoul grabbing his leg and pulling him under. It made every moment worse. He shook, and Stormrange shuffled nervously on his shoulder. Miraden wanted to run so badly. He was really struggling with his leg being stuck when Lovo turned and quietly pulled him forward out of a vacuum of mud.

Lovo patted him on the chest and whispered, "I got ya, Miraden. Stay close."

Then Miraden saw them. Lovo and Miraden stopped dead and remained as still as the gray reeds.

A band of men were battling what Miraden thought were ashenkin. He'd never seen the monsters before, but the rumors didn't do them justice. They were slightly shorter than the men but muscular, bearing sharp black claws and long fangs. Their crimson skin was mottled and ashy. Eyes were glowing pits, and tongues were long and purple. The rain and muck sizzled on their skin.

One of them held a dagger that looked just like Hellshy in its claw. The devils fearlessly battled and worked together to surround the men. Miraden realized there were way too many ashenkin for Lovo and him to join the fray lest they be killed. Miraden looked over to Lovo—his eyes couldn't get any wider than they were upon seeing the ghoul, but they did. Miraden wondered if he'd soiled himself; he certainly felt scared enough to.

Stormrange turned in circles on Miraden's shoulder. He knew this was what he had seen before when his companion was scared. He quietly lifted him and held him close and shared his fear.

Miraden felt cowardly, even foolish, watching the ashenkin slay several of the men with just their teeth and claws. Perhaps the men were sent on a similar bounty. Perhaps they knew where an Ashengate was, but he was fearfully content to survive and look for it himself. Then Hellshy twitched hard, and all the devils turned at once to look in their direction. Miraden's heart nearly leaped into his throat.

They stood still those extremely brief moments of terror, but Lovo sprung from cover, turned, and splashed away through the swamp like an angry cow. Two distracted devils were cut down by the remaining men as all the ashenkin splashed through the muck toward Miraden.

Miraden pushed Hellshy under his belt, tossed Stormrange into flight, and ran after Lovo. The ashenkin were even faster than the ghoul. There were screams and the sing of steel slicing flesh between their splashing footfalls. The duo ran toward a thick wall of trees. Stormrange flapped around Miraden, screeching and following.

Miraden spotted a cabin in the marsh just beyond the trees. But between them and the wall of trees lay a river and no bridge. Lovo didn't care and charged into the water, splashing and slogging his way to the other side. Miraden pulled Hellshy from his belt and placed it in one of the naagling chieftain's bags. He lifted an arm, and Stormrange landed upon it. He quickly tied the naagling bag around Stormrange and sent him into flight. Miraden then ran through the river after Lovo. It was only waist-deep, and there was no real current, luckily. They were completely out of breath and stumbled up the bank and past the trees. When he looked back, he saw the ashenkin scattering, all of them looking up at the sky, watching Stormrange fly out of sight.

They approached the cabin quickly and peered through a broken window—the place was completely wrecked, but, thankfully, there were no signs of ghouls or ashenkin. Lovo shoved the rotted door open. They rushed inside, dripping wet, then barred the door behind them with broken furniture. They searched inside the house. Lovo found a panel in the bedroom that led to a small crawlspace. They shuffled inside and pulled the panel shut.

Miraden wasn't sure how long they remained silent in the dark crawlspace. It felt like a week to him though it was likely a day. The dankness, the closeness of the walls, the lack of room were hard for him to ignore. He had no way of knowing if the devils were waiting outside or if his distraction of sending the blade elsewhere worked.

"I've not heard a thing. We should have a look," Lovo said.

"Okay," Miraden said and pulled the bow off of his shoulder.

Miraden quietly followed Lovo out of the crawlspace. He peeked out the windows—nothing but the sleepy bog beyond the river filled with thick fog. The air was crisp and cool. No sign of devils waiting for them. He suddenly remembered his father's words, *danger does not wait long.* He felt if the ashenkin wanted them, they'd have come into the cabin by now. They left the house.

Lovo found a small boat sitting on a drying rack behind the house that they used to get back across the river to investigate the battle. There were five ashenkin and ten men on the bank, all dead. A few floated in the river. They looted them and found less than five kams and a fistful of lumins, weapons, some food, and a note. The note was a bounty from the town of Muckmog to kill ashenkin in the swamp.

"Muckmog is somewhere on this river, I believe this direction. We could use the boat," Lovo whispered.

"I hate being on the water," Miraden complained.

"Would you rather be waist-deep in the swamp?"

Miraden realized he had a good point. "How do we know there's not more of them?"

Lovo shrugged. "We best go. Better to get to Muckmog before nightfall than wait to see if they come back."

Miraden wasn't eager to find the town, but perhaps he could find clues about the Ashengate.

"Help me take their horns. Let's collect that bounty," Miraden said. Miraden shuddered that their bodies were still warm to the touch. Their skin was coarse like a stone and cracked like burned wood. He removed his hunting knife to cut out a horn and realized quickly that he'd dull the knife and have no horns. He decided to try and hack off a horn with his silver saber. It was worth a shot. If it didn't work, he regrettably would have had to take their heads instead.

He swung the sword straight through the horn. Lovo's eyes widened at how easy it was. Miraden didn't expect it either.

"That must be relzyian silver. That's a treasure nowadays," he said. Miraden looked at the blade and realized how fortunate he would be to have it when the time came. He'd have to remember to have Ceychell thank Bryndyke in his next letter.

"Should we bury them?" Miraden asked. He wasn't eager to lose the daylight but felt remorse for leaving them.

"We have no shovels and little time. I will say a quick prayer." Lovo kneeled beside a man and whispered a quick prayer as he put his hand upon the fallen's heart. He prayed for each of the ten men as Miraden looked around to check for anything they'd missed.

He walked past a dead man and saw something gleaming in the dirt beside a cut bag upon his waist. Miraden fished out a golden ring with an emerald gem. The color reminded him of Ceychell's eyes, and it hurt him to remember her. It'd been so long since seeing her last. He used his cloak and wiped a bit of the mud from the ring to find serpents etched in detail along the band. It was beautiful and just about her size. He put it in his pocket and would send it to Ceychell with the next letter. He missed her so much.

They got into the boat and quietly rowed through the stagnant water to what Miraden believed was northwest, and hopefully, toward Muckmog.

It was peaceful rowing down the river and not nearly as miserable as dredging through the swamp. He realized it would very soon be Valdenfest, and he wouldn't see Ceychell this year. He remembered what she wore last year, a red dress with a green oak tree embroidered on the chest. He knew her mother had made it for her, and he thought it was her finest work. Ceychell's hair was so beautiful—it was a weave of mastery as if the gods were guiding her hands.

He then thought of the last time he'd asked her to go with him. She was cold on the hill, like she had been for some time, but there was a change. He felt she was pulling out of that sad place and coming back to him. He felt it so strongly. He was so glad he finally did because he wrote a letter to her the night before and placed it under his pillow. He'd forgotten about it until now, but the thought of what he wrote saddened him greatly.

The night was starting to fall, and more bugs were coming out. Miraden ended his daydream by imagining putting the ring in his pocket on her finger and holding her hand.

Stormrange flapped down and landed on the boat next to Miraden. He reached out and scratched his feathers and offered him a treat of cooked rabbit he kept a bit of in his bag.

"Can you row for a bit? I must finish this letter quickly and send it," Miraden whispered.

Lovo patted his back, and he knew that meant to go ahead.

Miraden removed the letter he worked on the last few nights and wrote of their trek through the swamp, the ghoul, escaping ashenkin, and his love for her. He rolled it up, tucked it in the scroll case along with the ring, and sent Stormrange off into the night.

SEVEN

CAUGHT

THE MORNING WAS COLD, THE coldest it's been all year. The breeze was brisk; it helped Ceychell wake up after a short sleep. She could hardly keep her eyes open as she trudged down the hill toward Kaehrn, carrying a new dress. Her backpack held a regional map she took from the village, but it was otherwise nearly empty with only a few reagents she couldn't sell in town. Miraden's recent letter was sticking slightly out of the side pocket. She had walked to Bilore Des and back. She camped and slept little each night to make the trip as quick as possible. Her legs and feet throbbed in pain. She looked forward to starting a hearty fire in the hearth, jumping under her warm blankets, and sleeping for a day. She had pushed herself to travel fast, having no intention of being caught by ashenkin, or worse, being reprimanded for leaving the village without telling her father.

She spent much of her time thinking of Miraden, missing him, and wishing Kyradel was home. She thought of his letter and how she rejected him the morning he left. She wanted to tell him she would go with him to Valdenfest; she just kept thinking of how much it would crush Kyradel all over again. And after turning down a lord she didn't know in Bilore Des, she realized she also didn't want to go to Valdenfest with Hydracks. He was cute, but not for her.

At last, she entered Kaehrn early that morning, unnoticed. In her short time gone, part of the wall was assembled near the north road where she entered the town. Seeing it made her very sad that her father didn't listen to Miraden. She recalled Chandar dismissing Miraden's advice as *nothing but boyish ignorance.* Chandar even talked her father into using some of the coin Miraden sent back to hire a few builders along with the mercenaries.

Ceychell scoffed as she recalled Chandar's conversation, then quietly opened the door to her store and shuffled inside.

"How was the trip to town, Ceycha?" Hydracks asked.

Ceychell screamed. "By the gods," she said and placed her hand on her chest. "You scared me."

"Where were you? Didn't see you all week?" he asked, stepping out of the shadows of the new shelves and leering at her.

She found his stare unnerving. "I didn't realize you were watching for me. Or that you saw it fit to come to my shop without me here." She walked past him and placed her pack and new dress onto the counter.

"Did you find that dress in the woods?" he asked.

Ceychell turned her bag and dress away from him. "No. It looks like you've finished my shelves," she said as he drew closer. She gasped a bit when she stared into the blacksmith apprentice's deep blue eyes. She ignored the feeling of danger and wanted to run her fingers through his dark hair.

Hydracks stepped up and took Ceychell's hand in his own. He looked at the dirt under her nails and stains on her fingers. "Looks like you were digging this morning," he said.

"I go out looking for herbs each morning," she said. She was attracted to him, but now that he held her hand, she didn't like it.

"I'm sure you do. Tell me..."

As she looked into his eyes, she felt her chest tighten. He leaned slightly closer, and she could feel his breath upon her face. She felt uneasy.

"Yes?" she asked.

"Would the chieftain's daughter be willing to take a blacksmith's apprentice to Valdenfest?"

It took every ounce of her willpower to look away. "I'm sorry, I've already accepted someone else's request."

Hydracks's eyes went dark as he frowned a bit. "I… see. I guess I misread you," he said and then noticed the edge of a note in the side pocket of her backpack. "What is that?"

She panicked when she saw it too. "It's nothing. An order I picked up in—"

He finished her statement, "—in the forest, I suppose. Well, I better get to the forge. I look forward to seeing you in that dress." Hydracks walked toward the door, opened it, and looked back at her. Ceychell felt her face flush red and knew she was caught staring lustily at him.

"Hey," Hydracks said, "have you heard any news from Miraden?"

His name brought her back into the moment. She clenched the ring in her hand and replied, "Yep."

Hydracks nodded and left.

Ceychell spun the ring and looked at the emerald. She could see her reflection on the face of it but looked and felt more like she were trapped inside. She felt awful for not writing Miraden back, and she wouldn't let it happen again.

EIGHT

VALDENFEST

EARLY WINTER FLURRIES OF FINE snow swirled on a frosty breeze and dusted the village of Kaehrn on the evening of Valdenfest. A giant tent was set on the village square and illuminated by torches and many candles that stood on tables laden with food and drink. Children and adults sang and danced, whirling around trees and circling past a bonfire in the village center. Kegs were tapped one by one. Mulled spirits and spiced ales filled wooden mugs faster than they were emptied. Brightly colored, carved forest animals dangled from trees. The whole town celebrated the annual festival, and Ceychell could hear their laughter up the hill where she sat and watched from the Kaehrnstone.

Lying upon a blanket, chilly in her sleek new dress, Ceychell listened to the fleeting notes of flutes and mandolins. She yearned to join the celebration, but she still mourned losing both loves in her life. Deep within her, she felt Kyradel was alive, but Ceychell was coming to grips with the idea that she would never see her again. Never see both of them again. Worse, she was haunted by the notes she'd received from Miraden, who was foolishly risking his life to save her sister. She had treated him so poorly for the past few years. As each day passed, she regretted it a little more. Her gut twisted in knots as she realized all the days she couldn't get back. She felt tired and had little appetite, and when she did eat, the food burned through her. Whether it was the gods' punishment or just plain guilt in her heart, Ceychell felt she deserved to feel terrible. She prayed to the Daughter of Forests, begged her to watch over Miraden on his journey.

Ceychell looked at the glow of the celebration from above the tree line and realized she would soon be missed. The last thing she wanted was to cause a panic, not tonight. She got up, folded her blanket, and headed back down the hill to her store, her home.

When she arrived there, she nudged the door open with her foot, stepped inside, and lay the blanket on the counter. Then she dug through a storage chest and found a handful of candles. She gathered them up and took them to Miraden's cabin not far from her shop.

She walked slowly through the woods, holding the candles in her hands, down the old path to Miraden's home. It was dark and lonely, cold and empty like a robbed grave—a place left forgotten, now simply a chapter of the village's memory. She placed a dozen candles on the windowsills of the house and lit them. After backing away to see the house glowing, she remembered Miraden's parents, who passed away from a sudden illness and then Miraden himself, who was now gone. They always made a bright festival display in their home. Miraden helped his father make candles for most of the village each year, and each year Ceychell's window glowed a bit brighter and with the more intricate waxwork. She remembered the beautiful candle Miraden had carved of her last year. It was tall and thin, and the gown she wore was made of leaves. Her hair was beautiful and long, her face perfectly carved into the yellow wax. It was as if Miraden stole her likeness. It was as if Ceychell looked like the candle and not the other way around. She didn't want to burn it; she wanted to save it forever. But in her arrogant, immature anger, she pushed it from her windowsill into the snow while he watched. Tears streamed from her eyes as she remembered the look on his face as if she had just slit his throat, and she recalled the look she returned to him that said *I will never love you* even though it would never be true.

Ceychell finally dried her tears and walked back to her parents' house. She saw a few mercenaries walking the paths through the village. They'd been in Kaehrn for a few days now. They didn't speak to anyone, slept during the day, and watched for ashenkin activity at night.

When she arrived at her parents' house, Hydracks was waiting at the door for her. He was wearing a suit of fine dark cloth and an open, bear-hide cloak that covered his broad shoulders and hung below his knees. He smiled at her.

"You look cold, milady," he said.

Ceychell forced a tight grin and shrugged. "I *am* cold." She admired his bear cloak, imagined how warm it must be.

"Well, you'll warm by the fire," he said and stepped out of the cottage.

"Why did you stop here this evening?" she asked, finding his visit unwarranted.

"Just thought I'd drop a gift off to your mother," he said. "Care to walk with me to the festival?"

She nodded, and they walked the short snow-dusted road to the festival square in silence. They sat down near the massive bonfire at the village center where everyone had gathered. She thought Valdenfest would make her happy. But the joy of the festival deflated rapidly as her thoughts drifted elsewhere.

She imagined Miraden sitting next to her. He might be whittling or getting her treats. Unlike Hydracks, he'd have offered his coat if it were the last he had.

Though she remained preoccupied with her daydreams, she occasionally noticed how much Hydracks was laughing at his friends' comments. She glowered and realized he was talking about her.

"She coaxed me to build her shelves, you know. She wanted me in there, keep the lot of you out," Hydracks said. A few of his friends chuckled. A few looked back. Most of them glanced over at Ormus sitting not far away at a long table and talking with Bryndyke.

Ceychell looked away as Hydracks downed the rest of his mug of ale. She tried to ignore his boasting and drinking. After a few minutes, she realized they had gotten quiet. She looked back, and Hydracks was sitting down right next to her but almost fell back. He was certainly tipsy.

"Hey there, Ceycha," he said. He grinned.

"Enjoying yourself?" was the nicest thing she could say. She looked out of the corner of her eye and noticed his friends watching.

"Yep." He slapped the empty mug against her chest and said, "Why don't you be good and go get me another?"

"She's not the fetchin' type," one of his friends said.

"Nonsense. You'll get it for me, won't you?" Hydracks said.

She decided to ignore him. She stared into the fire, feeling dead inside, and felt Valdenfest was incomplete without Kyradel's voice among the songs. For years, Kyradel had led many of the upbeat tunes and played her lute or pipes—everyone loved her songs, especially Ceychell. Even after their falling out, she still enjoyed Valdenfest with her sister.

She felt a shove. "I don't need to tell you twice, do I?" he said.

Worst of all, she sat next to a wretch she used to find attractive. She knew there was only one person she should be sitting next to, and he was not there. She looked up from the fire, and sitting on the other side of the fire from her was Vera, grinning and alone. The old woman's face was red from the fire. Wisps of her hair blew about in an untamed flurry. Vera grinned and nodded, and Ceychell struggled to return the good cheer.

Ceychell then tried to snatch the mug from his hand. He didn't release it. When their stares met, her teeth clenched. She flushed hot and felt intense heat within her body. She wasn't sure if she'd sat next to the fire too long or was just that angry.

"I'll let you have that. Now, go get me an ale."

Ceychell took the mug over to the tapped kegs. Standing next to them was a man as round as the pale moon in the cold sky. It was Hansejel, the brewmaster, and he was already struggling to stand.

"One more for Hydracks?" he slurred.

She smiled. "Nope, this one is for me. He's had enough." Hansejel didn't say a thing when she held her mug under the tap as he filled it. Her thoughts drifted to Miraden while she waited. She took a drink out of the mug and let it burn down her throat.

Then she looked back at the fire, pushed everything from her mind, and remembered one of Kyradel's songs. She closed her eyes and drifted far from Kaehrn. The sounds, the heat of the fire, everything faded. She was suddenly sitting next to her sister by the river, and they were young again. They splashed and chased each other. Then they were swimming together at Arrowheart Lake in the summer. They held hands and paddled, always within arm's reach of each other. Kyradel adored Miraden. She talked about him ceaselessly when they were out playing. He was a shy boy in his youth, but Ceychell had known Miraden truly loved her, not Kyradel, since her earliest memories.

Ceychell was ripped out of her daydream by Hydracks jostling her.

Hydracks pulled her in for a side hug and laughed. "Guess I wasn't clear about wanting that beer."

Ceychell glared at him and decided she'd had enough. She handed her mug to Hansejel—who proceeded to drink it—and when she started to walk away, she felt a stern, painful grip upon her arm.

"Where are you going?" Hydracks said.

She realized he wasn't asking. His bloodshot eyes were fixed on hers, and his grip was strong.

Ceychell had not known Hydracks for more than a year. He had moved to Kaehrn from Bilore Des after his sister was taken by the ashenkin. He seemed mostly quiet. She didn't expect such brashness from him. She'd catch him staring when she'd pass by the smithy, or he would make a flirtatious comment, but it all felt harmless. She wasn't sure if he was just drunk from the festival ale, or there was something worse lurking behind his unsettling gaze.

Ormus stepped out of the darkness to their left and said, "I think you've had enough, Hydracks." Hydracks's friends stopped laughing and began to disperse, but Hydracks sat firm.

"We're just having a bit of fun," he said. "It's Valdenfest."

"My daughter isn't having fun," Ormus said. His large hands curled into white-knuckled fists. Muscles twitched along his temples and clenched jaw.

Hydracks seemed to suddenly notice the grip he had upon Ceychell's arm and released her. She stumbled and nearly fell, then walked away.

Ceychell left the festival, trying to suppress her tears, but they flowed anyway. She retreated to her shop instead of her parents' home. When she reached the door, she saw Stormrange perched on her sign. She reached up, and he screeched and hopped into her arms. She smiled and held the bird tight as if he were the only ounce of hope she had left.

NINE

THE BLIGHT

CEYCHELL SHUFFLED INSIDE HER SHOP with Stormrange in hand and closed the door. She set him on the armrest of her chair and then quickly opened the scroll case. Out slid another letter and two sprigs of skor laurels—her absolute favorite tea leaves. She held them up to her nose, sniffed them in, and enjoyed the minty-licorice tingle on her tongue. She smiled from ear to ear. She threw some kindling into her fireplace and blew at the embers. The fire began to take while she prepared a pot for tea. The gift was exactly what she needed to calm down and forget that tonight's Valdenfest ever happened.

As the pot boiled, Ceychell lifted a sprig to her nose and inhaled its delightful aroma again. She dropped it in the pot. Moments later, the steam turned a bright green and filled the shop with its minty scent. She looked forward to setting the leaves in her tiny bedroom in the back of the shop to help her sleep. She ran her fingers over the letter and petted Stormrange while she waited for her tea. She unraveled the map she'd taken from the village archive. She had traced Miraden's journey so far and looked forward to updating it.

She couldn't wait any longer; she unrolled the letter.

My beautiful Ceychell,

I'm writing to you from a cramped room in Muckmog...

They traveled for more than a day on the swamp river but still hadn't reached Muckmog. They only stopped to rest last evening, but there wasn't much sleeping with all the insect noise and constant rustling in the swamp.

It was nighttime again. They paddled their boat to the shore. The bank was mucky and smelled, but it was still solid ground and far better than floating in the darkness and hoping nothing happened. Miraden sat next to a tree where they tied the boat. Miraden was first on watch tonight as Lovo was last night. He was ready to take his turn to sleep but figured it would be anything but restful—in fact, he hadn't had a good night's sleep since he left Kaehrn.

Miraden started to doze off after being relieved. Lovo shook him, and he started awake as a tiny red devil with wings absconded with Hellshy in its grip. The blade was so big in its small claws, it might have been a claymore, which humorously bounced in its grip, but Miraden wasn't the least bit amused. The little creature tried to fly away, but the dagger was too heavy for it. Miraden pulled himself out of a drowse and drew his bow, somewhat reflexively, and fired at it. The arrow missed. He fired again and missed it. It moved so erratically and was so small, he couldn't hit it! He ran after it— avoiding the trees and getting constantly whacked by branches— Miraden couldn't really see. Finally, after exhausting half his quiver, Miraden hit it in the back.

Lovo ran up afterward while the little pest snarled and hissed and bled. Miraden grabbed the dagger from it and stabbed it twice, then stomped it into the mud.

They didn't sleep after the little devil nearly stole Hellshy, just quietly rested. Miraden never felt grimier. The humidity and mud just stuck to him, along with the splattered bugs.

They decided to continue on the river, and Miraden remained stiff as he prayed everything would ignore them for the night. He couldn't see anything. Little bugs bounced off his face, and some crawled through his hair until he swatted them out. He stopped slapping them because he was afraid someone or something would hear him.

They slowly drifted through darkness. The only thing that broke the monotony was a cacophony of sounds he didn't recognize. He could hear everything, all the creatures growling, howling, the insects chirping. He had no idea how dangerous they were. They'd bump a root or slip against the bank, and he thought something might jump up and attack them. It was a horrible, constant nightmare through the night, and the uncertainty of where he was going or what they would find gripped Miraden like a vice. Every moment passed, and he hoped it would be the last before they reached Muckmog. That is, if they were going the right way.

The night felt the longest in his life, but when he opened his eyes in the morning, everything seemed okay, then he realized what woke him was the shuddering dagger. He feared what it meant.

When screams rang out that sounded like children, both of them sprung up in the boat. Hearing them shriek left Miraden's blood cold.

Lovo and Miraden didn't say a word, but when they exchanged glances, Miraden knew Lovo was thinking the same thing—just float on by. They passed under some low branches, and Miraden stood and grabbed one and pulled them to shore. Lovo looked uncertain, but he unstrapped his mace anyway, and Miraden readied his bow. They moved silently up the mossy bank toward a long reedy berm, wide-eyed and jerking at every sound. Miraden was so scared. The children's screams terrified him. He wasn't sure if they'd find a large host of ashenkin, or possibly dying children, but he didn't think he could handle either. He secretly hoped Kyradel would be there so that his journey would come to a close. The possibility of Kyradel being over the next berm was what pushed him to continue toward the screams.

When Miraden reached the top of the riverbank, he saw them: each dragging a child. Vapors of heat streamed from the creatures' bodies. Miraden swallowed the knot in his throat as he imagined their sharp, black claws tearing his skin open.

The kids weren't even fighting them, just screaming. Miraden took aim and offered a swift prayer to any god listening that he wouldn't miss the ashenkin and hit a child. He tried not to think about only having a few arrows left. He let one fly into the shoulder of an ashenkin. The devil roared, and both of them turned and growled. They released the children and charged them. Miraden drew another arrow and fired, striking one near its heart. But they ran so fast he had to drop his bow and reach for the saber. Miraden backed away and tripped on a root before he had fully drawn the blade. Lovo dodged a few claw swipes before he cracked one right in its skull with his mace. It fell to the ground a few feet from Miraden. Miraden stared into its wicked black orbs with a yellow burning around them. The eyes twitched, and he could only assume it was just dazed. It suddenly reached for Miraden's leg. He finally drew out the saber and stabbed it in the throat. Its blood sputtered out and started to sizzle on his leather boot.

Lovo screamed. The devil with the arrow in its shoulder had raked Lovo's arm inside the elbow. Blood began to well at the claw marks. Miraden scampered to his feet, darted behind the devil, and sliced his blade through its back just above its hips. It squealed and fell to the ground. Lovo swung his mace down on the back of its skull, and the ashenkin's head burst like a ripe melon.

Lovo had three large gashes on his arm and began praying to the Mother of Light while holding the wound and trying to staunch the blood. He muttered the prayers quickly as blood leaked out between his fingers. Miraden panicked for a second and froze. Then he dug through his pack for anything that could help, though he knew he had nothing that could stop a hemorrhaging artery. He grabbed the needle from his sewing kit. He'd sewn up wounds on animals, but never a wound like this. It was gushing too much blood. Miraden abandoned the needle, tore a strap from his pack, and tied it around Lovo's upper arm like a tourniquet. He might lose the arm, but at least he might live until they get to Muckmog. Without even letting out a whimper, Lovo shoved him away and continued his prayer. Within a minute, the wound was closing, healing! Miraden never saw anything like it!

Miraden stood, stunned. He jumped when the children screamed and ran up to them. He had nearly forgotten about them between the ashenkin and Lovo summoning divine aid. When he took a good look at them, he realized they looked as terrified as he felt. Their eyes were wild and nearly vacant. He thought they were in shock even though they were safe now, at least for the moment.

Miraden kneeled between them and whispered, "We have food and water, but we are heading to Muckmog. You're safe now, but we must remain quiet." He looked at the girl then the boy, who wide-eyed nodded without a word.

They left the ashenkin and quietly got back into the boat and kept going down the river.

Hours passed as they floated in silence for most of the day. Stormrange caught up with Miraden; he was so glad to see him. He realized the scroll case was empty again and wanted to cry. He shook and held his tears back, realizing the kids couldn't see him falter when they were already on edge.

Miraden looked at the young girl's large eyes. She was covered in mud and small. He knew she had to be scared.

"Here, he loves it when you pet his cheek," Miraden said and ran his finger behind the bird's beak. Stormrange closed an eye and leaned against the finger.

"Can I pet him?" the little girl asked.

"What's his name?" the boy asked.

"Sure, one at a time. His name is Stormrange. And he is quite the mouse catcher and naagling slayer!" Miraden whispered. The kids relaxed and giggled a bit. They slid closer, eager to pet Stormrange.

Lovo was doing most of the paddling, and even though his robes and leather were bloody, he seemed fine as if nothing had happened. Miraden wanted to ask him about his prayers but didn't feel the time was right. By nightfall, the river brought them to a large wall of trees reinforced with patchwork wooden barriers.

"We're home. This is Muckmog," one of the boys whispered.

There was a closed gate on a small tributary with watchmen holding torches and crossbows. They held out their torches, but Miraden wasn't sure they could see them.

"Can you open the gates? We have rescued two children," Miraden said.

The guards moved with a purpose, and the gates started to swing forward and open.

They eagerly paddled inside the gate to the first small dock of bobbing planks they could spot. A gathering crowd of folks helped them moor and get the children out of the boat.

"Thank you for bringing these children home!" a woman yelled and hugged both of them. More villagers were sharing their gratitude, patting them on the shoulders, many hugging them. But they soon started to disperse as the kids ran off on the docks to their parents.

Miraden was amazed by Muckmog. Most of the village was built around trees and on floating platforms. Some houses were built into the trees all the way up to the thick canopies over the dark swamp. The canopy was so thick that it was likely dark as night in the city all the time. Thousands of lanterns held small iridescent bugs that made the entire village glow blue. Townsfolk spilled out from their homes when they heard the children crying for their parents. Strangers continued to greet Miraden and Lovo, many hugging them. It felt good to Miraden, really good. He just wished Kyradel would have been with them, but perhaps they were getting closer.

The rescued girl came back with her mother. The mother was a gangly woman.

"I'm Jinoben, tanner here in Muckmog," she said. Her hair was matted into a single dreadlock that drooped over her shoulder, and she chewed a reed that she twiddled around missing teeth.

"Your gear looks in bad shape. Why don't you come back to my shop so I can fix that?" she said and held her daughter's hand.

Miraden and Lovo followed her along the dock. Miraden looked over the side briefly and saw a large red and gold snake slither out from beneath the dock and into the water. He shivered a bit and tried to push it from his mind.

A passing man greeted them and handed them each a piece of fruit. It was brown and smelled sweet but squishy to the touch. Miraden wasn't sure about it, but Lovo took a big bite. It gushed green juice onto his chest.

"Mhmm, it's good," he said.

Miraden decided to give it a try. It was almost too sweet and a bit sour, but he ate it anyway.

After a bit of trying on gear, Jinoben provided them with thick leather that was boiled and dried, and as Miraden looked closer at the leather, he could see faint scales.

"Not from stags," she said. "It's naga leather, preserved with fish oils." She hugged Miraden and kissed his cheek. He smiled, but he was gagging a bit from her odor that smelled something between swamp water and garlic. Lovo gave her a good strong hug, and she even laughed at it.

"Thank you for the gear," Miraden said. He was grateful.

"Thank *you*, heroes, for bringing my Kalada back safely. Daughter of Forests be your shade."

"Mother of Light," Lovo said and waved his thanks.

Miraden stretched his arms out. The leather was hard from being boiled yet comfortable, smooth, and warm. Good thing, too, because the ashenkin blood drenched his leggings and part of his boots. He didn't think they would have lasted much longer. Even if it were not for the devil's blood, his old leather was crusty and splitting from the swamp and the river crossing. It was a great relief to get into some dry leather.

A few of the villagers approached Lovo with a gray wooden shield of wormoak. It was polished and gilded. One man also had two fistfuls of arrows.

"We pooled a few coins. Thought you adventurers could use these." Miraden was grateful because he was nearly out. They also offered rations of dried fish, pickled tubers, and something that looked like dried worms. Miraden thought the worms looked disgusting and may only eat them in an emergency.

"We also paid for a room for both of yas, over at Kagan Jack's," a man with matted hair and brown face paint said. He pointed to a large lodge built around two trees. They nodded, thanked the group, and went to Kagan Jack's, which was more like a large house that sold booze built around a tree.

They went inside. It was musty. The floorboards creaked and

squished at the same time. There were two people, including the bartender, inside.

The bartender, Kagan Jack, wore a coverall and smelled like urine. His missing teeth left him with a black smile. His lips were stained, probably from the root he was chewing, which Miraden thought was millweed. He normally never drank, but Miraden decided he'd earned a few and had some with Lovo. They needed some after what they'd endured. If only for the night. Despite the bartender's nasty breath, they stayed there at the bar. Jack didn't charge them after hearing they rescued the missing children. He only asked that they tell him the story.

Lovo started to regale him with their travels through Pinderfang and then eventually got to Muckmog. Miraden was quiet, sipped his drink, and minded his own business. He glanced over at the robed person sitting next to him with a small drink. They wore gloves and had a staff beside them. Once Lovo mentioned killing two ashenkin when they found the children, the stranger at the bar turned to face Miraden.

"You're hunting the ashenkin," the man whispered. His voice was soft. Miraden had to lean in to him. "I heard you tell Kagan you're after ashenkin."

Miraden nodded. "We are. But I'm really trying to save my friend. She was captured by ashenkin. In my village, to the south." He sighed hard and took a sip of his spirits.

"I see. I'm so sorry. As a wizard of Kander, I'm hunting them for my research. My master has sent me to investigate all that I can about them and the Ashengates."

Miraden was surprised the stranger was so open to discussing the ashenkin. "You, you're a wizard?" His head spun a bit.

"Yes, an ice mage. I'm here to investigate a disturbance southwest of here but haven't found much. Where are you heading from here?"

Miraden thought of where Hellshy pointed after they left the docks and before they stepped into Kagan Jack's Inn. "North, I suppose. My compass is leading me there," he said.

The mage looked at Lovo while Lovo chatted about music with Kagan. "This is your guide?" he whispered.

"No, he's my companion. A cleric of the Mother of Light."

The wizard nodded. "I see. Well, I would very much be interested in where your compass is taking you. It could further my findings, and hopefully, I can collect some reagents from the ashenkin," he said in a soft tone.

"I imagine we are leaving first thing in the morning." Miraden's mind swam as he struggled to put his thoughts together. "I think we're staying here. We are leaving from here tomorrow?"

"Fair enough, I shall be here to follow in the morning. My name is Simigrin," he said and extended a gloved hand. His skin was dark and thin, from wrist to robe sleeve.

Miraden nodded and shook Simigrin's hand. "We welcome your help. As thanks, let me buy you a round," Miraden said.

"You're buying another round!" Lovo shouted and grabbed Miraden with a strong one-armed hug. "My buddy Miraden wants us all to be a little happier tonight!" he shouted.

Miraden woke up in his bed and realized he celebrated far too much last night. The world spun. His stomach even more. The close walls in his room felt painfully small. His blanket was overly heavy on his chest. Every little creak of wood squealed in his ear.

Miraden got up an hour later in a certain, unavoidable misery. He walked out of his room and into the bar where Lovo sat with a plate of breakfast. Miraden joined him for a small breakfast of bread and fish broth. Mid-bite, Miraden dropped Hellshy and saw it flip toward the north.

Mid-chewing, Lovo said, "I hope it isn't Keldenfeld Plains."

Miraden didn't know anything about the region, but his concerns evaporated quickly. They ate breakfast quietly and then stepped out of the inn.

"Good to see you both up," Simigrin said. He met them promptly at the front of the tavern. He was dressed only in a heavy blue robe with a thick cowl that hid his face. He had a large bag over his shoulder filled with supplies and the corner of a large book sticking out the top of it. He said he knew someone who could help them with their hangovers. Miraden hadn't drunk this much in his life, and he would have fought a dozen ashenkin for a bottle of Ceychell's sickness elixir that morning. He definitely needed it—his head pounded, and his stomach churned like he'd eaten a poisonous mushroom.

Lovo told Simigrin they were bound north, possibly far north. Simigrin nodded and waved them along. He handed them each a large fur coat.

"You'll need these if we are bound for Keldenfeld," he whispered.

Miraden and Lovo gladly accepted them. Simigrin pulled them along impatiently, saying they needed to get going soon. Miraden thought he was quite frail-looking, and his staff looked more like a battle staff than how he'd imagined a wizard's staff would look—no markings, engravings, or serpent's head handle. It was just smooth and black and seemed light but sturdy and ordinary.

Simigrin spoke in whispers, so Miraden found himself having to lean in to hear him. His skin was also dark. Miraden assumed he was from the South—but didn't ask.

They reached a herbalist named Aganu at the edge of town, near where their boat was moored. She was old, and her gray hair was long dreads that were spun with fabric. She smelled something fierce—

nearly upset Miraden's stomach—but the elixirs she made cured their hangovers. Lovo drank two. Miraden found it overly sweet, like the janga fruit that grew near Pallow Lake. Lovo let out a loud burp.

"I feel so much better," he said. Miraden agreed. It was a miracle. Miraden noticed she put some skor laurels in the tonic she gave them. Ceychell's favorite tea was made with skor laurels. They spoiled fairly quickly, so he'd need to send them soon.

"I need to finish a letter and send it, then we can head out," Miraden said. Aganu let him use her desk. He removed his writing equipment and continued the letter he'd worked on.

...I promise I will find Kyradel. Thinking about our long walks as children has really helped me through the past few nights. I could almost hear your laughter while we were floating along the dark swamp. It even made me smile and forget my fears. I try to remember my mission, but with each free moment, I think of you...

Love,
Miraden

Ceychell sat on her comfortable chair next to the fireplace with a cup of freshly brewed laurel tea in her hand, the note in the other, and Stormrange perched on the armrest. She read it again with tears in her eyes and suddenly felt her troubles on this Valdenfest were trivial. She felt thankful and so happy Miraden was still alive. Her throat tightened as she considered Miraden risking his life each day not only to save her sister but with the hope that he might regain her affection. She felt like such a fool for shunning Miraden in hopes that it would regain her sister's love. It didn't, not even a little.

As Ceychell sipped from the bottom of her teacup, she realized she was smiling and felt a comforting warmth in her chest. She sank into her chair, gathered all of Miraden's letters from the side table next to it, and read them again. She imagined Lovo as large and clumsy as he was strong, like an ox with a big heart. Her skin chilled at the thought of a putrid swamp. She could smell the moistness of the moss and rottenness of the wormy old trees. She shivered to imagine cold, murky water despite basking in the warmth coming from her fireplace hearth.

Ceychell looked at Stormrange. He preferred mice and rabbits, but she'd fed him hazelnuts in the past. There were a few left in a bowl on her counter. She finished her tea then retrieved a small wooden mallet from a box and the nuts from the counter. She whistled, and Stormrange flapped over to her counter, where she spread out a handful of nuts and smashed them open with the mallet. He munched while she ran her fingers up and down his neck and smiled. His presence calmed her.

With the thought of him, she held up her ring and adored the smoky green emerald. The longer she looked at it, the more something seemed to be moving inside it. It seemed as if the emerald were smoke being exhaled by the serpent's mouth on which it was mounted. She started to put it on her finger when the door shuddered.

She wasn't sure what to think. There were no robberies in villages as remote as hers. She fetched a paring knife from under the counter. Its razor's edge gleamed, but it was merely for cutting reagents and not much of a weapon. The door bucked a few more times, then burst open. She caught a glimpse of Hydracks and ducked behind the counter.

She held her breath and tried to stay calm. She heard the door slam and uneven footsteps approaching the front of the counter. Stormrange squawked, and there was a crash, something falling off a shelf. Ceychell screamed.

"I knew you were in here. Come on out, Ceycha." His speech was slurred. She heard another crash, a ceramic jar breaking.

"Please, just leave!" she yelled. He was far more drunk than he was at the festival. She was nervous about what he might do if she provoked him.

While she was thinking about standing up and trying to talk him away, he leaned over the counter and grabbed a fistful of her hair. She screamed as he pulled her up from the floor. When she was fully standing, she lunged and stabbed the knife in his arm. It was so sharp; he hardly noticed he'd been cut until he saw the red blade in her hand. He punched her in the face.

Her vision danced into a blur. The knife fell from her grip onto the counter before she dropped to the floor. Disorientated thoughts bounced in her head as her world spun in nauseating waves. She heard Hydracks pick up the knife from the counter, heard him growl, heard his boots on the floor as he stepped around the counter. He was leaning over her with the knife poised to plunge it in her neck when Stormrange screeched and swooped into him. Hydracks screamed. She opened her eyes and saw him holding his ear, blood dripping over his hand. He swatted the preddlehawk. Stormrange fluttered and gashed at his eyes with his talons. Ceychell saw the bird had a big chunk of Hydracks's ear in its beak. Hydracks took another swing at Stormrange, missed, and the bird tore a gash on his forehead. Hydracks howled and swatted and ran for the door with Stormrange clawing at his head. He opened the door and was gone.

Ceychell stood up. Her eye throbbed with enough force to make her head hurt instantly. She stepped around the counter and found Stormrange bleeding on the ground.

"No, please, no!" She scrambled through the shop for ointments to stop the bleeding. She pulled out everything she could find quickly, dropping a few jars in the process, then kneeled by the bird. Tears streamed down her cheeks as she carefully rubbed some juniper sap underneath his feathers, though she wasn't sure it would help. Miraden was the only animal medic in Kaehrn; the next closest was in Bilore Des. To her relief, the goopy sap clogged the wound. She lifted Stormrange to her chest to comfort him while she prayed to the Mother of Light to save Stormrange for Miraden.

She carefully dabbed tears from her swollen-shut eye. It hurt with every touch of her finger. The pain burned in her, she felt unnaturally hot, and her hand shook. Her anger got the best of her for a moment when she stood up and lifted the paring knife. When she threw it, it stabbed into her counter so hard she thought it impossible. The blade was all the way in the wood, and it made a loud thunk as if she drove in there with a great hammer.

She felt nauseous while standing at the counter where a half-written letter lay next to a large lit candle and a few broken hazelnuts. She took the nuts and tossed them to Stormrange. He hobbled happily toward the treat. He was no longer bleeding and seemed fine. She'd sewn extensively, but she was not skilled at stitching a wound, especially on a bird. She ignored her pain and continued praying for Stormrange every time she looked at him.

The shop door shuddered again. Ceychell screamed and ran toward the door, picking up the fire poker on the way. She leaned against the door and yelled, "Who is it?"

"Your father, why are you barring your door?" His voice rumbled with anger.

She lifted the bar and opened the door. Her father stood in the doorway, a dark shadow before a winter's flurry.

"Ceychell, I was just coming to check on you," Ormus said. He stepped into the shop and then forced the door closed against the wind.

Ormus looked tired and frail despite his enormous size and strength. He'd been suffering since Kyradel's abduction. He was made of iron, but from his trembling jaw and worried eyes, he appeared more like clay growing dry and cracking. Ceychell kept the injured side of her face away from him.

"Why are you turned away from me, daughter?" he said, his voice barely more than a whisper. She knew this quiet fury and turned to face him. Her eye was swollen shut, her face heavily bruised. She saw a fit of rare anger in her father's grimace, the kind of anger that can leave men hanging.

"Hydracks did this?" he muttered.

She said nothing, knowing her silence answered his question. His face softened a touch when he saw the hawk hop over. "What is Stormrange doing here?"

She picked up Stormrange and sank to the floor, unable to stand steadily. She petted the hawk and sobbed uncontrollably, not from what Hydracks did but from guilt.

He kneeled beside her and placed his large hand upon her shoulder. "My daughter, what have you not told me?"

"Miraden has written me three times," she cried.

"Thank the gods he still lives. Has he found Kyradel?"

"No."

"Have you written him back?"

She wasn't expecting the question. His face hardened when she didn't answer.

"Why not? That boy needs every ounce of support you can give him." Ormus removed his hand from her shoulder and waited silently for an answer.

"I'm going to. The first time I didn't, because… I was just struggling, but last time, Hydracks…"

Ormus stood up over her. She saw the frustration in his tight-lipped expression. He continued, "I know he's too much at times. But that boy has shown you nothing but kindness for years. As for Hydracks..." He ran his hand through his thinning hair, turned, and left the shop without taking time to close the door after him. Stormrange sprung from her grip and flew out into the storm.

His abrupt departure stunned her. She looked back to the counter where the pouch of juno beans still sat next to her letter to Miraden. She wept and crumpled up on the floor. She prayed that Miraden would forgive her and prayed to the Daughter of Forests to watch over him.

A week after the incident with the blacksmith's apprentice, Ceychell sat on her porch, her hair blowing in the chill morning breeze of winter. Her eye was still tender but mostly healed. Two days after the incident, Hydracks was whipped for assaulting her, and she struggled to suppress her memory of his agonized screams and wailing cries as he spent the rest of the day tied to the post at the center of the village. She knew his punishment was attended by most, if not all, of the village—everyone but her. Though she had no interest in witnessing his beating, she clearly heard it from the front of the shop.

The day after Hydracks was punished, Ceychell's mother visited her to tell her that the blacksmith apprentice was banished and could barely walk away. The news didn't affect her; she didn't care. All she cared about was seeing Kyradel, Miraden, and Stormrange come safely home.

As if the Daughter of Forests had heard her, she saw a black shadow dive through the trees. She leaped up to catch the bird and hugged him tight, kissed the top of his head, and rushed into the warmth of her shop to see what the scroll case tied to his chest contained.

She fumbled over the case as she removed the pages and a small wooden totem. It was a carving of three coiled fishes, a fishing totem. She recognized it from her youth.

She hadn't seen the totem since her 12th Passing. Her family had been at Arrowheart Lake for a week in the summer. They went every year, and she loved the holiday. She'd spent most days swimming with her sister or helping her father fish and cook over their campfire. The fish always smelled oily, but she loved the saltiness of the delicate flesh. She remembered devouring her meals and sleeping near the shore in the evenings. She loved listening to the calming water and dreaming of the sea.

One morning during their stay at the lake, when Miraden's 12th Passing was just a few weeks away, Ceychell followed her mother into Ildoo to buy giant pike oil and snapper scales for her poison antidotes. She looked through the reagents in the fishmonger's market. There was a barrel filled with pickled bass partially covered by a wooden lid. Atop the lid, she saw a few totems carved from drench wood. The surface of the totems was worn soft from the long years soaking in the lake.

"They bring luck," the fishmonger had told her. He smiled a toothless and wrinkled smile and brushed a tuft of white hair from his face. "The Lady of Lakes helps us fill our bellies when we wear them on her waters." He pointed to an older and cruder carved totem hanging around his neck.

"Can they help a boy learn to swim better?" she asked. Miraden was fond of luck tokens, and she wanted to give him something for his Passing. She wasn't sure how expensive they were but was willing to find out.

"Erm… I suppose it could," the old monger replied. "This one right here prevented a fisherman from drowning in this very lake." He picked up a pale white totem tied to a necklace of twine.

"What happened to him?" Curasca asked.

"He died of consumption. Totems don't help with that."

"I see. I'm sorry to hear that," Curasca said.

"Mother, I'd like to get this for Miraden. How much for this, sir?" Ceychell asked.

"Sir?" he scoffed with a hint of amusement. He ran his oily hands through his white hair again as if to prepare it for the proper addressing. "I'm 'fraid I don't make up much of a sir. This boy needs help swimming, you say? Well, I can't let him be swallowed by the Lady, can I? Is he a friend of yours, young lady?" he asked.

Ceychell nodded. "Yes, sir. He is my best friend."

The fishmonger placed the totem in her hand without another word.

TEN

THE TRAIL GOES COLD

CEYCHELL HELD THE TOTEM TIGHTLY in her palm as she read Miraden's latest missive.

My dear Ceychell,

We have finally reached Ildoo!

They finally had Pinderfang Marsh at their backs, and Miraden couldn't have been happier, that is until he saw Keldenfeld Plains. He wasn't sure anyone traveled this route, but it was the direction Hellshy was pointing them to. There were no roads, no landmarks, just fields of stone and shrubs covered in snow as far as he could see. Their fur cloaks saved them from the cold wind whipping over the flat landscape; otherwise, they would definitely have frozen. Though there were now three of them, Miraden felt very lonely in the barren open and away from the forest. He didn't see a single animal, even a bird. Keldenfeld was utterly devoid of life this time of year. The sight of such desolation chilled him to the bone.

Each hour of walking, Miraden hoped to see Ildoo on the horizon or even Arrowheart Lake, but they were in a sea of gray and white and following Hellshy's direction. Miraden thought about turning them around and heading back to the swamp, where he could at least hire a guide. It nagged at him constantly; he even stopped in the middle of nowhere. After standing for a few moments, pondering turning around, Simigrin patted him on the arm to keep going.

The only break in the sounds of crunching snow and the wisping wind was Lovo's continued pestering of Simigrin.

"Do you have a campfire in that bag of tricks?"

"I'm definitely wishing you were a fire mage."

Miraden groaned with the occasional comments. It definitely added to his misery.

"Any chance you can make it less cold?"

They shivered and trudged. Simigrin ignored Lovo's pestering for the most part, but Miraden swore he heard him threaten Lovo. Something about making it colder, which shut Lovo up for a bit.

The snow really picked up as they trekked. It was miserable. So miserable that Miraden had to remind himself why he was doing this before taking each step. It was so bitter cold he wanted to lie down in the snow, in the middle of nothing, and just die quickly to be done with the cold, but he couldn't. His feet were numb, and he couldn't feel his fingers. His eyes burned. It was so difficult to see anything.

They stuck together in a tight line when it started snowing hard lest they lose one another. Lovo groaned about being hungry, and Miraden was as well. He felt like his stomach was turning inside out. He was certain Simigrin was also hungry, but the mage was quiet. It was too cold to stop and eat.

Miraden was exhausted, Lovo's arms hung from his sides, and Simigrin was hunched forward as they continued. It was getting late and a bit colder. Miraden was worried if they tried to rest without shelter, it was likely they'd never wake up. His vision was blurry, and he could scarcely feel anything… he thought he was freezing to death.

Constant snow flurries pelted them as though they were walking through an avalanche. While they walked slowly through the night, something fell on Miraden and knocked him into the snow. Miraden panicked; he couldn't get up despite pushing with all his might. It was Lovo. He had fallen asleep while walking. Simigrin helped roll Lovo off of Miraden. Lovo wasn't shaking anymore, had snotsickles, and didn't look alive except for his teeth that continued to chatter. His skin was gray, and his eyebrows and scrubby beard were covered with frost. Simigrin pulled out a book and a small marble from his bag. He recited words onto the wind that were foreign to Miraden. A blast of light took his sight briefly, then, as the blurriness cleared, he found that they were below a dome of pure ice about the size of a very small bedroom. Strangely, Miraden felt warm for a moment. The wind and snow could no longer reach them. It was dark and cramped, but there was enough room for the three of them, or at least should have been if Lovo weren't so big.

After propping up Lovo, they huddled together in the dark, icy prison and rested there for several hours. Miraden wasn't sure what tomorrow would bring, but for the moment, at least they weren't going to die.

Normally, Miraden couldn't have stayed in such a cramped place, but he was happy to make an exception and welcomed the ice prison over the freezing cold outside. After they rested, they shared food and huddled close. No one said a word.

Miraden woke to water dripping on his face. It was steamy warm inside; it was such a relief. He could feel his fingers and legs again; he didn't even care that it smelled and he was semi-squished. Simigrin and Lovo were sleeping soundly against him. The icy dome was a blinding light that appeared to be melting.

"Let's get up. I believe it's melting," Miraden said.

Lovo moaned, and Simigrin leaned up. They had a quick meal of some dried meat Kagan Jack had given them. When Lovo bumped his head for the tenth time, he became enraged and struck the ice barrier with his mace. It split and cracked, and he kept smashing it until it broke open above them, revealing a clear sky and cold wind. In the distance, Miraden saw a black speck on the snow-white plain.

"I sure hope that's Ildoo," Miraden said and shielded his eyes. He tried not to think of it because he feared that they would freeze if it wasn't. He wasn't wretchedly cold like the night before, and he thought of Ceychell. He remembered her sitting by a campfire one summer's day. They went fishing and shared a meal. It was quiet, and the fireflies were just starting to buzz. He was so happy she—

Lovo slapped Miraden's back. "That's Ildoo, buddy. Let's go."

Miraden lost his daydream. Simigrin was already a bit ahead. The mage turned and waved them both along.

When Miraden saw a vast field of ice that could only be Arrowheart Lake, he felt better immediately. Though, now that he was not focused on the possibility of freezing to death, he felt Stormrange should have returned by now. He started to worry that he might have tried to fly to him during the storm. He was a strong flier and a northern bird, but that storm was too intense. Miraden prayed to the Daughter of Forests that he remained in the swamp until the storm passed.

Miraden's mind raced more as they grew less than five miles away from Ildoo. He knew Valdenfest had passed. He really missed not seeing Ceychell there this year… it was a memory he'd lost that would never be found. He thought of how she was at Valdenfest in the past and how much he enjoyed it. The warm memories had helped him so much on this journey, but they seemed to be fading.

Lovo tried passing the time by learning more about Simigrin.

They walked out front of Miraden, but he didn't mind. It didn't seem Simigrin was open to the discussion, anyway. He was content being a quiet mage in a blue robe and dark hood with a dark face. All he offered Lovo at times was a nod or the shake of his head. Miraden didn't pry for any details, either, but he was just as quiet.

Strangely, when Lovo was busy telling Miraden about his life story, Lovo didn't ask him anything about his. Miraden related more to their new companion and was grateful for their mage's ingenuity to survive the storm. Miraden wasn't sure if Simigrin's lack of responses, or perhaps the cold, got to Lovo while they hiked through the snow, but Lovo stopped.

"It's been too quiet for too long. Miraden doesn't say much. I can't have both of you quiet as temple mice." He sounded more jovial than upset. Miraden and Simigrin just stared at him. He dug both hands in the snow, packed a large snowball, and threw it at Simigrin. It hit him right in the chest. Miraden almost laughed but wasn't sure what would happen next as the mage stared at his dumb and impatient cleric friend. But Simigrin just raised a finger as a warning and turned again toward Ildoo.

Miraden sighed with relief that Simigrin didn't summon a lightning bolt or turn Lovo into a temple mouse. He hoped the little event was over, but as he turned to follow Simigrin, he saw another snowball whiz by and splat onto Simigrin's back. Simigrin leaned over, made up a small snowball, and threw it at Lovo, but it hardly poofed against his chest. Lovo laughed loudly, but then Simigrin raised his hand, palm forward in front of his chest, and a wave of snow rose far taller than any of them and crashed onto Lovo, completely covering him.

Miraden thought that Lovo must certainly be cold. He shuddered and left Lovo to work his way out from the snow by himself while he and Simigrin walked ahead. There was a bit of cursing, but Lovo finally caught up to them, and there were no more snowballs or questions for the taciturn mage.

Miraden remembered Ceychell's family coming to Ildoo every summer, but he'd never been this far north. They received a warm welcome, though, when they finally arrived after nearly freezing to death. The town was built of wood cabins around Arrowheart Lake. Great icy peaks clawed up the brisk blue sky beyond the large lake. On this side of the lake, there were dozens of log cabins that were snow-covered and sturdy-looking. A few cabins were multi-story, and the shops were centrally located next to the harbor. Smoke rolled out of the chimneys, but the town was otherwise pretty frigid. In fact, the boats were frozen at the pier, and fishermen sat on small stools on the lake where they ice fished.

A pack of locals greeted them and walked with them through the fishing village.

"Do you all need directions?" a man with a white fur hat and cracked brown skin asked. He'd spent a lot of time in the sun and was wind burned. But he smiled all the same.

"We don't get many visitors. We're happy you're here," a woman said. She had a string of fish over her shoulder, each large and pink with red scaly rings.

Miraden heard Ildoos were friendly—he was glad it was true.

"We could use a warm meal and a place to rest," Miraden said.

"Yes, first order. I'm starving," Lovo added. Simigrin said nothing and looked around town. Miraden thought an ice mage might find this place fascinating, but he didn't want to think of the cold.

"C'mon with ya then. The Bait Bucket's got stew on," the fisher lady said and took them to a lodge near the lake.

They had their fill of fish and potato stew and started asking around the village for information on the ashenkin. Unfortunately, either people were reluctant to speak to them about the matter, or they knew nothing. Miraden grew concerned that Hellshy had led them wrong. It almost seemed like the ashenkin didn't raid Ildoo at all. The Ildoos were far more concerned with bandit activity to the east and the ice krins to the north that actually had attacked their village. There was a hefty bounty on both, but neither would help them because last time Miraden checked, Hellshy now pointed due west past the lake, and the jobs would take them too far out of their way. Miraden still had plenty of coins. Simigrin and Lovo weren't interested in the money, either.

They picked up rations of salted fish and stale vegetables for their journey west at a market near the fishing dock. It was all they would part with. Miraden couldn't believe how expensive it was—ten times the reasonable cost for food for a week. Lovo was distracted and kept looking back to stare at one of the boats. Miraden began to wonder if it was the boat he worked on when he spilled the barrel and lost the catch. He hid a bit more beneath his cowl and remained quiet.

"Should we stay for the night?" Lovo asked.

"I don't think so. We've warmed up. We should stay on the trail," Miraden said. He wanted to stay and thaw for a week but couldn't.

"Miraden's right. There might be fog on the lake at night. We should go before we lose the light," Simigrin whispered.

Three villagers approached them, hats in their hands. "Excuse us," a fisherman said. He was thin, like the others they'd seen. His face was gaunt. "Very sorry to trouble visitors, but our village stores are running low because the krins kept raiding our food supplies."

Miraden wanted to sneak away since their misfortune wasn't his burden, and the faster they found Kyra, the sooner he could go home. Simigrin and Lovo looked to Miraden to make a decision without giving him an ounce of input.

Miraden was a bit angry at being begged into helping, but he tried not to let it show.

"We are hunting ashenkin and have no—"

"Please, we can give you information about the ashenkin in exchange for your help. Most of us ration one meal to a family a day. We eat rats when we find them, but soon we'll have to eat our dogs and cats."

Miraden's heart started to hurt. They were desperate. He couldn't withstand their begging any longer. "We will do it, but if we kill the krins we want warmer clothes, the information we asked for, and fifty kams." He'd ask for far more, but fifty was probably a hefty sum for this poor-looking village. They shook their heads without a moment of debate. Miraden realized he should have asked for a mansion on the wharf so he would have somewhere to live should he make it out of this alive.

"These krins are blue-skinned creatures, violent and cunning," the fisherman said.

"Aye, similar to bog ruks or the naaglings, just larger and smarter," another added.

Miraden already regretted his decision.

"Can you all come to help?"

They backed away. "We've lost many men. Many of us are weak. We can give you what supplies we have."

They followed the men to a tool shop, where they picked up climbing gear and rope. Miraden wasn't sure if he disliked the walk across the tundra or the thought of climbing icy mountains more, but he was not one bit excited about this mission.

"Should we be chasing krins into their territory?" Lovo whispered.

"You all looked to me earlier. It's too late for that now," Miraden said.

"These people will starve if we don't help. They're already skin and bones," Simigrin whispered. The others didn't hear him, or perhaps they didn't care.

"We leave at first light. You get to stay your night, Lovo."

The next morning they journeyed without issue to the northern mountains—except, of course, for constantly slipping on rock and ice and climbing into the wind. If only Ceychell could see him know, he thought. She probably wouldn't believe what he was chasing into icy mountains. Miraden had no trouble finding tracks in the snow that he assumed were krins. Still, it was the number of footprints that made him question the decision. He found it like tracking a single deer in a herd that's run over the same path dozens of times.

"There are definitely krins this way, a whole army of them," Miraden whispered.

Simigrin tightened his grip on his staff, and Lovo shrugged the wormwood shield in his grip.

"Guess we need to take 'em by surprise," Lovo whispered.

"We need to go back. We're not able to take on a horde," Simigrin whispered.

"Let's just look further," Miraden said. They carefully hiked up the trails of frozen stone, which were quiet enough until he looked up to find a hulking krin with a bow staring down at them, still as a statue. The sight of its dark-blue flesh beneath its open furs made Miraden's skin crawl. He drew his bow and fired an arrow straight into his skull. Lovo and Simigrin stared in surprise as Miraden simply drew another arrow and crept forward. He pretended that he wasn't actually the most shocked of them all and dropped the krin with a perfect shot.

"I didn't realize you were a sharpshooter," Simigrin whispered.

"If we took them on at a distance one at a time, I might have a chance. Otherwise, I hoped your magic would make up the difference," Miraden said. Simigrin did not reply.

They looted the big krin. He smelled like sweat and feces and had coarse skin like a lizard's. The pockets in his furs held only some rotten meat and a few bone tools. A sword at his feet was crafted but dull, stolen most likely. His bow was crude, and arrows were warped.

They left him there and carried on.

Nightfall provided them cover, but it came with much stronger and much, much colder winds. They huddled under a rocky outcrop to warm up a bit, but they eventually had to press on. It was miserable. Similar to being back on Keldenfeld Plains except for the sheer cliffs and slippery trail. Miraden was really starting to *hate* the cold.

An hour or so later, Miraden heard the krins' guttural barking. They sounded angry and fought one another just like the naaglings but worse. He waved them closer, and they hunched beneath a cluster of snow-covered boulders and listened. Miraden couldn't believe how loud they were. It sounded like the tribe was as large as the village of Ildoo, maybe larger.

Simigrin pointed to a large cave that glowed from a fire. A few dozen krins were outside, tearing through something. It was hard to tell what they were ripping apart, but Miraden thought they were bodies. It was not encouraging.

That was when he heard a familiar squawk. Stormrange flew down toward them. Miraden was so happy to see him that he almost cried. Then he noticed his pet favoring one wing, but now wasn't the time for inspection. Miraden waved him away and saw a few arrows fired in his direction. He thanked the Daughter of Forests that they all missed.

It began to snow again while they remained stilled, slowly froze, and watched the krins. Miraden wasn't sure if the snow was good or bad for them, but suddenly Simigrin motioned for Lovo and him to stay put. He withdrew the book from his bag, along with what looked like a small container of spider webs. He removed some of the gossamer with his fingers, but it was so fine it was hard to see. He whispered incantations, and then he completely vanished. Miraden couldn't believe his eyes. After a bewildering moment, Miraden saw a glimpse of him, blending in with the snow. He climbed over a boulder then vanished against the gaggle of krins.

Lovo and Miraden exchanged a nervous look then peeked over the boulder. They waited for a few minutes, all of which made Miraden increasingly nervous. Then the earth shook. He and Lovo stared at each other again as Miraden heard the krin colony erupt in even more raucous shouting and screaming over the mountain's rumbling. At first, he wasn't sure what to do, but the horde was going wild. Miraden nocked an arrow, Lovo drew his mace and shield, and they started to climb up the boulders. When they reached the top, he saw Simigrin running full stride toward them with the whole village of krins behind him. There was a violent rumble as if the whole earth were splitting in half, and then the mountain face of ice crumbled and plunged toward the camp. Miraden fired at the krin closest to Simigrin, then another, then another. He wasn't even aiming. He only wanted to slow them until Simigrin reached them.

They fled down the mountain trail as fast as they could, with the krins screaming and shooting at them from behind. Then their cries stopped as snow and ice plowed over the krins. Simigrin pointed to a slight incline on their left. They sprinted across the mountain and up and out of the gully that the avalanche was rumbling down. They barely escaped the massive wall of snow as it spilled down the mountainside, punishing everything in its path.

They couldn't rest long as another wave was coming directly toward them. Their spot would be covered, and so they ran again. Miraden glanced over his shoulder, then felt a cut across his face and fell into the snow. He wiped his face and saw a slather of blood on his glove. Miraden looked up and found a krin on a ledge above him. Unfortunately, the avalanche hadn't killed all of them. It fired another arrow, and this one struck Lovo's shield, moved in the path of Miraden's chest. Lovo charged up after him while the krin was nocking another arrow and slammed his mace into the krin's chest, knocking it down. Then Lovo bashed it several times on the head until it stopped moving. He removed something from the krin's body, and then he ran back to his companions.

They ran further and ducked under a giant jutting stone as the next wave of snow and ice cascaded around them like a raging river spate over a rock. Miraden watched below as the avalanche crashed along a ridge and finally smashed through the ice of Arrowheart Lake. When the danger had passed, and Miraden was able to catch his breath, he asked Simigrin, "What did you do?"

Miraden wasn't expecting high-pitched laughter, but he stopped quickly. After a few more heavy breaths, Simigrin whispered, "There were great ice spikes, like dragon's teeth, above the cave entrance. I cast a spell to make the ice explode into shards, and it brought the mountain face down with it." He pointed to Miraden's face then, which was still bleeding. Miraden's face was cold, so he couldn't feel it, but he then noticed blood dripping on the snow around his feet.

Stormrange fluttered down and landed on Miraden's arm and helped him forget about the krins and his face. He was thrilled to see him. He hugged the bird, got several loving headbutts and beak nuzzles. The bird was cold. Miraden gave him a few treats and started to tuck him under his cloak to warm up. When he did, he saw the scroll case empty again.

He dropped to his knees in the snow, and it took everything he had not to cry.

Lovo put his hand on Miraden's shoulder. He patted it and kneeled next to Miraden.

"It's okay." He carefully tied closed the scroll case without another word. He side-hugged Miraden and helped him back to his feet. "Let's get back to Ildoo."

Miraden nodded and then noticed cuts on Stormrange that he didn't remember. There was an infection just starting to take hold.

He started to tear up as he held him.

"We need to hurry. I need supplies to clean his wing and stitch him up."

Lovo and Simigrin nodded, and they headed back at a brisk pace.

They returned to Ildoo and went straight to a lodge. They weren't even questioned; they were given rooms after hearing about the krins' defeat. Miraden used the brown vial Ceychell had given him and rubbed most of it on Stormrange's infection. He was so preoccupied that he didn't see that Lovo was crouched beside him praying. Lovo put his hand up to Miraden's face, and he felt warm vibrations on his cheek.

"The krins poison their arrows. I healed the cut and tried to pray for the cure, but the poison could still be inside you," Lovo said. "You may need medicine."

Miraden then removed the yellow vial Ceychell had given him and nodded to Lovo before drinking it. He'd have to thank Ceychell in his next letter. She saved them both that day. And broke his heart again.

The village of Ildoo was rattled by the avalanche. No one else was hurt. They weren't showered with coins when Miraden told them they had taken down the krins, but their cheers made him feel far richer. Lovo was overjoyed at the attention, but Simigrin shied from it and escaped the gathering. A child jumped into Miraden's arms and thanked him. The child was frail, and Miraden felt like he was holding a bag of clothes. He set the child down and shared a bit of food from his pack with the boy. The boy offered Miraden a small fishing token that he carved. It was just like the one Ceychell had given him when he was this boy's age. He'd be sending it to her along with another letter, possibly his last, he thought. He'd tell her of their deeds here in Ildoo before heading west.

"I am lucky to have one of these already," Miraden told him and smiled.

"Who will you give it to?" the child said and looked up at Miraden. He smiled a mouth missing teeth.

"To the finest maiden in the world," Miraden whispered.

The villagers hugged them; some even kissed, which Miraden found a little awkward, but he accepted it as their way of thanking people. They were told the village could survive the winter now. It was hard for Miraden to believe, but he started to wonder if Ildoo would have perished had they not come by. Even if that wasn't true, Miraden knew they made a difference for these people.

As promised, one of the villagers told them that ashenkin were often sighted in Bleak Gale Pines to the west. The journey was long and cold, bearing south then west around the Arrowheart but not as far if they crossed the frozen lake. The thought of walking over a deep lake was terrifying. Miraden didn't fare well riding on the raft as a kid in a shallow river or on Pallow Lake. This was far deeper and frozen. No matter how much he wanted to go around, he needed to save time after their detour to the mountains.

They kept the warm gear and climbing supplies and ate their fill of fish gruel and fried freshwater squid for dinner at The Bait Bucket. The innkeeper let them stay the night for free and allowed Miraden to use his own wooden desk to write Ceychell a letter. One of his barhands fetched him more paper from the provisions shop in town; otherwise, he'd have soon run out of paper and ink. M i r a d e n would send Stormrange first thing tomorrow and then would be crossing Arrowheart Lake.

It was the right choice.

Since Stormrange is doing better, thanks to you, I'm sending him with all my heart.

Miraden

ELEVEN

THE PROWLERS

THE NIGHT WAS YOUNG. CEYCHELL wiped the tears from her eyes after finishing Miraden's letters. She was relieved that Miraden survived the krins and the dreadful cold. She embraced Stormrange, held him tight. She was proud of the big hawk for making the journey back and forth to Miraden again. She would pack more medicine for his flight back north along with a letter and juno beans.

She drank a few blissful sips of her skol laurel tea and started her hearth fire again to make more antidote. She then sat behind her counter on top of a box. She removed some paper and her inkwell from below the desk and set them on top. She'd already written a letter to him but wanted to add a bit about Valdenfest and wishing he was here with her. A thousand thoughts raced through her head.

Ceychell was a few lines into the next page of her letter when she heard a rustling outside. At first, she thought it might be an animal foraging in the snow, but she wasn't going to wait and see. She blew out her lantern and candles and grabbed a dagger from under her counter. It was heavy in her hand, unlike the little reagent knife she was used to. She hoped she wouldn't need to use it. She snuck to the back of the shop, into her small bedroom, and looked out a window.

She saw nothing but the darkness of the woods.

Something scraped the outside wall of her shop. She saw something slowly pass by near the bottom of the window but couldn't tell what it was. Her heart raced as she shuffled to the back door. She clenched her knife tightly, opened the door a crack, and stepped into the snow. She pressed her back to the door and waited to ambush the intruder. Slow footsteps shuffled closer in the dark.

She didn't want to hurt anyone, but she wasn't going to be victimized again… ever.

She sprung from the hiding, lunging with the dagger. Vera screamed and staggered back with her hands up. The knife whipped by inches from her eyes. Ceychell dropped her weapon and grabbed Vera's arms before she fell.

"You scared me," Ceychell said. She breathed heavily, holding her chest. She realized how scared she was. "What are you doing out here at this hour?"

Vera coughed and took several short breaths. She was ghostly white.

"You almost killed me, child. Since when do you leave your home armed?" Vera asked. As the old woman trembled in Ceychell's grasp, she dropped something into the snow. Ceychell leaned to pick it up, but Vera grabbed her hand and fell into her. She asked, "Would you happen to have any tea? It would certainly help my heart. I feel so dizzy."

"But didn't you—"

"It's nothing; leave it. Just a root I picked on the way here," Vera said.

Ceychell helped Vera inside and let her sit in her favorite chair. She poured Vera some of her special laurel tea, and the old woman smiled.

"Oh, child." The old woman ran her thumb over the lingering redness on Ceychell's face. "What did that man do to you?"

Ceychell looked down in shame and didn't answer. The thought of

Hydracks made her angry. Angry that she was so easily fooled. She lifted a blanket from a shelf and laid it over Vera's lap.

"Oh, thank you, dear."

"What were you doing outside my shop?" Ceychell asked.

"Oh, I couldn't find my cat, Nomed, and I followed his little tracks this way. I am sorry I frightened you."

"It's okay. I'm just…" She felt uneasy but wasn't sure why. She didn't want Vera sticking around but wanted to be kinder to her. After all, she didn't know for sure that Vera told Kyradel after she'd caught them together. She'd always suspected Vera told her, but it just didn't matter now.

Vera sipped the tea then asked, "Is it true Miraden is still writing you?"

"He is. I just got a letter from him earlier," Ceychell said. Her face flushed as she thought of the last time she saw him before he left the village.

"You're writing him back, aren't you?" Vera asked. When she smiled, it was as if all the wrinkles in her face smoothed into eagerness. When Ceychell didn't respond, the smile slowly sank to a glower, and she sipped her tea again and muttered something to herself.

"I am sending him a letter tonight," Ceychell finally answered. "And I'm sending him medicine." She petted Stormrange, who still perched on the arm of the chair, though Vera occupied it now and not Ceychell. "His bird is so brave."

Ceychell walked back to her counter. She rolled up the letter she'd written Miraden, and the vial of medicine was now cool. She placed the letter in Stormrange's scroll case and tied the small vial of medicine to the strap.

"That boy is brave, too. And he has always loved you. I hope you won't break his heart."

"I won't," Ceychell said.

Ceychell let Stormrange out to hunt for a meal after Vera left. If he left for Miraden, he had her letter. Ceychell was exhausted and nestled in under a pile of blankets on her small bed in the storage room. She thought of Miraden; she missed him so much, she missed her sister so much. She faded quickly into a dream…

Kyradel dug her fingers into the cold mud and crawled silently, deeper into the dark forest. She shook violently as she crawled between the trees. Her hands trembled as she pulled a strand of hair from her face. There were no sounds of creatures or insects, only Kyradel's panting breaths, gasps, and grunts.

A whip wrapped around her leg. She winced and frantically clambered to her feet only to have another whip yank her legs out from under her. Her breath wheezed out of her lungs with the drop, and she was dragged back through the muck. She rolled over sticks and mud before she was lifted from the ground. She screamed and kicked, but claws grabbed her legs and arms and threw her onto a pile of crying, squirming children.

Her legs dripped blood, but she was alive…

The other children, mostly smaller and younger, clung to her, and she told them to be strong. She held a pair of scared girls and wept with them. Dark yellow fire burst into the air around them, and they froze, terror in their eyes. Then she stared at something, something that growled and hissed.

Ceychell screamed herself awake. Her sheets were soaked with sweat. She had seen Kyradel, clear as day, captive with other children, possibly being forced toward an Ashengate. She was both relieved and terrified. She thought of Kyradel every day but had never dreamed of her, not like this. She thought it might be a nightmare but felt like this dream was her actually seeing through Kyradel's eyes. It felt too real to be a dream. She wondered how her little sister could remain so strong.

Still trembling from the nightmare, Ceychell pulled on a warm robe and her boots. She left her room, walked through her shop, and out the front door into the cold snow. The chill helped settle her; the silence soothed her spiked nerves. The woods were quiet and dark and icy.

She remained outside the shop for a few moments and tried to clear her mind. The lantern on her porch held a flickering light that barely pierced the darkness of her wooded shop. When she turned to open the door again, she screamed.

Stormrange was pinned to her front door by an arrow. The bird was hanging stiff, mostly frozen. She crumpled to her knees and raised her hands toward the bird, asking the gods for mercy.

Hydracks sprung from the corner of the shopfront and grabbed her from behind. She screamed again as he muscled her inside, but she managed a single shrill cry for help before he shoved her to the floor.

He put his boot on her chest to hold her and slammed the door closed behind him, pulling the locking bar down. He stood over her, deathly pale in his blacksmith smock and scraps of hides and clothes he must have stolen. His fingertips were black, and his hair and eyebrows were frosted white. He twitched and coughed. With a quivering hand, he drew a knife from his belt, kneeled beside her, and grabbed the front of her robe.

"Now you die," he muttered through chatters.

She jerked and screamed. She grabbed his knife hand and kicked at him frantically. Hydracks struggled to control her as she writhed from his grip and let go of his knife-hand. She stood up and kicked him to the door. She looked at him and saw the whip marks festering as black wounds just above his torn shirt.

Ceychell kicked him again, but she fell when he grabbed her. He leaned over her, and she kicked his face. He howled and sliced her calf with the knife. As she screamed for help, he grabbed a handful of her robe again and then grabbed her belt. He reached his blade back to plunge it through her. She kicked him again in the chest and pushed him back just far enough to untie her belt and wriggle out of his grip.

She limped behind the counter to retrieve her dagger, then realized she had left it outside when she'd nearly slashed Vera. Her hands fumbled through shadows and little jars, vials, and tools until she found the reagent knife and a flask of alcohol.

He stumbled around the counter. Hydracks's face was bleeding from her kicks. She threw the vial at him. It crashed against his chest. Shards of glass dug into his chest as the liquid sizzled on his wounds. He shrilled and struggled to remove his shirt. Ceychell grabbed another vial from below the counter and fled into her bedroom.

There was a loud pounding at the door. It sounded like it was about to come off its hinges within moments. She thought it might be the mercenaries and hoped it would scare Hydracks. Her heart pounded, and her chest heaved panicked breaths. She scanned the room. Just her bed, a small dresser, a small chest—no good hiding places. She could escape out the back door, but he would be right after her, and she would quickly freeze. She would have only one chance. She quaffed the sweet liquid and instantly saw her hand fade to nothing. She slipped off her robe and slid it under her bed, then crouched down.

More pounding on the front door. "Ceychell? Ceychell!" She recognized Bryndyke's voice. Multiple people banged on her front door. "Go, go, out back," Bryndyke shouted.

Hydracks stumbled into the bedroom but recovered his fall.

Ceychell moved the knife to the small space between the wall and the dresser to keep it out of sight. Her chest was hot; she felt something burn deep inside her, and with it came violent thoughts. She ducked and forced herself to be patient.

Hydracks frenetically whipped his head back and forth. Fresh blood covered his chest, and his black wounds bubbled. She held her breath for fear of gagging.

The shop door crashed open.

Hydracks stepped farther into the room right next to Ceychell. She screamed and brought her knife up, but he saw it and grabbed the blade before it hit his throat. His eyes widened as blood dripped from his hand. She let go of the knife, then raked her hand across his throat and tore her fingers through it with ease. Blood gushed on her arm and chest. She backed away from him and felt her body go numb. He dropped to the floor.

Bryndyke reached her bedroom—the sound of a blade singing from its sheath rang into the room.

The mercenaries crashed in through the back door.

"Hydracks?" he shouted.

Ceychell watched Hydracks choke, wide-eyed, on his own blood. She emptied her gut.

"What in the devils?" Bryndyke said as she felt a flash of heat and spewed vomit into thin air.

Ceychell's flesh started returning to normal. She wrapped her arms around her chest, crouched, and wept. She looked at the blood on her hand and couldn't believe what she had just done. Didn't know how she did it.

"It's okay, lass, it's okay," Bryndyke whispered as he averted his eyes. "On your way, men, I'll take it from here." The mercenaries stepped out the door and closed it. Bryndyke glanced at his former apprentice slowly writhing in a pool of his own blood as Ceychell grabbed a nightshirt from the dresser. Bryndyke didn't end his misery or add to it. He stared at the boy and watched him slowly die.

An hour or so later, Ceychell shivered on her chair with a warm cup of tea. In her lap was Stormrange. She ran her fingers through his soft feathers. The bird was curled in her lap and otherwise looked asleep. She remembered when Miraden found Stormrange as a hatchling who fell from his nest in the large tree next to his house. Discarded by his mother, the bird would have died were it not for Miraden. The young ranger nurtured him from a chick and spent every day with the bird. He would be devastated beyond words. Her eyes were red after shedding every tear she had.

It would soon be morning, but the day was already too much for Ceychell. Bryndyke and a few other villagers had carried the wrapped body out of her bedroom without a word.

Ormus sat across from her. "Ceychell?" Ormus said. She looked up at him. "I cannot take back what happened, but perhaps I can help."

She hardly managed to ask, "How?"

"I can—"

"I failed him, father!" she cried. Ormus dropped his head into his hands. "All he asked for was a few juno beans and maybe a kind word from me. He is risking his life for Kyra—he's already a hero! He saved the villagers of Ildoo from starvation. He rid Bilore Des of naaglings!" She tugged at her ring until it came off and showed him. "He sent this to me because it reminded him of my eyes!" She laughed. "I found out he just saved Ildoo from ice krins and sent me this totem a child gave him so that *I* would have good luck!" Ormus's eyes pooled with tears. "Now, Stormrange is dead because he sent him back to me." She looked at the closed scroll case and broken medicine vial still attached to Stormrange. I finally managed to send him a letter, but now he will never get it!" She covered her face and sobbed. "I don't deserve his love."

"Ceycha?" Her father never called her that. In all her years, she'd always been *my daughter* or *Ceychell* but never *Ceycha*.

She pet the bird wishing there was something she could do. "Please, just leave me."

"I have a friend in Bilore Des," Ormus continued, "who uses runners to conduct his business. I can talk to him, have a runner sent to Ildoo and one west to Oddion. Write two letters, and I will do my best to see Miraden gets one." He stood and put his large hand upon her shoulder. "I know this is hard, but you must be strong. You must be strong for him. Write the letters and get them to me before noon."

She wiped her tears away and nodded.

As soon as Ormus had closed the shop door behind himself, Ceychell grabbed some paper from her counter and began writing. Her penmanship was choppy and stressed as her hand ran feverishly over the page. She made a mistake and scratched it out. It happened again and again. She crumpled the paper and threw it in the fire, then calmed herself with a deep breath and started to write.

TWELVE

THE CONFESSION

DEAREST MIRADEN,

I wish my letter was good news. I know your journey is difficult, but you are a hero to Kaehrn and to me. Your dearest friend and wonderful bird lies beside me. When you saw him, he had been hurt defending me, then he was killed by the same horrible, jealous, and now dead man. I wish I could take it back, like so many other things, but I cannot. I am so so sorry.

I tried sending you a letter several times, but each time I failed. You have helped me look beyond myself. I remember being so angry that my sister was captured and mad that you volunteered to bring her back. Initially, I lay awake at night thinking that if you did manage to save Kyradel, I would be indebted to you, and each day I did or didn't repay you, my sister would hate me more.

Kyra and I were so close growing up. We'd finish each other's paintings, sew each other's clothes. We talked about everything, but more than anything, she talked about you.

You couldn't have been much older than seven when she saw you firing arrows with a training bow, missing the target with every shot.

That's when something about you jolted her. She begged me, and I finally followed her to say hi to you. I remember when she asked to pet your fox, Allegro. She looked so silly with all her braids, but I remember her petting Allegro and smiling up at you. I remember how each time she looked down, you smiled at me.

She pulled me through the woods after our chores to find you. Some days, you'd be hunting, other days, you were training animals, but it didn't matter; she just wanted to see you. Kyradel was… is a dreamer, so she swore you never knew we were there in the forest watching you, but I knew better. Especially when you started making your animals do tricks or fired your arrow at a tree then split it with a second shot.

I'll never know for sure, but I think Kyradel took up poetry and singing only to impress you. She was a natural, but her adoration of you fueled her to practice. We'd sit entire summers up on the Kaehrnstone, where she would sing and write. I loved hearing her while I looked to the sky and daydreamed about being swept up by a valiant knight. His steed was white, and his tall keep overlooked a lush green valley. He was a hero, wonderful in every way imaginable. But I wasn't looking to be saved. I wanted to ride into adventure with him. I wanted my own steed, my own sword; I wanted to be a hero. We would leave my meager life behind, and I would be his companion. We'd help peasants, stop villains, rescue people. I had it all planned out for so many years. I saw it clearly from that hill. Until I didn't.

You dreamed below the hill, left me love notes in my garden. Left treats upon my windowsill. I'd catch you staring at me when I walked by.

Remember the time you found me bathing in the stream and wouldn't give me back my clothes unless I gave you a kiss? It was just over two years ago, before Valdenfest. It was near my 15th Passing, and I was so excited to be asked out to the festival, and Kyradel, of course, wanted you to ask her. Then my perfect friendship with my sister shattered. It was the day I suddenly hated you.

I rarely returned any of your attention, but I left you a note to meet me just outside of town, at the ancient pine-tree tunnel, where you often trained. You met me, and I was going to tell you how much Kyradel wanted you to ask her to Valdenfest. Before I could speak, you took my hand in yours and told me you loved me. I always knew it, but I was so stunned.

Then you kissed me. For that moment, I wanted it, but a sickening feeling in my chest brought me to open my eyes, and I saw Kyradel running away and out of my life.

Since that day, we've rarely talked, and I have blamed you for taking her from me. Now that she's gone, I feel dead inside. Even if you return with her, I fear she will only resent me more. But I would gladly take her hatred until the end of my days just to have her home alive and safe.

I am wearing your ring and will wear it until you return to me. I pray to the Daughter of Forests every day and twice at night that you will return to me safely, with Kyradel. Know that whatever happens, you will always be in my thoughts and forever have my gratitude. I hope Lovo and Simigrin continue to help you on your journey and return safely as well.

All my love,
Ceychell

Ceychell copied the note onto a second parchment. She dripped limebloom oil from her perfume vial and spread it on the corners of each letter. Then she rolled them up and placed them in two identical green scroll cases she took from the village library. She would use them to store her recipes, but this was a far better use for them. She added a small pouch of juno beans and extra medicine to each case. She carefully tied them closed with a firm knot.

It was nearly high noon when Ceychell left the shop. She winced in pain as she dredged through thigh-deep drifts to the edge of the village. There Ormus stood, packed for a journey.

He smiled proudly at her. "Did you write both letters?"

"Aye, my father. You're not sending someone to deliver them?"

"Is there something more important I should be doing?" He raised a smile as she had rarely seen before.

"I suppose not. May I join you?"

Ormus embraced Ceychell. "I must move quickly. I need you to stay here where you are safe. I'll be back soon, don't worry."

Ceychell bit her lip and nodded to him. She handed him the scroll cases.

Ceychell returned to her home and remembered to fish the dagger out of the snow before it completely rusted. She walked along the side of her house and found no small footprints nor Vera's; they'd been hidden from the mercenaries running to the back door and partially by the night's snowfall. She raised a brow.

In a few patches, she could tell the snow was dug out by hand. She found a fresh pile of unpacked snow where she thought she had dropped her dagger and several pits in the snow around it. She pushed aside much of the powder and started to dig. She grew frustrated and then found a piece of charred wood. It was oddly warm to the touch and left black soot on her hands.

She stared at the item for a few moments. She wasn't sure, but it looked like the item Vera had dropped. She placed it in her hip pouch.

THIRTEEN

THE ICE GREW THIN

ORMUS RETURNED TO KAEHRN AFTER a few days and told Ceychell he had paid two riders to deliver the messages to Miraden. He offered them triple should they return with any letters from Miraden. Ceychell hoped one would, but as each day passed, her focus began to falter. Two weeks later and still not a word from Miraden.

After eating a light dinner of soup and bread, she stepped out of her shop and looked up into the twilight for Stormrange. It made her sad, but she believed the bird still watched over her, though she had buried him beside the oak tree near Miraden's cottage. Nevertheless, she felt him nearby whenever the pain started to be too much.

She walked to the large oak and placed a few winter flowers on the snow above his grave. The flowers nearly glowed blue and purple upon the fresh white snow. She whispered prayers that he kept watching over Miraden. When she visited, she was reminded of how hard Miraden would take the bird's death. She imagined him reading her letter and abandoning his quest. She believed he might lose hope.

She trudged back to her shop slowly. Her calf was throbbing where the stitches had been, but she refused to stay off it. Resting too long was when the fears and doubts crept in. The guilt was too much.

She shoveled out snow from her front porch and around her walkway. She'd shoveled her parents' house as well, so her back ached almost as much as her leg. Several villagers offered to help her, but she refused them. She suffered in silence and didn't complain.

She was about to go back into the shop when she heard footsteps crunching on the snow. She gripped the shovel tightly, ready to swing it. A stranger in black leather pants and a winter coat approached her from the snow-covered road. Two mercenaries down the road also started heading in her direction. She held the shovel in one hand and tucked her hand beneath her long bear pelt. There she unsheathed the new dagger she had purchased from Bryndyke. Her long hair billowed in the wind while she waited cautiously.

The man was long in years but sturdy and steadfast in his gait. A black beard speckled gray hung long below his chin. He swung his hands at his sides instead of stuffing them in his pockets; he seemed to ignore the cold.

"Mother of Light, maiden. This is the village Kaehrn, is it not?" he asked.

"Mother of Light. It is. Where do you come from, stranger?" She was kind but not inviting.

"I am Fendel, a messenger from Oddion."

Ceychell rushed up to him. "You're from Oddion?"

"Yes, I bring a message for Ceychell… are you alright?"

Ceychell's eyes teared immediately. She pushed them from her eyes. "I… I am Ceychell. Can I offer you some warm cider inside?"

"That would be kind of you," he said.

She opened the door and ushered him into the shop. It was not quite warm, and the hearth fire was dying down to embers. Fendel handed her a scroll case, and she gave him a cup filled with a golden liquid. She asked him to sit in her chair, which he did. He nodded his thanks. "Did you also bring a letter from my father to Oddion?"

Fendel leaned back and pondered her question. "I am not sure. I deliver many messages. I *do* work from Oddion, which is where I'll return when I leave Kaehrn."

"My father, Ormus, is a very large man. You'd remember him. He is the chieftain of Kaehrn, and he paid two messengers in Bilore Des to deliver letters. One was to Oddion."

He shook his head. "I'm sorry, but I was not that messenger."

Ceychell saddened. She nodded and then stared at the scroll case in her hand. It was not her own. "It is freezing out, and night is nearly upon us. You should stay at the inn here in the village. I can take you there."

"I think I could definitely use a warm bed tonight," he said. He finished the cider, ran his hand along his face and down his beard.

Ceychell retrieved his coat. She also filled a wineskin for him from a bottle she hadn't had the opportunity to open yet. He was grateful and thanked her. Then they headed out toward the center of the village. The Trendle Inn, a sleepy cabin three stories tall with two chimneys, was the only inn in town. Lights flickered in the window, and Elonor, the innkeeper, stood at the counter inside, looking like she was nodding off. Fendel thanked her again as Ceychell grabbed hold of his sleeve.

"I would gladly pay you to take a letter back to Oddion," she said. "If you would."

He nodded.

"I shall ready it," she said, smiling for the first time in recent memory. "Father of Night to you then."

"I leave at first light. More clients await their letters. So, be prompt." He gave her a slight bow. "Father of Night, Ceychell."

She hurried home from the inn, went inside the shop, and sat down near her fireplace. She smiled again and happily unrolled the letter. When she read the first two words, she stopped and choked up.

Dearest Ceychell,

I hope you are well. I survived the hardest weeks of my life. There were a lot of surprises…

They left Ildoo early that next morning. Miraden hugged Stormrange and sent him into the sky. He watched his bird fly up until he disappeared into the cloud cover. He felt sorrow and then started west. It was bitter cold, and the blistering wind blew at his back. It was like a storm was pushing them to the lake. He was grateful they weren't trekking into the wind. Long wisps of snow flew off the lake and blurred into a white-and-gray swarm on a valley of ice. He began having doubts when he stepped on the ice and heard the ice squealing beneath his feet.

"You sure this is okay to cross?" Lovo asked.

"It's sturdy enough," Simigrin whispered.

Miraden really didn't know. He wanted to avoid the lake; he truly did. But then he remembered his father telling him, *never let fear become failure.*

Miraden didn't like the idea of being on the water, and frozen water made him feel no better. As he thought of traveling south into the wind, back into Keldenfeld, and taking the long way around, the lake suddenly seemed like the right choice.

The storm slowed for a bit, and Miraden spotted some townsfolk from Ildoo fishing through holes in the ice. He suddenly felt better about heading across. He shuffled at a steady pace, the others beside him, despite the feeling in his stomach that screamed to run back to town.

His heart dropped with each slip, twice as fast when the ice squealed.

A few spots creaked rapidly as they passed over them. Miraden found the ice especially frail at the center of the lake, and the wind was really punishing them. He grew nervous and sped up. The others did too. He shuffled at a breakneck pace. They were covering ground quickly with the wind when Lovo slipped and fell onto his back.

Simigrin and Miraden slid to a halt. They turned, looked at Lovo, and watched the cracks racing out from under Lovo toward the shore as if they were trying to flee before the collapse. Miraden and Simigrin stood utterly still for what felt like an hour. He was unsure of what to do. He didn't want to move and cause a break while they waited for Lovo to get up.

"Can you freeze the lake?" Miraden whispered through his teeth.

"I need to put my staff in the water to freeze it. I could try to puncture the ice, but it could cause it all to break," Simigrin whispered back.

Miraden wasn't sure what any of them could do other than wait for the lake to refreeze, which wasn't really an option. He looked in every direction, not able to distinguish where the lake ended because of the blinding snow. As each moment passed, and with each squeal and crack below them, he expected an instant and inevitable plunge to his death.

Miraden felt waiting was the worst thing they could do. He shuffled to Lovo, who stared in fear at him. Simigrin joined him, and they both slowly helped Lovo to his feet. The cracking intensified.

"Go, go!" Simigrin said. They all swiftly shuffled toward Bleak Gale Pines in the west. They couldn't turn back and certainly couldn't afford to stop.

Miraden looked at the twisted tops of the dead trees ahead of him on the shore; they rose into the storm like icy teeth. It looked more like a thorny black jungle dusted white than a forest. It was a frozen curse, gruesome and full of brambles and twisted trunks. It looked like a nightmare.

Miraden moved faster. He was terrified of slipping but somehow maintained his footing. He didn't even look at the others, or the ice, or the horrible forest in front of him—he just looked at the shore where the solid ground beneath the snow would save them.

They finally reached the other side, plunged into the snowy bank. They kicked, cheered, and threw snow in celebration. Miraden was cold but so happy he didn't even care. Lovo, Simigrin, and Miraden hugged each other. He was pretty sure they wouldn't make it; he felt they thought the same.

"Did you hear something?" Simigrin whispered.

"Other than us celebrating?" Lovo asked.

"There it is again," Simigrin said.

Miraden didn't hear anything. They were quiet, and this time he heard growling. Miraden looked past Lovo and saw a tundra wolf staring at them from a ridge. It wasn't far away, and its white fur blended into the snowy hill. He could only make out two large black eyes and an outline. It was much larger than the brown wolves that roamed Baregorin. The brown wolves were easy to tame, but without a snare and a ready pack of meat, Miraden didn't think it to be an option for this white one. He drew his bow and nocked an arrow.

He'd heard tundra wolves could easily kill humans. The fear of being ripped apart made his heart race; he held his bow tighter. When it moved, Miraden could see just how big it was. When it shook the snow from its mane, it looked as big as a bear. Miraden tried to scare it by firing an arrow over its head. It growled loudly, and a dozen more wolves appeared over the ridge. They stood between the trees, licking their fangs and breathing hot steam.

"Do something, Simi," Lovo whispered. "Simi?"

Miraden and Lovo turned their head to see Simigrin running toward the forest. They turned in fear as the white wolves started barking and creeping toward them. Miraden soon realized that Lovo's stories had to be true because, for a large man, he could run fast. He got ahead of Miraden and even passed Simigrin.

As the snarling and barking grew closer, Miraden could feel the wolves getting closer. He was already exhausted from running and didn't know what to do. But one thing he did know was that running was not going to save them this time. His thoughts raced. Even if he turned to fight them, he figured they would become overwhelmed.

"Run into the forest! Climb!" he yelled ahead at Lovo and Simigrin. Simigrin heard his cries and veered toward the trees, but Lovo either didn't listen or refused and turned to run right back onto the lake. Lovo screamed at the wolves and slid and tumbled on the ice. The wolves all turned and ran after him.

Miraden drew an arrow to cover Lovo, hoping he would turn back toward them for escape. He made it back to his feet and sprinted fast and steadily away, but the wolves weren't deterred. They ran right onto the ice after him. Simigrin came back and stood next to Miraden, panting, and he yelled, "Come back, Lovo! I'll cover you!"

"Come back!" Simigrin yelled, and Miraden wasn't expecting his higher-pitched voice. Miraden fired an arrow, striking a wolf in the neck. It hit the ice and slid, tripping two others. The other wolves pursued Lovo farther onto the lake. He refused to look in their direction even though they continued to scream.

Then the ice broke with a roaring crash, and Lovo disappeared.

"No!" Miraden screamed. Simigrin held Miraden's arm as he screamed and pulled him toward the lake, though it was swarming with wolves. The ice continued to splinter and crack, and the wolves were swallowed by it as well. They cried like pups and desperately tried to paw back onto the ice. Lovo's arms burst up for a moment as he struggled. There was frantic splashing for a few seconds, and then all was calm.

Within a minute, the wolves had vanished under large drifts of ice. The danger was gone. And so was his friend Lovo. Miraden dropped to his knees along with Simigrin. Miraden wept into his hands and couldn't help but blame himself for Lovo's death.

"He's gone. He's gone. I'm so sorry," Simigrin whispered.

Miraden's tears froze on his cheeks, but he didn't care. He didn't know Lovo long, but he was a good companion and followed his lead… which led to his untimely death. The irony that Miraden thought Lovo would be *his* undoing struck a massive chord.

Miraden stared at the ice patches where his friend fell through. He didn't know why he ran toward the lake, maybe to save him and Simigrin, but he should have stopped him. All the misfortune he managed to survive in life abruptly ended when he followed Miraden. He realized that if it were not for him sacrificing himself, they would likely have died here today.

Miraden slumped on the snowbank with Simigrin, staring at Arrowheart. He prayed to the Lady of Lakes that Lovo would pop up, but after some time, he finally realized it just wasn't going to happen. Even if he were brave enough to try and swim out to where he dropped, they would never make it back to town before freezing. Miraden was responsible for his death, and it was ripping him apart.

It would for the rest of his life.

He would have something not so courageous to share with Ceychell, should he write her again...

FOURTEEN

BLEAK GALE PINES

CEYCHELL FLIPPED THE NEXT PAGE in the letter. She could hardly see through the tears as she read of Lovo's death…

Simigrin held Miraden at the snowy bank. He was a wreck, crying, shaking. He felt terrible, like a failure. Fearful he'd make another wrong decision and doubtful he could keep himself or Simigrin alive. But still, Simigrin stayed beside him and helped him to his feet and walk toward the forest.

Miraden repressed his sorrow and checked their direction with Hellshy. The icy lake was at their back, and the dagger pointed straight into the black, dead woods. Miraden grew nervous about what might lurk inside.

The woods were ominous in that he felt it hid unspeakable terrors. He'd heard nothing good about Bleak Gale Pines. Looking at the place up close, those tales seemed justified if not kind. As they stepped under the trees, everything fell silent. The trees seemed to creep in at them as they approached. The leafless branches spiraled like barbed vines. The trees were tall; their tops formed a cavern-like canopy of gloom and shadows. Even the snow couldn't penetrate it. Little grew upon the forest floor. The few critters spotted were sickly thin; some bore poxes, others dragged themselves along the dirt with a decay that would soon claim them. His stomach rumbled, and fear set in that, once their food supplies grew short, there would be no food to hunt here.

Bones were everywhere. Partially buried and scattered about as if a graveyard had unearthed itself. It was a macabre scene, and he was very afraid.

Miraden thought Simigrin might share his fear, but he was quiet as always. He supposed mages were taught skills to deal with such things, but there was nothing like this in his forest. He never wanted to know a reality like this dark and silent place.

At last, he found an old path leading west. They followed it, and he hoped it was the right way. He tried Hellshy again, and it pointed in the direction of the path, but who knew if the trail would run straight?

"Do you know anything about this place?" Miraden whispered. Simigrin's silence unsettled him.

After a couple of hours, something caught his eye. Something moved ahead. It was a shadow, or, he thought, perhaps his imagination. It was hard to tell, but he *knew* he saw something. The woods were so thick he knew he wouldn't get a good shot, so he drew his sword in one hand and Hellshy in the other. They crept forward.

A man sat on the ground, resting his back against a tree. He started to shift around in his slumber. At his side were two empty scabbards. Two bloody sabers were next to his hands. Four others lay near him. At first, Miraden thought they were sleeping, too, but as they neared them, he could see they had been killed. They lay there with their severed arms or hands near them. Their faces were frozen blue.

Simigrin shook his cowl and placed a hand on Miraden's shoulder.

He whispered, "Leave this man to his own fate. They're Henslemen, untrustworthy mercenaries."

Miraden had never heard of them, but in this place, he thought allies were more important than reputation. When he looked over the dead, he realized they were all dressed in similar uniforms. Their boiled leather was studded and dyed bluish green. Each had worn a black hood, and black sashes wrapped their right arms at the elbow.

Though Simigrin was against it, Miraden insisted that the man could help them find the Ashengate and even get them out of here. Simigrin pleaded with Miraden, then the stranger opened his eyes. He spotted them immediately and grinned. The first thing out of his mouth wasn't "hello." He asked, "Were you the ones I heard screaming like painted whores?"

Miraden didn't take insults lightly, and when he approached him with his blades drawn, the Hensleman merely leaned his hood back and let him see his grin.

"You intend to stop men trying to save children from ashenkin?" he asked. Miraden could see the flicker of his eyes as he looked at Hellshy. "That blade you carry is what brought you here because there is an Ashengate. You'll need my help." The comments stunned Miraden.

The Hensleman stood up and stretched. He removed a bit of ointment from a pouch and slathered it on a chest laceration and then on a welt on his head. He ignored Miraden's drawn blades and said, "I'm Neandra, and I'm the best chance you've got at getting out of here alive."

"What killed these men?" Miraden asked.

"They weren't in this to kill ashenkin and save children. They wanted to take the hydras they were paid and make a run for it. I simply couldn't have that on my conscience."

So Neandra joined them.

For a very fleeting moment, Miraden was glad to have another pair of eyes. They walked through the unpleasant Pines, but what was worse than the creepy silence was listening to Neandra. Unlike Lovo's innocent blather, Simigrin and he got to listen to stories of the brothels he'd conquered. He spoke as if that was what made him a hero, not taking the job to find the children here. When Miraden asked him about the Ashengate, he said they were still quite some ways away, then went back to talking about a woman he'd met in Southern Jolumn. Miraden started to block him from his thoughts when he suddenly put out his arms to halt them.

A blackness sat in the air, like a fog that swallowed the light, not far away. It shuddered and passed farther into the woods away from them. It was sickening, unnatural darkness. It seemed to be hunting for something.

They stood still for quite some time without a word until Neandra turned to whisper, "The devils know we are here. Those black clouds are them looking for us." The creeping dark continued away from them, and finally, Neandra whispered, "We found the ashenkin camp near an Ashengate a few days ago. There was a horde of children in front, but very few ashenkin. The devils were out hunting; it's difficult to say. We have a real opportunity to save them." This got Miraden thinking, but he was mostly curious why they didn't try to save the children right then. The way Neandra told them made him feel like the children were not his priority. At least that's what his smirk made Miraden think. His suspicions continued to rise about their new companion.

Though they stood there for several minutes, they saw nothing except that creeping darkness. It eventually floated out of sight, so they continued westward through the woods. Neandra asked Miraden how they got there.

"We're looking for children." Miraden was brief, and Simigrin said nothing. He sensed the mage was not thrilled by Neandra's presence and purposely avoided any interaction with him. Neandra wasn't insulted, though. He patted Simigrin on the back and said, "Met plenty like you, the quiet sorcerer. It's how they bred you, yes?" He chuckled.

Miraden thought it was night because it became even darker than before. In the Bleak Gale Pines, it was terrifying. He thought Pinderfang was terrible, but Bleak Gale Pines was truly a place out of nightmares. Large insects crawled out from the ground and the trees just before the light went out. Unfamiliar sounds he couldn't even describe rang out from every direction. It was completely black, with only the slightest hint of moonlight able to penetrate the forest canopy. The pale moon rays dotted the floor to reveal the foul things that crawled or slithered by.

"We need to get in the trees before it's too late," Neandra suggested.

Miraden was already climbing.

Simigrin settled on a cluster of branches next to him. Neandra stayed in another tree just below. Suddenly, it seemed they were the only things silent in the Pines.

In this near-complete darkness, Miraden could feel Hellshy occasionally twitch and turn. He held the blade close to his body to contain its movement.

As he lay with his eyes pressed shut, he saw Ceychell. She stood near the fire pit in the town center. It was a warm summer night, and her yellow sundress billowed near the flames. Kyradel was singing and playing her lute nearby, and the people of Kaehrn were in good cheer. Ceychell finally came over and sat next to him, and before he could tell her how he felt, how she'd know he'd always felt, she said that she would never love him.

That dream, though, was Miraden's reality. He wasn't sure why, but when he sat there in the darkness of that place, even though he felt she was right next to him, he completely lost hope. When he opened his eyes, he lost that dream and kept the nightmare. He trembled as it sank in that he would never be together with her and realized that knowing the truth now was better than returning home to face the pain he'd avoided for years. It was more real than anything else he'd ever felt; it burned through him, he ached. It swallowed him up and left him bitter. Tears ran down the sides of his face as he wondered why, why did it have to be this way? He wondered how she could hate him so much that she couldn't bear to look at him when he left to die for her sister. She couldn't even send him a letter! He sat in the darkness of that place, far from the comforts of his home with devils and who knows what else waiting to end his life because he blindly chased a childish dream. All he ever wanted was to make her happy—and he had lost his own happiness trying to achieve that. He wished she knew how badly this hurt, and he would tell her in his next letter. There were moments he wished the devils would find him in the night and end this unbearable—

Ceychell stopped reading the long letter because she could no longer see through her tears. These last few paragraphs had burned through her. She screamed into her sleeve and shook in anger. Obviously, her courier hadn't found Miraden, and maybe he never would.

Ceychell tried to imagine the darkness and fear Miraden lived through that night and only found solace in the fact that his letter had arrived. She looked out her window, which was nearly blocked from snowfall. She could not remember the last time it snowed like this. A rumor from Bilore Des was that the ashenkin were causing the change of climate and that the world would fall into eternal winter should the Ashengates remain open. The rumor troubled her, but only for a moment. Miraden's letter weighed on her far more.

FIFTEEN

THE NIGHTMARES GROW DARKER

CEYCHELL CRIED HERSELF TO SLEEP before finishing Miraden's letter. She slouched in her chair and twitched...

Kyradel stepped slowly across the sharp stones and through the thorny weeds with a group of children. She carried two small girls, and a third grasped around her neck and rode her back. Her hair was matted and tangled, her clothes ragged and dirty, and her feet bruised and bleeding.

Most of the children were younger than Kyradel, but there were a few her age as well, also helping the smaller children. The children were covered with filth, cuts, and bruises. They had been dragged, beaten, and pulled through swamps. They smelled filthy but not nearly as bad as the ashenkin, which gave off a sulfurous stink.

At the misty edges of her dream, Ceychell saw the devils prodding the children ahead. They were red and motley and often twitched as if something unseen yanked at their bodies. When the twitching seemed to drive them out of control, they took out their anger on the children.

They stopped at a clearing in a ghastly forest. The ashenkin barked at each other in their crude language, and a few of them corralled the children by throwing and shoving them into groups. Kyradel pushed to the edge of her group. There, several dead ashenkin lay on the forest floor. Their blood was black, but their bodies did not appear wholly frozen despite the cold. Despite getting shoved back into the circle, Kyradel laughed at the devil. The devil growled and lunged at her. It was held off at the last moment by another ashenkin.

Ceychell screamed. She sat up from the nightmare. She could still see the ashenkin lunging, its jagged teeth the color of bloody black stone. She feared the worst, but the thought that Kyradel was still alive brought a reprieve that let her momentarily smile, too.

She flushed with panic and stood up from her chair. Daylight shined in her window—she had overslept. She ran out of her shop down the snow-packed road to the Trendle Inn. She shoved open the front door to find Elonor at the counter reading. The old woman with a cracked spectacle raised a brow and set down her book.

"Is the messenger from Oddion still here?" Ceychell asked, out of breath.

"He left early just before daybreak," Elonor said. "A very nice man. I gave him some bread and a chip of pork to take with him."

Ceychell dipped her head so Elonor would not see the tears welling in her eyes. She was so angry at herself. She shook her head, thanked the innkeeper, and left the inn.

She walked back to her shop. Each step was heavy, but the weight of her failure made her sag as if she wore an iron yoke. She didn't hear the hellos, didn't enjoy the beautiful morning. She returned to her shop but couldn't continue the letter. Not yet.

She shoveled the new snow out front of her shop onto the drifts.

She thought of Miraden and tried to block out the pain. When she finished clearing the path, she stretched her aching back. She saw Wermen across the way, grumbling as he shoveled. Suddenly her back felt just a bit less achy. Ever since he and his wife lost their son Kjod, Lolia rarely left the house. Ceychell heard she watched her young daughter day and night.

"Hello, Wermen," Ceychell said.

Wermen nodded, hardly looking at her directly.

"Let me shovel for you today," she said. "Why don't you get out of the cold?" She tried a friendly smile, but it was difficult for her. She realized how cold she'd become these last few years.

"Not known you as one to do chores," he said. "Figured you'd be buried in your shop without Miraden here this winter." When Ceychell started shoveling his path, he shrugged and returned to the warmth of his home.

Ceychell tried to push the comment from her mind as she tossed the snow vigorously. She cleared the path around their home to the common road. She caught her breath for a moment next to a window on the side of their house. It had not been boarded up since Kjod was taken. She brushed away snow from the windowsill, stopping when her hand went across claw marks carved into the wood. She ran her fingers over the cuts and imagined how scared Kjod must have been. She looked for other claw marks and then noticed something behind the snow. She brushed more away.

After uncovering the section below the window, she found a smear of black on the wood, partially faded now. When she ran her finger on it, some of it stayed on her glove like purple chalk. She stared at the fine dust and back at the window. She rubbed her scarf on the purple substance and tucked it under her coat.

Her back throbbed. She walked back to her shop and left the shovel just outside her door. She went in, made tea, and dropped onto her favorite chair. She noticed a new bundle of firewood beside her fireplace. She was grateful that her father had brought it. She was too tired to split wood.

She sighed and sipped her tea while her thoughts drifted to Miraden. The snowstorm picked up outside the window, darkening the shop and her mood. She lit her lanterns and candles and sat back in the chair. She glanced at the letter she hadn't finished reading on a large red pillow near her chair. She was eager to read the rest, but not until her day's duties were completed.

After a few hours, she finished brewing the remedies she needed and placed them in a leather potion pack of multiple compartments cushioned with wool. Then she pulled on her fur robe and stepped into the snowstorm.

She struggled with each step, but she knew the sick needed her. She knocked on Vera's door and pressed her ear to the frost-covered wood. Vera called faintly for her to come in, and she entered the warm home.

The old seamstress sat on a large chair facing a fire. Next to her was a small pine table with a cracked leg. It was shoddily repaired, but it managed to stand. Three large books and a cup sat on it. There was a dusty kitchen table with four cats sleeping on it next to cluttered cabinets. Vera's cottage was simple, a single room in the back and an outhouse just behind the back door.

Vera was wrapped in several blankets. She smiled at Ceychell. "Come, dear," she said.

Ceychell walked to the hearth first, stirred Vera's fire, and added a log. She set her pack down on the kitchen table, careful not to disturb the cats, and removed Vera's medicine from it. She set the vial on a small wooden table beside Vera's chair and collected an empty flask, which Vera had ready for her.

"Thank you so much for bringing it to me, Ceycha. This winter is truly abysmal, and it's only begun." She uncorked the medicine and drank only a swallow before replacing the cork.

"I'm happy to help." Ceychell placed the back of her hand on Vera's head. Her fever was weaker than yesterday. "I think my elixir is starting to work. You must stay inside and keep warm. Why do you keep going out before the fever is completely gone?" she asked.

"Oh, I like to keep myself busy—you know that. Last thing I want is to just die here in my chair."

"My elixirs will get you out walking more, but you must be patient. Perhaps soon you'll feel so fit you'll even shovel some of this snow."

Vera chuckled and adjusted the blanket over her. It was thick and brown like a piece of the earth covering her. "You know, your mother has great skill with herbs, too, but she said you're far better than she is now. I cannot tell you how happy she is that you've reopened her shop."

Ceychell fiddled with her potion pack. She'd always been adored, always the center of love. As she started owning her decisions, the small comments and the reality of how everyone loved her made her feel a little more undeserving each day.

"I know… it's hard, dear," Vera continued. "We are all praying for Kyra and Miraden. Ormus tells me a messenger arrived with a letter for you. Good news?"

Ceychell looked at her with a shaking smile. "Miraden is still alive," she said.

Vera smiled. "That boy is clever. He'll find a way. I'm not worr—" A lung-scratching cough cut her off. She wheezed for a moment, then cleared her throat and smiled at Ceychell. "He truly loves you. A love that strong can do anything in this world."

Vera's words took Ceychell's breath as if a horse had kicked her chest. She poured some water from a jug into a cup and handed it to Vera. She didn't hide. She instead forced a smile. "Then I am the luckiest woman alive. I have five more stops before heading home. I think half of Kaehrn must be ill." She pulled her hood up and stepped to the door. "I'll see you tomorrow. Oh, I have that coal stick you dropped at my shop. Do you want it back?"

"No, it was just something I found on my walk," Vera said.

Ceychell nodded and left.

By the time she returned to her shop, her legs were numb, her back throbbed, and her fingers felt as if they might fall from her hands. She sat by the fireplace, brewed a pot of tea, and picked up the half-read letter. She started to shake but read anyway.

Morning finally came, but Miraden was still exhausted from the night terrors and lack of sleep. They resumed their trek through the thickets. They managed to avoid scavengers, a bear, and a few krinish-kin.

"We must move with the shadows lest the ashenkin find us," Neandra said. "We needn't tussle with the roamers. We need our full strength for the Ashengate." Miraden agreed with him.

They barely spoke that day. Whenever they stopped to rest, Miraden focused on the forest. Its floor was blackened, brittle, rotten. The trees were plagued with strangling vines and cracked with ridges of diseased bark that caused the wood to break apart at a touch. The air smelled rotten, like the open chest cavity of a decaying deer but far fouler.

Large icicles dangled from the dying trees. A piercing breeze carried dustings of ice that spiraled through the sparse branches as well as a few sharp icicles that nearly clipped his head. Miraden muffled his coughs not to give himself away, but the cold and dank bitterness seeped inside him.

The second night in the forest, Neandra drew them close. "We need to rest," he said. "We must be still as statues until morning. Whatever you do, do not close your eyes, or you will draw them closer." Miraden and Simigrin stared at him without a word. Miraden wasn't sure how he'd stay awake all night.

"It's been quiet for a few days. I feel they are about to hunt. If they do, our chance will be to invade their camp tomorrow when many of them would be out on the prowl," he whispered. Miraden was scared. He wondered how Simigrin was; he hadn't said a word since they found Neandra.

It was hard to find suitable trees to climb because most were rotten, but one giant tree still stood strong. Unfortunately, its branches were far out of reach. Miraden threw a rope over a thick branch and secured it. There was a large hole high up in the trunk, where at least one of them could rest if it was vacant. Neandra was the first to climb and took the lowest resting point. He pointed for Simigrin and Miraden to take higher positions.

Simigrin hesitated even to start climbing, so Miraden went up next. It was easy for him, but he'd climbed trees all his life. Simigrin tied the rope around his waist and climbed slowly. It was painful for Miraden to watch, and he finally pulled the line to help him up. As Simigrin got close, he rested his arms, but Miraden noticed the knot coming free around his waist.

"Grab the rope!" Neandra whispered. And Simigrin did. Just before it pulled free, Miraden grabbed his arm. When Miraden reached down around his chest to pull him up, he jerked and grabbed his arm defensively. He thought it strange, and he felt frozen as Miraden pulled him up by his arms. Lucky for him, he was light.

"Thank you," Simigrin whispered and retreated to get comfortable in the empty den of the tree. After coiling the rope, Miraden scooted back into the tree as well. He could hear Simigrin breathing heavily and wondered what had spooked him.

Though that night was more comfortable than the first, Miraden felt anything but safe. The moment his eyes closed, his thoughts went straight to terrors. He accidentally dozed a few times, then finally resorted to memories to help him stay awake. He thought of chasing Ceychell and Kyradel through the woods when they were kids. He thought of when he saw Ormus talk to his father after he found a note Miraden had written to Ceychell. He thought he would be in trouble, but his father never spoke of it. His father looked upset when Ormus spoke to him, but Miraden figured he genuinely wanted to respect his space. The faint memories helped him pass the time. But the night grew very long in the darkness. The sounds of crawling things, strange scratching sounds, the chatter of bats and insects. He felt like his mind kept deceiving him when he'd drift asleep several times even though his eyes were open.

Simigrin jostled Miraden's leg whenever he'd drift off, and he did the same for him. It made the night feel unending. Sitting helplessly in the dark was feeding his fears. He had no idea what was going to happen from one minute to the next. The fact that nothing happened almost made it even worse. His chest pulled every which way, and the only thing that helped him not scream like a madman was wondering if his companions suffered as he was. There were times he thought he'd heard Neandra mutter in a panic. Then it would stop. It was difficult to distinguish from the other noises of the forest. Miraden assumed he was dozing, but he was at least ten feet below him, and he couldn't see him. The pitch-black forest engulfed Miraden like a hungry beast.

Then he heard it. A harsh, growling chatter filled his ears. Miraden shook in place as he listened to it. He sat upon Hellshy's hilt to keep it still, praying it would not call the ashenkins' attention.

Twenty feet below them, the ashenkin passed through the woods.

Their flesh was lit as if they were burning through a sea of darkness. The floor smoked where they stepped, and bodies released heat waves. It was as if they were hotter en masse. Simigrin shook and held onto him. There were so many of them he suddenly felt their efforts were in vain. Even if they did make it to the Ashengate, they would easily be killed. No one would even know. As he watched them tramping hastily below, he seriously considered abandoning this quest.

He felt like a coward and didn't want to die, at least not like this. Not being devoured by devils. Though Ceychell wasn't with him, he felt like her prayers were. He could not explain it, but it comforted him and helped him maintain resolve while he trembled silently and gaped at the horde of horrors from his tree.

The devils continued past them like cinders blowing in the wind. Eventually, they were plunged back into darkness and, strangely, that brought some relief. There were so many, though. He wondered if they would return in the morning or just how many more would be waiting for them at the gate.

Morning came. Miraden was rattled from the tense night. Simigrin pulled a few roots out of his pouch and offered them.

"I harvested them along the way. It will help with exhaustion," he whispered. Miraden remembered him pulling a few roots after finding Neandra but thought nothing of it. He ate one; it tasted a bit like licorice. They were awful, but he did feel a little better.

"Why don't you speak up a bit, mage?" Neandra asked when he took one of the roots. Simigrin didn't answer. "Seems like you're hiding something," he said with a wink. He took a large bite of the root and carried on.

They followed and exchanged a glance. A few strands of purple hair hung out of his hood; his eyes were wide and looking at Neandra's in question. Miraden took another bite and listened when Neandra spoke.

"The Ashengate is no more than an hour's walk. Their camps are often deserted in the morning in this region, but we must still be on our guard."

"There will be a leader with a necklace. We must kill it immediately and take the necklace." Neandra turned around midbite with a surprised look on his face, a chunk of root hanging from the side of his mouth. "They are gate guardians, larger than the others. The necklace allows the gate to open and keep the devils in our world."

Miraden wasn't sure why Simigrin kept the information until now but was relieved to hear there was a way to close the gate. Recalling last night's horde, he felt no better about their chances.

"Is this the only gate, or how do we stop them from opening another?"

Simigrin shrugged.

Neandra patted Miraden's shoulder. "Let's just focus on closing one gate at a time."

Miraden found his comforting unhelpful.

They headed deeper into the forest. He could only hear his own breath and their footsteps. His nose stung, and eyes watered from a pungent stink. Some bare brush was smoldering despite the recent snow. The eerie canopy blocked most of the daylight. The air was deathly still; he had to take deep breaths just to keep from getting light-headed.

Neandra quietly drew his two long swords from the scabbards at his sides. Miraden's heart pounded; he drew and nocked an arrow, searching for whatever Neandra was looking at. Then he saw it. Through a gap in the trees was a ring of floating flames. Inside the ring was a cluster of pale, filthy children. There were dozens of them, and they were sitting still as the dead. Pox and burns covered their skin. Their faces were sunken in and flesh stretched over gangly bones. Clothes draped on them like rags. Their eyes stared out in the distance; most appeared to be in shock.

Miraden crept slowly behind Neandra and was closely followed by Simigrin. With each step, he expected ashenkin to spring upon them.

Maybe fifty children sat together. He couldn't believe they were alive, and when one caught sight of them, they all turned. None of them spoke. They just stared with wide-eyed terror. Though Miraden wanted to save them all, he searched for Kyradel, and with each miserable face, he felt more desperate.

Soon, one of them, a boy about ten years old, broke the silence. He begged loud whispers, "Do something!" The others joined in whispered pleas. Miraden put his hands up to quiet them, but it wasn't working. He was afraid the ashenkin would hear them.

"Remain calm. I'm going to try and break the fire ward," Simigrin whispered. Neandra nodded and continued scanning the camp. Miraden heard a crunch from behind, then turned and fired an arrow directly into the throat of one of the devils. It gargled on its own blood and dropped to the rotted earth.

Miraden and Neandra turned in circles looking for any others. "That can't be the only guard," Neandra whispered.

"Why can't it? Should there be more?" Miraden whispered back.

"It's going to get much colder," Simigrin whispered. The wind suddenly picked up, and it started to snow hard. Then gusts grew violent, and large flakes swirled around them… worse than the storm in Keldenfeld. Miraden turned and saw Simigrin with a spellbook and staff out. Snow dust fell from his staff.

The children cried out. "Run! Save us! Help us!"

Neandra shuddered. The ends of his blades bounced as he moved away from Simigrin and turned circles looking for ashenkin. The sentry lights finally went out, and the storm subsided. There were now roars growing louder, fast.

Neandra waved his hands to the children. "Follow me, hurry!"

Weak and injured, they scrambled to their feet and swarmed him. He led them away down the darkened path.

"We need your help!" Miraden screamed at Neandra's back. He ignored the cry and kept running, the children unable to keep up with him. One at the rear tripped. Miraden ran over and helped him to his feet and noticed many of the children struggling to walk. Meanwhile, Neandra was gliding through the woods like a spooked horse.

Suddenly, a fire spread in the camp. Miraden returned to Simigrin and drew another arrow. "Neandra!" Miraden yelled, but he was gone.

Miraden aimed at the wall of flames. He didn't know if this was the Ashengate, but he was scared of what would come next. The heat was intense. Simigrin whispered a spell next to him. The air chilled to a crisp frost, swirled around his staff, and hardened into solid ice. He held an arrow ready.

At last, a horde of ashenkin emerged from the flames. He shot arrow after arrow at them, many finding their mark, but they were coming fast. Simigrin bent down and dug his hand into the snow, then stood up and blew it from his hand. The snow billowed like a cloud, surrounding the ashenkin and froze them in an icy shell. It looked almost like the shell they'd slept in a week ago. The few devils who escaped the ice were distracted and close enough for Miraden to pierce a skull with each shot.

But more ashenkin kept springing from the flames. They were surrounding the camp, but Miraden kept firing. He was backing up, ready to run, when he heard Simigrin yell, "Be still!"

Miraden looked at him, drawing another arrow, and Simigrin had his hand and staff pointed at him. A gust of freezing wind blew below Miraden. He rose into the air and out of ashenkin's reach. It took him a moment to steady mid-air, then he loosed arrows down on the devils while they jumped and clawed for his legs. Miraden killed several of them this way before they realized that they had no chance to reach him.

The four monsters that remained abandoned Miraden and scrambled after Simigrin. He fired at them, splitting two right through the spine and another through the neck, but the fourth one raked its claws across Simigrin's midsection, breaking the spell that held him in the air.

Miraden screamed and fell to the ground, stumbling a moment before the ashenkin were on him. He drew his saber, and the glow of its relzyian silver blade stopped them in their tracks. He cut through their mottled flesh as if he was slicing through a tender roast.

The ones he didn't kill backed away from him, growling and roaring. Beyond them, Miraden saw devils clawing at an ice barrier Simigrin had created around himself. Miraden charged and cut down more of the creatures until he heard a roar that made the earth tremble.

He killed another ashenkin and turned to find the source of the roar, only to see a small flame explode into a fire-wreathed portal of darkness. Out stepped a devil that stood as tall as two men. It had great black horns, and its eyes burned like the portal itself. It grinned scalpel-sharp pointed teeth at him. The steel-and-red-bone, thick plate armor that encased it made Miraden's silver blade seem like a pathetic toy. In one clawed hand, it held a great steel ax. Rotting heads dangled on flesh ropes tied to its pommel. On its other claw was a gauntlet that burned with intense flames. It stood in front of the gate so Miraden couldn't see it.

Hope drained from Miraden's body as he stared at the monster. Then he saw the black necklace around its neck. The gate guardian said something to him then. He couldn't understand the words, but he shook regardless. They were harsh and loud. Miraden froze until two ashenkin were nearly upon him. The gatekeeper gripped its ax with both claws and swung it across its body. Miraden dove out of the way and heard the ax cleave the ashenkin surrounding him, but something else cut his leg.

Miraden rolled to his feet and backed away from the gate guardian. He circled around and put an ashenkin between them. The gatekeeper suddenly slapped the devil out its way with the broadside of its ax and then rammed Miraden. He flew through the air and smacked a thick tree trunk. He slumped to the ground.

Miraden gasped for air and realized he was no longer holding his sword. It was nearby but too close to the gatekeeper. He crawled toward the sword as the gatekeeper stomped toward it as well. He scrambled and jumped, grabbed the sword as he trembled to his feet, and turned to face the devil towering over him. It grinned. It laughed at Miraden's pathetic effort.

The sword twitched in his grasp. He couldn't move as the gatekeeper raised its ax to cleave him in two. Then it roared so loud Miraden shut his eyes and dropped the sword to protect his ears. When he forced his eyes open, the point of a huge spike of ice jutted from its chest. Boiling blood gushed from the wound and sizzled on the frostbitten forest floor. Simigrin stood behind the devil. He broke another icicle from a tree and hurled it. It tripled in size and plunged into the gate guardian again. To Miraden's astonishment, it turned and ran toward the Ashengate. He thought about following it through the gate to look for Kyradel but was afraid he'd never return. He drew his bow and fired an arrow into the back of the gate guardian's neck, but it didn't even seem to notice. Then he carefully aimed and fired his last arrow at the band of the necklace. The necklace dropped to the stony ground near the portal as the gatekeeper stumbled through it and disappeared. The Ashengate burst into cinders. Then the ashenkin screamed and burst into flames. The fire burned out, and they were suddenly gone.

SIXTEEN

THE MAGE'S SECRET

CEYCHELL COULD HARDLY BELIEVE HER eyes. She had to reread the passage a few times before she could believe that Miraden actually closed an Ashengate. She flipped the page, eager to read more.

The gate was gone. Miraden sat there for a moment, incredulous, trying to catch his breath. He couldn't believe the battle was over. It took him a few moments to realize everything was calm, and he was grateful to still be alive. And though he felt triumphant, he still felt defeated because he was no closer to finding Kyradel.

His reprieve was cut short when he heard Simigrin fall to the ground, clutching an oozing chest wound. Miraden rushed over, recovered a needle, thread, and the last of his alcohol from his pack, and then pulled his robe back. His chest was wrapped in heavy cloth that was soaked with blood from three slash marks. Sweat and blood shined on his dark skin. As he started to unwrap Simigrin, he grabbed Miraden's wrist.

"You're bleeding really bad. You have to let me help!" Miraden said. After wrestling his weak grip for a moment, Miraden said, "You could die." Simigrin stopped wrestling.

Miraden cut the wrapping with a knife, and it popped open. Miraden stood there in shock. Simigrin leaned her head back; her hood slid back. She lay there with her breasts exposed amid three gashes and said, "This can't be the first time you've seen a woman."

Miraden was stunned and couldn't answer. He shook his head and grabbed his wineskin to wash her wound with water. The blood oozed fast, so he started to stitch. She moaned in pain as his hand trembled. He stitched her, but the skin around the wounds was blackened and partially cauterized. Almost as if she was cut by a weapon heated in a forge, but the blackness resembled rot more than burns. He tried not to panic as he stitched her closed, but he feared she was infected by the ashenkin's claws.

Simigrin leaned up and pulled her robe closed and hood up. "Miraden, promise me you won't say anything to Neandra. I know his type," she said.

"I swear," Miraden said. He helped her to her feet. Her tight wrappings were ruined, and it was far more apparent *she* was no longer a *he* once she closed her robe again. "I feel dizzy," she said. Miraden led her by her arm. He knew they needed to hurry to a doctor or temple to treat her wounds, but he had no idea how far they were from a city.

"Any idea if we are near civilization?" Miraden asked.

"Oddion is west of here, I think. I'm not really sure."

Miraden was thrown off by hearing her non-whispered voice. It was light and soothing, and she spoke very clearly. He realized now her whispering was only to hide, but he wasn't sure why. He also noticed she had recovered the gatekeeper's necklace, which he had almost forgotten about in his panic. She was gripping it tightly in her other hand. Its amulet was a black rock embedded with a red gem. It was cracked from falling off the gatekeeper's neck onto the stones, but it was not broken. A smoky substance spiraled within the gem like a whirlwind.

"Put that in your sack. Let's keep it quiet," Miraden whispered. She struggled with the weight of it as she placed it in her sack.

Before he put away his sewing kit, he checked his gashed leg. He had a nasty large cut on his calf, which he quickly stitched and wrapped with a torn part of his shirt. Not the best job he'd ever done, but we had to keep moving.

He helped her to her feet and pulled her along. He limped, and she walked awkwardly not to jostle the stitches, but she whimpered with each step.

Miraden followed the children's tracks down a hill covered in brown mushrooms. There were dozens of broken stalks that created a path down to a dried stream. They continued to follow the fresh trail through the woods until they finally caught up to Neandra with the children. The children cheered when they arrived.

"So good to see you're both alright!" Neandra said with a smile.

Miraden didn't feel alright, not one bit. "Neandra, why didn't you come back to help? There were swarming devils. We had to face that giant demon without you!"

"I wanted to come back, but I had to protect the children. What if ashenkin came in and took them away and through a gate the moment I left?"

"The ashenkin were up there, fighting us, not looking for children," Miraden yelled and pointed up the way where they fought. Miraden was enraged at his cowardice.

"We saved these children—the three of us. I got them away, for that gate guardian would have started killing them indiscriminately. He is the one who sacrifices them!"

Miraden saw the children grow uneasy and let his anger slide.

For now.

"We must head straight to Oddion because Simigrin needs medical attention. It is urgent."

He went toward her and said, "Perhaps I can help." But Miraden stepped in front of her and shook his head.

"I already closed the wounds. We must waste no time." Neandra gave him a peculiar look, then nodded.

Neandra started heading in a direction and waved for everyone to follow. "Come, children, let's get you to Oddion and to a warm bed!"

The children were so emaciated. Miraden held back tears whenever he looked at them. They struggled to walk; their heads nearly bobbed on wiry necks—hair ratty and missing, skin filthy and covered in sores.

They walked for hours. Despite their condition, they didn't complain or whine. Miraden could see it on each of their sickly faces, a brightness, an unmistakable happiness that they were no longer being dragged to their inevitable deaths. Even the littlest ones smiled with relief. Sometimes though, he'd catch them staring at nothing. He could only imagine what they were remembering. He grew concerned about feeding them soon so they wouldn't get weaker or starve.

They followed Neandra through the forest. Little surroundings changed, but everything just felt better. It was like he could breathe a little easier than before. But there were few tracks, worn devil tracks, but definitely no game tracks. He began to wonder how the ashenkin fed the children because they certainly didn't have enough food to feed even half of them for a single meal.

Miraden realized they would soon be desperate.

"We must feed them. Is there anything you could do to help?" Miraden whispered to Simigrin. She dug into her pouch, rummaged around a bit, and pulled out an acorn-sized seed.

"Only two left. We must ration them," she whispered.

Miraden thought about holding off in case the journey took a week or longer, but when he saw the filthy skin barely wrapping the children's bones, their hair falling out, and black pox festering upon their skin, Miraden looked at Simigrin and nodded. She returned the nod.

She held one seed to her staff and whispered a spell. The children watched her then started to back away and chatter.

Miraden turned and hushed them with his hands waving them to calm down. "Everything is okay. My companion is trying to make you something to eat," he whispered.

Simigrin placed the seed on the dirt and then pushed it into the ground with the top of her staff. A large tree sprung out from the rumbling ground, budding an assortment of fruit. Gourds, potatoes, and other vegetables sprang from the soil. The spell produced a bounty of food, but to Miraden's rushed estimation, only one meal for so many children and the three of them.

Miraden enjoyed the long break eating. He was sure the children did as well. They probably hadn't eaten like this in weeks or more. Nothing but ravaged vines, and a bare tree remained when they left. Most of the children only ate a little, but they carried what they couldn't eat. The meal lifted their spirits, and for a little while, the Bleak Gale Pines wasn't so dismal.

Neandra stepped over and patted Simigrin on the back. She winced. It was evident by a perched grin that her concealment no longer fooled him. He stared at her red-stained robes and asked, "Can I take a look? I may be able to help." She shook her head.

"How far is Oddion?" Miraden asked. He wanted to pull his attention away from her.

Neandra turned around to Miraden. "Four days' walk at this pace, perhaps farther."

It wasn't what Miraden wanted to hear. He knew they had to pick up the pace, and that was a troubling thought.

They walked for three days through the woods. It was not an easy pace to maintain, but they luckily found small streams along the way to refresh their water. He saw very few creatures, certainly nothing Neandra said they'd encounter. The nights were quiet and without devilry. Now the Pines seemed just a dark and gloomy forest.

Along their journey to Oddion, Miraden made a point of asking each child if they knew Kyradel and described her in great detail, but none of them knew her... they seemed genuinely sorry and confused. Most of them were quiet while they trekked. He thought they might tell tales of the ashenkin, but none spoke of it. They trembled when asked about the devils. He decided not to push hard, not knowing if he really wanted to hear their stories.

On the fourth day, Miraden was beyond exhausted. He'd spent a great deal of energy helping Simigrin walk and encouraging her to continue. She shook uncontrollably at times and held her chest a lot. Miraden was dreadfully concerned for her. His leg ached more with every step. It was a mind-numbing pain. Focusing on her was all Miraden could do to stop himself from passing out from the pain.

Miraden really started to miss Stormrange and thought about him during the quieter times of the journey to town. He hoped Ceychell was taking good care of him and would remember to ask her about him in his next letter. It just wasn't the same not seeing him in this long.

They woke the next morning. Simigrin used her last seed, and everyone enjoyed their meal. Neandra walked over with a smug grin.

"We should be in Oddion tomorrow," he said. "We'd be there by now, but you know," he nodded back at the sicker children. They'd held them up quite a bit. He took a bite out of an apple from the tree Simigrin had summoned. "Need me to carry you? I'm not sure Miraden can handle helping you with that leg." Simigrin moaned and leaned against Miraden. He didn't think she had the strength to defend herself.

"Anything else?" Miraden asked. His leg was numb with agony, but he didn't show it.

Neandra chuckled. "Let's get them up and moving."

After a quiet day, they stopped to camp for the evening. Everything was much greener. Needles were on trees so thick he could smell the sweetness of the sap. The chirps of forest creatures were good to hear as if he had left the dying part of the Pines.

"Miraden, can you help me? Away from them?" Simigrin whispered. Miraden nodded and helped her walk away from camp. She opened her robe to show her wound. The cut was black, and Miraden's stitches hardly held the infected flesh closed. She winced and shut her eyes when he pushed near the cuts. It oozed. It was getting far worse, and he wasn't sure what to do. She certainly wasn't healing, and they were out of options.

"I— I'm starting to see things. Things that aren't really there," she said. "I can't… remember much of the day." Miraden felt her head, and it was burning up.

"I promise I will get you to a healer. We'll move faster in the morning." But the guilt of lying to a dying friend made him feel terrible. He had no idea if there would be a healer in Oddion or if they were even near the city.

She grasped his hand and squeezed. She smiled. "Thank you."

Neandra approached them, and Simigrin pulled her robe closed.

"Everything all right here? You… don't look so good," he said.

"We are running out of time. We may have to move faster than the children tomorrow or split up so I can get her to town."

"I really think you should let me see that wound," he said.

Miraden hesitated until Simigrin squeezed his hand. "I'm sorry, but no."

"We leave at first light and go at a faster pace to make it to Oddion tomorrow."

Neandra threw his hands up. "Suit yourself. Hope she makes it through the night." Miraden could hear him cursing as he walked away.

Miraden didn't trust him at all.

They returned to camp. It was a long night, for sure. Simigrin asked him if he would hold her while they slept in case she passed to the next realm. She didn't want to be alone. The question startled Miraden, but he couldn't refuse her potentially dying wish. He felt awful when he realized how little he knew her. The person who had ventured with him and saved his life might die in his arms tonight.

She held on to him tight, not as a loved one, but as someone scared of dying. He didn't think she slept even in her weakness, and Miraden certainly didn't. He was not sure why, but in his sleeplessness, he found it strange that he hadn't even seen her face clearly. She already had dark skin, and her face was painted dark purple with faint silver lines. Intricate silver shapes on her cheeks, chin, and forehead. It somehow held the shadows on her already dark skin. They'd experienced so much on this journey. It was a silly thing that he didn't even know her face or why she kept herself a mystery. He started to imagine what her hair really looked like. He'd only seen loose purple strands, but it was tied up under her hood, he thought. She had high cheekbones, almond-shaped eyes that were so yellow they reminded him of bright lights. His mind was restless, but the foolish game kept him sane through the night.

The next morning finally arrived, and he got the children moving fast. They groaned when they pushed them at a feverish pace until they broke from the tree line and saw sprawling Oddion in the distance. The children cheered. Miraden wanted to cheer, too, but he couldn't. He was biting his lip from the pain, and Simigrin was nearly unconscious. Oddion was her only hope, and he was destined to get her there, despite his exhaustion and sore leg.

The people rushed them that morning when they entered the city gates. He didn't think it would ever get old, receiving the praise for a good deed and feeling the joy of putting smiles on all those beaming faces. The kids were ecstatic. The townsfolk showered them with attention, which Neandra quickly accepted as if he were their leader. Miraden hated him. He was not sure they would have succeeded without him, but he acted as if he alone had saved everyone.

Townsfolk helped Simigrin and him straight to a temple of the Mother of Light. It was a large temple, meager, with a square red door and built of stone. It was sparse inside but large. When Miraden passed the doorway, he thought of Lovo and had to hold back tears. He

should have been there with them…

Miraden's leg was numb and infected. He could barely walk and was so tired he collapsed right there in the temple. He hadn't eaten much in days, and he'd nearly carried Simigrin that whole time. The clerics rushed them both, and Miraden started to fade in and out of consciousness. He heard muddled words while the clerics examined his and Simigrin's wounds.

"It's a wonder she's alive," one said. Miraden couldn't make out much else. He was carried along with Simigrin into a room to be cleaned and examined. He started to wake back up.

"She's cut badly," he said. He grew nervous they were treating him and not her.

"Yes, we know. We will help," a cleric said. He was short and had large hands. Older, with bushy brows, but his eyes were very kind. "Ashenkin claws can leave poison. Someone might have been watching over her," he said with a wink.

He wondered if perhaps Lovo watched over them or the gods were merciful. The clerics prayed and performed rituals to cleanse their wounds. Miraden slipped in and out of consciousness.

Miraden awoke sometime later to find his leg cleaned and wrapped. He could feel it again, and by "it," he could feel all the pain in his leg. He was in a soft bed. Simigrin was in one next to him. She lay asleep. Miraden leaned up and found a lone girl, not much younger than Kyradel sitting near the door.

She smiled at Miraden. "Are you thirsty? You must be hungry," she asked.

Miraden nodded and said, "How much is this going to cost us?"

"There were donations collected to pay for your treatment and to stay here," she said.

Miraden was relieved. He looked around and realized there were baskets of food and flowers and a few bottles of spirits. "What is all this?"

"Many of the people are so thankful, they practically lined up with gifts, but we didn't want to disturb you both, so we are just keeping the gifts in here."

Miraden smiled and nodded. He looked down and realized he was sitting on an actual bedsheet. It'd been so long since he had a nice night's sleep and been comfortable. He looked over to his friend. She slept quietly; her back was turned to him. Her purple hair was extremely long and fell over the bed like a waterfall.

"She is strong, but we are not sure if she will make it," the girl said.

Miraden turned suddenly. "Why aren't the healers in here helping her?"

"They've done all they can. Even the clerics from the house of the Father of Darkness brought holy salves to clean her cuts. It can cure the rot from wounds. There are even elixirs from the house of the Son of Seas that can cure sicknesses. They gave her plenty of both and left you some extra of each here," she said and pointed to a small pouch on the ground by the gift baskets.

Miraden leaned over and put his hand on her shoulder. She didn't move. He held back tears and swallowed a knot in his throat. "Can you please fetch me paper and writing ink? I may need a courier as well," he asked.

She stood and bowed her head and left without a word.

Miraden watched over Simigrin the whole night while she slept soundly.

He spent hours writing to Ceychell about all that had happened. He asked about Stormrange, told her about Lovo's death and how Simigrin was possibly dying and actually a woman. He passed his regrets and pain of her not writing or caring for him. He struggled to write to her. It hurt so bad. He would pay the courier to deliver the letter tomorrow...

...I want to see Stormrange so badly, want to pet him, so please give him a lot of love. I have had little talent for art in recent years, but I needed to draw something to help me abandon my thoughts while we rest, if only for a while. I hope you'll find this memory of you to your liking. Know that I almost stopped writing to you, but I made a promise and will keep it.

Wishing you the very best,
Miraden

Ceychell finished Miraden's letter and held it to her chest. She cringed in pain as if she'd been struck. She felt how hurt Miraden was, how much he felt she abandoned him. She couldn't believe Simigrin was a woman and hid it that long. Jealous thoughts crept into her mind as she wondered how close they might get on their journey.

She turned over the final page of his letter and admired the sketch he made of her. In it, she was wearing the embroidered oak tree dress she'd worn to Valdenfest last year. Her bangs were braided and pulled back and fastened by a metal clasp shaped like a bird. Her locks dangled over her shoulders and down behind her, just like they did on that day. Her eyes were kinder than she deserved, she thought, and her smile was softer than she felt it should be. The sight of it brought her a shudder of regret.

She prayed her letters would reach Miraden.

Early the next morning, just before dawn, a fierce wind blew a window open. Ceychell awakened to the shutter slamming against the wall. Her head throbbed. She drank too much wine the previous night and struggled to catch her wits. It was hours before anyone else would rise for the day, but she lit a few candles and decided to write two more letters.

After she finished the letters, she rolled them into her last two scroll cases. Only this time, she wasn't leaving delivery to chance. She packed her bags with medical supplies, food, and water and dressed in her heaviest fur-lined leathers. She tied a cape of pelts over her shoulders and slid on thick, black boots.

She exited her home into a whipping snowstorm. Her father was just stepping up to her porch, holding a bundle of firewood. He stared at her in surprise, then dropped the wood next to her door.

"Ceychell, where are you headed?" he asked. He brushed snow from his shoulders then crossed his arms.

"The couriers failed to get Miraden my letter. I must get word to him."

"Even if they did, do you realize what you're saying?" His voice wasn't filled with doubt or anger but concern. He placed his large hands on her shoulders.

"I do. He is risking his life while I am sitting here making potions. He was in Oddion taking care of a companion. He may still be there. I plan to pay a courier in Bilore Des to deliver a message in case I do not make it to Oddion in time. Otherwise, I plan to be there in just over two weeks."

"This is possible," Ormus said, scowling. "You could make it in that time if you take the path over the mountains, which are filled with krins. You would need gold to hire a band of guards for that long journey. When you get to the mountains, how will you climb them? How will you defend yourself from whatever decides to stop you on the road? Or if you plan to venture to Oddion unnoticed, how will you do that?"

Ceychell stared into the storm, considering. She felt strongly that she should go but knew her father was right. Ormus embraced her, and she could hear him choke up.

"Please, Ceychell. I cannot lose you too."

Ceychell heard the despair, the frailty in his voice. Her tears surfaced; they burned from the wind on her face. "How can I get this letter to him?"

"When the storm clears, I'll take the letter back to the courier and make sure he knows."

"Father. The last couriers have yet to deliver a message."

Ormus shook his head. "How do you know this?"

"Because he would have mentioned it. Please, father, I must get this message to him!" Ceychell had never felt so strongly about anything in her life. "I would love to see him, but I fear it will deter him from his journey. I just need to safely deliver my message to him."

Her father nodded. "Very well. I will take the letter to him," Ormus said.

Ceychell didn't want her father to solve her problem for her. She stood defiant. "You cannot. Kaehrn needs you here."

"Since I've never taught you to use a sword," Ormus said with a smile that looked forced, "I must bear this burden. Besides, I sent a boy to do something I should have done in the first place. I will have to live with that, but perhaps I can make this right. I will leave after I tell the elders of the four villages that you are in charge in my stead. It is paramount that Miraden gets your letter. He is the only hope we have to see your sister again."

"You want me to lead? I—"

"You will. I know this journey west is too much for you without proper guard, and we must have a leader here. Use your judgment and trust the village council." He stared into her scared eyes. "I know you can do this. Trust me to get the message to Miraden." He held out his hand for the scroll case. After a moment, she handed it to him, took the bundle of wood from him, and he turned away.

She watched him walk through the snow back to his home and felt confused. She loved her father; she'd always admired him, but she did not understand why he chose her to lead Kaehrn in his absence.

SEVENTEEN

THE DESPERATE JOURNEY

CEYCHELL WAS ASLEEP ON HER CHAIR, the first time in two weeks she'd slept so long. Miraden's letter lay on the floor just below her fingers. She shifted in her sleep and yelled incoherently.

Kyradel stood amongst the children, her face gaunt and dirty. The children looked exhausted and malnourished. The ashenkin were shouting at them, growling and waving clawed hands in the air. There seemed to be fewer children around her, and several still clung to her.

She and the other children were cramped into a cave, huddled together against a wind that still fluttered Kyradel's matted hair. The devils gave a small chunk of meat on a large bone, which she and the others ate raw. The devils watched her with burning eyes like candles hovering in shadows.

She began to sing a song of hope, and her voice rang out over the ridge and carried along with the wind. The other children calmed and listened to the song; even the ashenkin seemed entranced by the sound of her voice. Eyes closed above tear-stained cheeks; she sang her heart out.

The children began to lie down to sleep, and the ashenkin dozed sitting up behind them.

Ceychell sprung awake in a pool of sweat shortly after midnight. She could still hear Kyradel's song swimming through her thoughts. She remembered the first time she'd heard it. Last year's Valdenfest, and she remembered every word.

She was exhausted—she'd barely slept since her father left for Oddion. She prayed to the Daughter of Forests that he arrived there safely and found Miraden. She prayed that Simigrin recovered, and she prayed most fervently that she would gain Miraden's forgiveness. Then she sat and listened to the winter wind pelting snow against her windows.

She made a pot of tea and read through the old letters. She felt desperate and alone and hoped each hour that news would arrive. To escape her worries, she got a head start on the next day's remedies, brewing until late in the morning. She'd nearly finished with her daily batch of potions when she heard a knock at her door. She took a deep breath. She pulled the hair out of her face and tried to compose herself. Then she ran to the door, cracked it open, and found Fendel standing on the porch. Snow covered his cowl and shoulders; some even clung to his beard. She was startled at the sight of him and put her hands to her face to forestall her tears. When she failed, Fendel put his hand on her shoulder, and she hugged him.

"Are you alright, lass?" he asked.

When she let go, he had a letter in hand. Tears seemed to well in his eyes, and Ceychell realized he must have understood the message's importance.

"You have a letter from Miraden?" Her voice broke as she asked.

"I do, yes… he asked one of the hillmen to find me and have me bring it to you. I paid the hillman to return his coin. Miraden saved my son, Halos—" Fendel stopped. He pushed tears from his eyes. "He rescued my only son, along with nearly thirty others. Miraden has gained quite a bit of respect in Oddion, especially from me. I would have told him you said hello, but he had left just before I returned. I hugged my son, good and long that night, then left that morning to make my trek here. Since I cannot thank him in person, I thank you. Please, tell him so."

Ceychell couldn't stop crying. "Of course. I'm so happy for you," she said. Her lips trembled. "And I cannot thank you enough for bringing me his letter. Please, come in." Ceychell held the door open for him. When he had entered, she immediately offered him a cup of tea.

"You don't know if my father, Ormus, arrived in Oddion, do you?" she asked as she poured the tea from the pot over the fire.

"He sent your letters before, didn't he?" Fendel accepted the cup and sat on a barrel next to the counter.

"He did."

"Hmm, can't say that I've seen him. Are you sure he was bound for Oddion?" He dried his eyes once more.

The news was not what she'd hoped for. This time, she kept her resolve, perhaps because she was now chieftain of Kaehrn, and answered, "Yes, he was to deliver a message to Miraden."

"I see," he said. "Well, Miraden must have headed south through the mountains. The hillman said nothing of him returning to Oddion. Perhaps Ormus found him before he left town? Or perhaps on the road?"

"By the gods, I pray… you must be weary. I'm sorry to bother you with such things." She took his wineskin and filled it with a cider mixed with spirits that she brewed. Then she took a vial of potion to help with the cold from a shelf and offered it to him.

He graciously accepted the gifts. "It's not a bother, Ceychell. Thank you so much. If Ormus is not in the village, who is presiding here?"

"I am. Until my father returns." Ceychell answered the question confidently as if she had rehearsed it. "Are you bound for Oddion from here?"

"Not directly. I have a few stops, but, yes, I'll be heading back to Oddion eventually."

"Can I ask you to stay here in town? I want to read this and send back a letter with you for Miraden. I promise to get it to you within a few hours. Perhaps you could give it to him should he return to Oddion."

Fendel nodded. "I'd be happy to. Take your time. I think I may stay and get a warm breakfast from Elonor at the inn."

"Wait, let me get you a few lumins for the meal."

"No need," he said, placing the empty teacup on the counter. "I'll be back in a few hours."

EIGHTEEN

THE TREK SOUTH

CEYCHELL SMILED AND HELD THE letter to her chest. She walked over to sit in her chair and opened the letter.

Miraden's journey stopped while his leg healed and the clerics cared for Simigrin. Luckily the cleric's salves and prayers healed them quickly, but Simigrin didn't wake up for a few days. He remained by her bedside, fearing she might pass. Those days were long indeed, worse than his time in the Pines. Every moment he watched her, he prayed and convinced himself that she'd make it. It was quiet and haunting in the temple chamber. He could do nothing but join in their prayers and make her comfortable.

Meanwhile, Neandra took the public recognition for saving the children and continued to parade about town getting handouts and taking advantage of the citizens of Oddion. He came by once to check on Simigrin and only grinned. Miraden had scowled when he said a woman as pretty as she shouldn't hide behind a robe and cowl. He disliked Neandra even more now. Luckily, the clerics got rid of him after telling them he wanted no one, especially him, visiting.

Miraden's leg felt much better, thanks to the clerics. He had a full quiver once again, additional medicine, and food for the next part of the journey.

Miraden spent hours by Simigrin's bed and watched Hellshy twitch on a side table. It pointed south, and he never really noticed since he usually had it sheathed, but it steadily moved. Almost as if it were alive. He knew he wasn't its master. And, he would rather be rid of it, honestly. Nevertheless, it was his only clue to finding Kyradel and hopefully bringing her home alive. There were no two things he wanted more in this world.

Simigrin was up and about now; her color returned. Her wound no longer festered black. It was a bit strange seeing her out of hiding. She still didn't talk much. She mentioned she was from the Trade Cities in the South. Her complexion was dark brown. Her eyes were large and bright, amber, almost the color of honey. She had high cheekbones and thin lips. Her voice was soft and pleasant on the rare occasions when she spoke. Like many Southern women, she had dyed hair. It was a vibrant purple that shined in the glare of the lantern in the room. It was in a tight weave behind her head, which was why he never saw it. Now that she'd pulled it out, he was amazed that it stretched down to the back of her thighs. His mother had once told him about Southern women; they never cut their hair until marriage. She seemed to confirm that rumor, though he'd never traveled south of the village Yoldro.

"I am so glad you are fit to travel, but you do not have to join me from here," Miraden said. "We are both lucky to have survived." He wondered if his luck would run out or if she wondered the same thing.

She smirked at him. "I think I've gone a bit too far to turn back now. It looks like we are going south," she said.

A brief knock and the young cleric girl who'd attended them

entered. She'd not told Miraden her name; the others referred to her as "acolyte."

"Miraden, Simigrin, Mayor Madrannasus is here to see you."

Miraden nodded, and she closed the door. The mayor of Oddion visited them at the temple a few times. Her visits during their stay were overly kind. Several villagers delivered food to them three times a day, often with a pitcher of ale. They also hung paintings that the villagers had made for them.

They followed acolyte down the hall and turned left into a meeting room where the mayor waited for them. Acolyte stayed by the door and blocked others from entering. Unlike in the mayor's earlier visits, this evening, Mayor Madrannasus's face did not bear the cheery smile she might have learned to wear from years as town leader. She wore a grimace that showed deep concern. She was in her final Passings, full gray hair but her eyes were sharp. Today she was dressed in a formal dress that was low-cut and dyed blue and purple. It was cut to her portly shape exactly and made her look more noble.

Miraden regretted to but asked, "What is it? Is something wrong?"

She nodded. "There is. Have you ever heard of Baron Pezqeron?" Miraden and Simigrin shook their heads. "Don't suppose you would have. He lives south of here in the Meate Mountains. A wealthy lord who keeps to himself."

Miraden remembered seeing the ridges in the distance when they arrived here. They were jagged cliffs, mostly invisible on the horizon.

"My council paid the Henslemen to investigate the ashenkin and traced activity to the mountains, near the baron's territory. They reported a lot of recent activity of ashenkin there, and it seems odd because he's grown recluse, even bricked up the windows of his keep. Anyway, Neandra recommended you both should journey with him to the baron's manor to investigate and bring him to justice should you find any evidence. We could really use your help, and Neandra is so crucial to stopping this ashenkin uprising."

Miraden clenched his fists as he heard her talk of him as a hero. He hesitated to get involved, but Hellshy was pointing south, and if there was ashenkin activity, it might lead him closer to Kyradel.

"Won't you help Oddion once more?" she asked.

Miraden looked to Simigrin, who appeared to be just as conflicted as he was.

"We will need horses and climbing gear that we can keep," he said.

Madrannasus smiled and dipped her head a bit. "I can arrange that at once."

Miraden added, "You should know that Neandra is a coward, not the hero of Oddion, and you should be careful trusting him."

Judging by the grin on her face, Miraden thought she wasn't shocked by the information but nodded as though she needed just a nudge of affirmation to confirm her suspicions. "Your things will be ready by sunrise. I wish you both good luck."

Miraden turned around to acolyte after the mayor left the room. "Any chance you could get me a bit more paper and ink for the road?"

Acolyte grinned, nodded, and left the room.

"Are you sure about this?" Simigrin said.

"No, but it's our best option."

NINETEEN

THE BARON

CEYCHELL WAS SO RELIEVED TO hear Miraden and Simigrin had recovered. She worried about the journey south into the treacherous mountains full of ashenkin. She poured herself another cup of tea and continued to read.

Miraden was packing up his gear in the temple room he shared with Simigrin and was captivated watching the mage pull her hair into intricate weaves and tails so quickly. She must have memorized the movements. It was so involved, Miraden thought it might be a ceremony and decided to ask her if she needed help. He hadn't helped anyone with their hair since that skunk sprayed Ceychell several years ago—he would never forget that.

She laughed at him and, without a word, shook her head. Then she removed paint vials and brushes. She painted her face black and then drew purple lines from both sides of her chin up to her cheeks, coiled them around her eyes, and drew them out to her ears. They were faint yet delicately intricate patterns. She was loosely wearing an undergarment acolyte had retrieved for her in town.

"Mir, could you help me suit up?" she asked. Her back was to him, her head turned in his direction. He was surprised she asked him. He walked over, took the straps from her hands, and carefully looped them through the holes, criss-crossing them behind her back.

"Why, why do you wear them so tight?" he asked and finished tying the straps.

"In my city, I am respected, treated as an equal. I don't even whisper or wear my hood. Outside, in the rest of the country ruled by men, I will not give others permission to treat me like I'm lesser. So I pretend to be one of them."

Miraden was surprised at how secretive she was and how immodest she was now. It saddened him she had to put on a ruse for equality. She was right, though, and he hated it.

"But not you, Mir. You are a good one, and I have little to hide from you now." She looked up and winked.

Miraden tried to remain serious but managed to grin. She grinned back, then pulled her hood up and closed her robe around her.

They exited the temple early that morning to find Neandra already horsed, grinning like a fool and holding the reins of two more horses.

"I'm so glad you could join us, but you sure you are up for this, milady? You were at the gates of death," he said.

Miraden heard her sigh, but it was subtle. She reached for the reigns, and Neandra leaned down to say, "Southern women are some of the finest lovers. Their hair is silkier than Northerners', and they are even more beautiful than the islanders of the west. I think—"

"I do not care what you think," she blurted and got on the horse. She grabbed her side for a moment where her cuts were but sat up straight.

"Well, I know your side is probably stiff. Those were some deep cuts, after all," he said and winked to Miraden. "If only you had proper medical attention. Anyway, if your saddle bothers you, mine is much more comfortable."

Miraden wasn't sure who disliked Neandra more, but he was precisely the kind of person he hated the most. He reminded him of Hydracks. He never liked the way he stared at Ceychell.

"We are not going with you because we are happy to. The mayor asked us to, and we are going along to look for clues to find my friend. Can we be off?"

"Ah, of course," he said and kicked his horse into a ride.

Spending the day on horseback made Miraden realize how much he wished they had them back in Kaehrn. They were so expensive, not even Ormus owned one, so he was most fortunate when his father tamed Shira years ago. She rode much smoother than this black mare, but Miraden wasn't about to complain. He couldn't believe the difference they made.

They traveled a great distance today. Miraden daydreamed about Ceychell. He missed her, thought of things he would write about and perhaps a few things he'd leave out, mostly around Simigrin. He figured they would make it into the mountains tomorrow.

They didn't speak much that evening. Miraden asked Neandra if he knew much of the baron. But whatever he knew, he didn't share it. He spent most of his time singing a mellow tune and smoking cloves in a pipe. The smell reminded Miraden of Ceychell's mother's store in the early spring when she'd place herbs in a small bowl and light them inside the shop. He wrote to Ceychell some while they were in camp and held back tears as he missed Stormrange. He *desperately* hoped he was with Ceychell. At one point, he almost stopped writing her, even told her the same, but remembered his promise and kept writing.

They reached the mountains the next day. The noon sun was obscured by heavy cloud cover. They had the day to get to the baron's manor. The path was steep, craggy, very difficult. He was glad they got the equipment in Ildoo and Oddion for this trek.

He followed Neandra deeper into the mountains. By late afternoon, Neandra slowed the pace, then dismounted. They crept around a shallow ridge and saw a massive stone tower built directly into the side of the mountain, across a ravine. Grand windows that once faced ridges were wholly blocked with stones, which seemed weird since this place would be unlikely to attract prowlers… other than them.

The baron's home was a black stone citadel with cold, sheer features, high towers, and balconies overlooking a gorge. No banners or colors flew from tower tops. Battlements lined the main catwalks around the keep, yet no guards patrolled them as he had expected from reading about such castles. It looked deserted.

Miraden noticed many tracks along their path for some time but didn't pay extra attention until they were on foot, leading their horses. When he examined them closer, he realized they were ashenkin footprints. Their four sharp claws and heel spike were hard to mistake. Miraden pointed to the tracks. Neandra nodded.

"They come here often," Neandra whispered. "We just need a little proof to bring back to Oddion without getting killed or captured."

"How do we get inside?" he whispered.

Neandra pointed to a small shaft below Baron Pezqeron's main entryway. It was tiny and perhaps forty feet below a rope-and-plank suspension bridge that led from the mountain trail to the main gate.

Miraden studied the gorge for a few minutes. He saw several

outcrops below that would make it possible to leap to the other side. Apart from those jump points, the gorge faded to darkness and was fatally deep. He was okay with the climb but concerned about Simigrin. She was not even a novice climber.

"We head in tonight. Get some rest," Neandra said. They tied their horses to a dead tree that grew out of the mountain face. It was sheltered and kept the horses from standing in the freezing wind or being seen.

Miraden was very cold and miserable waiting as the night grew darker. The wait to enter the keep was cold and windy despite their little enclave, and once the sun went down, his misery went up. Clusters of snow pelted them when the wind intensified. Miraden kept busy by meticulously suiting up Simigrin and acquainting her with the gear. He explained everything she should know about climbing in great detail, hoping that she might remember something that would save her life. He could tell she listened intently as she never took her eyes off him while he spoke, but he felt she was still very nervous. She eagerly nodded and squeezed his wrist when she leaned in to listen.

The storm eventually settled as darkness fell, leaving a dense fog that blanketed the mountains. They secured their ropes to a thick tree trunk growing between the stones and repelled down the gorge's rock face. Neandra went first. Miraden went next, helping Simigrin with her steps. She did well and slipped only a couple of times, which made him panic, but she didn't scream and caught herself quickly.

Next came the hard part. Neandra kicked off the wall, sailed easily thirty feet, and used his climbing spikes and pick to catch the rock face on the other side of the gorge. Miraden went next and caught the wall, then waved for Simigrin to follow, but she froze. He was so frightened for her. He could not imagine how she felt. She told him earlier that she never climbed anything, and nothing scared her more than heights. He had already let go of his rope and would have to descend far into the gorge to find a way to jump back across. His arms were starting to burn a bit, and he knew he didn't have the strength to rescue her and then climb back across again.

He gripped the cold stone and ice and looked back at her while howling gusts tore through the gorge. He couldn't even yell encouragement. They were stuck.

"She should have never come," Neandra whispered. "Let's go. She'll get herself back up the ridge." Neandra started to shimmy toward the shaft. Miraden didn't follow him. He waited. He prayed to the Daughter of Forests and the Father of Darkness that she would gain her courage if he remained there for her. He saw her shivering on the stony face of the gorge and occasionally looked to see him reaching out toward her. The gap was significant. He realized his error in expecting her to jump.

Neandra was far ahead of him when Simigrin suddenly kicked off the wall. She sailed toward him, and he reached and grabbed her robe and pulled her to the wall. She was so tense and hit the wall hard. He thought it would knock her unconscious, but she didn't even yelp. He whispered over and over that he had her and for her to grab the wall. She finally released the rope. It sailed back to the other side, and she dug her picks in and secured herself.

Neandra made it to the shaft without much difficulty, but their journey was slower, much slower. In addition to focusing on his effort, he helped her every step, told her to follow each move he made as they spidered down the rock wall together, and finally reached the shaft. He had to lower her into the opening, then pull himself down. When she was finally standing on solid ground, she shook uncontrollably and curled into a ball on the stone floor, covering her face with her sleeve and crying. Miraden leaned over and pulled her head gently into his chest to comfort her and muffle her screams.

Neandra stood there, tapping his foot with his hands on his hips.

"It's okay, everything is okay," Miraden whispered to her. When Simigrin finally realized she was safe and composed herself, she stood up and walked out to the edge of the shaft and broke off icicles from the ceiling. She took several and placed them in her bag.

They traveled up a waste tunnel with overhead holes and reached a dead-end. Above them was another crapping throne hole, and above it was a high ceiling. It was so dark and stinking that he found it difficult to breathe. He wondered how he would get up there.

"Let me boost you, you're light and a good climber," Neandra whispered.

Miraden secured the last of his rope around his shoulder and stepped one foot into Neandra's clenched hands. He threw Miraden up to the hole, and he grasped onto the forward edge of a crapping throne. He closed his eyes and tried not to think about what his gloves were grabbing. He kipped up his legs until he got an elbow over the throne seat and then pulled himself up and out of the hole.

Miraden was in an open and empty prison cell. Chains attached to empty manacles hung from the stone wall. Outside the barred door, there were many more cells carved into the rock but no guards, or at least none that he could see.

His arm muscles burned. He was so exhausted. It took him a few minutes to get his strength and steel his wits, and he was finally able to run the rope around a bar on the cell and lower it for Simigrin and Neandra.

Once they were all out of the shaft, he heard a whisper from one of the cells, "Free me. I hear you! Hurry!"

They were careful to head over to the cage where a large man clutched the rusted bars. He wore thin rags; you could see the poxes covering his skin. Miraden pitied him, but Neandra laughed at him.

"You look right in this cage," Neandra whispered.

"Gahh," the prisoner growled and tried to reach for Neandra.

"Who are you?" Miraden whispered.

"I'm Hestos of House Hornfaur. If you're here for the baron, I can help you."

"The Hornfaurs are all liars, and you're in a cage, so we don't need *your* help."

"Henslemen are liars. You are just devil chasers and extorters!" Hestos whispered. His voice was raising too much.

Miraden was fairly sure Hestos was right, but Hestos was in the cell, and Neandra wasn't.

"We should find the keys and free him. We can't leave him in here," Simigrin whispered.

Miraden had never heard of his House and wasn't sure they had the time.

"No, we are here to do a job, not free criminals!" Neandra was staunch and even raised his voice. Miraden tried to calm him down and feared they might attract attention.

Hellshy fidgeted on his hip, then vibrated erratically. The others didn't know what to think of it, but Miraden was instantly on his guard.

"Ashenkin are near. Let's hide," he said, and they looked around quickly.

"They're always here, sometimes with children," Hestos whispered. "Help me get out. I can show you!"

They hid in an alcove near an empty cell and remained still. Miraden held Hellshy tight to his hip and slowed his breathing in hopes it would slow his pounding chest. He focused on every step and growl.

They came in a drove, a dozen of the ashenkin hauling prisoners down the steps and nearly yanking their arms from their sockets. All of them were in leather and had a yellow sash, like Neandra. They were Henslemen—five of them. They were beaten, bruised, and cut and only screamed when tossed in the filthy cells. The ashenkin, bickering to each other in their harsh tongue, locked the prisoners up and went back up the stairs.

After they were gone, Miraden expected Neandra to want to free the Henslemen immediately.

"Should we free them before or after we captured the baron?" Miraden asked.

Neandra shook his head. "Don't know those men. They're not our responsibility. We need to get the baron to stop this."

Miraden couldn't believe he didn't want to save his guildmates.

They silently left the dungeons and went to the stairs leading up into the keep.

Hestos kept calling for them, but they ignored him and entered the main hall of the baron's keep. The smell reminded him of burned meat but far fouler. The entire main floor was empty, as if the baron didn't even live here, and it was just as cold as outside. Broken furniture littered the main hall, stains and bones covered the floor. Tattered rags of red and yellow that once must've been tapestries hung from the walls. There was a dark passageway leading out of the hall. There was also a large stone staircase that led up to a second and third level. There were many cracks and broken bits in it. He didn't want to walk on it.

Neandra pointed at the stairs, so they shuffled toward them. Miraden pulled the bow from his shoulder and nocked an arrow, just in case. They were almost there when an ashenkin stepped into view on the second floor and stared right at them.

Miraden was trembling when he fired the arrow, and so it flew over its head. His second arrow pierced its eye and dropped it. The ashenkin tumbled down the steps and slapped the stone floor in front of them with its face. Miraden felt momentary relief until he heard the rest of the devils coming from the second floor.

They ran into the mostly dark passageway. There was a single lit torch that illuminated another set of stairs leading up at the far end. Simigrin dug into her bag and pulled out some melting ice and her book. The book sprung into the air, turned pages, and floated in front of her. Miraden couldn't believe it and almost forgot they were in danger. Simigrin read a passage and threw the ice. It expanded until it completely blocked the tunnel and even pressed into the walls on each side until it cracked the doorway's foundation. It was one of the most amazing things he had ever seen. He saw ashenkin behind the ice, pounding on it in vain. Then they turned and rushed up the stairs.

Two more ashenkin waited at the top of the stairs. In one swift movement, Neandra decapitated one and stabbed the other right through the chest. Miraden was suddenly glad he hadn't challenged him back in the Bleak Gale Pines.

Miraden heard a man shouting from down the corridor at the ashenkin to stop them. They ran down a hall over stone tiles and barged into a large room. Miraden dropped two ashenkin with three arrows, and Neandra dodged the vicious claws of another two, swung his sword at them, and missed. As they circled him, Simigrin grabbed a jug of water from a table, touched her staff to it, and while she spoke a few words, she slung the water from it. It coated the floor and froze instantly. The ashenkin slipped and fell and rolled around on the ice, trying to get up, making it easy for Neandra and Miraden to dispatch them.

The room wasn't destroyed like the rest of the keep. A bronze table stood near the door next to Simigrin. There were hundreds of books in large wooden bookshelves. The covers appeared dusted and well-kept, from what he could tell from a glance. Then there was an altar made of steel with a red silk sheet over it. As he stared a moment more, he realized the basin next to the platform was nearly full of blood. A large, black armoire was near an exit leading toward stairs to the third floor. Hiding behind it was Baron Pezqeron.

The baron cringed; they had him trapped. Miraden dragged him out by his full-length fur coat. He was short and thin in a fancy, threadbare suit, and he was terrified of them.

"Are you robbers?" the baron said. "I have hydras, lots of them. Do you—" but Neandra smashed him in the head with the pommel of his sword and knocked him out.

"We didn't even interrogate him about the prisoners! What if there are any children?" Miraden yelled.

"Feel free to look for them," he said. "I'm taking him. I'll cover your escape and wait for you at the horses."

Miraden didn't believe one word. He thought about skewering Neandra with an arrow right there. He *really* wanted to, but he couldn't bring himself to murder him.

Simigrin surprised him when she screamed, "Liar!" Neandra just grinned and hoisted the baron over his shoulder. He ran out of the room and up the stairs. Miraden heard the ice crumble downstairs and knew the ashenkin had finally broken through. It sounded like a *lot* of them.

They ran after Neandra, who seemed to know exactly where he was going. He ran fast up the stairs, quicker than he'd expected someone carrying a body could go. They scrambled up the stairs after him. Simigrin's book was still floating in the air next to her head.

Miraden heard the devils closing in from behind. He turned and fired arrow after arrow. Simigrin cast something he couldn't see just yet, and they ran up the stairs.

When they reached the top of the stairs, a burning gate opened in a large bedchamber to their left, and two hellhounds emerged from the darkness. Neandra ran to a passage on the right, leaving the others as their dinner. The flaming dogs were muscular and as large as horses. The floor shook from their paws. Their harrowing howl echoed down the halls, and their mouths spat fire. The hungry monsters ran at them, and though Miraden fired several arrows into them, they didn't even slow down.

Miraden panicked and froze. Then the windows along the corridor burst open, and the icy wind and swirling snow whipped through them and gathered in a cyclone in the middle of the bedchamber. Simigrin's spell momentarily distracted the fiery beasts, and he felt her hand grab his shoulder. She yelled, "Run!" and he did, as fast as he ever had, down the corridor to the right. A group of five or six ashenkin came at them from that direction. Simigrin thrust her staff into the face of one of the devils. It froze in place. Then her book whirred around her so fast it looked like a blur and batted away several ashenkin.

Miraden looked back and saw ice soldiers climbing out of Simigrin's whirlwind and attacking the hellhounds. It was so amazing that he almost wanted to stand and watch, but he had to get out of there. The hellhounds' fire was already starting to melt the ice warriors, and the drapes and rugs were on fire. The wind was spreading flames all over the corridor. The ashenkin ran away, screaming from Simigrin's book, but they had to follow them or else go back toward the hellhounds.

They reached the end of the corridor. "Not off to find the children?" Neandra called out from a balcony. Miraden and Simigrin ran toward Neandra's voice. The devils cowered away from the spinning book as they stepped out an archway onto the balcony and right into Simigrin's blizzard. There was a rope tied to the railing. Miraden ran to the edge and looked down. Neandra was just clambering off the line onto the ground floor near the baron's body that he had dropped there—and possibly killed. He picked him up and ran toward the suspension bridge.

Miraden climbed over the ledge after him, jumped down, and then reached his hands up for Simigrin to follow him. She fell the short distance, and he caught her. Then they ran after Neandra, but he was already across.

Neandra held his sword to the ropes and smiled from the other side of the bridge. Then he cut the lines, and the bridge plunged toward their side of the ravine and slapped the face of the chasm below them. Miraden burned with anger and forgot all about the dangers closing in from behind.

Neandra withdrew a green scroll case from his pocket. Miraden stared at it; his chest tightened, and his heart pounded.

"I figured you for a fool," Neandra said, "but she confirmed it. I'll kiss Ceychell goodbye for you!" He threw the scroll case into the abyss, and Miraden almost jumped in after it. Simigrin grabbed onto his pack to keep him from reaching toward the scroll as he watched it fall until it faded into the snow and darkness.

Neandra ran up the path with the baron on his shoulder. Miraden regretted not killing him earlier. He drew an arrow, but Simigrin patted his shoulder. Miraden looked up, and the ashenkin were clambering over the balcony railing above them; others were pushing through the front door that was barricaded.

Miraden stared down into the deep ravine that disappeared into a swallowing blackness and questioned if he had any strength remaining to climb. Simigrin looked up at the book hovering over her head and cast an ice bridge toward the other side that seemed to be strengthened by the freezing wind as it stretched, crackling toward the opposite cliff face.

The ice bridge wasn't complete, but the devils were upon them. He drew his silver saber and cut down the lead one. The sight of his silver sword once again caused them to pause briefly, but, luckily, Simigrin finished her spell and started over the bridge.

"C'mon, be careful!" she yelled.

Miraden backed up and slipped and almost lost his footing as he stepped onto the ice.

The devils rushed him. He dodged a few claw swipes and dropped onto the bridge, and straddled it facing them. An ashenkin charged him, slipped on the ice, and fell howling right down into the gorge.

The rest of the devils came after him undeterred. He sliced a leg off one, and it fell from the bridge. The next one raked its claws across his back. Miraden screamed as it felt like lines of fire burned across his skin.

He needed to buy Simigrin time, so he swung his saber wildly and straddled the ice bridge. One of the devils grabbed his pack strap and tried to throw him off the bridge. He sliced its arm off, and half its arm still clung to his pack by its claws. Then he stabbed it right through its gut.

Miraden tried to shimmy away from the devils and toward the other side of the bridge, and he noticed the ice getting wet, melting from the devils' boiling blood. He nearly slipped over the side.

He shimmied as fast as he could and watched them slip as they ran haphazardly after him. He enjoyed watching them fall one by one into the gorge. The blood and ice made the bridge so slippery that the ashenkin got down on all fours trying to follow. The weight from the pack of devils was too much for the melting bridge. It started to tremble—deep cracks spread along the ice. Simigrin grabbed his bag as the bridge collapsed.

He didn't even realize he had reached the other side of the bridge until Simigrin groaned as she held him up by his pack straps. The devils shrieked as the bridge gave way and dove for him. All fell except one that grabbed onto his leg and held on. They swung there with Simigrin holding up all their weight. Miraden stared into the eyes of the devil, and it stared right back. It took all his strength to hold the straps instead of falling with the devil into the abyss.

"I can't hold on!" Simigrin screamed.

"Let me go!" he screamed back. The devil reached his claws up and swiped his chest. It sliced through his leathers, and he felt sharp burning. He screamed; his shoulders started slipping. He clutched the straps with his hands. His front pocket was torn open, and the broken vial of slow hunger spilled yellow liquid onto the devil's eyes. It howled. At last, the devil released him and plummeted into the gorge. Simigrin pulled him onto solid ground.

Simigrin and Miraden lay in the snow for a few minutes to catch their breath but knew they couldn't linger.

"Oh, thank you, Simi. Thank you, gods thank you," Miraden muttered. Their chests heaved, and their breaths spewed clouds into the frosty air. He knew he would be dead were it not for her. He leaned up, held his face in his hands, and just thought about how terrifying it was. Then he yelled from a painful jerking on his back. It was Simigrin removing the claws and half an arm still attached to his pack.

"You're cut pretty bad. I should stitch you up," she said.

"No, let's see if we can catch Neandra. C'mon," he said, and they ran toward their camp.

When they got back to the alcove where they tied the horses, they found the dead tree, but of course, no horses. Miraden fumed. He wouldn't make that mistake again. Should they meet Neandra again, it would be as enemies.

They stood there, looked back, and saw the entire keep engulfed in flames. They stood silently in the chilling wind. He couldn't hear anything but the distant crackling of the fire.

The wind froze his tears, and Simigrin took his hand. He knew she shared his anger and regret.

Despite the blistering cold on the mountain, Miraden took off his shirt and cleaned and stitched the cuts on his chest quickly while Simigrin took care of his back. He did not want to risk infection. She created a magical light that floated near them, making this otherwise painfully tricky job a little less stressful. When she rubbed the holy salve onto his wounds, they flashed hot for a moment then felt immediately better.

After he was stitched and re-clothed, they huddled close behind a large, jutting stone. It was cold, quiet, with only the howling of winter wind whipping through the gorge.

"Is Ceychell the woman you write to?" Simigrin said. She'd never asked about his letters before.

"Yes." It was so painful that she wrote him, and someone like Neandra got a hold of it.

"Tell me about her. Is she smart? Talented? Pretty?" she asked.

"She is. She's my… she was my best friend. I grew up with her in Kaehrn."

"Why does she think you're a fool?" Tears streamed down his cheeks as he imagined what she wrote. He wondered if it was full of venom if she called him a fool like Neandra had said.

"I don't know," he said, clearing his throat. "Maybe because I promised her I'd save her sister. Leaving my village to hunt things I never wanted to see in places I never wanted to go." Miraden realized he sounded a fool, a cowardly one.

"This life suits you, Miraden. Perhaps she is the fool," she said. She held onto him tightly, and they shared warmth. He was glad she was with him on the mountain pass that cold night. "Do we return to Oddion tomorrow?"

Miraden took out the dagger and stared at the blade that pointed southwest. Kyradel was not in Oddion, and chasing Neandra would do nothing to save her.

"No, we will find him. But not tomorrow."

TWENTY

THE UNFORTUNATE CHOICE

CEYCHELL SAT IN HER CHAIR, furious that her letter made it somehow to Neandra, him throwing it away, and then abandoning them. She squeezed her wooden cup so hard it suddenly crushed between her fingers. Hot tea spilled on her and the letter. She shot out of her seat and grabbed a cloth to dry the pages. Her heart raced while she patted them dry, but her tears started to drop on the pages as well.

Ceychell got another cup off her shelf and poured more tea. She was unsure how she could have crushed the wooden cup. She took a few deep breaths and held the tea close to her chest while smelling the herbs.

She missed Miraden so much and knew how angry he had to be at her. She wiped her eyes then continued reading…

They left the baron's mansion and traveled south over the mountains, speaking very little about the mansion and not a word about Neandra. Their passage slowed to cold, grueling clips through the jagged terrain. On the second night, Simigrin pointed to a light on the ridge ahead, so they approached the encampment.

Smoke rose over the hill in front of them, and the wind carried low chatter. They crawled through a small tunnel onto a rocky outcrop to get a better look. It was a small camp, with less than ten tents. Tribesmen in heavy furs were gnawing meat off bones next to a large fire. Their faces were green. Miraden thought they might be krins, but after a few moments, he realized their faces were painted. There were no women. He thought it odd but wondered if they might be in the hide tents in the small valley.

One of the men spoke loud enough for him to hear, and even though he didn't understand him, it didn't sound barked and broken like the krins' tongue. Simigrin turned to him and whispered, "They said if we meant to rob them, that we would be tomorrow night's dinner, but if not, we were welcome to join them by the fire." Miraden was quite relieved she understood them. They shared a nod.

They climbed down the rock and did just that, despite how uncertain he was. He pulled a bottle of blackweed spirits from his pack. One of the townsfolk had given it to him in Oddion, and he had no intention to drink it all. After a swig, his tension drained away. He then offered the bottle to the tribesmen. They took it without a word and passed it drink by drink.

The tribesmen were friendly but didn't talk much, not that he could understand anyhow. Luckily, Simigrin spoke to them a little without any trouble. She said something that pleased them, and they raised their meaty bones toward them. One offered his leftovers to Miraden, half a rabbit, another handed Simigrin a hunk of meat. Miraden was confused but accepted the gift, then devoured it. It was a bit burned, but he gladly ate every bite down to the bone.

"I told them we burned the baron's keep," Simigrin said. One of the tribesmen finally began to speak, and Simigrin translated it in whispers. "They said that the burning gods are here now because we have grown greedy for power and unnatural magics." The tribesman pointed to her staff, and she handed it to him. The tribesman examined it for a moment, then another took it, twirled it a few times, and swung it downward. He nodded in approval and spoke a few words. Simigrin translated, "He said it was a good stick for killing rabbits. I told him I am an excellent rabbit hunter!" She winked at Miraden.

"Can you ask them if they would provide us safe passage south over the mountains? Oh, and ask if they would take a message back to Fendel in Oddion," Miraden asked. She discussed the matters with them, and they finally nodded. They said something that made Simigrin sulk.

"They..." she started, "will provide us a guide, some food, and deliver your message... but they want your silver sword."

Miraden put his hand on the hilt and shook his head. "I have a few hydras. I'll trade anything but this or Hellshy."

Simigrin nodded and pleaded with the tribesmen, but they waved their hands and spoke aggressively.

Miraden was reluctant to give up the sword. Though he wasn't skilled with it, it cut through the ashenkin beautifully, and just the sight of it brought fear to the devils. It was a precious gift, and he would likely never find another like it.

Simigrin looked back at Miraden and shook her head slowly. "I'm sorry," she said. The decision became difficult. Their packs were light with food because their horses carried most of their supplies. He looked at the landscape of craggy peaks and sheer cliffs ahead of them. He wondered if he or Simigrin could survive the climb down. Miraden checked Hellshy a final time, and it pointed directly through the worst of the mountain peaks. He removed the saber, stared at it, the gift that saved his life multiple times this journey, and then at the dagger, which was the compass, and his only hope of finding Kyradel. With a heavy heart, he handed the sword to the tribesman. He would include an apology to Bryndyke in his next letter and hope should he make it back that the blacksmith wouldn't kill him for it.

Today was Miraden's 17th Passing. A year ago, he would have never imagined that he'd be atop these mountains so far from home. He stared into the rocky landscape and felt he might never see Kaehrn again.

As he sat there with his aching back and burning cuts, he dreamed of asking Ceychell to Valdenfest, and by some miracle, she accepted. He dreamed she forgave him for everything. Her love was the only thing he ever wanted. He wanted to cherish her and be part of her life...

After Valdenfest, he would ask Ceychell to marry him. It would be perfect. He would take her down to Shilo Pond at dusk and bring a jug of her mother's delicious honey ale. He'd give her the fur gown he'd made for her over the past year that now collected dust in his room. He would tell her that she was the center of his world, that he would lay his life down for her. He'd tell her he'd make any sacrifice for her happiness, that the sun wouldn't rise without her on his mind. That when he carved wood, made candles, or hunted food for their village, it was all done with care because every detail was an expression of his love for her. He'd tell her that when he closed his eyes at night, it was her eyes he saw.

It was a perfect dream.

It was... only a dream.

Ceychell dropped the tear-stained letter onto her lap. Her shattered heart took the breath from her, and she wept. She covered her eyes, and within the darkness, she saw Miraden. She deeply regretted wounding him. She and he had had the same dream, but she never told him. And now it was too late.

She also burned with jealousy of Simigrin, the worthier and kinder soul.

Thoughts of her father not making it to Oddion or getting caught in the mountains made her feel worse.

Her gut swam with hatred for Neandra.

She thought about making her way to Naponian Cove just north of Crestain, where Miraden must be headed. If she could meet him there, she could set this right.

TWENTY·ONE

A STEP INTO THE PAST

CEYCHELL LEFT HOME THAT EVENING. The pain in her calf was nearly gone. She waded through the snow across the village carrying a shovel and went straight to Miraden's small home.

She dug out his front door, pulled it open, and stepped inside, not knowing what to expect. She tried hard to remember but couldn't recall ever being in his home. Though she'd known him all her life, he had always come to her.

Inside, the air was cold but stale. A stillness took her breath. There were two comfortable chairs with blankets drooping off the backs. A table between them held a few dusty books and a small wooden figurine of a bird. She picked up the hummingbird figurine. The carved feathers showed such detail; she just stared at its beauty for a long moment.

She set the bird back on the table and walked to the fireplace. Next to it were two shelves where a few books rested, and more figurines stood: a familiar razorback bear, two wolves, Miraden's fox, Allegro, and one of Stormrange. The details were perfect on the bird, down to the tiny spots on his feathers. She held the figurine and thought about how much she missed Stormrange. She decided to keep the carving until Miraden returned.

She looked on the fireplace mantle where the portraits of his parents hung. She remembered them so well. They were always kind to her, always treated her like their own daughter. She missed them so and remembered how crushed Miraden was when they passed. He didn't leave the house for weeks except to hunt for food and fetch water in the spring. She could have been so much more supportive to him then. She felt so stupid.

Only two rooms were leading off the main hall. One door was shut, the other open. Outside of the open door was an overturned trunk, clothes spilled out of it. She turned it back over, placed the clothing inside, and shut it.

She was curious yet hesitant to venture into Miraden's bedroom. She stared at the ajar door that she assumed was his room. She'd imagined sneaking in so many times but never did.

She stepped inside and was surprised at how sparse his bedroom was. He never was one for possessions, but there were a few. The candle of her likeness that she had rejected stood on a shelf beside his bed. The very sight of it made her choke back tears. Several hunting knives lay on his hutch, and a dozen bows hung on his wall, even the smallest and shoddiest, the first he'd ever made. She lifted the old bow from a hook. Its string sagged, and its frame was brittle and dry. Ceychell was seven when she first saw it...

"Ceycha! Ceycha!" Miraden called as he sneaked around her house with a newly carved training bow in hand. Ceychell waited just around the corner, where she suppressed her giggling. As Miraden stepped into view, she stuck her foot out, and down he went.

Ceychell grabbed the blunt arrows out of his moleskin quiver and pinned him down. "You can't catch me," she said. And she sprinted away. She loved it when he chased her.

Miraden reached into his quiver and rolled his eyes. "Hey!" he yelled and scrambled to his feet. Kyradel came out of the house and laughed at him as he ran after her sister. Miraden chased Ceychell through the woods and down to a small brook no more than three feet deep. Ceychell jumped from the bank and landed on a stone at the center of the creek. Miraden ran down and stood on the bank, staring at her with contempt.

"Give them back," he said.

"Ceycha, give them back!" Kyradel yelled, wandering down to the bank.

"You have to come get them," Ceychell answered. She knew he was scared of the water. She grinned and watched him looking for secure footing or a path of stones. "You better hurry before I drop them," she said, then jumped to another rock.

Miraden backed up and leaped for the rock she stood on, falling short and splashing into the brook. He flailed at the surface, grabbed onto the rock she stood upon, and climbed onto it.

"Miraden," Ceychell called. As he looked up, an arrow bounced off his head. Ceychell lobbed them with better accuracy than he shot with his bow and did it with a smile. "Maybe I should be a ranger," she said.

Miraden took another arrow in the chest then jumped after her. Ceychell jumped onto the bank and fled, running a path she knew well. Miraden was close on her tail and finally grabbed her hand holding the arrows. She dropped them, and she tripped, and he rolled over her on the soft brush of the forest. When they stopped, Ceychell was on top.

Miraden pushed against her, but he was pinned.

"You cannot escape, Miraden." And though he tried to escape, Ceychell leaned down to kiss him twice before letting him get up.

She set the bow gently back on the wall, exactly how it previously hung. She looked down at his bed and saw something sticking out from below the pillow on his bed. It was a folded letter.

She lifted the pillow and felt a little guilty, taking it without Miraden's knowing. She wondered if it was a love note, like so many she'd read, or something else entirely. Her hand shook, holding it until she stuffed it in her pocket.

Ceychell ventured to his closet and found the fur robe he mentioned. It was so beautiful it took her breath away. The furs were vibrant gray-and-blue, made from malicans, small, adorable, fearless forest creatures. Ceychell had only ever seen one and recalled how cute it was. But she also remembered running from it. She ran her hand along the beautiful robe, perfectly sized for her. It was precisely her style. It came down to a *V* in the front and was slender on the arms and waist. Hidden pockets were cut into the inside of the lining and fitted with soft leather. The robe had a cushy hood that she could imagine nearly engulfing her face in bliss. An attached scarf could completely wrap her face. She wasn't surprised Miraden had so accurately guessed what she'd like, but she wished he had given her the robe as he described in her letter. Despite her better judgment, she took it. It felt so good, warm and comforting in her arms.

She left Miraden's cottage and walked across the village. She saw her father stumbling into sight. His usually bold gait was cautious and shaky. Snow flew in Ceychell's eyes as she ran to him. She couldn't see any injury, but he was pale, sweating, and piqued. She helped him back to her shop, and he did not say a word. His stoic expression brought the tears right out of her. She feared what news he might bring.

TWENTY·TWO

IN THE GODS' HANDS

"WHAT IS IT?" CEYCHELL ASKED. "Did you find Miraden?" She wasn't sure she wanted to hear the answer. She laid the robe on the counter and started some tea—her father, worn from a journey that he was more than capable of completing. A thousand questions came to her mind, but she didn't want to overwhelm him.

"I arrived in Oddion… I—" Ormus's composure cracked. He collapsed into a chair and dropped his head into his hands. Ceychell started to cry, though she wasn't exactly sure why.

Ormus collected himself and looked up to her from a slouch. "When I arrived, I visited Mayor Madrannasus. She told me Miraden and two companions left to bring a baron in league with the ashenkin back to Oddion. She said only one companion returned, and that he said… he said—"

He shook like a tree in a violent storm.

"What?" Ceychell asked.

"Miraden perished in the baron's keep. Hellhounds devoured him."

Ceychell walked away from her father, over to her table. She lifted Miraden's last letter and brought it back to him. "This *companion* who told Madrannasus these *lies* must be Neandra. The bastard who left Miraden there to die! But, Miraden *did* escape and made it south to the I'la tribe. He sent me this letter days after they left the baron's mansion."

Ormus leaned back in the chair and stared at her in shock. Then he smiled and started to laugh. He laughed so hard he almost had a coughing fit. "Thank all the gods then. I didn't want to believe it. I truly didn't. Wow, that boy has real grit. He may very well make it out of this yet!"

Ceychell wasn't as amused. "Yes, perhaps he will. When he returns home to Kaehrn, he will resent me, and I will have to live with it for the rest of my life." It took everything she had to clench her quivering jaw.

Ormus nodded but said nothing. "He is on a selfless quest to rescue your sister. He made his choice, and we must support that. Let us focus on that for now." He stood and hugged her.

"Father?"

"Yes, Ceychell."

"What did you do with my letter?"

"The mayor mentioned Miraden used a messenger named Fendel. She said she'd take it to his home for me. That was before we received news from Neandra," he said and squeezed her shoulders. "It is so good to see you again. I must go to your mother," he said. He got up from the chair, still smiling, but hobbled a little when he left.

Ceychell was so agitated that she had forgotten to offer her father some tea. She worried if Fendel would deliver either the letter she gave him or the letter her father had left for him should the messenger hear of Miraden's false demise. She wasn't sure what to do. Now that her father was back, her council meeting duties were over. She started inventorying ingredients to make potions: camouflage, slow hunger, blinding flash, cure poison, and levitate. She needed to leave for Crestain to find Miraden. She needed to journey in stealth.

Nearly a week had passed since she received Miraden's last letter. Most of the potions were ready, and she made plenty of elixirs for the villagers. She stared at the ring Miraden had given her often when she stirred her cauldron. The fishing totem sat on her counter. All his letters were neatly stacked in order beside it. She read them twice each day and imagined the details that he *didn't* write into the notes. She imagined him clipping bird feathers to fletch more arrows beside a low fire in the mountains. She saw him blowing on a stew of wild rabbits; he always cooked his meals well but hated hot food. The daydreams and memories of him made her feel a little better.

She left her cauldron for a moment and returned to her counter, where his letters sat next to the folded, unread note she took from beneath his pillow. She desperately wanted to read it, but she was unsure if he would be mad at her. She picked it up along with a cup of tea and paced away from the counter, then walked back and set the folded paper back down on the table again. She tapped her fingers next to the note.

It was another love letter, she thought. Or perhaps a drawing. Or maybe something he received and not for her at all. She wasn't aware of anyone having feelings for him other than Kyradel, but she had to be sure. She sipped her tea and unfolded the letter.

Kyra,

I'm writing you this because I'm too cowardly to tell you in person. I know you love me. You always have. You were always kind to me, kinder than I was to you. You followed me and would have done anything I asked of you. For years, I kept my love for Ceychell a secret. I knew it would break your heart. What I didn't realize is that it would drive you two apart. I never wanted that or to hurt you in any way—I am ashamed that I caused this rift. Two years have passed, and even now, I continue to be selfish and foolish. I am leaving my home this morning to pick lunarcaps for Ceychell and ask her to Valdenfest one last time. I expect her to say no, and if she does, I plan to leave Kaehrn. Forever.

I hope in my absence, you and Ceychell can be close again.

I will regret the pain that I have caused you both for the rest of my life. I am sorry.

Miraden

Ceychell cringed and shut her eyes as she finished the note. She remembered the morning vividly, remembered him standing there and kindly waiting for her, remembered hearing her mother's scream. She pushed the tears from her face and checked the levitate mixture boiling in her cauldron with a silvery hue. She pulled out the map she had borrowed from the village archive. It was old but well detailed. She'd traced his journey many times and even estimated where he was likely headed, down the mountains to the Naponian Cove and finally the Port of Crestain, a large harbor city.

Ceychell went to Crestain once, long ago. Her family had sailed from Oddion around the Meate Mountains and up to Crestain. Her father had imported salted fish and potatoes to their village when a pestilence ravaged Kaehrn's farms. An atoll of tiny islands was visible from the harbor, and during certain tides, sandbars would surface where folks could walk and enjoy the lagoons and harvest shellfish from the beautiful shallows.

She was twelve when they sailed to Shinder's Bay, outside of Crestain, past a large island where natives lived. The natives swam nude in the waves and sunbathed on the beach in the warm summer sun. She always wanted to visit them; they looked so happy. Her mother would tell her, as she stared over the side of the ship, that the islanders were the best alchemists and healers in the world. They fascinated Ceychell, but Kyradel could not share in the wonder. She always got seasick and remained below deck. She loathed their sailing journeys.

Ceychell thought of the islands and hoped that, should she reach Crestain, Miraden would be there and take her swimming near one of those islands. She dreamed of the perfect day she could give him, for his birthday, when he would not have to worry about ashenkin, betrayal, and the icy northern wind. She would cook a stew with herbs from her garden and simmer black shrimp from the bay for him. She would mend his wounds and keep him warm at night. Then she would join him in finding her sister.

That night, Ceychell lay in bed thinking about Miraden. She tried to get the sleep she needed to start her journey, but she could not stop thinking. She was afraid she would sleep in too late or that a storm would roll in overnight. The snow was so deep outside she had strapped her snowshoes to her gear. She packed plenty of dried food and wineskins of water along with her potions. She packed a mending kit, flint, a compass, a bedroll, and extra clothes. When she placed her pack on earlier, it weighed heavily on her shoulders; she wondered if she could carry it even a full day.

She was so tired, yet she couldn't sleep. She couldn't help but feel Miraden was in danger tonight. She wasn't sure why; she just couldn't shake it.

A knock on her door in the middle of the night brought her out of bed. She sprang to her feet in a panic and ran through her shop to the door, hoping to see Fendel, but it was Curasca standing on the porch when she opened it. Her mother was draped in warm clothes, and her eyes were red.

"What is it?" Ceychell asked. Only an emergency would bring her outside at this hour.

"I need your help, Ceycha. Your father is sick. I didn't want to worry you. I thought it was just a sniffle. I sent word to Bilore Des for a healer when it quickly worsened. Tonight, he is not doing well at all."

Ceychell pulled on her robe and rushed across the village with her mother. She pushed open the door to her parents' home, waded through dogs and cats, and entered her parents' room, breathing heavily. A robed man she didn't recognize stood near the head of her father's bed. Ormus's skin was tight on his face, and his flesh was moist and pink. Sweat poured from his brow onto his pillow. Ceychell looked to her mother in a panic. "What has he caught… and who is this?" she asked.

"I… I am unsure, Ceycha, but this is Gonan from the temple of the Fath—"

"Why did you not get me sooner?" Ceychell shouted.

"It was only a fever, but his condition has suddenly worsened. I sent Steljen to Bilore Des to bring back one of the healers. Gonan, here, is from the temple of the Father of Darkness."

Ceychell looked at the man across the bed. He was stout with a piggish nose, small mustache, and gray hair parted perfectly in the middle of his head like two slices of moldy bread. His cheeks were as swollen as his black suit that barely contained his belly.

"You must have got here by coach," she said.

"Hello, Ceychell," the man said, nodding. "I am sorry to meet you at such a bad time. Your father has caught something quite unnatural." Gonan's eyes opened wide, and his chin dipped into his chest. "When your father was conscious, he couldn't remember anything about how he could have contracted such a malady, which is no matter at this point. We've seen similar cases in Bilore Des. They call it the Devil's Dream. He has slept the entire day, and now I fear it may be out of my power to help him. I've prayed to the gods—it is all we can do now." He pursed his lips, took a cloth from the side table, and wiped some of the sweat from Ormus's pink forehead.

"Perhaps a wizard could help father?" Ceychell said. She refused to sit and pray. All the praying she'd done for her sister had gone for naught. Miraden was still gone; now, her father was fading fast.

Curasca just shook her head and muttered, "I don't know."

"What about the islanders? You told me they are the world's best healers." Ceychell thought of her quest to find Miraden. Perhaps she had a more urgent reason to travel to Crestain now.

"A shaman is unlikely to help your father," Curasca said, wiping her nose with a handkerchief. "They are simple people and have little interest in money or travel to our shores."

"Besides," Gonan added, "your father is unfit to be moved, especially through the cold."

"I can go," Ceychell said. "I will convince one to help me." She placed her hands on Ormus's arm. The slick, cold sweat terrified her. She tried not to cry, tried to stand tall and proud for him.

"Even if you left to get one," Curasca said, "it could take you two to three weeks to bring a shaman back here. Your father would… would want you here with him."

"What are you suggesting? That we do nothing?" Ceychell said.

"We can pray to the gods," Gonan said. He extended his hand for Ceychell to take it. With his other hand, he lifted a red book from Ormus's bed and prepared to read from it.

Ceychell scoffed. "The gods haven't brought my sister back. Why would they listen now!" Her words elicited a frown from Gonan, but she continued undeterred, "I'm getting a message ready; then I'm going to Bilore Des to pay a riding messenger to find a shaman and bring him back here." Ceychell stormed out of the room, down the stairs, and out of the house.

When she arrived back at the shop, Ceychell doused the fireplace and hiked her pack on her back. She quickly wrote a plea for any shaman willing to return with her to Kaehrn to heal her sick father and promised them any price. She described the sickness in as much detail as she could, then rolled it up and realized she'd need to purchase another scroll case in Bilore Des. She heard a commotion outside and pulled on the robe Miraden had made her. Then she headed back out into the snow.

"Ceycha, you had better come quickly. I think there is a messenger," Bryndyke said. Quill and note in hands, she followed him to the town square where a small statue of Kaehrn, the village founder, stood. The simple tribute to the long-bearded woodsman held a hatchet in one hand and an always lit lantern in the other, extended hand. Hanging below the lantern-bearing arm was a giant black bat, as large as a man, with a scroll case on a belt strapped to its back. The creature flapped its large black-and-red wings whenever one of them drew close.

Ceychell immediately regretted her statement about the gods. She slowly approached the bat. It stared at her with beady red eyes, opening its wings slowly as she moved closer. It screeched and startled her, then closed its wings.

Ceychell calmly stepped around the bat and carefully removed the lid from the case. Out dropped a message and a beautiful, blue seashell. She placed her message inside and was barely able to tie the scroll case before the bat flapped its wings, rose into the air, and disappeared into the snow flurries.

"I pray to the gods that this message finds you," Ceychell whispered. Then she picked up the scroll and the shell and headed down the snow-packed road toward her parents' house.

TWENTY·THREE

INTO CIVILIZATION

CEYCHELL WAS EXHAUSTED, AND HER mind buzzed with activity. Her father's sudden illness weighed heavily on her every step as she still considered leaving to find Miraden. Many of the townsfolk followed her, asking if the letter was from Miraden. She asked them kindly for privacy, and when they finally left her alone, she opened it.

When she saw that the letter was for her, she decided to forego leaving Kaehrn to find Miraden, at least for the moment. She rolled up the message and continued pushing through the snow until she reached her parents' home.

She opened the front door to the house and smelled the foul remnants of a brewed potion. It smelled of licorice and vinegar. She knew too well, it was a powerful fever remedy. Even the dogs were quiet; the cats were out of sight. Most of the candles were out. The fireplace smoldered on its final embers.

She felt an uncanny sensation as she walked through the still house and into her parents' room. The fat cleric from Bilore Des and Curasca were praying quietly beside her father's bed. They looked up at her without a word as she stepped into the room, across the bed from them.

"I was wrong," Ceychell said. Her hand holding the letter trembled.

Gonan and Curasca exchanged a glance. "Wrong about what?" her mother asked.

"The gods. I, too, will pray for my father."

"Hopefully, you have not angered the gods with your actions," Gonan said. He adjusted the book at his side as if it shielded him from her impiety.

"What is that you have?" her mother asked. She rose carefully to her feet and steadied herself on their bed.

"It is another letter from Miraden." Ceychell leaned down and kissed her father on the forehead. She placed her hand upon his sweating head. It felt rough and gritty like wood. There were cracks along his face and arms that oozed yellow fluid.

"I managed to send my letter requesting a shaman. If Miraden indeed sent the bat, then he is near the islands. He will find a shaman."

"A shaman would take weeks to arrive here," Gonan said. "It is time to kneel and pray for mercy. Pray for your father."

Ceychell wiped tears from her face and left without replying to the cleric. She did not need his help to pray for her father.

After another fight against wind and snow, she stepped into her shop and made a pot of tea. Despite her exhaustion and looming sorrow, she was thrilled to hear from Miraden. She ran her fingers over her ring and didn't even bother starting a fire. She hurried back into her chair with Miraden's robe around her, pulled it tight as if it were hugging her, and unrolled the letter.

Miraden and Simigrin lost their tent and blankets with their horses, and their I'la guide saw no reason to share a shelter with them. It was a freezing night, and he huddled with Simigrin together on the ground between some jutting stones. He could barely sleep and thought the wind was going to freeze them solid before dawn.

Miraden woke early the next morning feeling lucky they survived the night, and when they left with their guide, he was glad to be on his way. Hiking was what he needed to shake feeling back into his bones after the night.

He wasn't even sure of their guide's name. He was just a tall, wide man with a heavy brow and thick jaw, covered in furs. His thick, black hair was like a pelt, and he smelled foul, precisely how he imagined a bear-like man living in the mountains would. The guide didn't speak at all, just walked forward on a path that he seemed to know as if he could see it—Miraden certainly couldn't. When the guide saw them struggling to keep up, he would stop to wave for them to follow, as if they purposely traversed the sharp rocks and slippery ice slowly.

There was little to distract Miraden from the misery of the howling wind, cold stone, and many, many steep drops. Simigrin was silent and often held Miraden's hand around sharp drops. She squeezed his hand as if trying to crush it on dicey spots of the path. He felt her fear and held her hand tightly as if to give her mild assurance that they wouldn't freeze or fall a thousand feet.

"How far is it until we are down the mountains?" Miraden yelled onto the whistling, snowy breeze. The guide shook his head to discourage further questions, he assumed. Miraden heeded his dismissal and focused on avoiding loose rocks or ice patches that could take him over the side of the mountain.

Their guide didn't stop to rest, ever. His stamina was beyond human. Miraden was freezing and was pretty sure Simigrin did as well. She moaned about her feet. Though his leg muscles burned with pain, they were also so cold he could barely feel them. In a sick sort of way, this was good because they made a lot of progress despite the icy trail, but exhaustion soon overtook him. Miraden began dreading every step, and at one point, he had to hold Simigrin's furs and pull her along behind him to keep her on pace. Miraden wanted to ask him to stop, but he feared he would ignore the plea, and they'd lose him in the snow squalls ahead of them. Even more, he worried if they stopped to rest, he'd never wake up.

When they journeyed nearly a whole day without stopping, he began to wonder if their guide was trying to lose them. He thought the I'la must be part krin, or perhaps monsters that just look like men. He didn't recall him eating, drinking, or even stopping to relieve himself the entire day. He wasn't sure about the men of I'la, but every time he would catch a glimpse of his guide's face under his shaggy black hair, he saw prominent, primal features—a heavy brow, thick nose, dark eyes—that led him to believe they were more krin than man.

After what felt like a week of walking, but it was probably only a day and a half, Simigrin yelled something in a language that sounded like his. The guide turned to look at her and said one word back. Miraden had no idea what it was, but it didn't seem pleasant. Simigrin pleaded with him, and he finally pointed his hand to a few flat rocks jutting out of the snow ahead of us. He stopped there and pulled food from his pack.

Miraden collapsed beside Simigrin. It was just getting dark, and he felt like he was going to pass out immediately. He was so tired he didn't want to set up camp; he didn't want to eat. He just wanted to sleep and pretend that he'd wake up, and this problem would be over. It took him a bit to recover enough just to set up a lean-to to protect them from the wind. Their guide merely curled up behind a rock that blocked the wind. Miraden wasn't sure if he even fell asleep. The guide just held his spear and remained still.

Simigrin and he devoured a few roasted grubs and lizards that they'd traded a pelt for in I'la. They were disgusting, but he didn't care. He ate them, and so did Simigrin. He was so hungry he would have eaten a barrelful of them.

A heavy hand shook him awake. He scrambled from such a deep sleep that he immediately grabbed his bow, expecting the worst, only to be seized by the guide. As the daze faded, he could tell he was powerless within the guide's grip and released his weapon. Rather than allowing Miraden to wake Simigrin, the guide shoved her from his side, and she screamed as she rolled awake. He wanted to yell at the guide, but he started to venture on without them. So, they scrambled to brush off their snow-dusted gear, threw it on their backs, and resumed following him. They went down the mountains for two more days, and at last, they reached a flatland of sparse trees and thick grass. Thankfully it was much warmer. There was a soft glow on the horizon that shined a dull yellow below a pink dusk sky. Their guide pointed toward the setting sun and then turned to head back up the mountain. Simigrin thanked him in his language, but he didn't seem to hear her or care.

They walked for an hour toward Crestain before they slowed their pace and stopped to camp that night. Miraden could see the city brightly lit in the distance and the sea beyond it. The buildings glowed with a thousand lights. He'd never seen anything like it, and it made him a little anxious. He scratched his arms as he thought of being among so many people. He knew the air must stink, and thieves must be everywhere. And the vast sea beyond stirred up a world of hidden horrors in his imagination.

His view of Crestain made him realize how tiny Oddion was, even though it felt big to him when he was there. He stared at this new city and almost wanted to return to the mountain pass, but when he pulled Hellshy from his belt sheath, it pointed right at the heart of it. What started worrying him was that the dagger pointed past the city to the sea beyond it.

They did not bother to make camp that night since the lowland weather was so much warmer than the mountains had been. They slept under the stars, and the next morning they woke to the cold rain. They hiked down to the port city in a rainstorm and arrived just before noon. He welcomed the warmer weather and didn't mind being wet after nearly freezing to death in the mountains. But the rain felt dirty. It passed through the smoke of the city and stuck to his face like soot. Crestain was just as awful as he'd imagined.

Every step he took was on something unpleasant, whether feces or garbage or a dead bird. It was hard to breathe; the air was thick with a myriad of offensive stenches. He constantly wanted to vomit.

Fortunately, he was distracted from the gross smells by the buzz of activity. As he carefully pushed his way through crowded streets, he was jostled by merchants, commoners, sailors, mercenaries, orphans, and lots of other kinds of people he couldn't even recognize. He'd never seen such a diverse mix of people, nor thought he ever would. Races he'd never known existed were thick in this place. He wasn't even sure where they hailed from or by what name they were called. Simigrin stayed close, even held his hand at times, as they minded their business and tried to avoid attention.

It was stifling, seeing how the homes were built atop and beside one another and stretched in long rows separated by trash-strewn alleys. The poor took up residence in them. He felt terrible for them living in filth under makeshift roofs and walled in with broken boards.

After wandering for hours, they finally reached the harbor, where at least twenty ships docked. Nearly fifty more were anchored out less than a mile from shore. It was a strange sight, looking out to the sea. He felt vulnerable and small. He was first very anxious nudging his way through throngs of people in the stinking city, and even more so now that he looked out on a vast, featureless expanse that was far more intimidating.

There was a sullen grayness in the stormy sky over the white-capped waves and a rich blueness to the water that hid what he knew must be terrifying creatures and unfathomable depths. When he'd swum in the lake or rivers as a kid, if a small fish touched him, he screamed. After seeing the size of some of the great monsters hanging in fishmonger shops and strung up on yardarms on the dock, he nearly soiled himself with the thought that even more massive creatures must lurk below the shimmering surface. More terrifying than the ashenkin.

As he looked at the boats and realized sailors went out to fish and returned alive each day, his nerves started to calm. Just as he began to lose his childish fear of the ocean and realize that sea monsters were simply a sailor's yarn, he saw one.

A massive, silver creature burst from below the surface in the distance, caught a huge bird in its gaping maw, and disappeared back into the water. He swallowed the knot in his throat and instantly hoped he wouldn't have to sail on this quest.

Simigrin rubbed his knotted shoulders for a moment. "Try not to think about it," she said. It seemed kind, but that massive sea creature was all he could think about other than a boat capsizing with them on it. He pulled Hellshy out of his pack and hoped it would point any direction but west. After it settled, it appeared to point directly where the sea monster was. Miraden slouched in dread.

Simigrin dragged him away from the water toward the harbor stalls, which were full of fish, jewelry, exotic weapons and baubles, and fishing supplies. Vendors were stiflingly close together. The merchants shouted their wares over one another and waved their trinkets while rag-clothed beggars jostled passersby and demanded alms.

The stench of fish guts rotting beneath the docks made him gag, and the extreme poverty of the beggars and the fishmongers' houses beyond the stalls made him lament leaving Kaehrn to learn such squalor existed. He'd seen beggars in Bilore Des, but this was a different level of poverty that he did not understand. Entire communities of beggars and peasants and miscreants seemed to live in filth and fight over scraps. They seemed hardly human at all. And the townsfolk treated them as such, throwing trash at them and calling them all sorts of names.

But that was not the worst of it. Everyone coughed. Some had hives; others had poxes, most showed dark pockets under their eyes. And there wasn't a child in sight. It was as if the ashenkin had already harvested this city and left a plague as their payment. It was horrible.

He realized he was scratching a lot. He ran fingers through his matted mess of hair to comb away imaginary bugs. He started fidgeting like many of the locals did, though he had no affliction. Or so he hoped.

They wandered through the city until early evening. Despite the gruesomeness that was Crestain, he was hungry and needed a warm meal. They stopped at a soup kitchen that was little more than a shack with a stove. The roof leaked and dripped on them, but he didn't care. They sat at a long table with a bench on each side, squeezed between others waiting for food, and enjoyed a few large flagons of ale.

At last, the cook brought them steaming bowls of fish stew, which tasted terrible but was far better than surviving on lizards and bugs from the I'la, and they ate their fill. He felt human again and chatted with the other folks sitting next to him. Most of them were willing to discuss fishing woes or taxes, but no one wanted to talk about Ashengates. Just mentioning them sent some folks to find seats at other tables. Others started telling stories of people murdered or children lost. What was sad was not their tales but how numb he felt hearing them. He didn't mention fighting the ashenkin or freeing children. What caught his interest were the stories about dying neighbors and the sickness. Everyone talked about how the contagion was killing Crestain ever since the ashenkin arrived. Everyone called it "the devil's payment."

He started to think they'd never find out anything about the ashenkin in Crestain. Then, one of the patrons, an older man with matted gray hair, wild green eyes, and brown age spots on his face, shuffled over to him and said he saw an Ashengate in the early morning, outside the atolls. He was fishing when he saw a black pit wreathed in fire hanging over the water and spewing fiery red devils that swam with great speed toward the mainland. After the gate dropped a few dozen of them in the water, it closed and disappeared as if it were never there.

A few eavesdroppers scoffed at his story, called him a drunken sailor, a fearmonger, and a liar. He may have looked crazy, but he wasn't. He described the Ashengate precisely as Miraden recalled it, and it troubled him that this one might be tough to reach.

Simigrin elbowed Miraden. "Ask him," she whispered.

Miraden looked at the sailor, drunk and troubled. "Sir, do you remember exactly where you saw the gate?" At first, the sailor stared in thought, but then he finally nodded.

"There are islands to the west, some larger, some so small they disappear with the tide. The gate I remember was near one of the largest islands, full of people."

"Them islanders are why there are ashenkin!" a drunk blurted out. "Those… shamans are summoning the devils!"

"The Crestain Legion should swarm their beaches and kill the savages!" another yelled. The comment was disturbingly popular among the other patrons. Still, Miraden didn't dare fight or fuel their murderous prejudice, fearing they'd become an angry mob and take to the islands immediately. Still, he was disgusted by their racism all the same.

The hateful talk dissipated fairly fast, and the drinking continued.

Miraden bought the fisherman who saw the Ashengate a glass of spirits, even though he didn't need another. "I'd like to ask you, sir, would you mind taking us back to where you saw the gate? I have a friend I'm looking for, and I think she may be there."

The sailor grumbled and shook his head. He lifted the drink in a dirty glass and tipped his green wool cap before taking a drink. "Never sailing there again," he said.

"How about just taking me to the nearest island… I could pay you well?"

That he did listen to.

"Meet me at the dock tomorrow, on the north side. You'll find a blue boat with a copper-lined hull. That one's mine." His face sank for a moment. "The copper's green from the weather, and it only floats thanks to the barnacles."

They agreed to meet at the vessel. That is, if the storm outside didn't take it first.

One of the women in the kitchen, which was just a stove behind a counter, mentioned that wealthy visitors, which she mistakenly assumed they were, often stayed at a nearby inn called the Farley Back. They left with full bellies and walked down the street until finding a two-story inn with a broken sign. Half of the sign hung from two chains and a pole. The other half was in the mud.

A few town guards were standing out in front of the inn. On their belts were sheathed long swords. They each carried a wooden shield rimmed in iron. Upon the shield was the painting of three fish chasing one another nose-to-tail in a circle. They wore greenish chain mail and had visored helmets. Miraden had seen many of them in town. Even saw one flog a thief at the market.

As he walked by the guards, he nodded, and they nodded in return.

He walked inside the inn. It was large, dry, and warm—exactly what he needed. A lone innkeeper, small and pock-nosed, sat at a table where he was carving letters into a new sign. He had the "Farl" finished.

"Five lumins per room, two copper more for a room with a bath and bed," the innkeeper said.

Miraden paid for two of the better rooms. After all, they'd been so miserable the last few days, and soon he'd be on the water. He wanted to enjoy a relaxing evening.

It was pleasant to be alone with his thoughts after a bath. He could feel his skin again; it tingled and calmed him down. His shoulders ached; he realized how tense he was in the city. As he lay in his bed in a room just large enough to house it, he tried to remember the last time he bathed, maybe two days before leaving Kaehrn? He felt safe for the moment. It was hard to remember that feeling, so he cherished it and just listened to the rain and thunder outside his window.

He wrote to Ceychell. The first time he had in a few days. He got lost in his thoughts and started to reminisce as he wrote her. He remembered how cold the river was at home. There was a spot he always went to once he found out Ceychell went there as well. Kyradel would visit often. There were so many times she took his clothes and threw them into the trees and then laughed as he scrambled to climb for them. Other times she'd just dangle her feet in the water and lean over to flirt with him. Once, she even stripped down and came into the water without him knowing it. She snuck up and grabbed him while he was washing his hair and nearly scared the life out of him. He was so scared that he got out of the water immediately. He'd always feared her father and thought he might get a beating or banishment if Kyradel whispered a word of them bathing together.

Miraden always loved Kyradel, just not in the way she wanted. She'd flirt, but he never led her on. Deep down, he never wanted to hurt her, he just wanted to be with Ceychell, and now he wondered if she even cared at all.

They were as close as two sisters could be or at least used to be until that day. He regretted kissing Ceychell and getting caught by Kyradel. His throat tightened as he remembered the look on Kyradel's face when he opened her eyes and saw her watching them. Like he'd just shattered her entire world. It was the biggest mistake of his life, and he'd lost both in the act. And his quest to atone would likely do little more than kill him.

Now he was farther from home than he had ever wanted to travel, and he would be leaving in two days to go to the islands. He stared out the window at the moon, hiding behind a cluster of clouds. He thought of sitting on the Kaehrnstone. It was strange to see the same moon in such a different place, the same moon that he stared at many nights wishing Ceychell would join him. Sometimes she did, but never after the incident. He went up there every night after that, hoping to get a chance to talk to her, but she never came. What a fool he was to think she would. He finished writing as his eyes started to close. He lay back on his bed and prayed that he wouldn't get eaten by that giant sea monster.

TWENTY·FOUR

GEARING UP FOR THE JOURNEY

TODAY WAS THE DAY TO resupply and rest. Miraden had a few hydras and kams left after buying three dozen relzyian silver-dipped arrows from a merchant. It was hard to find anything silver, and they soon discovered that devil hunters were buying all of it.

He wanted to buy an additional quiver full of iron arrows and stepped into a store in town that had some. Miraden held them; they were finely crafted. The shopkeeper coughed a lot, like many of the townsfolk. He almost looked green and sweated, his parted hair stuck to his forehead.

"You can fire those out back if you want to test—" The shopkeeper began coughing. Simigrin was looking around the shop, so Miraden took two arrows and stepped out back where a shoddy target was set against a soggy hay bail. As he drew his bow, he realized a heavy crack. He hadn't noticed it until now and wasn't sure when it happened, perhaps when he fell on the ice bridge.

He nocked an arrow and could carefully fire the one, but he couldn't fully draw the string. It would fail soon. Now that his saber was gone, he was desperate and defenseless.

Miraden stepped back into the shop.

"You want those arrows?" The shopkeeper placed a soiled rag to his mouth and coughed into it.

Miraden looked at a battle bow hanging on the wall behind the keeper. It was about his size and looked to be made of white spirewood. Spirewood grew far to the south; he'd only heard of it and never seen the wood before.

"Can I see that bow?" Miraden asked. The shopkeeper motioned for him to take it from the wall between coughs. Miraden lifted it and was amazed at how light it was yet solid in his hands.

"How much?" Miraden asked.

"Twenty hydras, not a lag less."

Miraden didn't have that much left. "You couldn't lower it a bit? I am out hunting ashenkin," he said.

"Yeah, you and everyone else," he coughed into his rag. "You want the bow, you pay the toll."

Simigrin came over to Miraden. She was holding a pair of silver vambraces. "New bow?" she asked.

Miraden showed her the crack on his bow. Her eyes widened. She set the vambraces down and pulled out what little money she had. They pooled their coins, but Miraden was still a few short. Miraden looked over as the shopkeeper's coughing fit got worse. He and Simigrin stepped back a bit. He was nervous he'd catch it.

"Sir, my bow is cracked, I really—"

"How is that my problem? Can't you see I have enough problems?" the shopkeeper coughed.

"We killed several ashenkin in Bleak Gale Pines, even stopped a gate guardian," Miraden said. Simigrin pulled the cracked amulet out of her bag and showed the shopkeeper, who simply shrugged.

"Broken jewelry doesn't prove you're heroes. You could be liars and swindlers, even killed someone for that," he said.

Miraden wasn't sure if they were receiving such animosity because they were outsiders, but haggling seemed pointless. They stepped out of the shop without another word.

Miraden had enough arrows, but his bow was in bad shape. He had to shop for a cheaper one or head south and start chopping—which was not really an option.

"We probably have enough for those bracers," Miraden said and offered the coins to Simigrin.

"No, you need a bow. Your arrows aren't going to fire themselves. We need to find another way to convince him," she whispered.

"Maybe we can do a small job or two," Miraden said.

"Our ride leaves tomorrow. We don't have time," she whispered. "I will go in. I will get you that bow."

Miraden wasn't sure exactly what she meant, but he took her by the arm as she walked by. He stared into her amber eyes beneath the shadow and saw her smile. She said, "I believe in you, Miraden, but you will need a bow, and I'm going to get you it."

He couldn't remember a kinder and more selfless gesture. He desperately needed a new bow, but he couldn't let Simigrin do whatever she'd planned. It was his problem.

"No. Wait here for me. I'll be back in a moment," he said and left her there.

He stepped back into the shop. The shopkeeper folded his arms, and if glares were dangerous, the shopkeeper would have bored a hole through him. His back tensed, and his neck started to tingle.

"Going to give you a moment to walk out of here before I call the guards. I don't need beg—" He started to cough again.

Miraden emptied his bags and placed on the counter medicine from Ceychell and a few other items he received as gifts from the temple of the Father of Night. As he set the last one down, out fell the pouch he looted from the naagling chieftain. It had been deep in his bag since then, and he had forgotten entirely about it, never even searched it. As he loosened the twine and opened it, out dropped several small stones, each with a glowing symbol on it, plus a charcoal stick and a jeweled bird.

The shopkeeper's eyes lit up when he saw the jeweled trinket, but he focused more on the medicine jars.

"They're healing elixirs," Miraden said. He wasn't sure how much everything was worth, only that this was his last chance to haggle. "I want the bow and the vambraces," he added. The shopkeeper didn't even answer him. He handed the bow over and an additional two quivers of silver arrows, which Miraden gladly strapped over his shoulder. The shopkeeper put the jeweled bird into a box at his counter and then chugged the medicines indiscriminately as Miraden picked up the charred stick and left the shop.

Miraden examined the charcoal. He wasn't sure why a naagling would have it. It left a strange purple residue on his fingers. He decided to toss it.

Simigrin leaned against the wall of a stable next door. She turned and asked, "What happened?" He wasn't sure if she was smiling, but when he removed the vambraces from his bag, she shook with joy. She pulled up her sleeves to reveal slender, dark-skinned arms with serpent tattoos. She let him put them on her. They were a perfect fit. They were ornamented with jeweled wyverns and a plume of fire that burst at the wrist. She adored them for a long moment, as if observing art, then hugged him. He held her back and enjoyed it. She didn't ask again how he got everything; maybe she didn't care.

They spent the rest of the day trying to gather more information. By evening they visited the city hall, three taverns, a supply warehouse, and a library. Unfortunately, most people were ill, and many just shouted curses and said they were all damned. At the library, they were told of a few heroes that had tried to enter the Ashengate, some that even came back but died from wounds later. All the stories were awful. One widow told Miraden about how she saw devils eating her husband during an attack on the city one night. Another man said how he and his wife set their son in bed and came back upstairs to give him water, and he was gone. He'd heard all the stories before but hearing them over and over again left him with an aching heart. When he heard Simigrin sobbing, he could tell their efforts to get any useful information were taking their toll on her as well, so he stopped for the day.

They stopped to stay at the Scaled Lady's Inn, near the harbor. He paid for the nicest room, figured they should enjoy a potentially last night of comfort. Who knew how long it would be before they had warm shelter again?

Miraden gave Simigrin the bed, and he would sleep on the chair. He hoped it would be a quiet night. She was already sound asleep, and he had his boots off and his feet kicked up on the shoddy table in front of the chair. He wrote to Ceychell before he got too tired. He tried to include as many details as possible but wondered if he would be able to send it. He realized he should have sent it before leaving Crestain. His eyes finally closed, and the paper dropped from his hand as he drifted to sleep.

Miraden sprung awake after hearing a crash from outside. He looked around, saw it was dark. He hadn't slept for long. Hellshy thrashed on the nightstand like a fish desperate for water. Miraden looked out the window and saw a torrential rainstorm, and despite it, a fire at a nearby temple. It was so consumed—there would be no putting out the blaze, even with this rain. Simigrin rushed up to the window next to him. They stared at the fire without speaking and then suited up. He was groggy, and his hands shook when he grabbed his bow and arrows.

They rushed out of the inn and toward the temple. On the street, a few town guards gathered around two dead clergymen. But Miraden was more surprised to see children, the first he'd seen in Crestain. His bravery faltered when he saw the dead clergymen bore deep gashes from their arms and faces. The wounds still smoldered. The smell of sulfur and blood turned his gut, and he gagged several times.

He was about to ask a guard to point them in the direction of the ashenkin, but then he heard shouting from a couple of blocks over and knew where to find them. They dashed down the road and through an alley and finally saw the rest of the guards battling the ashenkin in the moonlit city square. Careful not to hit the guards, he loosed a silver arrow that tore through two ashenkin as if a ballista struck them. He fired another that split a devil's head in two. He was amazed at how light and easy it was to fire the battle bow.

The remaining ashenkin saw where the arrows were coming from and charged Miraden, the guards right behind them.

Simigrin recited a spell from her book. Frost grew around her extended arm and captured the rain. Miraden backed away from her as shards of ice spiraled around her. She thrust her staff toward the devils, and the bits darted at them like blades. Hundreds, maybe thousands, of sharp ice fragments pierced their bodies and ripped them to shreds. The guards ducked behind their shields; the ice shards that missed the devils crashed against their steel shields and left dents and bits of sizzling ashenkin gore.

After the ashenkin fell, he ran up to retrieve his silver arrows and met with the guards.

"There are still some at the Temple of the Son of Seas," a guard said. They trembled. One couldn't even look at Simigrin. He knew they feared her. "We'll take these children to safety. Go help the temple," the guard added and went to the three remaining children.

Miraden and Simigrin ran to the temple, which was still ablaze. The door was open, and they must have seen them coming in the light of the fire because there wasn't a single devil in sight. His bow was drawn. When he stepped inside, he choked on the thick smoke. He had to bring his cloak up over his mouth to suppress his coughing.

Joists had crumbled from the ceiling and burned like pyres in the center of the large room. Benches were beds of smoldering coals. He heard someone crying.

"Call out so we can find you!" Simigrin said. A woman covered in soot and a young cleric in charred, blue robes sat up near a bench. Simigrin ran for the woman as Miraden drew back his bowstring and waited. An ashenkin dropped from the ceiling toward Simigrin, but he shot it through the chest and immediately nocked another arrow. The ashenkin spun and flopped to the floor. His boiling blood nearly sprayed Simigrin as she sprinted toward the cleric.

Another devil leaped up from behind a bench, and Miraden shot it through the throat. Simigrin reached the girl and screamed, "Miraden, I need your help!"

His eyes teared from the smoke, and he coughed so loud, he couldn't understand her. He plodded forward and held his bow in front. He didn't see anything until he made it to Simigrin. She pointed at a cleric who was either dead or unconscious on the floor. He put his bow over his shoulder. As he crept closer to lift him, he heard an inhuman shriek. He looked over at Simigrin and saw a devil spring from behind a tapestry and rake its claws across the throat of the young woman Simigrin was helping. The woman didn't even have time to scream. Her head toppled off her shoulders and sprayed Simigrin with blood. Then the devil grabbed Simigrin by the throat and hoisted her up.

He fumbled to draw his bow, but he was too close, so he pulled Hellshy from his belt. He brought the dagger up, and the devil stared at it with narrowed black eyes. He was afraid it would puncture Simigrin's throat if he stabbed the ashenkin. So, he extended the blade toward it. It nodded and motioned for Miraden to give it over. He coughed and inched forward toward the bench. At first, he couldn't see Simigrin's face, just a blackness beneath her cowl. Then the tapestry burst into flames, and he saw her staring at him as scared as he'd ever seen anyone. He couldn't lose her. They'd come so far together.

When he was a few feet away from it, he extended Hellshy out for the devil to take and began coughing, faking most of it. He slipped a silver arrow from one of his new quivers while he hunkered over in a feigned fit of coughing. When the devil reached out for Hellshy, Miraden thrust the silver arrow into its chest. The devil screamed, dropped Simigrin, and clutched the arrow shaft. Rather than lose the arrow, he sliced the devil's claw off with Hellshy and tore the arrow out of its chest. Miraden screamed when the blood burned his arm like hot oil. Despite his own screaming, the ashenkin's screams nearly deafened him.

A joist fell from the ceiling and struck Miraden in the head.

He woke up with a severe headache and a harsh cough. He wasn't sure where he was. The devil's scream still rang in his ears. When he glanced over, he saw Hellshy on the table next to the chair he'd slept in. It seemed like it hadn't moved. It was still dark outside, but he knew it couldn't have been a dream.

He turned his head and saw Simigrin. Her hood was down, her face mostly wiped clean of paint and ash, and she was smiling. There was a bruise on her neck and a few cuts on her face. Her long braid of regal purple hung over her shoulder and down into her lap. He then realized she was in the chair, and he was in bed.

She dipped a rag in a bowl of water, wrung it, and wiped his head. The knot on his skull burned with the touch. Suddenly, he was sure it wasn't a dream.

"A beam fell and knocked you unconscious," she said. "I managed to carry you out, but the guards helped carry you back here."

He didn't think she had the strength in her, but he didn't question it. She saved his life once again, and he was thankful.

Miraden sat up in bed despite his spinning, aching head. He then realized her hand was on his. He hugged her. He was so happy to be alive. When he leaned back, she stared at him for a long time. Then she pulled him back to her until their lips touched.

TWENTY·FIVE

THE SHAMAN'S CALLING

THE MORNING AFTER THE TEMPLE fire, Miraden and Simigrin geared up and walked to the end of a long dock where dozens of people were not fishing but praying. The temple still smoked from the night before. The sailors and fishers quietly faced the ocean with their heads down. Their buckets were empty, and their lines were not in the water. Some of the fishermen stared intently at them as they walked, but not one said a word. Miraden definitely didn't want to disturb them.

It was difficult to contain his nervousness. Just being on the dock with the ocean below it made him shake. He hated the smell of fish and brine and all of it. They found the boat—the Saddled Serpent—exactly as their new guide had described it. Calling it shoddy was too kind. It creaked and shifted as if all the planks were barely hanging on to each other. The copper on its hull was an ugly green and nearly covered in barnacles, and the paint above it was peeling back from its rotting wood. The mast swayed a bit, and the whole thing listed in the slight breeze. He couldn't imagine it being able to hold full sails of wind. He thought he was going to crush the railing as he pulled himself aboard and felt the deck below his feet sagging. He could not remember the last time he was so unsure and uncomfortable at the same time.

There was no hiding his fear. He was the only stiff thing aboard and didn't move unless he had a tight grip on something, even if it were Simigrin's hand, which he thought he broke a few times. The sailor made some off-color comments about him. "Land nurse" and "milk pup" were his least favorite. But he didn't care. He held his new bow tight to his chest and focused on breathing.

Looking into the water and not being able to see the bottom was terrifying. He imagined a sea creature lazily bumping their boat and smashing it into a jumble of flotsam. Or worse, something larger deciding to swallow them whole. These visions played in his head constantly. He wanted nothing more than to be back in the forest. Even Crestain was better than being out at sea on a barely assembled pile of rotting wood.

Everything caused him agony: the rocking from choppy waves, the salty smell of sea air, the creaking of the hull. He focused on the nearing islands so intently that the water around him seemed to vanish. But then he imagined getting stranded on one and felt even worse.

At last, they approached a large mass of solid land with thick vegetation and yellow sand beaches. The sailor told him not to get excited. They would not be landing there. They were sailing *far* beyond the horizon. Miraden turned and looked to where the blue waters fell off the world and almost soiled himself. The sailor laughed and whistled a tune.

The rolling waves picked up in the late afternoon. He'd already vomited several times since they left the harbor. He felt sick but hungry, yet he couldn't eat. When night fell, at last, the blackness of sea and sky surrounded them, and he felt as if the nightmares became real. He shivered on the deck of the boat all night long. It was worse than floating through the darkness in Pinderfang; at least he could swim to a mound of grass there. Here, if anything happened, it would be the end of them. He couldn't sleep and could barely think. His only saving grace was that nothing remained in his gut, though his side ached from vomiting so much.

They sailed another day, then another, then another. The weather became much warmer. The heat wasn't helping him at all. There was a hint of an island on the horizon for some time, but it eventually vanished. There was nothing but water everywhere. He spent most of his time crouched on the deck, looking down at the wood and praying to the Son of Seas that they would just land… anywhere.

Finally, it wasn't the first, second, or tenth island they passed, but from the looks of the islands he'd seen, it was the largest, and it lay straight ahead. On the beach were natives dressed in skimpy, simple clothes. Bright red, yellow, and teal paints were on their arms and faces. They stared at the newcomers with confusion as they landed the boat, but at least they weren't holding weapons or yelling at them.

Simigrin paid the sailor and stepped off the boat into the surf. Miraden leaped off and ran up to collapse on the sand. The fine yellow sand felt strange, not like the sand near the rivers and lakes back home. It was coarse, and there was a tiny crab that burrowed into the clump of sand he held. He dropped the sand and stood up. Everything felt unstable below him, as if he were still on the water. The world still swayed around him. He thought perhaps the island was floating.

When he looked back to the boat, the sailor was already leaving. He was amazed the boat got them to the island and suddenly felt very hungry and even more nervous. The islanders spoke to each other in a strange tongue. As Miraden watched the boat float away, he felt hopelessly stranded.

The islanders stared at them with skeptical curiosity. His plan seemed quite faulty when he realized they spoke a language he didn't understand. Even though he tried to wave and offer a handshake to the natives, they were much more fascinated with his clothing and bow.

The islanders spoke to each other but not to them as they escorted them to their village. There was a central bonfire that appeared to burn a kind of stone. It was quite a blaze, one that couldn't keep burning with only the trees on this island. Fanning out from the bonfire were groups of huts made of dried leaves and wood. Most didn't have walls, only a roof with thatched mats suspended between support poles. Past many of these similar huts, there was a huge, walled hut in the middle of a patch of high palms. Smoke rose from its roof.

It was built on stilts, like all the dwellings, between five large palms, roofed with woven palm strands that draped like gray hair from its apex. Cages below it held... dogs? They barked like dogs and had snapping jaws and sharp teeth. Other cages were empty but looked baited. While being escorted, Miraden hoped whoever lived inside would have answers.

There was an islander in front of the great hut that gave him pause. He was quite possibly the largest man Miraden had ever seen. Fierce and muscular, with a face painted red like a stern warning. The spear he held was taller than Miraden. He stood before a red and yellow cloth barrier that blocked the entrance. The man's nostrils flared the many rings in his nose when he looked at them. Miraden tensed, stared at the spear tip near his face. Miraden realized they were unwelcome, but he raised his hand in peace.

"We're here to fight the ashenkin," Miraden said. He wasn't sure if the guard understood him, but he reached his hand out and grabbed Miraden's bow before he could move. He tugged on it, but it was strapped to his shoulder. Then he growled something that sounded very threatening. Miraden didn't find it hard to imagine getting killed with one punch. Simigrin handed the islander her staff and said something in his language. By now, Miraden shouldn't be shocked that she knew their language, but he was, and so was the guard. Simigrin took the bow off Miraden's shoulder and handed it to the guard, who then held aside the red and yellow cloth over the opening for them to enter.

Miraden's senses were overwhelmed by the smoke that billowed from a small fire inside the hut. A man and ten older women sat around the fire, which burned a strange mix of herbs. The scent was dizzying. Miraden had to watch his step not to fall over. As he approached, the man stood. He wore a large fish jaw around his neck, and bone strands hung from a reed necklace that also bared teeth of something foul—whether it be fish or devil, Miraden was unsure. He wore so many rings and studs and even fish teeth in his nose and cheeks that it was hard to see behind them. His eyes were large and filled with calmness. His arms and legs were thin and long. His belly was round; his feet were large.

His bare-breasted female companions stood and left the tent immediately. The man held out his palm for them to sit at the fire, which they did.

"You have come to walk into a fire," he said. His voice was deep and full.

It wasn't what Miraden wanted to hear. Simigrin put her hands over her hooded ears and leaned forward as if trying to drown out his words.

"How is this possible?" Miraden asked. He couldn't understand how the shaman knew their mission.

The shaman shrugged as if it was not something worth discussing. "We don't choose such destinies, and we cannot avoid them. The firewalkers, the graja, are scared of people like you, and soon you will be hunted," he said. He grinned. Miraden found this curiously disturbing. He never wanted to be whatever the shaman thought he was, but in a strange way, it felt good to hear it.

"I am Gorgundi, the shaman of O'kokra. I've been expecting you for some time."

"You have?" Simigrin asked. "How could you know we were coming?"

"Ah, I have seen much of your long journey. I saw the house of stone where graja hunters screamed their final breaths before their bodies boiled. The house breathed fire before a bridge of ice. The stone mountain held a man without a soul."

Miraden couldn't believe it. He wanted to hear more.

"You met where the water swallowed the earth—even the dead walked freely. You even brought young souls to a town where the trees hid the people, and the water rested below their beds. That is, before you went north, where a hungry lake swallowed your careless companion."

Miraden's legs were shaking. He was nervous about what else he might say but also entranced by his every word. It felt as if he had taken the journey with him.

"Now you are here to save the red-haired woman with a voice that melts gold. She lies just beyond the womb of fire. The birds listen to her sing in the mornings when the great spirit in the sky rises, and the world shall weep if we do not act soon because the devils will silence her forever."

Miraden felt his tears. The thought that Kyradel was not only alive but so close to peril brought on a rush that made his palms sweat. He wanted to run. He wanted to save Kyradel right away. But as he stood up, the shaman calmly stared at him, and he knew there was more.

Miraden was jittery. He felt like someone was watching them. His mouth dried, and his eyes watered. He wanted to run, run, and not stop. But he couldn't.

"Please, good shaman, won't you tell us more?" Simigrin said.

The shaman reached up from where he sat and held Miraden's hands. "Be calm," he said.

Miraden wasn't sure why, but he felt much better and sat back down.

"I must join you to break the imbalance here. I'm pleased you've finally come with your soul companion."

Miraden looked at Simigrin, and she looked at him. Before he could say anything, Gorgundi said, "Your bird friend still watches over you." Miraden felt that pinch in his chest, and his eyes tightened. He cried and couldn't help it. He wanted to believe Stormrange was still with him. "A bird so magnificent could never be grounded, and he is always watching over you…"

Suddenly Miraden completely lost control of his tears. At first, he thought Gorgundi was telling him that Stormrange was safe back with Ceychell, but then he realized that the shaman was telling him that Stormrange had died.

The comment shook Simigrin, too. She had asked Miraden several times about Stormrange since he stopped returning. He never spoke of him. It was too painful. Since leaving the baron's manor, he hadn't thought much of him, but the memories flooded back as he sat next to the fire in the hut, and it took all his grit to press the conversation forward.

Miraden wiped his tears away and asked, "Do you really wish to join us?"

Gorgundi nodded. "Only to close the womb of fire." He ran his hand through his long beard that hung from his face like a saggy banner. "Rendeekra!" he called out. The spear-bearing giant stepped into the hut.

Rendeekra bowed his head to Gorgundi. They spoke for a few moments. Miraden wasn't sure what they said, but he noticed Simigrin listening intently. Rendeekra looked at Miraden with sharp eyes, as if he were a devil, then bowed to Gorgundi. Miraden swallowed the knot in his throat.

Gorgundi led them out of the great hut into the mid-afternoon sunlight. Miraden enjoyed it beating upon his face for a moment, but he felt he might regret his next steps. However, the thought that he might be so close to Kyradel helped that concern melt away. He suddenly didn't care what happened next or what happened to him. He was here to save Kyradel and would likely die trying. At least it might be all over soon.

When he stood and looked out at the ocean for a moment, Gorgundi took his wrist and placed two blue shells in his hand, then he whispered, "Give one to the person you love most in this world lest you be lost in theirs."

The shells were beautiful the way they spiraled and glowed a deep sapphire blue. He wasn't sure what to do at first. While he stared at them in his hand, he wondered if he would live to see Kaehrn again or Ceychell. Gorgundi believing Kyradel was alive gave him hope. But he wondered if Ceychell would ever love him again. He missed her so much but missing her was painful now. Now that he realized she didn't miss him. It was foolish, and he thought for a moment of keeping both shells or giving them both to Simigrin.

He didn't realize it initially, but Gorgundi watched him standing there, staring at the ocean while conflicted thoughts of Ceychell raced through his head.

Gorgundi reached out and closed his hand around Miraden's hand. "You need to give one shell to the woman with a soul of fire." When Gorgundi squeezed his hand holding the shells, he knew he meant Ceychell.

That evening Miraden sat on the sand and thought about his day here on the island, about everything Gorgundi had said. It was clear now that he might not return, so he finished writing the letter to Ceychell, recounting all he could and sending her this final token. Though this time, it wasn't a token of his affection. He had courage, strength, faith, and a healthy fear of what he might face on the other side. He asked for Gorgundi's help earlier to send a message along with the shell. He summoned a bat from a nearby palm to carry the message. The creature was enormous but friendly; it hung from a palm next to Miraden, waiting for his message pack. Miraden finished the letter, reread it, and wished more than anything she loved him as he loved her. He found so many places in the letter where he said so. He used to tell himself it was easier that she didn't know that, but now, in what was likely his final hours, he realized it was not…

The final words he wrote to her were:

I don't know if I would have ventured to save your sister if we were in love. Would I have traveled into that wretched bog or the freezing north, crossed icy Arrowheart, or watched burning devils pierce the darkness of the Bleak Gale Pines if I knew I could stay safe with you in my embrace? Probably not, but then again—I'd still be that coward you knew.

Miraden

Ceychell shuddered. Tears flowed. Was Miraden really so close to finding Kyradel? She felt terrible again that her actions had made him so despondent, and she felt even worse that she might lose him now to Simigrin. She was jealous of her, knowing how silly and petty she felt and knowing it was her fault. Still, nothing could be worse than losing Kyradel and Miraden from this world, Ceychell thought, even if he no longer loved her as he had.

She shivered, thinking about how much Miraden loved her and how cruelly she had rejected him. Now he might pass into the next world without ever knowing that she had always loved him.

She plunged into dark thoughts filled with regrets and missed opportunities. She wished she could just disappear from the world. She clutched the blue shell in her hand and spent the rest of the night in prayer for her sister and Miraden. Her final thought before drifting to sleep: *My soul is on fire.*

TWENTY·SIX

THE CONFESSIONS

CEYCHELL SPENT THE NEXT DAY and night at her parents' home, by her father's side. She held onto the blue seashell the entire time and remained quiet until she finally couldn't keep her eyes open. Ceychell woke in her mother's embrace. She didn't even realize she had fallen asleep at her father's bedside. She wasn't sure how long she'd slept, but all was quiet, and she could tell by the pinkish glow of the sun that it was early in the morning.

"You've held that blue shell tight all night," Curasca said.

"Mmm," she moaned and held it closer to her heart.

"You should go to your bed and get some rest. I'll watch over your father."

Ceychell let out a long yawn. "I have so many potions to brew… I just don't want to leave him," she said. She placed her hand on his reddened forehead and tried not to focus on his frailness. She wondered if her prayers and his strength would help him cling to life. Now that the portly healer left to get additional aid, she realized the three of them were alone. And he was getting worse.

"Your father wouldn't want you sitting here at his bedside. He would want—"

"You don't know what he would want right now. And it doesn't matter. I want to be close to him. He left Kaehrn in my stead to find Miraden and deliver my letters. That is why he's now sick. Should I just go back to my shop and brew potions? Forget all about it?"

Curasca started to respond, then choked up. She lifted her palm to her mouth and then hid her eyes.

Ceychell realized she was out of line. She hugged her mother tightly like she used to. "I love you, mother. Please, don't listen to an irrational girl who can't even stay awake long enough to pray," she said.

Her mother smiled. She ran her hand over the shell Ceychell held and asked, "Where did you get that? I haven't seen a shell in years."

Ceychell looked at the smooth, blue shell. It shone with an unnatural glimmer. She wasn't sure why, but she knew Miraden was alive and well. She could feel him. "It was a gift," she said and then quickly changed the subject. "I would like to make a long cloak of fine leather and embroidery but concealing and light. Can you help me?"

Making a cloak was a sign of endearing love in the four villages. It was considered an unconditional offering, one that Curasca understood very well. She took Ceychell's hand. "The shell is from Miraden, isn't it?"

Ceychell nodded. "Yes… it—" She immediately choked up as she remembered the end of his letter.

"What?"

"He told me Kyradel is close. He told me he must now pass through an Ashengate. This may be the last thing I ever get from him." Ceychell felt her jaw tremble. She wept into her mother's chest and held her tight.

Curasca spoke soothingly. "I remember when you were kids. Kyradel would come home, and she'd be humming to herself and smiling. Though she never told me anything, I knew she was in love with Miraden. It was obvious, her crush. She'd spend every ounce of her spirit searching for ways to catch his attention. I'd see her drawing his likeness on a long parchment. She drew him every day and then hid them under her bed. I found a large pile cleaning her room one morning, all stuffed underneath like a cache of memories. She'd sing songs that spoke of ranging the forest and of wild animals. She worded them cleverly, but they all spoke of the same hero."

Ceychell wasn't sure she wanted to hear this story. She could see the blue dwarf pines behind their house, now covered in snow, and remembered them basking in the warm summer sun over Kyradel's paint-splotched easel. Kyradel either had a flute strung at her waist or a lute strapped around her shoulder should the moment arise for a song. Her mother was right; most of Kyra's songs were about the forest, love, and freedom. She wondered if her sister, the great dreamer, would be forever traumatized should she ever return to Kaehrn. The world wouldn't be as beautiful a place if Kyradel never sang or played again. It was a dark reality that the wicked things from another world destroyed her spirit.

"While she'd sing, you'd stare off in another direction. I knew you were thinking of him, too. You were just too proud to admit it. I'm not sure why you decided to turn your back on him, but I know it hurt him. He would come by and chop our firewood, pick herbs for me so that *you* had fewer chores; he even brought clothes and blankets from his home after his parents died. I think your father really liked him, though he didn't encourage Miraden because he never wanted to arrange relationships for you girls. I think he always hoped you would come to accept Miraden in your own way, but I know he also dreaded what that would do to Kyradel."

"It's worse than you think," Ceychell said. The memories surfaced all at once. She felt ill as if she hid a great virus that had slumbered within her for two years and suddenly took hold.

"Oh? Did you ever hear how your father and I met?" Curasca asked.

"Let's go out to the family room, and I'll tell you." Ceychell sat up, and Curasca stood and motioned for her daughter to follow her. They walked out of the bedroom. Her mother hung a pot of water over the fireplace and prepared a kettle with tea leaves and some mint.

Ceychell's parents rarely spoke of their youth. Kaehrn's words stuck with his people; he always said, *The world of trouble lies behind you; the world of fortune lies before you.* In her village, stories of the past were often told as fables rather than memories. She thought of her father, the man who always supported, protected, and cherished her, and realized she knew so little of the person he was before he was the chieftain of Kaehrn. He was a quiet man, equally respected and feared by the villagers. Only once had she seen him draw a weapon when a lowly captain of Bilore Des came to town and left the inn staggering drunkenly and intent on taking any woman he could grab. Her father's anger was an ugly sight, but the mess he left of the captain was even worse. Bloodstains splotched the grassy beds outside the inn until the next rain.

Her mother poured hot water into the kettle and fetched a few warm blankets from a cabinet near the chairs. She set one next to Ceychell while Ceychell poured two cups of tea. "Your father was a military man," Curasca started, settling into a chair with her tea. "He served in Crestain and often sailed on ships to faraway places. He rarely spoke of the raids and battles he took part in, but he was proud nonetheless. He often told me that spending time in the service gave him a rich perspective on life. He learned that he wanted peace, and he tried to keep the peace for others. Mostly, he wanted to raise a family far from any war.

"I was young then, a bit younger than you are now. I was a fishmonger's daughter, if you can believe it." She held up her smooth hands as if they were rough from working, which they were not. "My hands were so gross I wouldn't have held my own hand. I scrubbed barnacles from ships, gutted fish, painted boats, anything you could imagine a fishmonger's daughter might do. I smelled terrible all the time." She laughed. Ceychell tried not to but laughed as well as she imagined her mother filthy, ratty, fishy. "I could never get the smell off me or all the fish scales out of my hair. I hated it, and I cannot eat fish to this day. But… my father was good to me, especially after my mother passed. He needed my help, and I was happy to help him for the lumins we sorely needed at the docks. And the sailors… they treated us so poorly, especially when they staggered down the docks drunk and looking for trouble.

"I remember it was a hot day late in the summer. My skin burned, and there was nowhere to escape the blistering sun. The coastal breeze was still, so the fish guts smell hung on the docks like a suffocating fog. A merchant docked in a slip next to my father's little sloop. Your father's war vessel was in the slip on the other side of us. The merchant's sailors threw sacks of grain, spices, and other things onto the dock, and I would haul, count, and place them in crates for shipment. The merchant lord… I can still see that bastard. He was fatter than any working man should be, obviously never had to want for a meal. He reeked of rum, urine, and low tide, if you know what I mean. I was hauling some of his goods without even a second thought when he grabbed me. I wasn't sure what to do. He ran his hand up my shirt, and when I saw the way he looked at me, I was so angry I wanted to pull my scaling knife and stab it right through his neck. But I froze, and my father—though I knew he wanted to—did nothing because he knew it would go badly for us. The merchant, chewing on a foul-smelling root, said, 'Why is a little fish whore working this side of the docks?' His men laughed while he groped me. I was so embarrassed. He just grinned his blackened teeth at me and wouldn't let go.

"Then I heard someone tell the merchant lord that if he didn't let go of me, he'd tie him to an anchor and watch him drown. I turned my head and saw your father for the first time. He was broad-chested and angry, not restrained as you know him now. He was in a gray shirt and black, tattered pants and held a broadsword in his hand. When the merchant lord's men flapped their lips at him, your father's entire crew showed up. The merchant lord threw me on the dock, and that enraged your father. I've never seen him so mad since that day. I crawled back to my father, and we both watched your father and his men beat every bit of will out of those merchant scum. It was unpleasant but satisfying, to say the least. The merchant's men all took off, and I have to say, I enjoyed watching your father tie a rope around that merchant lord and throw the anchor into the water. The merchant grabbed the end of the dock and held on for dear life, but that anchor was too heavy. I watched, and he gaped at me. His bulging eyes nearly popped out of their sockets. He begged me to help him, and though I pitied him, I wasn't about to do anything but watch him die. When his fingers gave up, he slipped into the water with a large splash.

"Then your father came over to me, kneeled next to me, and asked if I was okay. I knew I was in love, but I nearly blew it. I told him, for some reason, that I could take care of myself. He smiled at that. Then he offered my father and me some rum from his wineskin and returned to his men. After your father's ship left, the merchant's men came back. They didn't dare say anything to us, but they raided the merchant's ship like it was an enemy vessel."

Ceychell couldn't believe her ears. She'd never heard the story and thought someone arranged her parents' marriage, like the elders in the village had told her. Her mother's story made her smile, though, at least for a moment.

"Everyone in the village knows Miraden has loved me for years, but no one knows more than that, except for Kyradel, of course.

Miraden flirted with me all the time, out of sight of Kyradel. It was our best-kept secret for years. He was so good at finding the right time to be with me... until he didn't."

Curasca sipped her tea thoughtfully, then said, "I remember when you and Kyra suddenly drifted apart. It was so strange. Your father always thought it was just a normal sibling rivalry, but I knew it had to do with Miraden. I just didn't want to invade your privacy in the matter."

"It *was* Miraden." Ceychell ran her hands over her soft sleeves. "He made me this robe. Yesterday morning, I walked right into his house and took it after telling me about it in a letter. It is so beautiful. He's sent me tokens from his journey and wrote to me just as he promised..."

Ceychell choked up on her words, and her mother took her arms and asked, "Tell me about him, apart from being the sweet boy trying to get our attention. I don't know him as you do."

Ceychell rolled her eyes. She didn't know where to start, so she went for more tea to make time to think. She returned and sat again on the rug next to her mother's chair. "He's very thoughtful. He'd sometimes sneak a warm tart through my open window in the morning and leave it on my dresser. Then he'd close the window, so I might think Kyra brought it for me. Sometimes when I was out, he'd hide fresh flowers under my pillow, so when I went to my room at night, my bed smelled like fresh flowers. He was very good at smoking meat and often brought me deer or rabbit he cooked with his father. You remember that delicious rabbit stew I made on harvest eve a few years back?"

Curasca raised an eyebrow and nodded. "It was Miraden who made it with his father. I was just too embarrassed to tell anyone." Ceychell sipped her tea and thought about that stew and her little lie. She wanted to laugh and cry at the same time. She took a deep breath and continued, "He so loved his father. He trained with him every day and talked about everything he learned from him. His father was always so kind to me. He always called me little lady and would take his hat off whenever I came near. He would smack the dirt from Miraden's cloak when they saw me as if to remind him that he was in my presence. He knew how much Miraden cared for me, and Miraden inherited his chivalry and kindness… if not much else.

"Sometimes, Miraden would find me out walking in the woods just to ask me how I was faring. He was really just looking for how I might answer more than what I would say. The way he would try to look in my eyes, I knew he loved me more than anything in the world.

"He never stared at me as most men do. As I got older, a part of me believed he only loved me because he thought I was beautiful, but his actions when I wasn't my best changed my mind. When I was sick, he would sneak into my room and bring me broth. He once washed the stink out of my hair after I got sprayed by a skunk. He must have scrubbed my hair for four hours. At one point, I screamed at him to just cut it off, but he begged me to be patient."

Curasca laughed with Ceychell for the first time in years. "I never knew you were sprayed!"

"Oh, I was, badly. I vomited when I smelled my hair! This one time, three years ago, I ventured close to Preyno, near the farms on the northern edge of the village. They had large patches of sunsprig and needleweed that—"

"So, that's where you would get so much? You know, I thought you were raiding another alchemist's basement; you were bringing back so much."

"No, but I had to avoid the farmers because I didn't want them to know I was helping myself. I went through one afternoon; Miraden caught up to me. He had an uncanny ability to track me. You'd think I was leaving flower petals along my path. He went down to a stream to fetch water, and as I was gathering bundles of sunsprig, I looked up and saw a razorback bear. It stared at me less than twenty feet away. It was larger than anything I'd ever seen, brown as earth with a white line of fur that stretched from its black nose over its hulking back.

"I wanted to scream, but I froze in that patch of flowers. I knew if the bear attacked me, I would have been killed. It sniffed the air and kept its eyes upon me. When it walked toward me, a rock fell near its paw, then another. It growled and saw Miraden returning from the stream. He hadn't yet drawn his bow. He told me to get up slowly and back away and that when he told me to go, I needed to run. The bear raised onto its hind legs and looked like a mountain of fur and muscle.

"Miraden stepped closer and removed a piece of smoked meat from his pack. He tossed it right in front of the bear's feet. The bear dropped back down and started licking the meat. I backed away from it as another piece of meat brought the bear closer to Miraden and farther from me. He motioned me to run, and I did, but when I felt safe, I stopped and watched Miraden get close enough to feed the bear by hand. I was stunned."

Curasca's mouth hung open. Ceychell wrapped a blanket around her and poured a bit more tea for them.

"I didn't have to run. Miraden calmed the bear and even sat down next to it for a moment before giving it all his food and returning to me. I knew Miraden could tame animals, but I'd never seen anything like it."

"You have a small bear in your room. You've had it for a few years," Curasca said.

"I woke up on Valdenfest that year and found it beside my pillow. I thought it was a dream as I put my fingers into its thick fur. Even the white plume on its face and back matched my memory of the bear Miraden tamed. I love that little bear and used to ask Miraden how he made it or if he got the fur from the bear we saw that day near Preyno, but he would never tell me. He even told me once that he bought it. I almost believed him, but the care of the details in the bear's face, I just knew he made it for me."

Curasca's eyes filled with tears. She placed a hand on her daughter's hand. "Kyra really never knew about any of this?"

"No. For a long time, she would tell me things like he would weed our gardens for her. She said he has a real spirit, and it would take everything she's got to tame him. She even said the nice things he would do for me were just to make her more jealous. But as she got older, she started to realize that her dreams may not be true. No one told her, and I kept our relationship secret from everyone. I didn't want people to see Miraden flirting with me because I knew it would hurt her. At times, I think he believed I was embarrassed to be seen with him, but that wasn't true at all. I didn't want to hurt Kyra. I knew it would devastate her." Ceychell's throat tightened. "It did."

Ceychell looked away from her mother to hide a sly grin. "I really shouldn't have, but…" Her face flushed as she recalled the memory.

Curasca grinned. "Tell me, why hide it now?"

"I continued to discourage him. After rejecting him so many times, he sort of withdrew from me and became depressed. He just seemed to stop enjoying life, and he turned away from everyone. I… I was selfish and missed his attention. I missed him. Which was horrible because I would ignore him publicly. I went down to the river to bathe when I knew he might be out. He showed up, and he finally came down to the bank to talk to me. I hadn't talked to him in a few weeks, so I casually went over to him. He looked so nervous. I was too, but I knew he would never hurt me. I stepped out of the water and kissed him. He held me close even though I was dripping wet. We were both anxious. He was so stunned by the affection and my immodesty. He looked me up and down and then looked in my eyes, just as he always had. I let his curiosity take him for a moment, then told him that Kyradel could never know. He nodded, but before he removed his clothes, he looked back to the forest. He told me someone was coming and then ran for cover. A few moments later, after I went back into the river, Kyradel came to join me, happy as ever. I felt guilty. Too guilty.

"I was distant with Miraden after that. But he was way more attentive to me after that day, and I think I was just content with him loving me and happy again."

Curasca nodded over her teacup. "I remember Kyradel coming home in a fury. I've never seen anything like it. She went into her room and tore her paintings from the walls, threw her mandolin out the window, and screamed for me to leave her alone. It was so unlike her. I let her be, and when she finally collapsed, she broke into tears after destroying all of her things and told me she saw you and Miraden kissing. She was never the same."

"I know… she still hasn't forgiven me. I wouldn't forgive me, either, for the way I betrayed her and Miraden. Who could?" Ceychell stared at the warm blanket sitting on Curasca's lap as her heart sank again.

"Oh, my love, you cannot blame yourself. You must be strong for Kyradel and Miraden. They are experiencing things you may never fully understand, and now is the time to be selfless. Pray to the gods, be good to your village, and love the people who come to you. You never know what the day may bring."

Ceychell hugged her mother and knew her mother was right. "I will, mother. And when Miraden returns, I will love him no matter what."

TWENTY·SEVEN

THE SHIPMENT

THE NEXT MORNING WAS BITTER cold, but at last, the vicious snowstorm had ceased. The sun pierced the fresh blue sky beyond the thick pine branches sagging from mounds of fresh white powder. Ceychell woke up in her bed and shivered. She threw on the robe and a coat before fetching the shovel and snowshoes near her front door. She decided to open her window and crawl through it onto the top of the snow. She spent an hour shoveling a passage to her front door so sick villagers could visit her. She prayed to the Mother of Light while she scooped, and when she finished, she walked to her parents' house and started to clear a path there.

Ceychell tried not to worry, but her every thought was on her father, who she wasn't even sure lived through the night. For the past two days, his breathing was rough and short, his skin a stony gray.

A few villagers were out and about, knocking snow off their roofs or shoveling paths like she was. She waved hello to everyone, and most yelled back to her that they were praying for her father. Their support was comforting but not enough to stop her worry.

Then a screech overhead drew her attention. She shielded her eyes from the morning glare and saw a great shadow descending upon her. The large bat fluttered around her until it found a large enough branch on a nearby oak to grasp. Snow dropped on the bat from the swaying branch as it flapped wildly and screeched. Ceychell approached it and saw the scroll case strapped around its chest. She couldn't believe how quickly the message had returned.

"Please, stay, bat. Please, stay long enough for me to get my letter." The bat seemed to understand or knew its job and did not resist her when she got closer. As she opened the case, a scroll dropped into her hand along with a small gland filled with liquid. The gland was brown and sticky and looked like a creature's organ, or perhaps from a human, she wasn't sure. It was fragile in her hand; she was certain that should she drop it, the gland would splatter. She carefully opened the note and scanned it very quickly for some clue as to the gland's contents. She read the line:

I hope the remedy reaches your father before...

"Please, stay, stay right here!" Ceychell yelled to the bat then ran through the snow with the gland in one hand and the scroll in the other.

She rushed into her parents' house only to find it filled with villagers. Folks she'd known all her life turned to her and dipped their heads sorrowfully, averting their eyes. Ceychell rushed past them and brushed through several well-wishers—Bryndyke, Gonan, Vera, Chandar, Elonor, and others—in the bedroom where her father lay. Beside him, her mother prayed and looked up at the disturbance. Curasca was a ghost of herself, her thin frame hardly holding the robe on her body and her hair disheveled. She was nearly as pale as Ormus and trembled from a lack of food and sleep.

"Your father... is passing," Curasca whispered. "Come to me, my daughter."

Ceychell rushed to her mother's side. "Help me give this to him—he must drink this now!" Bryndyke and Curasca helped elevate Ormus to drink. Ceychell looked at the gland and wasn't sure how to open it. She fumbled it, nearly dropped it, then caught it carefully.

"What is this witchcraft?" Gonan said, approaching her. He pushed past Bryndyke and collided with Ceychell, splattering the gland on Curasca's robe and the blanket covering Ormus.

"Noooooooo!" Ceychell screamed. "No! No! Noooo!" She turned to strike Gonan, who tried to retreat but Bryndyke held him. Ceychell punched Gonan in the nose. Then she hit him so hard in the cheek he screamed. She felt something crunch—she couldn't believe how hard she'd hit him. Gonan wobbled in Bryndyke's grip, dazed.

"Help me, Ceycha! Help me fast!" Curasca said. She twisted her scarf to wring the stinking liquid onto Ormus's lips. Ceychell tried to do the same with the blanket, but the drink had already soaked into it. She screamed and twisted the cloth so hard it wrested free a small stream of remedy into Ormus's mouth. He shuddered in pain but remained asleep.

Ceychell slumped next to the bed and howled. She clutched the scroll against her chest and then glared at Gonan. She never hated anyone until now, and it twisted her thoughts. "Miraden sent that cure from an island shaman. He sent a potion to cure my father, and now he may not live because of you!"

"My lady, I am—"

"Because of you! I want this man tied and secured in the holding house."

"You can't possibly—" Gonan groveled.

"Ceycha," her mother said.

"My father bestowed the charge of Kaehrn to me. I want this false healer bound. If my father does not survive, you will hang him for it!"

"Surely, good people," Gonan pleaded to the villagers, "you could see it was a mistake! I came here from Bilore Des to help Ormus! To help him! I have committed no crime."

"You heard, the chieftain," Chandar said, scowling. "Bryndyke and I will take care of it, Ceychell."

Gonan struggled against the grips of the two strong men. "You have no authority to keep me here. I am bound to the laws of Bilore Des, and more importantly, the Father of Light's laws, not *yours*! Don't be a stupid little brat."

Ceychell stepped up to face Gonan and saw the blood crusted on his right nostril and his cheek badly swelling. "Say that again, and I'll have you tied naked to a tree and let the wolves eat you alive if you don't freeze first."

"This is the daughter you've raised, Curasca?" Gonan shouted though Curasca was just as angry as her daughter. "I can sense a devil inside you, young beauty," he seethed at Ceychell. "I hope you don't lead your people to ruin."

"Get him out of here," Ceychell yelled. "If he says one more word, take him deep in the forest and find him a tree." Ceychell watched Bryndyke and Chandar yank Gonan out of the bedroom, heard them drag him down the stairs pleading, then the slammed front door.

She addressed the remaining well-wishers. "Please, go about your day and keep my father in your prayers." She stared at them sternly. "Nothing more can be done now. Thank you for being here for my father."

"Did Miraden really send that?" Vera asked, leaning on her thick cane, her wrinkled cheeks damp from recent tears.

"He did…" Ceychell answered but found her emotions eclipsing her composure and could say no more.

Each of the remaining villagers touched Ormus's bed and whispered a quick prayer. As they left the bedroom, each of them touched Ceychell's shoulder and told her, "We shall follow the hunter," the traditional first words the people of Kaehrn recited to a new leader. They did not say the whole ritual out of respect for her father.

"Born under the Kaehrnstone," Ceychell responded to them in whispers. It bothered her to respond while her father still drew breath, but she would not break the tradition.

Ceychell changed her father's blankets and remained by his bedside with Curasca. She wiped his sweating forehead with cool, damp rags. She still shook from the incident with Gonan and found no comfort from her mother's embrace.

"I will never know why that happened," Curasca whispered. "And I pray to the Daughter of Forests to not abandon my Ormus. There is nothing we can do now but keep him comfortable and pray. I'll leave you to read Miraden's letter. I hope he has good news." She kissed Ceychell's cheek and exited the bedroom, leaving Ceychell alone with her father.

Ceychell opened the letter.

Ceychell,

I've tried writing more here on the island, but I've been so anxious to look for Kyradel that I can barely sit still. Then I received your letter. I was unbelievably excited! Then I read it and saw that it wasn't even a letter to me... Thank you for crushing me again.

I'm recounting what has happened because it may be my last letter. I need to write this quickly. Gorgundi's remedy for your father is cooling, and we will send it as soon as it's ready.

Gorgundi talks to me often about what I must do, but he speaks in riddles. I've tried to ask him about the Ashengate, but his answers are so vague that I can't understand what he's saying. He says things like when the lidless eye opens, you must be ready to shatter the key. And the devils' berthing can only be fulfilled in a world without children.

I've almost gotten used to his cryptic comments, but I'm growing more nervous each day. Any day now, we will see this Ashengate, and I must know what to do. Gorgundi pointed many times to a section of water where a sandbar often appears at ebb tides. He said that the last time the sandbar was visible, the gate opened. I've taken Hellshy out to the shore, and it also points in the direction of the sandbar. But for now, we wait. I'm not sure for how long.

It is interesting watching how infatuated the tribesmen are with Simigrin. They call her Boonja and say it with a bit of reverence. They believe anyone who can command magic is an extraordinary being, strong enough to enslave those who can't. They think she is a demigod. Several men brought her freshly caught fish. One even caught a fish with massive jaws. It was as big as a horse with glassy eyes and rows of sharp pointed teeth—exactly the kind of terror I knew lived in the ocean. Ten people helped the islander drag the fish to her. I think the poor man thought for sure she'd marry him for pulling the horrible trophy from the deep. Alas, Simigrin remains a maiden, but we all ate well that night. I have never tasted a more delicious steak than the meat of that terrifying creature. It was perfect with reed vegetables harvested from a nearby lagoon boiled in saltwater.

The few children who remain on the island carved trinkets for Simigrin, and the women asked to braid her hair. I'm not sure how many of the men have offered blessings to catch her favor, but it seems like all of them. She told me the attention was overwhelming, but she didn't dare offend anyone. She often retreated to Gorgundi's hut, where the others did not dare bother her. Rendeekra saw to that. Despite their affections, the islanders as a whole were not aggressive. I've not feared for our safety here at all. Especially after Simigrin whispered to me that she understands every word they say. She told me they love to gossip and talk about spirits and the Ashengate constantly...

Miraden and Simigrin sat near the fire in Gorgundi's tent. He'd finally gotten used to the smoke. Gorgundi chanted quietly to himself with his eyes closed.

"What is it?" Simigrin whispered to Miraden.

He couldn't help but think about Ceychell. He often wondered what she wrote in the letter Neandra threw in the chasm. He felt close to her, closer than he had in a long time. "It's nothing," he replied, but when he looked over at her, she stared right through his lie.

"Boonja," Gorgundi said. He stretched out his long arm toward her. "I will take that necklace now. The sandbar rises."

Simigrin withdrew the chain from her inside pocket, and Gorgundi scooped it out of her hands. The more Gorgundi stared at it, the wider the shadows grew in his eyes. Then he threw dust from a pouch at his waist into the fire. The flames crackled and hissed wildly. He reached his hand out to the wisps and then sliced his hand open with a tooth from the jawbone around his neck.

Miraden and Simigrin backed away from him. Miraden had no idea what Gorgundi said next, but he was crazed and shouted at the gate guardian's necklace. It started to burn in his hand, and the fire slithered up his arm like a serpent.

Then Gorgundi screamed. Miraden didn't know what to do. He finally couldn't listen to him anymore and started to stand up, but Rendeekra pushed him back down. He looked up at the large spearman, who shook his head without a word. Soon, Gorgundi was entirely engulfed by the fire, and Miraden expected the hut they were in would catch fire, and they'd be running for their lives.

Miraden froze when Gorgundi grabbed him by both shoulders. He felt a painful jolt as his vision went black for a second. He reeled afterward while his whole body buzzed from the shock. He wasn't sure what had happened. Something wasn't right.

Then, as fast as the fire came, it sucked into Gorgundi's skin until it burned only around his hand holding the necklace. The broken chain holding the red-and-black crystal burned wildly, and within its burning loop was a yellow flame and darkness that looked like an Ashengate. And then it went out, and the whole thing was over.

Gorgundi sat hunched and perfectly still for a few moments with his head hanging as if he slept. Then finally, he picked his head up and said, "It must be made whole to open the gate, and when it opens, upon their temple, you must shatter it."

He opened his long, withered fingers and let the chain droop over his hand. The smooth crystal was flawless as though never cracked. Simigrin took the necklace, and Gorgundi said, "Be ready, Boonja— it comes, and you must turn our flesh to frost."

Miraden and Simigrin exchanged a confused look. He really couldn't shake feeling so strange, as though he were lost, and he thought she could tell. She put her hand on his shoulder. Then, a commotion outside the tent got his attention. Gorgundi stood up and patted his back, then said, "The bat is here."

Miraden ran out to find the bat had returned with the case. One of the villagers removed the scroll from its case and brought it to him. Miraden opened it and immediately recognized Ceychell's handwriting. He was so excited he couldn't even look at the letter. He couldn't believe she actually wrote to him! She finally wrote to him!

Simigrin ran up to Miraden. "Is that from Ceychell?" she asked.

"Yes!" Miraden yelled with enough excitement that she and the islanders stepped back. Miraden ran; he jumped through the air. He held the letter to his chest. Miraden sat down next to a palm tree and got comfortable. He opened her letter with utmost care.

Then he read the letter asking for help. She didn't write a thing to Miraden. It wasn't even addressed to him! He sat there for a long moment. Tear streams would have normally run down his cheeks, but he felt an emptiness instead. It was as if she could hurt him no more.

He then thought of Ormus. Even though her father was their Chieftain, he'd always felt he was the father of their village. He was such a good man. Ever since Miraden's father passed, Ormus had treated him almost like a son, so long as Ceychell wasn't around. Miraden would help save him at any cost.

When Miraden turned his attention up from the letter, Simigrin pulled back her hood and stared at him with concern. It was the kind of look you see in someone's eyes when they watch you in peril.

"What is it? What happened?" she asked. She reached her hand out to him just as he stood up in a slump.

Miraden tried, but he couldn't answer. He felt sucker-punched and just dragged himself over to Gorgundi. Miraden proffered the note, and Gorgundi took and read it.

Gorgundi nodded and chuckled to himself for a brief moment. "I know what this is." The shaman rubbed his hands along all the large tooth piercings on his cheeks and nose and said, "This is a sickness a man gets when he has eaten meat tainted with insect venom." He then said something to the villagers. Miraden watched as a few villagers left and then returned with a goat.

"We are eating to goat tonight?" Miraden asked.

"We can, but there is work to do to save her father," Gorgundi said with a grin.

Miraden spent the next hour helping Gorgundi dress the goat and remove its bladder. As instructed, he carefully emptied and cleaned it afterward. Gorgundi was busy brewing something foul in his stew pot. It was pungent for sure. Gorgundi dipped a bowl into the liquid and set it aside to cool.

Miraden watched patiently until Gorgundi waved him over. He held open the bladder as Gorgundi carefully poured in the liquid, then Miraden was extremely careful tying the bladder closed.

"Go, now. Send your letter and that," Gorgundi said.

Ceychell cried. She fled past the cats and dogs and out of her father's home. Once outside, she realized how long she had been distracted.

Snow flew as her thin legs plunged into the deep drifts back toward the tree where the bat hung. When she reached the tree, the bat was no longer there. She dropped Miraden's letter onto the snow, stared up at the sky, and asked the gods why they meddled so much. Why had they turned her into a monster?

Despite her anger, she asked them why they let a soul as sweet as Kyradel be taken by the ashenkin.

She grabbed the letter out of the snow and stumbled back to her parents' house. As she passed Kyradel's window, holding back tears, she looked at it closely and noticed a dark smudge just below it. She waded through the snow and wiped her finger on the darkness. The stain was frozen, but she rubbed at it until some of its purple taints spread to her leather glove. It felt strangely familiar, but she couldn't place it.

TWENTY·EIGHT

THE ALTAR OF SACRIFICE

MIRADEN SAT AT THE SHORE late at night. Fully geared up, he rested just above the tide. He wasn't sure when they'd leave, but he wanted to be ready. His bow and quivers sat beside him. Hellshy stood on end on the other side of him, stuck into the sand. He stared out at the sandbar just beyond the shallow blue water near the shore.

He thought of Gorgundi's words while he sat there quietly. Tomorrow morning, the old shaman had said, they must open the gate of fire and enter. Gorgundi told him that they had lost most of their children and that they were the only hope to close the Ashengate permanently, and should they fail, the ashenkin would surely kill the islanders.

Miraden felt his quest had veered a bit off course. He felt no closer to Kyradel, but he continued to hang on to his secret hope that Gorgundi would help him locate her after he and Simigrin close the Ashengate. Every time he asked the shaman if he could sense where she was, he just chuckled and told him, "I've already found her, boy. You must be patient."

He heard the sounds of feet shuffling through the sand and turned to see Simigrin approaching. She sat down next to him and sighed. "Apart from our impending doom, what else is on your mind, Miraden?"

"I am thinking of everything since I left Kaehrn. I've lived more in these couple of months than all my years combined, but I've felt constant fear. I don't even know if the person I'm trying to save is still alive. And even if I do find Kyradel, what will be left of her? All night, I've thought, am I going through this gate just to be killed for no reason?"

"If you could stop ashenkin coming into this world, wouldn't that be a good enough reason?"

"For the world? Yes. But not for me."

"Why not? Don't you care?"

Miraden looked at his normally quiet companion. He sheathed Hellshy and slapped the sand off his hands but said nothing.

"It's Ceychell, isn't it?" Simigrin asked curtly.

She rarely mentioned Ceychell, but this time it stung with jealousy. Miraden wasn't sure why since she hadn't shown any interest in Ceychell. "I can't explain how it feels," he said at last. "Yes, it's Ceychell, but I want to rescue Kyradel more than anything. She is a dear friend of mine. But I honestly thought Ceychell would finally reach out to me. The hope of it has kept me going. But when I got her letter, and she didn't even address me, I just feel like I've lost my reason to be here."

"Perhaps you need to look beyond your own desires. I'm sorry she doesn't love you." Simigrin glowered and stared out at the sandbar, shuffling her feet in the sand.

After a few moments, Miraden said, "She used to, I think. But I've lost her by my own doing. Now I'm not even sure if I love her anymore. My love for her was my entire world. It was what I was desperately trying to save, and now it is gone."

Simigrin put her hand on Miraden's back. "I promise that if we make it out of that gate, I'll show you all the wonders of my city, and soon you will not even remember her name. I hear that burying the past is the culture in your region, is it not?"

"It is, but I find myself living in the past. But... perhaps you're right. Perhaps it's time to look forward."

"Perhaps, it is," Simigrin said. Then she stood up and left him to stare out to sea.

Miraden awoke to a hand on his shoulder. A dark silhouette stood over him, blocking out the sunrise. The sky above the shadow was blood-red, and clouds swirled violently over the sea. He shaded his eyes with his hand and saw Gorgundi, Rendeekra, Simigrin, and a host of armed islanders standing around him. He grabbed his bow in alarm.

"My friend, Miraden," Gorgundi said, "it is time to seal this Ashengate. I have seen our path."

Miraden stood up and lifted his quivers from where he'd laid them on the sand. He strapped one to his back and the other to his shoulder. He felt no better than the night before, but he returned a stern, confident stare. He was nearing the end of his mission, and perhaps it would finally lead him to Kyradel. "Let's finish this," he said.

Even Rendeekra smiled at this as the giant islander stepped up to Miraden. He held out his hand and offered Miraden the restored amulet.

"There is an altar of flesh and bone on top of the temple," Gorgundi said. "The amulet must be shattered upon it—it must be done, boy." The old shaman made a throwing motion. "There will be many terrors there, unspeakable things. There will also be children. But these are only distractions. Breaking that necklace on the altar is the only thing that matters." The shaman walked out to the shoreline's edge, where the sandbar was visible again in the ebbing tide. He waded out to it through chest-high water until he was again only ankle-deep in the sand. Then he kneeled in the surf. Rendeekra, Miraden, Simigrin, and the islanders followed him and crouched down in the surf behind him into two lines. Their faces were painted bright red, but on the front of their faces were drawn white skulls with horns. They each held a spear and mumbled a chant in their strange tongue.

Gorgundi chanted, whispered into the morning breeze, and Simigrin translated to Miraden. He called upon the devils. He shouted to the spirits.

Miraden stood silent. Gorgundi turned in the surf and stared right at him. The shaman waved for him to come forward but put his hand up to halt Simigrin. Miraden walked through the two lines of island warriors and reached Gorgundi.

The shaman stood tall and placed both hands on Miraden's shoulders.

"I'm sorry I did not tell you this sooner," he whispered. "But we needed a soul of fire, and though she does not know it, she has done her part by opening this gate and, should we succeed, by bringing us back. But there is also a price. The price we paid is your soul." Gorgundi lifted Miraden's hand that held the amulet.

Miraden stared at him, incredulous. He looked down and stared at the amulet that glowed white. He thought back to when Gorgundi grabbed him before he restored the necklace. He shook as he held it. It was warm, familiar in his hands, and comforting. He placed it over his neck.

"If you cannot break this upon the altar, your soul will be theirs forever. So will that dear girl's back in the forest. I'm… sorry, it was the only way."

Miraden didn't know what to say. He felt cheated but not surprised.

It was far more than he would have bartered if he were asked. Now he had no choice.

"Boonja, you must protect our flesh, or surely we die." The shaman reached his hands out to call her.

Simigrin stepped forward, uncertain. She and Miraden stood silently as a gate of fire opened behind the shaman.

"Boonja, Miraden, my brothers, we must do this, we must do this now," Gorgundi yelled and ran into the gate.

Miraden heard his name but didn't understand the rest. He pulled Simigrin into the burning portal, the islanders followed. Miraden felt as if he'd entered a forge without a vent. The air was brutally hot and steamy. A blackened field stretched before them. The ground was putrid filth, and flames jutted from crevices as wide as streams. Beyond smoke and flame and spirit, perhaps a half-mile ahead of them, a grotesque structure stood in the distance. It was a pale green, stepped pyramid more than a hundred feet tall. At its top, flames danced in shimmering heat. Above them loomed a chaotic sky of fiery vortexes.

Souls, twisted and deformed, drifted past Miraden and his companions, moaning in a harrowing chorus and reaching their dead hands out toward them.

Miraden couldn't believe what he was seeing was real.

"Boonja, Boonja," Gorgundi called. "There is the temple." He stepped up to Simigrin. "You must protect our flesh with your frost now, or we shall all die. This is something *you* must do."

Simigrin shook her head. Miraden saw her shaking and put his hand on her shoulder. He was starting to sweat and noticed the others were, too. He whispered, "Protect us from this heat, please!"

Simigrin nodded, reached into her bag, and withdrew her book and a vial full of ice. She held the vial in her clenched hand as the book flipped itself open.

"Where are all the ashenkin?" Miraden asked.

Gorgundi put a finger to his lips. "Shh, boy."

Simigrin chanted quickly then shattered the vial in her clenched fist. Frost wisped from her hand and surrounded them in a chilling armor, coating them in an icy fog. Miraden sighed in relief.

"Most of the graja are out hunting," Gorgundi whispered to Miraden with a grin. "That is why we are here now. We must not waste another moment. Come." Gorgundi waved for everyone to follow him.

Cloaked in their icy armor, they ran toward the temple half a mile ahead of them. They navigated fiery pits and fought off the souls that reached out to grab them. As they were getting closer, they saw hundreds of children huddled in groups less than fifty feet from the temple and guarded by ashenkin. Miraden's heart sank. He kept pace with the others, and when they neared the temple, he saw more devils standing guard at the base of the tall, stone-step pyramid.

Miraden looked over at the horde of children. He wasn't sure how they were still alive. He saw an ashenkin already halfway up the temple steps, pulling a child along behind it. The poor boy tried to kick and scream, but he was skin and bones and nearly dead already.

Miraden snatched the battle bow from his back and readied it. He prayed to the Father of Darkness that he had enough arrows. He gritted his teeth. If he were going to die, he would take as many ashenkin with him as he could.

When they reached the temple steps, they looked up at the monument of fused and melted bone. The ashenkin standing at the base of the temple saw them and started to charge. A few gate guardians came into view through the heat at the top of the temple steps and started walking down toward Miraden and his cohorts. The guardians barked orders at the ashenkin, and other devilish creatures ran at them with black-toothed grins.

Gorgundi stood at the front of his allies, lifted his bone staff, and roared. His battle cry boomed through the valley like a crack of lightning. The ashenkin stopped in their tracks and scampered away as fast as they could. Gorgundi held his staff up as the moaning spirits gathered around him. As more joined, they became a thick swirling fog. The dead wailed as Gorgundi turned his staff in the air and drew more spirits toward him. Their floating turned into fast darting as they circled him. More and more gathered around him until it was impossible to see within the tornado of souls.

"Go!" Rendeekra said to Miraden. He pointed toward the top of the temple. Then he shouted to the islanders, and they moved into a mob and charged the fleeing devils.

Miraden turned to Gorgundi just as the souls around the shaman separated. They were no longer moaning—they roared. Their faces were no longer agonizing but ghastly, angered. Their eyes burned red. The spirits suddenly darted through the air toward the devils. One ashenkin close to Miraden screamed and ran from them.

Miraden ran toward the temple and quickly reached the steps, where Simigrin had caught up to him. His mind was overwhelmed with the screams of the dead and the devils that followed them. The spirits ripped apart the ashenkin with ease, tearing their limbs and heads from their bodies. Miraden looked up the temple steps where devils were being lifted away by the dead. He focused on the top of the pyramid, where heatwaves and a strange glow illuminated the storming sky above.

"Miraden! Miraden, it's okay!" Simigrin yelled.

Miraden turned to her and shook.

"They are under Gorgundi's control. Let's—"

Miraden saw her eyes fix behind him and turned to see a gatekeeper approach the large group of children. It lifted a massive ax as it neared them. Miraden drew a silver arrow from his quiver. It felt hot in his hand. He nocked the arrow on his battle bow, aimed, and fired. The arrow sailed directly into the back of the gatekeeper's skull, releasing a gout of blood. The devil staggered and crashed down on the scorched earth. The children cheered.

Islanders screamed wildly and charged up the steps, spearing ashenkin as they climbed. Rendeekra led the pack, skewering the ashenkin like a madman with his dual-headed spear, running through one after another, stabbing the next before the last had even fallen.

Miraden and Simigrin ascended the bottom steps. He loosed several arrows into devils attacking the islanders. The ashenkin he hit dropped and tumbled down the steps. But behind them, three gatekeepers came charging down the steps from the top of the temple.

He looked over at Simigrin. She held her book at her side and pointed her staff at the gatekeepers. The staff shook as ice gathered around its end, then it burst into a stream of ice spikes that pelted the closest gatekeeper. The lead guardian crumbled and rolled down the temple steps. Its enormous body splattered devils and crushed islanders alike as it tumbled to the bottom. The other two jumped away to avoid the spikes and slammed down the steps. Miraden fired another arrow at one of the guardians, grazing its shoulder, a wasted arrow.

A tremendous roar shook the temple, louder and more ferocious than anything Miraden had ever heard. He looked up at the top of the pyramid. It was hard to make out anything from the heatwaves, but he sensed the roar came from the temple apex.

He glanced to Simigrin. Beside him, she was kneeling on the black stone and sobbing, heaving and panting. The ice armor around her began to melt away. He looked up at the islanders fighting on the steps and saw their armor beginning to melt away too. He kneeled beside Simigrin and put his arm around her.

"Simigrin, Simi, Simi!" Miraden grabbed her arm and shook her. "You must concentrate, or we are going to die!"

Miraden looked up at the temple again. A swarm of ashenkin poured over the top and began running down the steps. Miraden shot them down as best he could. One of the silver arrows plunged right through an approaching ashenkin and stuck directly into the temple steps. There were so many. He stood in front to guard Simigrin, screamed, waited for the final moment.

A sea of fog passed over Miraden from behind. He wasn't sure what was happening until he realized it was Gorgundi's mass of angry spirits. The ashenkin halted their assault. Some fell, others turned and collided into their brethren. The spirit wave crashed into ashenkin lines and tore them apart, red body parts flying through the air, black blood spraying the steps.

Miraden leaned back down over Simigrin. He placed his trembling hand on her shoulder and said, "Let us finish this. We can defeat them, but I need your help!"

Miraden looked back up the steps again. Three ashenkin had somehow evaded the spirits and were less than ten feet from him. He drew and fired one arrow sloppily into the chest of one, and the other two charged forward and tackled him. He dropped to the ground, and they all rolled down several steps of the temple. He rolled over a burning crevice, but his cloak caught fire. He swatted the devils away and screamed as he wrestled off his flaming mantle.

Miraden's scream snapped Simigrin back to consciousness. She grabbed her book from the step and yelled a spell that sent a wave of sharp ice shards swirling around the two ashenkin, cutting them to shreds in a whirl of red flesh and black blood. Then she chanted the frost armor spell again, and the cloud of ice reappeared around Miraden and the surviving islanders. She tossed her book into the air; it flipped pages in a blur and then stopped open before their eyes.

"Tear off his horn, quick!" she yelled at Miraden.

Miraden gaped at the shredded devils' remains. He removed

Hellshy from its holster, hacked a horn from one devil's skull, and threw it to her. She caught it and began chanting again. She held the horn aloft. Black ice gathered around the bone until it was nearly as big as her head.

"Miraden, look out!"

Miraden looked toward the children where the call had come from, only to find two ashenkin bounding toward him. He parried one's claw with his bow then stabbed it through the neck with Hellshy. The other devil grabbed the dagger. Miraden let go of the blade, then fired an arrow through the devil—the silver burst through several ashenkin behind the attacking one.

The devil holding Hellshy dropped to its knees. Miraden yanked the dagger out of its claws then kicked the devil over.

He hardly sheathed Hellshy when more ashenkin attacked. He dodged a slashing claw, stabbed an arrow through the attacking devil, turned, and fired another arrow through one approaching Simigrin.

Simigrin screamed as she completed the spell and held the horn up toward the temple apex. A dark frozen barrier formed around the horn and stretched out twenty feet on both sides. She held on tight to the horn as the barrier solidified and launched up the temple steps, ripping her off her feet and pulling her up with it. The wall of dark ice knocked ashenkin down on the steps and then detonated, sending shards of black ice shredding through every devil running down the temple. Then the ashenkin horn disintegrated in her hand.

Miraden ran up the steps through rising vapors of melted dark ice and reached Simigrin. "Are you alright?" he shouted. Then he felt the temple shaking. It rumbled, stilled, then shook again. Miraden looked to the temple top and only saw the glow and ripples of heat. A mass of spirits flew overhead toward the temple apex.

"Miraden!"

Simigrin and Miraden turned their heads toward the woman's

voice, back toward the yelling children.

Someone shouted, "Miraden, Miraden, please help us!"

Her voice was so familiar to him. His thoughts were distracted by the swarming dead wailing and closing to the temple fast. He waved smoke from his face and scanned the burning wastelands. He looked at the horde of children and saw Kyradel waving at him from amidst the crowd of captives. Her bright red hair stood out even against the fiery landscape.

Simigrin yelled and grabbed his attention back. "Miraden, I need your help. We must reach the top and destroy that amulet. There are fewer than a dozen devils and a lone gatekeeper near the top—now is our chance!" She grabbed his arm. Her purple hair flipped around her face from a torrent of wind. Her eyes were wide and focused on him, wet from tears. Her brow was furled. She squeezed his arm.

Miraden looked back at the circle of children. Many were dead, but a long stretch of over thirty dead ashenkin lay beside them. Fending the devils off was Gorgundi. His blurred staff sent streams of boiling blood from the attacking devils. The children gathered behind him, along with Kyradel.

"Kyradel is there!" Miraden screamed. "In that circle!"

Simigrin still held his arm. "We need to finish this. Where will they go if you free them? There is no escape from here!"

Miraden pulled the amulet off his neck and placed it on Simigrin's neck. He held it tightly and stared at it for a moment. He pondered the chance of dying and the amulet not being broken. He remembered his promise and felt the tears surface and run down his soot-covered cheeks. His hands shook when he let go of it. Her eyes widened from below her hood.

"I will be right back," he said. "I believe in you." He pulled himself away, tried to push her fearful stare from his mind, and then ran down the steps.

Miraden charged onto the blackened earth. He tore through the fray of ashenkin, clubbing and bashing them with his bow. He nocked an arrow on the run and fired at the ashenkin attacking Gorgundi. Children screamed and fled as Miraden pursued the devils, shooting them down, one by one. He fired an arrow straight through the side of a devil's skull just as it was about to grab Kyradel.

"Miraden, you came!" Kyradel yelled. She was sickly and frail. Her eyes were wide and dark. An unnaturally large smile was on her face. Her lips shook, and her eye twitched.

"Go, boy," Gorgundi yelled. "You must finish this, or we all die. Leave the children to me." He swung his staff through a devil's skull and started to chant. Miraden picked up Kyradel and tossed her over his shoulder, then ran back toward the temple and bounded up the steps, his leg muscles burning.

"Miraden. Miraden!" Simigrin screamed. She was less than twenty feet from a fighting cluster of ashenkin, islanders, and a gatekeeper. Rendeekra stabbed a devil through the face, then another through the heart, but when he pulled his burning spear from the devil's chest, it fell in two. He clubbed another with the broken end, turned to stab another as the gate guardian grabbed his arm, and drove a great ax into the mighty islander's collarbone. As he fell bleeding to the ground, he yelled, "Boonja—" but no more.

Miraden struggled to sprint up the steps with Kyradel on his shoulder. He nearly fell on a cracked step and had to catch Kyradel before she fell.

"Run!" Miraden yelled to Simigrin.

Holding her book in one hand and staff in the other, she ran up the steps, and the ax-wielding gatekeeper followed. The devil gained on her. She turned and yelled a word in it its face. Her book flew from her hands, then slammed shut. It released a wide blade of ice, severing the guardian's head just above its bone armor. The blade fell from the book and shattered as the devil fell backward and crashed down the lower steps.

Miraden watched Simigrin crest the top step of the pyramid. He felt exhausted and sagged with Kyradel on his shoulders. Every step burned in his thighs. He pushed hard, screamed, and charged the last few steps to the top.

Miraden set Kyradel on the top step, afraid he was about to drop her. He was covered in sweat and felt faint from the heat and exertion. The temple's top was a long plateau with a bone floor and a thirty-foot-tall altar in the middle. A wall of flames ten feet high surrounded an altar. Miraden inhaled a few deep breaths and saw Simigrin near the burning wall. A roar brought both of them to their knees. Miraden shook, pressed his palms against his ears, and felt his heart sink. Through the flames, a giant shadow grew larger. The temple thundered as the shadow approached him.

Then it came into view. A giant devil taller than ten stacked men stepped out of the wall of flames. Its legs were thicker than pine trees, its arms were muscular, and its claws were like curved swords. Its flaming horns spiraled back from its massive skull, and its eyes burned inside black sockets.

Simigrin was within its reach; she crumpled on the floor.
"Help her!" Kyradel yelled.

Miraden lifted his bow, drew an arrow, fired, fired another, and another. All three arrows struck, one directly in the eye. It shrilled and back-peddled into the flames. Miraden dropped his bow and fell to the floor, holding his head again.

He saw Simigrin lift her book, ruffle through its pages, and blurt incantations. She cried out her spell. A hurricane cloud of ice surrounded her, twisting and roaring. She grabbed her book and slammed it down to the bone floor. The spellbook shattered into chunks of ice that gathered and multiplied until they fused into an ice colossus standing high above the flames, as tall as the giant devil. The frozen giant was flat on top with no visible head. Its hulking shoulders hung from the sides of a solid chest that sat atop legs larger than the greatest tree trunks. It was bulky and massive and already dripping. The ice colossus reached down a hand and lifted her above the field.

The great devil advanced on them as it carried Simigrin toward the altar in the center of the burning plateau. The ice colossus stepped through the fire, hissing and steaming and melting fast.

The entire temple shook. Miraden drew his bow and fired two more arrows over the flames. They struck the great devil in the chest but did little to deter it. He reached back and found a lone arrow left in his quiver—the other two were empty. He ran up to the firewall to get a better shot and stopped, unable to move a step closer.

He watched Simigrin slide down the ice giant's arm and jump onto the top of the altar. The frozen creature stomped ahead and slammed into the giant devil, pushing it back a few steps. The devil clawed the ice creature's shoulder, and its large frozen arm fell into the flame wall and burst into hissing ice chunks. The ice giant swung a fist down onto the devil's head, stunning it.

The heatwaves were so intense Miraden couldn't quite see what Simigrin lifted from the altar and put in her bag. It was large, like a spellbook, but the heat was so blinding he wasn't sure. He saw her slapping what looked like the necklace against the altar. Nothing happened. She sagged against the altar.

The giant devil raised both fists over its head and smashed the shoulders of the ice colossus. An explosion of ice rain showered the fire field, sizzling and steaming, and evaporated in the flames. As the smoke and vapors cleared, the devil fixed upon Simigrin.

The giant devil roared and charged Simigrin. She screamed and slammed the amulet again against the stone altar and again and again.

"Simi!" Miraden screamed. He nocked his last arrow.

Simigrin lifted her head, held the amulet, and turned to look for him. Miraden aimed for the amulet. It was hard to focus through the shimmering heat, the thundering of the devil's steps, the sway of the amulet, but he held his breath and let the arrow fly. It sailed through the flame field and struck the amulet. It shuddered on the chain, and Simigrin slapped it against the altar. The amulet shattered.

The moans of thousands of lost souls wailed from the temple in a deafening cacophony that shook the entire pyramid. The great devil collapsed to its knees. The flesh burned from its body; its bones turned to ash. The wall of flames puffed out in a plume of black smoke.

Miraden ran up to the altar. Simigrin lay upon it, her arm dangling over the side.

"Simi! Simigrin, jump down to me!" he yelled. She lifted her head, started to get to her feet, and fell off. Miraden caught her, every muscle straining to keep them both from toppling to the hot bone floor. Simigrin wrapped her arms around him. She was still cold from her spell, but her robe was singed to tatters, and her hair was mostly burned off. He held her tight and then shuffled back toward where Kyradel was standing.

"This may be the end," Miraden said, "but I am glad it is over!"

"Are you? Is this the end?" Simigrin whispered.

"I think so, but I would do it all again if it were with you."

Miraden slowed as he reached Kyradel. She reached out to hug him, but she was suddenly grabbed by a dozen spirits and flew off the temple.

"Nooooo!" Miraden screamed.

He looked over the pyramid at a gate near where Gorgundi and the children were. The spirits carried Kyradel toward the gate. Suddenly, a pack of souls grabbed Miraden and lifted him from the temple. He held Simigrin with all this strength as the spirits flew them through the gate.

TWENTY·NINE

THE TURNING POINT

EARLY MORNING SUNLIGHT CREPT OVER the forest. It shone in through
a window a few feet from a bubbling cauldron. Ceychell dropped
freshly ground ginseng into the pot and stirred it. It smelled sour,
but she didn't mind. She heard a knock on the front door of the shop
and rushed to the door. Bryndyke stood there out of breath, panting.
His face was pale behind the usual layer of soot.

"You better come with me, lass," he said. "Your father is awake and
lookin' his old self."

Ceychell held back her tears. She grabbed a coat off the hook by the
door and followed the blacksmith into the snow. Her gut churned
as she took each step. She was so happy that her skin numbed with
excitement. She couldn't wait to see her father awake.

The cold wind whipped against them as they ran from her shop
to her parents' cabin. Ceychell covered her face from the flurries.
Bryndyke opened the door to her parents' home and stood like a
statue next to the front door. He said nothing, just pointed for her
to go inside.

Curasca was just beyond the door, smiling. Ceychell hugged her
mother. Tears flowed down Curasca's red cheeks and clung to her

daughter's long hair.

"Go to my room, Ceycha," she whispered.

Ceychell hesitated. She pulled her coat off and handed it to her mother, pet the dogs and cats on the way to the back of the house, and entered her parents' room. When she walked inside, she found her father upright and coughing. She ran into his arms and cried uncontrollably. Ormus hugged her tightly despite his weakness.

"I thought I'd lost you, father," she mumbled.

"Not yet, Ceychell, not yet." Her father sat up straight, though he was weak and pale. "I woke up late last night. I struggled to get out of bed, but I needed to. My back felt like it was broken, and I could barely feel my legs. It took me some time, but I finally got out of bed and walked outside. It was great to be alive, to feel the cold wind on my face." He ran his hand through his thick beard. "Outside the door on a tree across the road was a giant bat."

Ceychell's eyes lit up as Ormus lifted a rolled scroll from the side table and handed it to her. She took it into her shaking fingers. "Did you read it?"

Ormus shook his head. "Go. Read it and come back to me."

Ceychell ran back to her shop, stoked the fireplace, and sat down to read.

She struggled with every word when Miraden described running through the burning realm, escaping spirits, and fighting devils. She sweated while reading his climb up the temple steps with Simigrin. It seemed like a tale from legend. She almost didn't believe it, and then she saw Kyradel's name.

Ceychell held the scroll to her chest and cried what few tears she had left. She couldn't stop smiling, crying, and laughing at the same time. She wiped her tears on her sleeve and had to pause her reading because her vision was so blurry.

At last, she cleared her eyes and continued reading. She grew fearful as Miraden described the great devil and the altar and finally the escape…

He felt sand upon his face. It wasn't unpleasant. Honestly, he thought he'd died. It was surreal enough. He could hear birds, feel the warmth of the sun. When the cool breeze brushed across his face, he decided to open his eyes. A small black crab stared directly at him from its burrow in the sand. Beyond it, calm waves, the blue-green sea. There were no devils—nothing threatening at all. He thought he had found the afterlife and was glad for it.

He was so thirsty. At first, he wasn't sure if he was dreaming or even alive, but he soon realized that he didn't die. He sat up and turned and then lost his breath.

Next to him lay Kyradel. He couldn't make out dirt from freckle on her face. She was awake and just staring forward at nothing. She seemed happy, just like he remembered her, yet strangely absent as well.

Her torn red plumes of hair were knotted and filthy. Her legs, thin and covered in sores. The clothes she must have worn to bed when taken were tattered rags stained with dried blood. Miraden shook as he reached his hand out to touch her shoulder. He felt he was too late. She was alive, yet he had failed to save her.

He heard cheering. He turned and saw all the children lying on the sand. There must have been a hundred of them, now confused and just coming around. There were islanders in warpaint too, and then he saw Gorgundi stepping carefully over people. He smiled broadly and walked toward Miraden but still fifty-or-so feet away.

Miraden realized he didn't see Simigrin anywhere. He stood up and searched and searched. "Simi! Simi!" Miraden yelled. His heart raced.

Gorgundi quickly approached him. He was calm and started to laugh.

"Do not worry, the Boonja is fine. They are attending her now," Gorgundi said. "You see, I told you we'd find her and close the gate." The way Gorgundi grinned, he must have known that Miraden had felt the opposite.

"Bring your friend. We will care for her now," Gorgundi said and waved Miraden to follow. Miraden ached when he leaned over to lift Kyradel, but she was so light. He carefully picked her up. She didn't say a thing; she was light like a blanket and hung from his arms. He couldn't help but focus on how thin and frail she was. It felt like she'd break if he dropped her.

Miraden followed Gorgundi inside his hut and laid Kyradel down by the fire as gently as he could. When he kneeled, a sharp pain hit his leg. Cuts and aches were just starting to surface, but this was fresh. He carefully reached into his pocket and felt the blue shell. It somehow shattered in. He removed the big piece that had cut his leg a bit.

"Gorgundi, what were all those spirits?" Miraden asked as he stared at the shell.

"They are the lost, the ones sacrificed and unable to find their way to our ancestors. Those ones are now free because of us, because of your bravery."

Miraden stared at the shell and couldn't believe his ears. "How did we make it back if we were—"

"The woman with a soul of fire brought us back to our land."

Ceychell stopped reading and immediately reached into her pocket to find a shattered shell. She pulled a few pieces out and turned them over. Seeing them burned and brittle, she didn't know what to think—she hadn't done anything to bring them back.

She dropped the shell shards and jumped back. She wasn't sure if it was all shaman magic or devilry, but it scared her. She fetched a small jar from a shelf near her counter, then returned and collected the shell pieces. She placed them inside and put the pot on the small table next to her chair.

She took a deep breath, picked up the letter, and continued to read.

"You should thank her when you get home."

Miraden didn't know what to think about Ceychell somehow bringing them back. Then he remembered the amulet—with his soul—shattered on the altar. He felt Gorgundi staring, and he was afraid to ask.

"You worry far too much, Grazinya. Your soul is right where it should be," he said and placed a hand upon Miraden's shoulder.

Miraden sighed. He was so incredibly relieved. He realized he was just called "Grazinya" and asked, "What is Grazinya?"

"In my tongue, it means devil slayer."

He didn't mind it at all. He never was called anything impressive or even positive in his life. He smiled and looked down at Kyradel resting and couldn't believe she was there. It was like a dream that finally came true.

Gorgundi examined her as if she were a fine pelt. He ran his fingers over sores and cuts and detached blood-sucking insects. "She needs much recovery. She needs to stay here so I can heal her," he said.

"She has to come back to Kaehrn with me. I promised I would bring her back."

"You will, but she isn't going anywhere like this. And, there is so much for you to do after you finish your quest. Go, rest for now."

Miraden wasn't sure what he meant by that. "Is Simigrin okay?"

"The Boonja is a survivor, boy."

Miraden nodded to him, so happy they all made it out of that dreadful place. "Gorgundi, what does Boonja mean?"

Gorgundi grinned a mouthful of teeth. "It roughly means the bearer of doom." Miraden wasn't expecting that. "Write the letter to the woman with a soul of fire. Tell her of your triumph. My bat will deliver it, and when the time is right, I will send a message to Crestain for a ship to return these children and get you home soon enough."

It was hard to believe that everything might be okay, at least, for the moment. "Thank you for everything," Miraden said.

Ceychell sat in disbelief. She reread the letter to ensure she hadn't misread it. Then she ran out of her house into the snow, screaming over and over, "He saved her! Miraden saved Kyra! He did it!"

Her screaming alarmed the whole village. Everyone rushed out of their homes into the snowy street and stared at her as she passed. She ran to her parents' house, where the door was open. Inside the doorway, Curasca was helping Ormus put on his coat.

Ceychell waved the letter at them. "Miraden found Kyradel in an Ashengate and saved her life! He defeated a devil lord and closed the bloody gate! Kyra is alive!"

Ceychell hadn't even realized that everyone had followed her down the street until they all cheered behind her. Except for Vera. The elderly woman simply glowered and turned back toward her home. The woman's scowl aroused Ceychell's curiosity, but she was pulled back into the celebration by her mother.

Ormus and Curasca cried for joy and embraced each other. "Ceycha," her mother said, "does the letter say when they are coming home?"

"No," Ceychell answered. "They are on an island near Crestain. Kyradel must heal before she can travel home."

"As long as my Kyra is coming home, I can once again sleep at night." She turned to Ormus, grasped his arm, and whispered, "My Kyra is coming home."

THIRTY

THE BEARER OF DOOM

KYRADEL SPENT HER FIRST NIGHT of freedom in a few months sleeping soundly in Gorgundi's hut. She twitched a lot but slept through the night anyway. She woke up less than an hour ago and had just finished a small bowl of soup with a fish paste for breakfast. Miraden kept a close watch for fear she got sick. Gorgundi remained silent, preparing ointments in a stone cauldron.

"You really came all this way for me?" Kyradel asked.

"Yes, I've been trying to find you for months." He could barely remember a time when his whole focus was not on finding her. He felt good, having saved her, but he had not had time to think about what he would do next.

"The last few weeks," Kyradel said, "I thought for sure I was going to die. I stopped dreaming at night, and the devils killed more of us each day." Kyradel stared vacantly. She shook and fell into her thoughts.

Miraden shuddered as he imagined what she was reliving. Then he realized he did not *want* to imagine it and shook his head to dispel the images. He grasped Kyradel's shoulder and shook her out of the daydream.

She realized it, smiled, and then said, "I— I don't think you came all this way for me."

"Believe it or not, I did." Not even Miraden believed his own lie.

Kyradel dipped her hair into the jug filled with seawater. She struggled to run a bone comb through it and untangle the burned ends and knots but grew frustrated quickly. She took Miraden's cutting knife from a sheath on his belt and cut the tangles out. "You are not here for Ceychell?"

"Maybe at one point, but no longer," he said. He watched chunks of matted hair drop to the floor. He felt glad she was coherent enough to see through his ruse.

She stopped cutting her hair and looked at him in surprise. "How is that possible? You love her more than anything. That's all I used to hear."

"When did you hear that?" Miraden asked.

"Oh, Miraden. Don't think I didn't read every letter you gave her or that I didn't eavesdrop on your secret meetings in the forest. I was always there. You just didn't realize it because all you could see was her."

Miraden struggled to look at the pain in her eyes. It felt fresh as if it had just happened. Even after two years and this entire ordeal with the ashenkin, it was still fresh. She'd not spoken to him since that day. It was like he finally was tripped into the trap. His head sagged.

"You've always loved her, though I was the one who loved you."

Miraden remained silent, clenching his jaw at the bitter reminder. "I did. Yes, I did, but no more." He put his hand on her shoulder and squeezed gently. "I've sent a letter back to Kaehrn. Everyone will be so happy to hear you're alive."

Kyradel softened her expression. "All thanks to you."

"Thanks to me and many others… I left the morning you went missing. I just wish it hadn't taken me so long to find you."

Kyradel smiled again as she shook and struggled to keep her eyes open.

"Come now, Grazinya, you must let her rest. She needs my attention now," Gorgundi said.

Miraden stood up, nodded, then he left the hut.

He spent a few hours helping the islanders tend to the wounded and children. He had just finished stitching a head wound on a teenager when he heard Simigrin calling, "Miraden! Miraden!"

He saw her silhouette running toward him along the beach. He was looking right at the evening sun and shaded his eyes. As she broke into view, he sprung from his spot and ran to her.

She collided with him, and they embraced. Miraden squeezed her and nearly burst into tears. She ran her fingers along the scruff on his face.

Miraden pulled his fingers through her short hair and grinned.

"Do you like it?" she asked. "It was so burned I had to cut it. The people back home will think I'm married!"

Her hair felt so strange, running through his fingers.

"There is a strong tradition in my country. Women do not cut their hair, and I've never thought about doing it until I saw how singed it was. I am not sure—"

"I love it," Miraden whispered. "And I am so relieved to see you, so glad you're alive." What he wasn't expecting was seeing her nearly naked in the islanders' attire. He'd never seen her so clearly.

"As am I," she said. "I thought we were going to die." She leaned her head against his and closed her eyes. She ran her bandaged hands across his face.

"We survived," he said, "thanks to you."

"I couldn't break the medallion. You—"

Miraden kissed her. He held her close and felt so comfortable, like he was exactly where he should be, so far from home.

He broke off their kiss and opened his eyes. It was as if he looked into her eyes for the first time. They were amber like the sun. He loved her dark skin, dark as the earth and soft to the touch. "I told Gorgundi I'd help with the wounded. I'm having some trouble talking with the islanders."

"I'll help you," she said.

Night came, and Miraden's eyelids drooped. He sat in Gorgundi's hut next to Kyradel while she slept soundly. Gorgundi was less than six feet away, where he mixed a stew of roots and fish.

"Grazinya, how are the injured?"

"Much better now. They just need to keep from getting sand in their stitches."

Gorgundi tasted the stew and saw Miraden adjusting the reed blanket on Kyradel. "She is strong. She will heal in time."

"How long do you think before she can travel?" Miraden asked. "We live very far from here, and I promised her parents I'd bring her home safely."

"The spirits work on their own time," the shaman replied. "Could be a day or a month. I do not determine these things. Relax, now, you have earned it. Take it while you can." He smiled at Miraden.

"Thank you for helping her. And thank you for allowing us to stay as long as it takes."

Gorgundi nodded. "Of course, but, Grazinya, you have *much* to do."

Miraden was puzzled. "I plan to take Kyradel back to Kaehrn. That has always been my mission."

Gorgundi held his belly and let out a hearty laughter. "You cannot lie to Gorgundi. That was not your mission."

Miraden was insulted but realized he was hurt from the truth. Gorgundi was at least mostly right.

"This woman with the soul of fire you write to, she was your true quest, was she not?" Gorgundi asked, raising an eyebrow.

"She was," Miraden said and lowered his head.

"Grazinya, these things are your past, not your future. You have the gift. That gift is not hunting rabbits. Our entire world is in peril. Our world needs you."

"There must be others who can close the gates. If I died tomorrow, then what?"

"Such things are true, but you live. For now, enjoy my home, and let me help your companion so that she is fit to journey home with you. No more could be asked of her."

Miraden stepped out of the tent. His stomach rumbled, and his head spun. He looked up at the stars twinkling through the twilight. He used to stare at them when he lay upon the Kaehrnstone. His thoughts drifted to Ceychell, but he shook them off and started to follow his nose to the bonfire. There he saw Simigrin surrounded by the islanders. She was telling a story while the others ate dinner. He listened and got his fill of soup.

Sun warmed Miraden's face the next morning. He opened his eyes and felt the daggers shunt into his mind from a massive headache. He was lying on a reed mat not far from the embers of the bonfire. Simigrin lay on a mat next to him, still asleep. Thoughts of Gorgundi's words bounced in his head while he tried to remember the previous night. He wondered how Simigrin might feel about chasing the Ashengates. He wondered how she might feel about *him*.

"You drank too much last night," she mumbled, eyes still closed.

"Did I?" Miraden asked, but he was sure that was the case when his own voice thundered in the caverns of his skull.

"You did," she replied. "And it's still early. Why not lie here with me a little longer?"

Miraden sat up despite his world spinning. "I should probably—" he said, but when he felt her fingers rustling his hair, he changed his mind. She pulled him down onto her mat, crushed him against her chest. His previous thoughts vanished. His heart raced. Thoughts of her spun and spun until he closed his eyes and soon fell fast asleep.

THIRTY·ONE

THE BLOOM ON THE BATTLEFIELD

A DOZEN DAYS PASSED. THE kids were healing and able to help with the fishing. Miraden and Simigrin had helped clean them up, mended their wounds, even cut their nests of hair.

Miraden walked along the shore early in the morning.

"Hi, Miraden!" Kyradel said. She caught up to walk beside him. She was now wearing a grass top and skirt, like the other islanders. She limped, but her smile had returned.

Miraden kicked a clump of sand into the surf. He turned to her. "How are you feeling today?"

"Much better, thanks. I walked a bit yesterday, and I am only a little sore today. I can't wait to go home. I want to hug everyone in Kaehrn. I want to sit in my living room by the fire, drink tea, and listen to mom hum. I want—"

Miraden looked at her when she hesitated. He knew she was thinking about Ceychell.

"She misses you dearly. She missed you every day, long before all of this," Miraden said.

Kyradel looked down and kicked a shell near her feet. "I've missed her too. All of me died that day. The day I stopped loving my sister

274

and realized you would never love me. It was the day I drove a wedge between all of us… and I'm so sorry for that, Miraden. Truly I am."

Her words shocked him. Miraden was also so used to Kyradel's delicateness that he was ready to comfort her. Usually, she'd be crying, but her eyes only blinked. She didn't shed a tear.

"I am truly sorry too, Kyradel. You must know I never wanted to hurt you—" Miraden dipped his head. It was his deepest, most enduring regret, and it never healed. "I worried about you constantly. I left Kaehrn not knowing anything—where you were, if you were alive! Nothing. I'd never seen your father so frail… but when I turned and saw you in that prison, I was so happy you were still alive. But… I—"

"But you did it for Ceychell?" she asked.

Miraden flushed. "This is not about Ceychell at all. Many people, good people, died because of my decisions. My mission was to save you, no matter what, but the price others paid was high. Even in the devil's realm, I left Simigrin to fend for herself. I abandoned her to save *you*. I promised your family I would do whatever it takes."

Kyradel nodded, rebuked. "So… what will you do when we get home?"

"I'm not sure. I just want off this island as soon as you're feeling up to the journey. I am tired of sand in my boots and being trapped, being out in the open, being surrounded by water… everything."

Kyradel laughed. "You never were a very good swimmer. I remember Ceycha helping you out of the lagoon when we were kids. When the rope broke, do you remember?"

"You mean the day I almost drowned? How could I forget! I was swinging across the deep part to the shallow section you two were swimming in. I was going to splash you both, then the branch snapped."

"Oh yeah, it was the *branch*!" They laughed at the memory.

Miraden hadn't laughed in so long, and the gravity of his decision stilled his laughter. "I haven't fully decided what to do when I get home. I may turn right back around and hunt for the next Ashengate."

Kyradel's mouth fell open, and the pink left her face. "You mustn't! How could you leave home again? How could you leave us?"

"Why not?" he asked. The last thing he wanted was to return to his old life.

"You cannot leave Kaehrn again," she said, her smile fading. "You're our hero!" Her eyes watered as she stared at Miraden.

Miraden suddenly remembered the letter he had left under his pillow that he was going to give Kyradel. Had he delivered it a day earlier and left Kaehrn, she would be dead. "Perhaps my leaving will heal your bond with Ceychell."

"Don't you want to see her? Stay and be happy with Ceychell. You just can't leave us. Please, don't go. Please…"

Miraden noticed Simigrin approaching them and chose not to respond.

"Hello… I'm not interrupting, am I?" Simigrin asked. She smiled at Kyradel.

Miraden was certain Simigrin heard their last few comments.

"Not at all," Kyradel said. "I was telling Miraden that I can't wait to leave the island. We forest folk aren't meant for fishing and grass skirts." She grinned and glanced at Simigrin's skirt.

"I do love it here, but I know Miraden doesn't," Simigrin said and gently patted him on the shoulder. "And I should probably return to the university." She smiled at Kyradel. "How are you feeling today?"

"Better, thanks. Miraden was telling me how courageous you were in the Ashengate."

"I'm sure he left out that he saved my life a few times. Has he always been so modest?" Simigrin pulled her purple hair behind her ears, reaching for long hair that wasn't there.

Miraden clenched his jaw and tried not to stare at her. It was so unusual not to see her fully concealed.

"Not always," Kyradel said, returning Simigrin's smile. "Say, is it true that mages are born in the university? I read the mages of Kander never know a family life. Is that true?"

"It is true, and look at me now," she says with arms held out. "I am a mage without a book or staff! But I summon quite a dinner with my fishing pole."

Kyradel laughed. "Your skin is so tan and beautiful—you must not burn as I do. Isn't her skin beautiful, Miraden?"

Simigrin laughed. "I am not tan. I was born with dark skin. I am actually rarely exposed to the sun, but I burn like everyone else."

Kyradel laughed again. "This is what mages wear, is it?"

Miraden and Simigrin laughed.

"No, I wear a robe. I'm thankful one of the women in the village gave this to me." She spun, whirling her grass skirt. "Anyway, I am going to find some fruit. See you soon." She waved and walked toward the jungle, then turned. "Oh, Miraden, can you meet me at Gorgundi's hut in an hour?"

"Sure," Miraden said. Simigrin waved again.

Kyradel watched Miraden watch Simigrin walk away and whispered, "She certainly is cute, isn't she?" Miraden realized he was staring and looked out to sea. Kyradel laughed and continued, "That outfit doesn't leave much to wonder. I don't know how she doesn't come out of that top just walking."

"I haven't thought to ask her," Miraden said. "But you shouldn't talk about her like that."

"I'm just saying what I'm seeing. I know you're shy, Miraden, but it's okay. I bet you would love to cuddle up to those… and let her magic fingers run through your hair."

"That sounds like the Kyradel I remember," Miraden said with a grin, but it faded quickly.

"Yes. I am glad there is some of me left," she said.

"I… I am sorry. I didn't mean that."

"No, it's okay. I'm glad we can finally be honest with each other. Care for a walk before going to see Gorgundi?" she asked.

"Of course."

After walking around the island, Miraden left Kyradel at the soup fire, then continued to Gorgundi's large hut. He stepped inside. Simigrin was kneeling a few feet from Gorgundi. Between them was a large closed book.

Gorgundi waved him over.

Miraden walked closer, though he felt uneasy. He looked at the book, which reminded him a bit of Simigrin's spellbook but was far more gruesome. He could see heat radiating from it. The cover looked like a red stone with black symbols. He couldn't read it and had no interest in what it might say.

Miraden sat next to Simigrin and said, "What is that?"

"I found it on the altar. From their realm. I've never seen a spellbook like this in Kander."

"Wh— wouldn't a fire mage have a book like that?" he asked.

"There are no more fire mages. The last one vanished years ago."

"This book—it holds all dark secrets," Gorgundi whispered. "I dare not open it."

"Should we destroy it?" Miraden asked. He wasn't sure if that was possible.

"Such a thing kept in such a place means the graja do not want us to have it. This book"—he held his hand over it—"it is a weapon. A weapon of great power, but a power we should not use."

"I will bring it back to my order," Simigrin said. "Some of the most brilliant minds live in Kander. They will know what to do."

Miraden stared at it and wanted to throw it in the sea where no one could ever find it again. He didn't think it belonged in this world. He stood up and backed away and placed his hand on Hellshy. "Keep that out of sight. It will attract them," he said.

Simigrin lifted and slid the book inside her enchanted sack.

THIRTY·TWO

HOMEWARD BOUND

ON A BRIGHT SUNNY MORNING two weeks later, Miraden stood on the shore next to Simigrin and Kyradel. Dozens of children gathered near Kyradel, and two held her hands. They watched a ship approaching from the horizon. It was larger than any ship he'd seen with a tall mast and furled sail. Oars slowly rose and plunged back into the water, bringing the ship toward the island. They dropped anchor a quarter mile out and lowered two small boats into the water staffed by two oarsmen, who paddled them toward the island.

Every man, woman, and child of the village came out to see them off. The island children jumped and shouted happily, and the villagers stood smiling with gifts of food and water. Miraden was proud to have helped them, and strangely, he was sad to leave such beautiful people.

Gorgundi had a hearty grin as he walked over to Miraden. In his hand was Simigrin's sack. "Grazinya, I wish you great luck. The spirits are with you, and so am I and my people. Should you ever need of me, cut your hand with this in a safe place." Gorgundi handed Miraden a small devil claw painted white and ornamented with red beads and blue-green feathers. Miraden placed the gift in a new side bag of woven palm leaves, then extended his hand to shake. Gorgundi's long arms grabbed him like a sea monster and pulled him into a firm embrace. "You family now, boy, we do not shake hands on the islands, only with strangers. We do not shake their hands either." He burst into laughter. "Go now. Remember what it is you must do."

Gorgundi looked at Simigrin and spoke to her in his language. She listened, accepted her bag with a smile, and tied it to her skirt waistband. She looked back to Miraden without a word, then gazed out at sea. Their escorts greeted them with a hearty hello and asked them if they were ready to go home. The children cheered and rushed the boats.

Two days later, the ship reached the dock in Crestain. The children ran down the ramp and onto the pier. Fishermen, merchants, artisans, and passersby all stood in shock then started to cheer. A gathering of guards and armed men in leather with yellow sashes on their arms called the children over.

Miraden stood on the dock with Simigrin and Kyradel. He stared at the Henslemen, now corralling with the children, looking for Neandra, but he didn't see him. He wanted to get a closer look.

"The captain said we have two hours before they set sail south to Kander Bondare," Miraden told his two companions. "I don't know about both of you, but I'm willing to spend it on land."

"Can we go to a tailor?" Simigrin asked. "I feel... I feel very exposed here."

Miraden nodded. They hurried off; the citizens didn't seem to care to stop them.

"You need fresh clothes as well," Miraden told Kyradel.

"I don't know. I kind of like my outfit," Kyradel said.

"I can't wear these now that we are off the island," Simigrin said. "Even if I do look *cute*." She winked at Kyradel.

Simigrin adjusted her top, and Kyradel smirked and asked, "How did you run and battle wearing that?"

"I didn't. My robes burned to shreds, along with five feet of my hair!"

"By the gods! You had five feet of hair?" Kyradel shouted.

Simigrin grinned. "Yes, five feet. I woke up to an islander poking me with a stick. Apart from my vambraces and bag, there was hardly a thread on my body. I almost passed back out from shame!"

They stopped at a clothing shop, and Miraden gave them coins and waited outside.

Kyradel came out quickly with a thick green dress, black thigh boots, and a dusky coat. She handed a few coins back to Miraden. "Why don't you go in and help her get something to wear? She might need it," she said.

Miraden looked over and found Kyradel fluttering her eyes.

Miraden grinned and crossed his arms. He'd missed Kyradel's constant flirting.

"Already did. I got her those vambraces."

"Too bad you didn't buy her a matching brassiere. That's what she needed."

"They were all out," Miraden said and rubbed his hand along the side of his chin where a burn was still tender.

"I suppose they would need a lot of silver to cover those—"

Simigrin came out in a dark-blue, hooded robe. Kyradel stopped mid-sentence and broke into a toothy grin.

"You look… nice?" Kyradel said. "Definitely subtler."

Simigrin shrugged but leaned her head back so they could see her smile. Without another word, they returned to the ship.

THIRTY·THREE

THE VOYAGE SOUTH

FIVE DAYS PASSED AT SEA on route to Kander Bondare. Miraden spent most of his time hanging over the rail and avoiding everyone else. He hoped whatever his path would be after this passage, it would require no more sea travel. Kyradel's singing helped. Her songs also soothed the sailors, the few remaining children riding to Kander Bondare, even the windstorm. One of the sailors gave her a guitar, which she played beautifully. Simigrin remained below deck in one of the very few cabins, which she shared with Kyradel.

Miraden was overjoyed to know he'd be arriving at Kander Bondare the following morning. He wouldn't be more than a week's walk from home, and that gave him a lot of hope. The night was as black as the Father of Darkness. The stars sparkled on the water. The current was so calm it seemed like they were sailing through a vast twinkling blackness. The slapping of water against the hull was the only sound. He sat on a chock quietly. He was anxious—he was just ready to be done with the voyage.

He felt a hip bump and scooted over to make room for her to sit down. She pulled her hood back and grinned.

"You okay?" she asked.

"I will definitely be okay tomorrow," he answered.

Simigrin nodded. "I cannot wait to see the mountains, to see my home. From the moment we stood in the center of Arrowheart Lake, I thought for sure I would never set foot in the university again."

"I can understand that, for sure," he said. He'd made many poor decisions along the way, and that was a big one. If Lovo was watching him from the afterlife, Miraden hoped the unlucky cleric had forgiven him.

"But I will," Simigrin continued. "I'll get to study in the Magister's Grand Library. I'll practice in the Summoner's Alcove, and I will have the privilege to enjoy the enlightenment of Kander once again. And… it's because of you."

"What are you going to say when people ask you about your hair?" Miraden's heart pounded as he realized he had asked the stupidest question possible.

She shrugged and ran her fingers through her short locks. "I'll tell them a commoner took it…" She looked at him. "I'll tell them he took my locks and this." She placed her hand on his and lifted his palm onto her chest, and he felt her heartbeat.

Miraden was still. Simigrin leaned in to kiss him, and he enjoyed every second, wished it would never end. He'd not felt happy in so long it seemed like a dream. Everything was calm as he held her and kissed her. She pulled him in closer, and they held each other for a long moment.

At last, they parted lips and opened their eyes. He looked into her amber eyes; they shined with the starlight like shimmering pools. She was mysterious and deep and intrigued him more each day. He was thankful he'd finally gotten to know his companion better after they closed the Ashengate.

"I'll see you in the morning," she whispered and returned below deck. Miraden slid down and leaned back against the chock, closed his eyes, and smiled.

He woke the next morning and went up to sit on the chock he had sat on the previous night. He thought about the hard decisions he'd made and would still have to make. He felt no closer to knowing his own mind when the faint image of a cliff broke through the morning sea mist. Bells rang from a distant harbor.

As they sailed through the fog, the large sprawling city of Bondare appeared around a misty cove. From shore to mountain, it lay. Long trails wound up into the hills from the great cliff base and disappeared in the fog where Kander rested at the top. Miraden could hardly wait to visit the two cities.

When they reached the pier, Miraden and his companions prepared to leave. Many of the sailors held their hats to their chests and stared at Kyradel with puppy love in their eyes.

Kyradel waved to them, and then the three companions descended the ramp to the docks.

Simigrin pointed to where the mountains disappeared into the clouds. "My order is up in Kander, the city in the sky. You should be able to find someone willing to transport you to Baregorin Forest down here in Bondare."

"Do you know Bondare very well?" Miraden asked.

"Not really. I occasionally come down here on errands, but we have our servants run for goods most of the time. Most of this city is nomadic, so plenty of travelers come and go, and very few live here year-round. We in Kander have a saying that our economy flows out of the mountain." She pointed to a large opening in the mountain's base where a thousand tents and a hundred caravans stood. "That is called the Corral. It is where many travelers meet."

Miraden and Kyradel looked at the Corral. He saw dozens of horse-drawn wagons and hoped one could be persuaded to give them a ride home.

"Then that is where I will go," Miraden said.

Kyradel hugged Simigrin. "Thank you so much for helping rescue me. It was lovely meeting you," she said.

Simigrin nodded and squeezed Kyradel's hands. Then Kyradel stepped back and let Miraden say goodbye.

Miraden stared into her hood, met her eyes, and felt at peace. He already missed her. He wanted to ask her to follow him to Kaehrn but figured she wouldn't.

"Here," Simigrin said and removed a tied scroll from her bag. "Gorgundi told me to give this to you when we parted. I didn't read it, in case you're wondering. It smells like it's from someone pretty…"

Miraden took the scroll and immediately smelled the limebloom. He dismissed the urge to return to childhood memories and pushed it into his bag. Then he reached out and grasped the silver vambraces on her slender arms. Her hands gripped his forearms, and he didn't want her to let go. He was quite fond of his quiet companion.

"Thank you for everything, Miraden," she said. "Not only have you done a wonderful thing for this world, but for me as well. My master will be very pleased with my progress—" She choked up. Miraden's eyes watered. Her chin trembled for a few moments before she continued, "Hopefully, it will help him overlook my lost spellbook."

Miraden swallowed a lump in his throat, and she said, "He might make an exception. One tome for each gate closed." They both laughed their tears away for a moment. He reached up and wiped the tears from her cheeks. "I plan to train and meditate a while here but not for long. I will focus on the next gate, should you…"

Miraden hugged her tight. They held on silently for a moment, then released each other.

Miraden felt the lump in his throat again. "Take care of yourself, Simigrin. We shall meet again."

She placed her hand on his jaw and ran her thumb over the burn scar on his chin. "Until we meet again," she said. She turned and walked toward a dirt path that zigzagged up the mountain.

Miraden stared for some time, and the longer he did, the greater he regretted not following her. He missed her and knew she was already missing him. But he also knew he could not follow her. Not yet. He had to get Kyradel home first.

THIRTY·FOUR

FINDING THE CAUSE

ORMUS AND CEYCHELL WADED THROUGH the snow early on a brisk afternoon. The wind was calm, air with a biting chill. The bright sun shined through the frozen forest and glistened on the freshly fallen snow. Their snowshoes crunched on the fresh powder, a rhythmic crunch, crunch, crunch.

Occasionally, Ceychell stopped and dug out winter roots from beneath the snow. Ormus waited for her. She looked back and saw him smiling. She figured he was just happy to be up and walking. She enjoyed spending time with him like they used to. Since he'd gotten better, he'd walked with her each day while she harvested.

"Ceychell?" he said.

She pulled down her hood and let her long locks tumble down the back of her robe. She wiped the sweat from her brow; Miraden's robe was almost too warm for chores. "Yes, father?"

"Soon, Kyradel will be returning, and we will have to be very supportive of her. She will need our love to heal from this terrible experience."

Ceychell nodded, placed a root in her bag, and they continued tramping over the snow back to her shop. "I know. I pray she will have a normal life after this."

"All we can do is help her find peace here in Kaehrn. I would have never dreamed her life would take a turn like this, but I hope it will bring the two of you back together."

Ceychell suppressed her tears. "I know. I would love nothing more than to have my sister back."

Ormus unslung his wineskin, took a hearty drink of hot spiced spirits, and then handed the skin to Ceychell. "Yes, and… of course, Miraden will be returning with her."

Her father's mention of his name made her uneasy. His tone was expectant, and she was unsure about what he might ask of her.

"The boy is a hero," he continued. "I never even expected him to make it to Bilore Des. Yet, he trekked through the darkest corners of the world to keep his promise. I've sent notice to Bilore Des, Oddion, and Crestain to honor him."

Ceychell stopped walking and turned to her father. "I— I can't believe it myself." But she couldn't bring herself to say what she really thought. It was too painful, and saying the words would only breathe life into the problem. This time, she would not be selfish for Miraden.

Ormus placed his hand on his daughter's shoulder. "I have never meddled in your business, but I must know…" Ceychell wanted to stop him, but she was too curious what he might ask. He looked her in the eyes and said, "What will you do when he returns?"

Ceychell sighed. She fiddled with the ring Miraden had given her. She thought of the letters, the tokens, the resentment. "I would hold him, tell him everything, listen to everything he has to say… I would thank him. I would spend my life trying to make his better… if he would let me…"

"You are indentured to no one, not even Miraden. But you speak as if you cannot do these things—"

"Because I have lost him."

"Ceychell, I do not think Miraden would—"

"We don't know what he thinks!" she shouted and dropped the sack onto the snow. "He has risked his life for Kyradel, and I couldn't even be bothered to send him anything but a selfish request to help you. He must think me a monster far worse than any he faced beyond the Ashengate."

"Now, you know that's not true. I've seen that boy adore you with love—"

"He's not a boy, and that love is gone! I would be amazed if he did not return with Simigrin by his side!"

"I don't know who Simigrin is, and you are not a—"

"A hero? I'm just a village alchemist, and a cook, and most of all, a terrible friend to Miraden. You asked me what I would do. I will probably beg his forgiveness and live a life of regret. Hopefully, one day, he will find it in his heart to forgive—" Her flustered face froze as she stared at her shop.

"What is it?" Ormus asked.

Ceychell shuffled through the snow, and Ormus picked up her bag and followed her. She hurried until she reached her bedroom window. There were black marks on the wood below her window, just above the snow. She carefully pushed the snow away and uncovered a pattern she didn't recognize, but someone drew it.

"What is that? I've never seen anything like it," Ormus said.

Ceychell rubbed her finger on it, and the mark smudged purple on her glove. She turned slowly to her father, who returned a wide-eyed stare.

"Come with me," she said. It was growing dark. And she knew she must hurry. They went into her shop, and she closed the door. She lit a single candle and took her father through the shop. She opened a cabinet and withdrew the charcoal stick Vera had dropped. She drew a line on her counter, then smeared it.

"It's purple, the same as below your window," Ormus said.

"Yes," Ceychell whispered. "The same as below Kyradel's and Kjod's, too, though theirs was mostly wiped away. But whatever this *is*, it doesn't wash away easily."

Ormus examined the stick and handed it back to her. "This cannot mean—"

"It means we should be prepared because ashenkin could be coming to visit me tonight."

That night, Ceychell lay in her bed with her eyes closed. She thought of Miraden and Kyradel and couldn't wait to see them. She imagined cooking for them and hearing their stories. She imagined their arrival again, and again, and again until she heard her window open.

Ceychell sweated. She felt her skin buzz and started to shake. A gentle, cold breeze entered the room. Her hands trembled on two long daggers under her blanket as she tried to remain perfectly still. She felt a heat in her chest grow and a strength within, just wanting to be unleashed.

From the corner of her eye, she saw an ashenkin climb up on the sill, then another pop up behind it. They silently climbed on the sill, and both crept onto the dresser below the window. She waited... one... two... three...

"Now!"

Bows twanged, arrows whistled over Ceychell's bed. The two ashenkin howled as the arrows pierced their skin. One took arrows in the eye and chest, the other in the neck and forehead. She leaned up and stared at the monsters as they clutched at the arrows and toppled over onto the floor. She watched them twitch, scrabble their sharp claws, and bleed sizzling black blood on the floor. She climbed out from under the covers, bent over them, and slit both their throats. They stopped twitching.

Ormus, Bryndyke, Chandar, and Elonor's husband, Tip, stood

up and stepped out from behind the bed. Ormus hugged Ceychell while the other men retrieved their arrow shafts from the bodies of the ashenkin.

Ormus and the other men followed Ceychell when she stormed out her door and walked through town in the middle of the night. Bryndyke carried the body of one ashenkin and Chandar the other. The men were rattled but encouraged by their victory. The men didn't question where they were going. They only tried to keep up with Ceychell.

Ceychell stopped in front of a quiet home. "Break the door down," she commanded.

Ormus nodded. Tip slammed his ax over and over against the barred door, and Ormus kicked it open. Ceychell stepped in to find Vera sitting in a chair by the fire with her back to the door. The old woman didn't turn to look at them as they entered the house and Bryndyke and Chandar dumped the ashenkin bodies on the floor.

Ceychell walked over to face her, but Vera refused to look up at her. Ceychell tossed the char marker onto the blanket on Vera's lap.

"Thought you might need this back," she said. Her face was stone, and her posture tall. She looked down at Vera and held the bloody dagger to her side.

"Do what you must," Vera said.

"I will, but not until I know why," Ceychell said. "Restrain her. I don't know what other witchcraft she possesses."

The villagers grabbed Vera's arms and tied her to the chair. Vera simply laughed.

"Why have you been summoning these devils?" Ceychell roared. "Tell me now!"

When Vera stayed quiet, Ormus drew his sword and placed it at her neck.

"Like the Ashengates," Vera said, "there are many like me in this world."

"Why did you take Kyradel and the others? Tell me!" Ceychell said and stepped closer.

The glow of the fireplace cast dark shadows on Vera's deeply wrinkled face. "Don't take it personally… or perhaps *you* should take it personally. Kyra was a sweet girl but watching you break down was a joy. So, she had to go first. You're next." Vera laughed as Ceychell brought the dagger to her throat.

"Kyra is on her way home. So is Miraden. I won't be going anywhere."

"One of you will die—" Vera stopped as she stared into Ceychell's eyes that burned. "No, you can't, I didn't realize—"

Ceychell cut her throat.

"Tip, Chandar, search the house," Ormus said, sheathing his sword. "I want this place turned upside down. Bring anything suspicious to us. Then we will burn this place to the ground with these things and her in it."

Ceychell sat beside the Statue of the Huntsman at the village center early in the morning. She waited for a bat to arrive, just as she had each day for weeks. She was cold and pulled Miraden's robe tighter around her. She could still smell the smoldering ruins of Vera's house.

At last, Ceychell saw a shadow flit across the snow. She looked up and saw a black speck flying above the treetops. She jumped to her feet as the bat spiraled down toward her, grasped the same branch near the statue, and hung there upside-down. Ceychell had a letter prepared and opened the scroll case. A letter and a smaller note slid out into her hand. She placed her letter inside the case and closed it. The bat screeched when Ceychell petted it.

Villagers saw the bat and gathered around her. Ceychell opened the letter.

Ceychell,

I'm happy to tell you Kyradel is doing much better, thanks to Gorgundi and the islanders who have seen to it. Over a hundred children survived and are with us here now.

Gorgundi sent a messenger to Crestain to return with a ship to bring everyone back to the mainland, where I'll buy passage by ship to Kander Bondare, then head north along the road to Kaehrn. It is the safest journey for Kyradel and hopefully will allow us to return without incident.

I hope your father is much better.

Miraden

The short note made Ceychell's eyes water, but she rolled it up and was happy nonetheless. The villagers stood staring at her, waiting for her to say something, so she told them, "Kyradel and Miraden are coming home in a few weeks!"

The villagers cheered.

"Hello? Miraden is coming here?" She didn't recognize the man's voice. The crowd parted for a large man with short blond hair. White pelts covered the tall and broad man, and at his side hung a silver mace. His brown eyes were kind and curious. "I'm sorry, did you say Miraden?"

Ceychell turned to face him. "Hello, stranger, who are you?"

"I'm Lovo. I was looking for Kaehrn and thought I might find Miraden—"

Ceychell charged and embraced him. She crushed him with her

hug and felt his large arms hug her back.

She reached up and touched his face. "You… you died," she whispered.

"I am luckier than that," he said with a wink. "You must be Ceychell."

She nodded. "I am."

"Wow, Miraden sure missed you. I bet you must be as happy as I am to hear he's coming home."

Ceychell smiled and then pulled his arm. "Please, you must be hungry. I want to hear everything."

Ceychell cooked a large meal for Lovo and offered him freshly brewed cider. He made short order of it, cleaning his plate.

"My, you are quite the cook!" he said.

"Thank you, I have been wanting to ask you…" she started. The anticipation of it killed her.

"How I'm alive?" he said.

"I am sorry, it's just—"

Lovo held up his hand. "I wouldn't tell just anyone, but I know I can trust you. I remember falling into the lake. The ice went right to my bones, and I couldn't hear or think. I paddled and felt fur and water and knew I was going to die. The last thing I remember was that I knew I had saved Miraden and Simi. I was happy I could give them a chance. Then I fell asleep."

Ceychell's eyes were wide. She was stiff listening to his story.

Lovo's smile faded. He stared through the table for a moment. His eyes began watering and fingers shook beside his plate. "I remember being held and warm. I couldn't see but heard a voice. It was soft. She said my sacrifice and the deeds of my friends earned me a second chance. I didn't want to leave, but I woke up, right on the shore of the lake."

"You just came back to life?" she blurted.

"I think so, not sure really. I was dry and wearing these. They look like they're made from the wolves that chased me. I really don't know how long I was gone. Miraden and Simigrin were gone. The lake was frozen solid, and I just wasn't sure where to look. So I came looking for Kaehrn. I knew if he was successful, he'd bring Kyradel back." Lovo wiped the tears on the back of his large hand.

"You were right. Your sacrifice did save them, and they closed an Ashengate because of it. I'm thankful for you and so happy you're here. Miraden will be thrilled to see you."

THIRTY·FIVE

THE FINAL LETTER

MIRADEN AND KYRADEL WALKED THROUGH small encampments, trading posts, pack merchants, and fences selling anything they could get their hands on. They arrived at the Corral, sprawling out the mouth of the cave. The entrance ceiling stood nearly a hundred feet above them, gaping and partially filled with smoke from cooking fires. They were in the middle of a bazaar of traders in tents. Races of people, some Miraden could not identify, bartered and hollered and waved goods at one another.

After an hour of talking to traveling merchants, Miraden spotted the old ore merchant, Sulover, next to his cart. The elder was hunkered over his gut, lifting a large rock that had fallen off the back of it.

"Why, hello, Miraden and Kyradel. What brings you down to Bondare?" he asked.

"It's a long story. Could I tell you on the journey north?" Miraden asked and handed him the last of his coins. Sulover smiled and pointed for them to jump in the cart.

Three days passed while Miraden and Kyradel rode in the back of Sulover's cart. They had put some blankets over the rocks, which still wasn't very comfortable, but it was faster than walking. They rode over the snow and huddled under a warm blanket.

Miraden couldn't believe he was finally returning home with Kyradel, but she was still quieter than usual. She hummed a lot but otherwise seemed lost in her thoughts.

He was still unsure about opening the letter. He thought about just tossing it on the road behind them and forgetting about it. He feared what it might say, feared it could sadden him or, worse, send him into a rage. Why would it come now? So close to the end of his journey.

The thought of the letter gnawed at him for hours while he listened to the creak of the wagon wheels on the bumpy road, the crunching of wheels over snow, and the horse's hooves crushing the fresh powder. He finally gave in to temptation, drew the letter from his pouch, pulled the green ribbon free, and unrolled it.

Sweet Miraden,

I pray that this letter succeeds in finding you though the others have failed.

I am sorry for not thanking you when you left to find Kyradel.

I am sorry for never showing you the kindness you so often showed me.

I am sorry for ignoring you at Valdenfest year after year.

I am sorry for not thanking you for saving me from the razorback bear near Preyno.

I am sorry for not kissing you after you spent half a day cleaning the skunk musk out of my hair.

I am sorry for not kissing you after you helped me with chores.

I am sorry for not being a better friend to you all these years.

I am sorry for not making tea for you when you were sick.

I am sorry for not reading your letters enough, though I read them every day.

I am sorry, so so so very sorry for what happened to Stormrange. I couldn't believe Hydracks killed him, and I cried for days after I buried him.

I am sorry for Lovo. He sounded like a great companion and a kind man.

I am sorry Neandra betrayed you and me. I hope I find him before you do...

I am sorry you ever had to go on this terrible journey, one I think was fueled by your love for me. A love I did not appreciate.

I am sorry for not telling my sister that I loved you, forcing you to break her heart, and then breaking yours.

I am sorry I never told you that I loved you when you kissed me so long ago.

I think of you every day, and I like to imagine that I am on your journey, comforting you, being there to help you. I hoped that my prayers found you each night and that my warm thoughts would help protect you from the cold. When I finally realized how selfless you are and how much I love you, I changed. I've been so miserable for the past few years since that day I lost Kyra to your kiss. I wish I could take back all my cruel words and actions—but I cannot.

You're probably traveling with Simigrin and Kyradel soon. I hope my sister is doing better, and I look forward to meeting Simigrin. She sounds wonderful. You're lucky to have met her. I wished it would have been me who journeyed with you to the Ashengates, but I know I wouldn't have had the courage. Know that my love for you is true, but do not let it sway you. If you return to Kaehrn and have nothing left but resentment for me, I will accept it.

You are a hero, Miraden. I can never thank you enough for all you have done for my family and me.

All my love,
Ceychell

Miraden's hands trembled; he could barely roll up the letter. He wanted to crush it. He wanted to cry. A cruel joke befouled him, and there must be a god laughing so hard at Miraden's folly.

He stared off the back of the cart at the long trail through the snow. The letter shook in his gloved hand.

Miraden wasn't sure what it meant to him. For so long, he'd wanted to hear her words more than anything in life. He'd repressed his thoughts of her and tried not to think about what he would say when he saw her.

"What did she say?" Kyradel asked.

Miraden didn't answer at first. He lay against the covered ore pile and pulled the blanket over his chest. He felt the snow on his face and took a few calming breaths.

Then he choked out, "She said she's sorry."

END OF BOOK ONE

CEYCHELL'S CINDERS

CHAPTER ONE: REUNITED AT LAST

THE SUN BEAMED THROUGH CEYCHELL'S window, warming her store. Though she'd slept soundly since hearing the news, she awoke early each morning excited that today would be the day Kyradel and Miraden returned home. She brushed her auburn hair with a copper comb and pulled it into intricate braids. She admired how long and lush her hair had grown over the years.

It still didn't seem real that Kyradel was coming home. She had been taken by the ashenkin several months ago, and Ceychell had slowly begun to accept that her sister was gone. The sister she had been inseparable from for most of her childhood. The sister with a song in her voice that could make the flowers bloom. The sister that would no longer sing for the forest and the birds and the mountains. Everything would be grayer, duller, and uglier with her sister being silenced forever.

Then the young man she loved left to save her. Miraden, the young ranger, wanted nothing more than to share time with Ceychell. He wanted nothing more than to love her. She ignored his love and him for so long, for something so stupid, she hated herself for it.

But she hoped all of that was about to change. If Miraden got her final letter, it would mean the difference.

She was eager to see him, but she couldn't help but feel she'd lost him all over again. Worse yet, to Simigrin, his *lovely* and brave companion. Simigrin sounded too perfect, she couldn't blame him if her fears were true.

Miraden would be thrilled to find out that Lovo had survived his freezing plunge into Arrowheart Lake. Lovo showed up in Kaehrn looking for him just a few weeks ago and had been helping her brew her potions and chop firewood. He'd also helped out with smelting ore at Bryndyke's forge. Lovo's much friendlier than she thought he'd be. Always happy to pitch in and never complained. It was nice having him around, a wonderful reminder that Miraden was on his way home.

Regardless, time crept along slowly. It had been nearly a month since she last heard from Miraden after he closed the Ashengate and saved Kyradel. It was the single greatest thing she'd heard in her life, but every hour since had felt like a year as she waited and watched for Kyradel and Miraden to walk out of the forest and into Kaehrn's town square. She hoped that all would be forgiven between the three of them.

And then at last, on a warm morning in early spring… she heard yelling from the road. It grew louder.

"They're here!" someone yelled.

The comb fell from her hand. She grabbed her fur coat and dashed out of her cabin shop and into melting snow.

The entire village had gathered around Sulover's ore cart. As she approached, Kyradel darted out of the crowd into the arms of her mother and father.

Ceychell covered her mouth and dropped to her knees. The gods had mercy and her sister was home again, saved from the clutches of the ashenkin. Tears ran down Ceychell's face. She picked herself up and ran, slipping and sliding through the snow, and crashed into her sister. They held each other so tight. Ceychell cried, so happy was she to hold Kyradel after all this time. Two years had passed since she last hugged her sister. That lost time hurt, but the worst was the last six months since Kyradel was taken. She looked up at the sky and thanked the gods that her prayers had been answered.

Kyradel cried, too. Her fiery hair was cut shoulder-length, loose and messy. Ceychell could feel her sister's bones through her clothes. The puffiness in her cheeks was gone, neck was thinner, and collar was exposed. She looked frail like a bird.

Ceychell smiled and brushed tears from her eyes. She couldn't help herself and wiped a smudge of dirt from Kyradel's cheek.

"I thought I'd lost you for good," Ceychell wheezed. "I'm so happy you're home." She embraced her sister again and kissed her cheeks.

Kyra cried in her arms. "Me too. I never thought I'd see you again."

Ceychell's heart nearly stopped when Miraden stepped out from behind the cart. His rusty hair was nearly shoulder-length, and almost wavy. He had a scruffy beard she'd never seen before. He stared at her, his deep brown eyes bloodshot and misty. She lost her breath and thought for a moment that she might faint.

Miraden looked over at her father, Ormus, and reached out to shake his hand, but Ormus grabbed him and pulled him into a monstrous bear hug. Miraden looked like a small child in her father's arms. She never thought she'd see the day her father would hug him.

Curasca, her mother, reached out and wrapped her arms around Kyradel and Ceychell. She was crying tears of joy. She put both hands on Kyradel's face and kissed her forehead.

"My baby girl is home. Gods be praised."

Ormus released Miraden and pulled Kyradel carefully into a hug. Ceychell had never seen her father cry with such happiness as he gently squeezed Kyradel.

"Thank you," Ormus whispered over and over to Miraden.

Miraden nodded and turned toward Ceychell. Despite her tears, she calmly stared back at him. She wanted to run into his arms; she wanted to be swept away and told that all was forgiven.

At last, Curasca pulled Kyradel into a hug again to give Ceychell and Miraden some space. Ceychell abandoned her pride and ran to Miraden. She hugged him with every ounce of her strength. They both cried. Ceychell brushed his long rusty hair back, stared into his sandy brown eyes, and rubbed his stubbled cheek. She wanted to tell him how much she loved him, how much she'd always loved him, but instead, she whispered into his ear, "I am so sorry… for everything. I'm so happy you're home."

Miraden looked down, seemed distant, lost in thought. It was something she'd never seen in him. For a moment, she felt like she didn't recognize him. She finally raised his chin to look into his eyes and he came back to her. She saw a glimmer of the affection he'd always shown her since they were children.

"Perhaps Miraden can join us for breakfast. Someone special is waiting for him," Curasca said.

Ceychell was anticipating what Miraden might do when he sees his former companion, who Miraden thought drowned in Arrowheart Lake. The old Miraden would have screamed and ran thinking Lovo had risen from the dead—she was curious what the new Miraden will do.

"I…" Miraden hesitated.

Ceychell took his hand in both of hers. It was rough, dirty, and cold. "Please, Miraden," Ceychell whispered.

His eyes widened. "The robe… you… found it."   "Yes, I love it. It's so perfect down to every detail," she said hugging the garment around herself. They walked together to her parent's house.

The rush of heat from the hearth and the smell of cider and baked bread rekindled so many memories for Miraden. It helped him briefly forget his treacherous journey. He ran his right hand along the top of a couch with a warm brown blanket. The fireplace was burning hot where he could feel it on his face, just how he liked it. He wanted to dive under a blanket and slip into a long nap after the cold ride on the back of Sulover's cart for the last week.

One brown and one golden dog greeted Miraden and Kyradel with barking and whimpering. Miraden petted them eagerly, including the finicky gray tabby cat that tried to ignore him and prance over to Kyradel.

"Miraden!" Lovo shouted and held out his arms.

Miraden jolted so hard he almost knocked over Ceychell. "Lovo!" Miraden broke down immediately. It just couldn't be true. He watched his friend die—it was like a grinning specter had returned to haunt him. He couldn't speak and before he could crumple in disbelief, Lovo grabbed him in a bearhug. Lovo was real and just like Miraden remembered him. Like a blonde ogre.

"I missed you, buddy," Miraden sobbed, struggling to breathe. "You, you"—

"I missed you too," Lovo said, "but it's breakfast time, let's talk about it later."

Curasca brought Miraden a winter greens salad, two freshly cooked eggs, and a chunk of warm bread. It was the finest meal he'd had in months. He sat next to Lovo, whose plate was loaded near to toppling with eggs, greens, winter squash and bread with a layer of preserves. Ceychell leaned over Miraden from behind and placed a hot cup of juno in front of him, a dusting of cinnamon floating at the top. The smell was intoxicating; oh, how he'd missed it. He picked it up and took a whiff of the bitter juno and enjoyed the warm steam on his face. Ceychell ran her hand along his back as she sat down next to him. Curasca grinned and passed her some bread.

Miraden desperately wanted to ask Lovo what happened. He

knew something unexplainable, perhaps divine saved him. No one could have survived that plunge. He stared into space for a moment and vividly remembered watching the shifting ice and the stilling water on Lake Arrowheart with Simigrin until it was too dark to see anymore. For the moment, he didn't question it. He was so grateful to see his friend… who just ate an entire egg in one bite.

Miraden ate but said nothing. He'd always wanted to share a warm breakfast with Ceychell and her family, but never did. Curasca had often sent him home with bread or a pie when he finished a few chores for them, but he'd never shared meals with them.

He wanted to savor it, wanted to melt away and just be happy he was home in Kaehrn, but he felt forlorn. He wasn't even sure why. He got up without a word, left the table, and went to sit by the fireplace alone with the warm cup of juno Ceychell made for him. It was extra rich without milk, exactly how he liked it. He'd forgotten how good it tasted. It still didn't feel real to be back in Kaehrn. He stared out through a frosty window at his village. He could even see his little cabin in the woods over a snow drift and down the shoveled path.

"Here, son," Ormus said, stepping up next to him and offering him a metal flask. Ceychell's father was nearly two heads taller than Miraden and broad-shouldered. The sickness he caught took a toll, his shirt was loose and the belt was much tighter. Miraden had never seen him so thin.

Ormus never called him son, so he was thrown off guard by his comment and the offer. Ormus had mostly shooed him away before his adventure. Miraden took a hearty sip that burned his throat in a good way… or at least a way he had started to tolerate. He nodded and handed the flask back to Ormus, who sat down next to him. He couldn't recall the last time he sat next to Ormus like this.

"I know that look," Ormus said and looked out the window, too. "I know it all too well." He exhaled a heavy sigh.

"I'm not sure what you mean," Miraden said.

"That's a look of having seen far beyond your home, being changed by the risks you've taken and the mistakes you made. It's the look of someone who is no longer a boy. You've seen what torments this world, and by the gods, you found a way to beat them."

Miraden grabbed the poker next to the fireplace and stirred a few coals. He said, "I have closed one gate. I have no idea how many exist, but I know there are more. I... I am not even sure if they all close the same way."

Ormus sighed again and nodded. "Representatives from Storjn and Valijn, Adolehrn and Bilore Des are coming here soon to seek your wisdom. You have had a difficult journey, and I don't want to forestall your needed rest. If you want, I can relay your story to them so you can have some peace before you decide what you are going to do."

"What do you mean?" Miraden asked, a bit surprised.

"I know what's weighing on your mind, Miraden. It is a heavy burden, and I'm sorry, after all you've done, that you must carry it. But always remember this, as long as my family is in Kaehrn, you will have a place to come home to."

GET A FREE WORLD MAP AND THE FIRST THREE CHAPTERS OF THE SEQUEL IN THE HER SOUL OF FIRE SERIES.

I love writing. I really love worldbuilding, but what I love most is when people enjoy my stories. I want to stay in touch with you, not to send you spam, but to make sure that if you like my stories, that you get notified whenever I release a new book or have something special to send to my mailing list community.

I would like to share the world map with you. Also, as you can imagine, I'm working on the next book in the series and have a good deal of it written. As a member of my mailing list, I'd love to share part of it to give YOU insight on what's to come!

So, if you sign up for my mailing list at **jvfahl.com/#newsletter**, I'll send you this free stuff:

1. A map of the world in the *Her Soul of Fire* series
2. The first three draft chapters of the second book.

My promise: I **will not** spam you and you'll only hear from me when I have something to share that I think you'll be interested in. I do this because I love it, and I hope you will too, not for the spam and sales.

Thanks so much.

DID YOU ENJOY THIS BOOK? YOU CAN MAKE A DIFFERENCE

Your review is the **most powerful thing** I can earn to get more people to read my stories. What I do have, is the potential for a real reader who enjoyed my story to leave a review for others and encourage them to read my stories. That is what matters to me.

Honest book reviews bring me other loyal readers. Your review is very important to me, **I cannot stress that enough**.

If you enjoyed this book, I would be quite grateful if you could spend a few minutes leaving a review. It can be as short as you like.

Thank you so much, I truly appreciate you. And thank you for reading.

ABOUT THE AUTHOR

J.V. FAHL is the author of *MIRADEN'S FOLLY* (HER SOUL OF FIRE Series) and is working on another grimdark fantasy series as well. You can find him at **jvfahl.com**. He's on Twitter at **twitter.com/JVFahl**, on Facebook at **www.facebook.com/jvfahl** and if you really want to reach out to him directly, he'd love to hear from you: **jvfahl@thedarkwriter.io**.

J.V. Fahl has lived in all four corners of the United States, been to 20 countries, served in the US Navy, and now lives in the Smoky Mountains. He is always interested in hearing from his readers.

DEDICATION

C. DENNIS: I owe you a massive deal of gratitude. You were there breaking me down in the early times. You taught me how little I really understood. Your advice was endless, and so was your patience. You taught me the mechanics of writing I never learned in school. You showed me just how bad, *really bad*, I was at writing. It was so hard at the time but I needed it. You spent at least 8 years working with me, 8 YEARS. I can never say enough thanks, buddy.

K. FAHL: You weathered some real storms and kept me grounded. This wouldn't have happened if you let me walk away from the mission.

B. GABEHART: We served together. You helped me in the early times. You always sent me the best music to keep me motivated. I would have lost early inertia without you.

M. MYERS: Calling you a cruel editor wouldn't be fair. You were a just and excellent editor who made a difficult process doable and helped me reach the necessary growth to bring this book to publication. You gave me the clarity I needed to really turn my concept into a story. You are a fantastic editor.

H. DEWULF: You coached me to think about deeper concepts in writing. You taught me so much in a short period of time and gave me so much to think about after our sessions. Thank you for helping me turn wild ideas into storycraft.

R. HEMINGER: This is the man who dared me to write a novel (after I trashed the one that he let me borrow). Were it not for your nudge, I may have never found this passion.

HONORABLE MENTIONS:

M.M, A.J

If YOU are a fellow writer and looking for a great editor:

Find **M. MYERS** here: **www.sffeditor.com** and bring your coat of thick skin.

If YOU are looking for writer coaching and an excellent mentor:

Find **H. DEWULF** here: **harrydewulf.com**

www.ingramcontent.com/pod-product-compliance
Lightning Source LLC
Chambersburg PA
CBHW021103110726
47900CB00007B/2006